D0593772

CROSSFIRE

Also by JoAnn Ross

Available from Signet

FREEFALL

CROSSFIRE

A HIGH RISK NOVEL

JoAnn Ross

A SIGNET BOOK

SIGNET
Published by New American Library, a division of
Penguin Group (USA) Inc., 375 Hudson Street,
New York, New York 10014, USA
Penguin Group (Canada), 90 Eglinton Avenue East, Suite 700, Toronto,
Ontario M4P 2Y3, Canada (a division of Pearson Penguin Canada Inc.)
Penguin Books Ltd., 80 Strand, London WC2R 0RL, England
Penguin Ireland, 25 St. Stephen's Green, Dublin 2,
Ireland (a division of Penguin Books Ltd.)
Penguin Group (Australia), 250 Camberwell Road, Camberwell, Victoria 3124,
Australia (a division of Pearson Australia Group Pty. Ltd.)
Penguin Books India Pvt. Ltd., 11 Community Centre, Panchsheel Park,
New Delhi - 110 017, India
Penguin Group (NZ), 67 Apollo Drive, Rosedale, North Shore 0632,
New Zealand (a division of Pearson New Zealand Ltd.)
Penguin Books (South Africa) (Pty.) Ltd., 24 Sturdee Avenue,
Rosebank, Johannesburg 2196, South Africa

Penguin Books Ltd., Registered Offices:
80 Strand, London WC2R 0RL, England

First published by Signet, an imprint of New American Library,
a division of Penguin Group (USA) Inc.

ISBN: 978-0-7394-9888-0

Printed in the United States of America

PUBLISHER'S NOTE
This is a work of fiction. Names, characters, places, and incidents either are the product of the author's imagination or are used fictitiously, and any resemblance to actual persons, living or dead, business establishments, events, or locales is entirely coincidental.

The publisher does not have any control over and does not assume any responsibility for author or third-party Web sites or their content.

Again, to all the men and women of the U.S. military—and their families—for their service and sacrifice, especially my favorite sailor, MA3 Keith Danalewich, and Air Force Technical Sergeant Trae, who's currently deployed in Afghanistan.

And, as always, to Jay.

Acknowledgments

Heartfelt thanks once again to everyone on the extraordinary NAL team, especially my fantastically supportive editor, Laura Cifelli, and the super efficient and always cheery Lindsay Nouis. You all are the best!

Also, thanks and a wave across the sea to Maxim Popenker, of St. Petersburg, Russia—a lieutenant in the Russian Air Defense Force turned writer—who was kind enough to answer my questions about silencers and, more specifically, about a little-known Russian Special Forces rifle I wanted to give my serial sniper.

Go, bid the soldiers shoot.

—WILLIAM SHAKESPEARE, *Hamlet*

1

"Do you really have to leave so soon?"

"Now, darlin'." Brigadier General John Jacob paused while tying his spit-polished shoes long enough to nuzzle the neck of the lusciously naked blonde lying in the middle of the rumpled sheets. "You know I do."

"Just a few more minutes?" She arched her back like a sleek Siamese, displaying the voluptuous breasts, which, although not natural, were still damn fine.

He was tempted. What male wouldn't be? A former Miss Watermelon Belle, Meredith Hawthorne was one helluva good lay. But he'd begun to suspect that she had set her sights on marrying up.

Her husband—who hadn't even gone to one of the academies but had come up through the OCS ranks—had made only captain before joining the faculty of the Admiral Somersett Military Academy. While he was not only a retired brigadier general but had graduated from West Point, as had all the males in his family going back to the Revolution.

He was also, if Meredith was to believed—and it stroked his ego to accept her word—a better lover. But, dammit, he'd been honest about his intentions from the start. They were both married. Neither was looking for commitment. Both had reasons to keep their affair discreet.

As the highly visible commandant of a very successful athletic department (which brought in beaucoup bucks from ASMA alumni), he was on the fast track to be commander of the college whose roots had first been established in the Lowcountry to supply the government with a citizen corps of cadets during the War of 1812.

His wife, the daughter of a former chairman of the Joint Chiefs, whom he'd married solely for her social and Pentagon connections, had served him well. Loyalty prevented him from putting her out to pasture just because some blond beauty queen gave the best blow job in the South.

"Your husband's going to be home at eighteen hundred hours," he reminded her.

He should know, given that he'd been the one to send Captain Hawthorne to Savannah on a recruiting trip. Both VMI and The Citadel had their eyes on a seven-foot-tall high school basketball center, but Jacob had every intention of winning the phenom for ASMA.

One more trip to the Final Four, and he figured that plush commander's office with its stunning view of the Somersett River bridge, and the harbor beyond, would be his.

"I know." She sighed prettily, drawing his attention back to her breasts. "It's just that every time I'm with him, I wish I was with you." She touched a hand to his face. On a distant level, he admired the way she allowed the single tear to trail down her cheek. "In fact, just the other night, when he was upstairs, playing war games on that damn computer, I was thinking that maybe I should just tell—"

"Don't." He grasped her wrist. Tight enough to make her flinch. "You're not going to tell your husband anything. Because if you do, I'll make sure he's shipped out of here so fast that pretty blond head of yours will spin. And given that you dropped out of college when you nabbed yourself an officer and a gentleman, it's not as if you have a lot of career skills."

His face was inches from hers. His other hand tangled in her long hair, holding her gaze to his. "Unless you decide to take that pretty cock-sucking mouth of yours out on the pro circuit."

She frowned. Her eyes swam. This time the tears were real. "That's nasty."

"That's what we're about." His tone was hard. He could have been raking a cadet over the coals for an honor code infraction. "We get together twice a week to do the nasty. I get my rocks off, and you get a man who, instead of treating you like glass, knows you like rough sex and likes giving it to you the way you want it."

"That's it?"

Hell. Realizing that this could get out of hand, he backtracked. "No." This time it was he who touched a hand to her unhappy face. "You're right. It was cruel and uncalled-for. You know you mean more to me than that."

He stroked her cheek. "But we've got to be careful. If your husband gets so much as an inkling of what's going on, I could kiss my future good-bye."

"That's the most important thing, isn't it?" She sniffled, but from the tilt of her chin, he could sense she was regaining the spirit that came so naturally to stunningly beautiful women. Women accustomed to the attention of men. "You becoming commander of ASMA."

"It's important." He was not above lying. When necessary. But this was the absolute truth. "But you need to keep your eye on the big picture."

"Which is?"

"I'm going to need a proper hostess once I move into the commander's house."

Blue eyes narrowed. "I assume that would be your wife."

"You'd assume wrong." He stroked her arm and felt her body soften. "You know that Eleanor and I haven't been living as man and wife for some time."

"That's what you told me."

He could also tell she hadn't entirely bought the

story. He didn't blame her, but again, it was the truth. His bride had let him know early in their marriage that she found sex messy and distasteful. So long as he behaved discreetly, and never slept with any of her friends, she'd been more than willing to allow him his little affairs.

"Our marriage has always been"—he paused for effect—"complicated. But it's become more and more difficult for us to live under the same roof. So we have an agreement that as soon as I become commander, we'll divorce. At which time Eleanor will receive a substantial financial settlement."

From the way her smooth brow furrowed, he could tell she was sensing the lie. "Why would she give up the opportunity to play lady of the manor?"

"Simple. Because she's never enjoyed the role of an officer's wife."

"You could certainly have fooled me."

"She's a good actress." And a spectacular hostess. Having always believed in giving credit where credit was due, he allowed that Eleanor Longworth Jacob's inborn Southern graciousness was part of the reason for his success. "But she's growing weary of the part."

His lover's hair had tumbled over her shoulder. He smoothed it back, brushed his hand over her breast, and felt her heart pick up its beat. "Besides, there's another reason she wants to be free as much as I do."

"What's that?" Her flesh was warming. Tempting him even as he played her.

"She's in love."

"You're kidding."

"On the contrary. And there's more." Like putty in his hands, her mouth softened beneath his as he pressed a line of kisses from one side of her lips to the other. "Her lover just happens to be a woman."

Her head snapped back. "Your wife is a lesbian?"

"It seems so."

"When did you find this out?"

"I've always suspected. But that's all it was. A feeling. She confirmed it last month."

"Wow." He could see the wheels turning in her head as she absorbed the lie. "Talk about 'Don't ask, don't tell.' "

She tilted that busy little head and studied him. Despite her Barbie doll body and sugary Southern belle charms, Meredith Hawthorne was a cold, calculating female. It was one of the things he honestly admired about her.

"If that got out, it could really screw up your chances for making commander."

"Exactly." He kissed her longer. Deeper. Leaning her back against the pillows. "Which is why I'm counting on you to keep my secret."

He skimmed his lips down her rosy torso. He didn't really have the time for this, but neither did he want to risk her deciding to come clean with the cuckolded captain. "For just a little longer. Until we can be together."

Slender thighs opened. "In the commander's house," she said.

"Absolutely," he agreed robustly as he clamped his mouth over her and closed the deal.

Five minutes later, twenty minutes before Captain Hawthorne was due back from Savannah, Jacob, with his future firmly back on track, left the house six blocks from the ASMA campus.

It was a pretty neighborhood. Brick sidewalks were shaded by leafy green trees lined up like soldiers in front of tidy 1930s-style bungalows; the Stars and Stripes flew crisply from every porch; lawns were neatly trimmed, gardens darkly mulched.

It was dog days in the Lowcountry, the air so scorchingly hot it rippled along the ground as he strode with military bearing to the black Cadillac parked in the Hawthornes' driveway.

A sound like a tree branch cracking overhead shattered the summer silence.

Although he'd spent his entire life around weapons, Brigadier General John Jacob never heard the shot that penetrated his skull.

He was dead before he hit the bricks, crimson blood oozing from the hole left by the copper-penny-colored rifle slug.

One shot. One kill.

2

Afghanistan, eight months earlier

Quinn McKade never claimed to be psychic. But when you spend the first eight years of your life with your parents on the run from the cops, and the next nine years bouncing from foster home to foster home, you pick up a lot of survival instincts. Ones that had proven helpful during his years in the SEALs. And he wasn't getting good vibes about this mission.

He'd known, as his team had sat around the Bagram air base waiting for all those REMFs—rear echelon motherfuckers—to get their collective brass asses in gear, they were in trouble from the get-go. After a series of delays, they were three hours and fifty-eight minutes from sunrise, and if there was one thing more dangerous than humping up the side of a Kush mountain beneath the full moon, it was climbing it in daylight, when they'd be silhouetted against the white snow and gray sky.

While the mission would be challenging, it was still doable. Until a contingent of CIA, Marines, and Army Rangers crashed the party at the last minute, forcing a major change in logistics.

The original plan had been to do a rope insertion, the helo hovering low while they slid down in the dark. The number of troops now piled into the Chinook, awaiting takeoff, would require an actual skids-down landing. In a snowstorm. On one of the steepest mountains in the Hindu Kush.

Not, in Quinn's mind, a good idea, but since both the LT and Chief Zach Tremayne had already stated their case to the head sheds in command of the joint task mission, it wasn't exactly as if anyone had a choice.

His team—like all SEALs—were loyal servants of the U.S. government. They'd go wherever they were sent, do whatever they were told, face off against enemies anywhere around the world, all day, every day.

And they'd damn well succeed, or die trying. The lawless area along the Afghan/Pakistani border had already become destabilized as various factions struggled for supremacy; last week's earthquake, which had shaken up more than the mountainous land, had made things worse.

Conventional wisdom might have supposed having the quake take out one of the terrorist camps was a good thing. And it was. But like everything else about this crazy country—which just happened to be the dark hole of terror, where the deadly 9/11 plot was hatched and nourished—nothing was black and white.

Sure, some bad guys had conveniently been buried beneath tons of rock. But the downside was that another al-Qaeda leader—dubbed Rambo due to his tendency of going off on his own tangents rather than sticking with any united terrorist program—had taken advantage of the disaster to make a move to control the entire region.

That, along with the taunting videos he'd been putting out via the Internet the past six months had definitely put him in the U.S. military's crosshairs even before he'd started spreading the word among local farmers that the Great Satan had sent the infidel U.S. soldiers to destroy their crops. Which, given that poppies were their only livelihood, tended to make those enraged farmers fight like mad dogs backed against a wall.

Quinn was no fan of the drug trade. Nor was any

other military man he'd ever met. But they had more important things to concern themselves with than burning crops. Hell, there were fields of poppies growing right outside the gates of the forward command post, for Chrissakes!

According to the latest intel, Rambo was holed up in one of the many subterranean tunnels. Quinn's team had been tasked with finding the ratlines supplying him, locating the "bat cave," then calling massive amounts of ordnance down on it.

Which should have been just another day at the office.

"A trained monkey could plan a mission better than this," he complained to Zach.

"Trained monkeys *are* planning this mission," the chief responded.

Fortunately, their pilot, Shane Garrett—a member of the army's elite SOAR Night Stalkers—was the best copter jockey in the business. He'd shuttled the team on so many successful missions over the past nine months, they'd come to think of him as their lucky charm.

The helo, which had been flying nighttime lights out, had just flared to land, its huge tandem rotors churning furiously in the thin mountain air, kicking up clouds of ice and snow around the windows and open ramp when Garrett shouted, "RPG!" from the cockpit.

The rocket's fiery glare was blinding as it hurtled toward the left side gunner's door.

The rocket-propelled grenade slammed through the side, slicing hoses, spraying hydraulic fluid all over the team before blowing the M4 Quinn had been holding to pieces.

Then the shit well and truly hit the fan.

The first twenty minutes after the crash was a bloody blur of violence. With enemy fire turning the helo into a camouflage-painted colander, they had no choice but to evacuate.

The lieutenant was dead. As was the Chinook's copilot and many of the Rangers, who, following their creed, Rangers Lead the Way, had charged off the Chinook right into a barrage of bullets, grenades, and RPGs, pouring in at them from a well-camouflaged bunker that hadn't been visible from the air.

The Marines had also taken heavy casualties. If they'd been on Omaha Beach instead of in this damn Afghan snowfield, the scene could have come straight out of *Saving Private Ryan.*

Shouts and curses flew as the mixed team of SEALs, Rangers, and Marines tried to create order out of chaos. Bodies lay on the ground, too many of them not moving. A Marine was sprawled with his boots still on the ramp, his torso in the snow. Through Quinn's night vision goggles, the blood pooling beneath the kid's helmet took on an eerie green fluorescent tint.

Shane had caught a tracer round in the leg. Proving that an army flyboy could be as tough as a SEAL, he'd managed to drag himself off the bird and was now lying on his stomach with them, behind a dead donkey that had had the misfortune to become a casualty of war.

Proving the old military cliché about no battle plan surviving first contact with the enemy, their radio battery was too cold to work. Not that it would've been much help anyway.

"Don't have to check my handy-dandy J-Fire reference guide to know that we're too near the enemy to call in for close air support," Zach said.

Quinn agreed. No way would Command risk a friendly-fire incident.

Which was a good thing, because killing one of your own was about as bad as it got. Unfortunately, it was nearly as bad to have tangos whipping your ass.

SEALs preferred to work in the dark. Hell, as he'd been taught in BUD/S training, they fucking *owned* the dark. Unlike Rangers, who liked to go into a battle zone with guns blasting away like they were reenacting the shoot-out at the O.K. Corral, SEALs worked covert missions, getting in and out without drawing attention to themselves. Which is why they got away with their beards and long hair, the better to fit into the general population.

On those occasions when Quinn found himself in a firefight, a preternatural calm, which Zach insisted on calling his "spooky sniper zone," would settle over him. But now, as the damn bunker rats began targeting the injured who lay bleeding in the snow, a temper he usually managed to keep reined in set his blood boiling.

"The fuckers know we're not going to leave our wounded," he said.

Leave No Man Behind was a Special Forces motto. One written in stone.

"They're trying to draw us out," said Zach, who, since the LT had been killed, was now in charge of whatever mission they managed to cobble together. "Which means we've got three choices."

A tango popped up from the bunker.

Quinn casually picked him off with the M4 he'd retrieved from the snow to replace the one he'd had blown away in his hands. Unfortunately, its owner, who appeared to have been shot everywhere his helmet or armor didn't cover, no longer needed it.

"We can sit out here and die by enemy fire." Zach continued his assessment of the situation. He ducked as a bullet from some overeager Ranger flew over his head. "Or, dammit, friendly fire."

"Or get rid of the enemy fire," Quinn concluded.

He'd long ago accepted the fact of war that men—and, increasingly, women—die. And that the best way he could help the wounded was to remove the danger by taking out the enemy.

"Looks like door number three," Zach decided as

the Kalashnikovs' muzzles continued to flash from the bunker, shredding trees and making holes in the snow all around them.

"The only choice," Quinn agreed.

"Roger that," said Shane, who, despite his wound, had also grabbed a rifle from one of the fallen Rangers. The snow around his leg was beginning to look like a frozen strawberry margarita.

The enemy had already proven that they would do anything to win this war. They also looked prepared to shoot all day if that's what it took. Their countrymen had sent the British packing in the 1800s and early 1900s, and after years of warfare, they'd beaten the Russians' butts in the late part of the last century.

They were tough, brutal, and driven, willing to take the battle to the limit. And unlike the Americans they were currently trying to kill, these guys didn't have any rules of engagement.

Which meant they had to go.

Now.

Even though it involved close-in shooting, Quinn, being the designated sniper and therefore the team's best marksman, was the logical choice for the assault.

"You get to play cowboy," Zach said.

Despite the seriousness of the situation, Quinn grinned. "Yippee-ki-yay."

While the others provided cover fire, he rolled across the snow toward an outcropping of rock behind and about five feet above the bunker.

Meanwhile, the enemy kept blasting away with those damn AK-47s the Russians had left behind, the red tracers hitting all around him, looking like an outbreak of measles on the white snow.

A bullet zinged off the eyelet of his right boot. Quinn decided if he survived this clusterfuck he was going to have the boot bronzed.

He reached the rocks, wishing as he clambered up them that Mother Nature had given him Zach's long, lean runner's body. At six foot five, two twenty-five, he wasn't much of a mountain goat. But he did make one helluva big target.

He pulled himself onto the ledge, slid into the zone, and began blasting away.

Quinn had no idea how long he kept shooting. Even Zach, who was better at keeping track of such things, told him it could have been seconds. Minutes. Maybe even hours.

Afterward, they gathered up their wounded, dragging them into the bunker to get them out of the driving sleet and snow.

During that time Zach and Quinn stayed outside, atop the rocks, trying to reach anyone who could send in another Chinook to evacuate the wounded, but the radio refused to work.

One of the men left the bunker. "Excuse me, Chief," he said, "but I think I might just be able to help."

"Who the hell are you?"

"Tech Sergeant Dallas O'Halloran at your service. I'm a CCT."

Zach exchanged a look with Quinn, who shrugged. "What the hell is an Air Force combat controller doing on this mission?"

"Coming to your rescue?" O'Halloran asked with what Quinn thought was inordinate good cheer considering what they'd all just gone through.

CCTs were techs that hardly any civilians even knew existed. Although the Air Force had a reputation among Special Forces as "three push-ups and you're in," the selection process for combat controller was nearly as daunting as it was to become a SEAL.

Not only were they geniuses when it came to coordinating weapon-laden aircraft, they had to be able to fit in with SEALs and Delta Force on the ground. Which was why there were less than a hundred of them out there.

And hoo-yah, it appeared Quinn's team had drawn one of their own.

"I was a last-minute addition," O'Halloran explained. "But, Chief, this is your lucky day."

"Yeah," Zach drawled, "I noticed that right off the bat when that RPG took down our bird."

"That was bad," the CCT agreed with typical Spec Ops understatement. "But I've got the answer."

He dug into his rucksack and pulled out a radio with a thin whip antenna. "I learned about this handy-dandy gizmo from a female sailor I met while she was on shore leave in the Green Zone." He began twisting dials. "They have them on ships. It allows them to talk to anyone in the joint services, whatever the frequency."

"Cool," Zach said.

O'Halloran flashed a grin that could've lit up the Kush for a month of Sundays. "Fuckin' A."

He got through, but the news was not good.

"Sorry," the voice from the command and control center said. "We've gone way beyond the thirty minutes to daylight window."

"I realize that, sir," O'Halloran said.

He frowned. When he exchanged a look with the other two men on the rocky ledge, Quinn knew they were all thinking the same thing. Back in the first Gulf War, just as dawn had been breaking, a Spectre gunship had delayed returning to base long enough to help out an embattled unit of Marines. Unfortunately, the rising sun had allowed an Iraqi with a deadly surface-to-air missile to see the gunship, which subsequently crashed, killing all fourteen people aboard.

"But we've got wounded, sir."

"I understand," the voice said. "But—"

"Give me that." Zach grabbed the radio. "We've got men dying here, dammit," he shouted.

"Who is this?" the disembodied voice demanded.

"Chief Zachariah Tremayne, U.S. Navy SEAL Team 11. We were on Falcon 01 when it went down after taking a bullet at the LZ. And we need some exfil. Now." His jaw was clenched as tight as his fist. "Sir," he managed to tack on.

"I'm sorry, Chief," the voice said. "But attempting to evacuate your team now would be unsafe and unsound."

Damned if he didn't make it sound as if he was being asked to do them a fucking favor, Quinn thought.

"Are you under fire?"

"Not at the moment," Zach admitted on a frustrated huff of breath. "We managed to take out the tangos that shot down our bird, but—"

"Then hunker down and stay put. Your rescue copter will be there at eighteen hundred."

Zach continued to argue, getting nowhere.

"This is a joint mission," the voice said, finally cutting him off. "You're not the only players on the board today, Chief."

And that was it.

Over and out.

Quinn had never heard dead silence before.

But as they stood there on the mountain, which had gone as quiet as a church on Monday morning, he realized that despite the American military being the toughest, most well-armed in the world, they were truly all alone.

In one of the most dangerous places on earth.

3

The cops had already taped off the scene by the time FBI special agents Cait Cavanaugh and Frank Angetti arrived at the tidy little house. Given that crime in this leafy suburban enclave usually involved vandalism by kids whose embarrassed parents proved a lot tougher on the offenders than the justice system would be, the sight of seven flashing black-and-whites, two unmarked detective cars, a fire truck, a medical examiner's van, and an ambulance had definitely drawn a crowd of neighbors.

Adding to the carnival atmosphere was the flotilla of news crews from television stations as far away as Charleston and Savannah; satellite uplinks pointed into a sky that had turned from robin's-egg blue to steely gray as a storm rolled in from the sea.

The street was blocked off in front of the house by two black-and-whites parked nose to nose, forcing the rush-hour traffic to have to turn around, which only added to the congestion.

Cursing beneath her breath, Cait pulled the black SUV—which, with its dual whip antennas screamed federal government agent car—into the driveway of a house two doors down from the crime scene and parked beside a white WBUC van from the Somersett ABC affiliate.

Reporter Valentine Snow, who was getting ready to do her stand-up on the front lawn, beneath a bright pink canopy of crape myrtle, called out to Cait as she climbed out of the van.

"Can I steal a sec for an interview?"

Cait shook her head, wondering how the newswoman managed to run across grass in those killer high heels. "I don't even know what I'm dealing with."

"Afterward, then." The reporter flashed the coaxing smile that had, before she'd left the high-flying world of network television, won more than her share of high-profile "get" interviews with leaders all over the world. "This murder's going to hit the city like an IED. Better for you if you get a head start framing the message. Hard to put the genie back into the bottle once it blows up."

Cait hated that she was right. "Why should I talk to a reporter who doesn't know enough not to mix her metaphors?" she asked as she kept walking toward the barricades.

"Maybe because I'm right? And because I'm offering to take one of those kittens off your hands?"

Cait stopped in her tracks, the pause allowing Val to catch up with her. "How did you know about them?"

"I'm a reporter." The strobelike smile flashed again, making Cait think that if those straight-as-a-ruler, toothpaste-commercial teeth weren't caps, life was truly unfair. Two years of childhood braces, and *she* was still left with an overbite. "With a nose for news."

The brunette newscaster tapped a slender patrician nose as perfect as her pearly teeth. "You rescued a pregnant tabby who got stuck in a tree outside your apartment when a group of nasty boys were throwing rocks at her. Since the shelter warned you that there's not a big market for pregnant cats, you, harboring a generous heart beneath those ugly FBI suits you usually wear, took her home, set up a kitty nursery, and are now trying to unload seven kittens."

"Shows what you know. There happen to be just four."

Two had gone to the owner of her favorite Greek restaurant, which, with its beautiful waterfront location, had a bit of a problem with rats. She'd convinced him that what he needed was a pair of good mousers.

A third had gone to an ER doctor at St. Camillus, who, thanks to increased business during Buccaneer Days, hadn't had time to go shopping for her five-year-old daughter's birthday present. Cait had suggested that a fuzzy orange kitty with white paws would win huge mom points.

"Three minutes. Make that two," Val amended quickly, when Cait opened her mouth to argue. "And you'll be down to three homeless tabbies." She held up the appropriate number of fingers tipped by—what else?—perfectly manicured nails the exact same sea coral color as her snug, short-skirted suit.

"Stick around and we'll see once I know what I'm dealing with."

"Hey!" A man in a Somersett Buccaneers T-shirt with baggy shorts flapping around his knees came lumbering toward her. "You can't park there. It's private property."

"The news van's there," Cait pointed out.

"Yeah. Sure. Because the station paid the rental fee."

"Rental fee?"

"It's private property," he repeated. "Consider it pay-to-park."

"We're FBI." Cait's partner countered on a New Jersey accent straight out of *The Sopranos.* "We don't pay nobody to park nowhere."

"I don't care if you're the president of the freaking U.S. of A." the guy shot back. His face turned as red as his shirt. "This is America. Where we have laws protecting—"

"Private property," Cait finished up for him. She managed, just barely, to keep from sighing. "So, how do we even know you own this driveway?"

That stopped him. "Why the hell would I be renting out space in someone else's driveway?"

Cait didn't have time to argue. "How much?"

"Fifty bucks."

"Fuck that," Angetti growled.

"My driveway. My price." When the guy shoved out a gut that revealed a fondness for Lowcountry cuisine, Cait realized the two men were about to get into a pissing contest. Which she so didn't need.

"Here." She pulled two twenties and a ten out of her billfold and shoved them at him. "I'd better not come out and find anyone else parked behind me."

"I'll watch your rig for you," Val offered cheerfully. "Since I need to stick around for our interview anyway."

If she didn't get to the crime scene, there wouldn't be any need for an interview.

"Whatever."

"What a freaking circus," her partner muttered as they walked toward the scene.

Angetti, aka the Bane of Cait's Existence, was wearing one of his two black suits and dark shades, which made him look as if he were auditioning for *MIB III*. He was mid-fifties, less than a month—thank you, Jesus!—to retirement, with an ego off the chart. He also possessed the unique talent of annoying everyone he interviewed, which wasn't real helpful.

"Murder sells," Cait murmured. As entrepreneurial showmen—from Caligula to Shakespeare to Scorsese—over the centuries had proven.

"Maybe. But this murder just happens to be *local*. So what the hell are we doing here?"

"General Jacob was on the short list to becoming commander of ASMA," she said, sharing what the Columbia field office had told her when assigning them the case as she worked her way through the throng of neighbors pressing against the wooden barricades. "He's also connected in Pentagon circles."

"So?"

"So, apparently certain people above our pay grade feel that him getting killed just might be part of a larger terrorist threat picture."

"I'm sorry, ma'am." The uniform cop assigned to guard the ramparts held up a hand as she started to dodge around the wooden barricades. "No civilians allowed."

"Good thing I'm not a civilian then, isn't it, Officer?" She flashed her red, blue and gold South Carolina FBI Joint Terrorism Task Force shield. "Special Agent Caitlin Cavanaugh, and this is Special Agent Frank Angetti."

The patrolman's gaze moved from her light auburn hair to the white T-shirt and cropped khaki pants, which certainly weren't usual agency attire.

She'd been at a family barbecue when the call had come in, unfortunately just as her brother-in-law had taken her sizzling, mouthwatering, medium-rare strip steak off the grill.

At least, in deference to her mother, who'd been a what-not-to-wear maven long before that fashion show had appeared on cable, she was wearing proper sandals instead of flip-flops. Though they did bare her toes, which she suspected could well cause J. Edgar Hoover to spin in his grave.

Although the cop looked surprised, and more than a little curious to see the feds on the scene, he waved them through.

"It could be some cadet pissed about getting a bad grade," Angetti continued the argument. "Or one who had some other grudge to nurse. Jacob is head of athletics, right? Maybe some hothead jock didn't get a scholarship. Or could be some old grad pissed about them losing to Duke in the Elite Eight this year."

"No one would kill over a stupid basketball game."

"March Madness is a helluva lot more than a mere basketball game," he countered. "There's big bucks bet on that tourney. Besides, people have killed for a lot less."

She couldn't disagree. "Well, college basketball would definitely be one of the more ridiculous reasons."

Brigadier General John Jacob was lying supine on the brick driveway, a hole drilled dead center through his forehead.

One shot. One kill.

Even if she hadn't attended the bureau academy, Cait would've known the sniper maxim from the military thriller novel that had kept her reading all last night. The general's expression in death seemed to be one of annoyed surprise, making her wonder if he could have actually heard the shot that had nailed him.

Although classes wouldn't start for another two weeks, a new-class orientation was currently taking place on the ASMA campus, which undoubtedly explained why the victim was in summer uniform. A silver star winked on the epaulet of his snow white shirt, an inch-wide bloodred stripe ran down the knife-edge-pressed legs of his white trousers, and his spit polished white shoes shone like a glacier in the late-afternoon sun. The front of the still crisp, snowy shirt provided a billboard for the multicolored ribbons acquired during his army service.

Cait decided she'd gotten perverse when the sight of the body lying on the driveway caused a little boost of not exactly pleasure but definitely anticipation.

Most people went through their entire lives without ever seeing a dead human being. Or, if they did, the body was nicely dressed, coiffed, laid out on slick silk in a polished wooden casket, appearing to be merely sleeping.

To Cait, a body offered both a puzzle to be solved and a challenge to overcome. She hadn't realized, until now, how much she'd missed both.

She understood—really she did—that fighting terrorism was the nation's highest priority. Which meant that all the hours surfing the Internet, reading through ship manifests, and patrolling Lowcountry harbors were hugely important to the entire free world.

But the pitiful thing was that while Jack Bauer might be able to save the world in twenty-four hours, trying to accomplish the same thing in real life was, well . . . tedious.

She'd left the Somersett PD after her longtime partner, Detective Joe Gannon, had gotten married and gone to work for Phoenix Team. Murder just hadn't been nearly as much fun without Joe. He'd tried to recruit her to come work with him at the private international security firm based on nearby Swann Island, but about that same time Uncle Sam had come calling, bearing apple pies, waving the Stars and Stripes and singing "Yankee Doodle Dandy," and well, the possibility of having to play bodyguard to some pampered, self-indulgent pop star hadn't sounded nearly as appealing as tracking down terrorists.

After three years as a "force multiplier" in the JTTF, Cait had begun rethinking that decision. Especially after consulting on the recent case of the Swann Island Slasher.

She had no doubt that a guy as high up in military circles as Jacobs had been would go out with all the pomp and circumstance a general was due. A horse-drawn carriage with an escort platoon carrying the flag-draped casket, a military bugler playing taps, a gun salute over the gravesite.

There'd probably be enough military brass on hand to make up a full marching band, but *she* would be the one standing for the general. Making sure that whoever had taken this man's life paid for the crime.

"Not much of a house for a guy with all that fruit salad on his shirt." Angetti broke into her thoughts.

"It's not his." Coincidentally, the general lived across the street from Cait's parents. In fact, he'd probably been invited to today's barbecue. *Too bad he hadn't accepted.*

"Well, then, looks like he got caught making a bootie run." Angetti nodded his graying crew cut toward the thirtysomething blonde who was seated on a porch swing, dabbing tears as she talked with two plainclothes SPD detectives. "And got himself nailed by an angry husband."

"We don't know what the vic was doing here," she pointed out. "He could have dropped by on academy business."

"Sure. Or he could've been going door-to-door selling Girl Scout cookies."

"It's a good thing you're retiring soon. Because obviously all the years working in the Bureau have made you cynical."

He waved his hand in front of her face. "Hey, Special Agent Kettle. This is your partner, the pot. Calling you black."

She couldn't deny it. She'd joined SPD right after graduating from USC, and although she'd never considered herself naive, it hadn't taken her long to come to the conclusion that the much-more-seasoned Joe Gannon hadn't been exaggerating when he'd told her that everyone lied.

Even she did. Hadn't she, less than two hours ago, told her youngest sister, who'd recently had a baby, that the new short haircut looked great, when in reality it looked as if Little Orphan Annie had stuck her finger in a light socket?

Ignoring her partner's sarcasm, Cait glanced around, taking in the wrought-iron-fenced cemetery across the street. While some people might be unnerved living in such close proximity to a graveyard, given that Cait's apartment was located on the cobblestone street currently serving as Buccaneer Days party central, she found the idea of all those silent neighbors hugely appealing.

Scattered amid the smaller grave markers in that garden of stone were several large tombs the shooter could have hidden behind. Unfortunately, it didn't appear that the cops had sealed off the cemetery, thus risking contaminating what could be a crime scene.

One of the detectives glanced up, registered their arrival, said something to his partner, and came ambling down the steps toward them.

"Well, well, this is a surprise," Lonnie Briggs drawled. "Having the fibbies consult on my case."

"*Our* case," Angetti shot back before Cait could respond.

Terrific. That's all she needed, another turf war. Fighting over a parking spot was one thing; this was another. Having been on the other side of jurisdictional battles as a cop, Cait had planned to smooth things over with a little finesse. A word that wasn't in Angetti's vocabulary. Nor Briggs's either, apparently.

"That so?" The detective's lips, beneath a mustache the color of a rusted-out skiff, twisted in a sneer.

"Didn't the captain call you?" she asked.

"I've been a little busy to take calls," he pointed out. "Handling a homicide."

"Well, you won't have to worry about that now." Angetti plowed forward. "Because you've just been removed from the case."

"Like hell I have," Briggs countered.

"It's nothing against SPD, Lonnie." Cait's conciliatory tone masked her distaste for the detective, who, in her mind, wouldn't even still be in the department were it not for the fact that his uncle was a politically connected captain on the city's south side. "But while all law enforcement's overextended these days, JTTF still has more resources."

"You're kidding." His brows rose, like furry red caterpillars, up toward his bald, bullet head. "Are you suggesting the FBI thinks some muckety-muck ASMA guy getting shot after indulging in a nooner is terrorism?"

"I didn't say that."

Odds were the general's death wasn't related to terrorism, but that hadn't stopped her from jumping at the opportunity to handle a homicide.

"Told you it was probably about sex," Angetti said smugly.

He grinned at Briggs, the two former antagonists suddenly morphing into a couple of cops bonding over a body. Then, as if their heads were connected, they both looked over at the porch, where Briggs's partner, Detective Derek Manning, continued to interview the woman whose short red silk robe wasn't exactly late-afternoon attire. Perhaps she'd been getting ready for a night on the town with her husband and had just gotten out of the shower when the general dropped by.

Yeah. Right. And Cait had just been elected Pirate Queen.

"I take it the weepy blonde's not the vic's wife?" Angetti said.

"Nah," Briggs responded. "The general's housekeeper says his wife's in California. We're trying to track her down. Meanwhile, we've got a BOLO out for the blond chick's husband, who conveniently isn't answering his cell phone."

"Do me a favor?" Cait asked.

"What?" Briggs replied.

"Don't call her a chick."

The detective looked at her with the lack of understanding he might have revealed if she'd asked him to recite Einstein's theory of relativity. No big surprise. Back when she'd been on the force, whenever Briggs got to pick the lunch spot, he invariably opted for the harbor-front Hooters. Which was why no one in homicide was surprised when his fifth marriage broke up.

"Whatever," he said, slapping at a mosquito on the back of his neck. "Along with being an assistant basketball coach, Hawthorne teaches a course in computer science at the academy."

"Captain Ryan Hawthorne?" Cait asked.

"That's the guy. Why?" The distractingly mobile critters dove toward his nose. "You know him?"

"Yeah. At least, I did."

Cait had long ago come to terms with the fact that one of the givens about living and working in the city where she'd gone to high school was that she would occasionally run into old boyfriends.

But never in her wildest dreams—or nightmares—had she expected her former prom date to be involved in a high-profile murder case she was investigating.

"How long ago?" Briggs asked.

"Twelve years, give or take some months."

"So you haven't seen him in all that time?"

"As a matter of fact, I ran into him last week, when I dropped by the academy to take Dad to lunch." Her father, a retired vice admiral, taught military history. "He seemed fine," she said in answer to the question she knew would be next. "We only chatted for a minute or so."

Until she got a handle on the case, she decided, there was no point in adding that Ryan had suggested they get a drink some evening after work. It was probably exactly as he'd said, just an opportunity for two old friends to catch up on each other's lives.

"So, did you find the slug?" she asked, looking around at the ground.

His eyes narrowed at her not-so-subtle attempt to change the subject.

"Yeah." He glared up at the news helicopters hovering overhead. "It fragmented, but what came out the back of the guy's skull is a .223."

"Well, that narrows it down." Cait's tone was dry.

A .223 bullet was small and fast, designed to expand on impact, causing severe, usually fatal damage. They were common, used in both hunting and assault rifles. They could also be shot with a high degree of accuracy from as far as two hundred yards by a reasonably skilled marksman. Farther by someone who'd been trained to kill.

"You really need to cordon off the cemetery," she said.

"We've got the slug," he argued.

"But there's more to a crime scene than a body and a bullet. There's a good chance the killer shot from over there. Maybe left some clues that are already being compromised."

Knowing him to be surprisingly thin-skinned for a cop, she tried not to sound as if she were giving a Homicide 101 lecture. "This is already high profile, Briggs. Playing it by the book is going to look a lot better not only in the press, but it'll cover your ass when the brass jumps in and starts playing politics."

"Shit." He dragged a hand down his face. Took out a roll of antacids, thumbed two off, and popped them in his mouth. "I had my department physical the other day."

Cait had a feeling she knew where the seeming non sequitur was headed. "And?"

"My blood pressure is off the charts. I've got acid reflux and the start of an ulcer. And most of the time it feels like some maniac is tightening a piano wire around my skull."

"Typical Buccaneer Days syndrome."

"Yeah. But I'm getting too freaking old for this shit. Which is why I put in an application to be police chief in this small town out west. In Oregon, where I figure the worst I'll have to deal with will be jaywalking, barking dogs, and the occasional beaver chewing down trees."

"Sounds nice."

Actually, it sounded excruciatingly boring, and Cait allowed a moment of sympathy for the citizens of whatever town ended up with Briggs heading their police department.

She was just about to suggest that Angetti take

some uniforms and start clearing the cemetery, when her cell phone began to play the theme song from *The Good, the Bad, and the Ugly.*

She dug it out of the pocket of her capris and flipped it open. "Cavanaugh."

The curt message on the other end was not what she needed to hear. "We'll be right there," she said, wondering if Briggs had an extra roll of those Tums. She closed the phone.

"We've got another body down," she told the two men. "At the academy."

4

The shooter was an expert at camouflage. Sure, killing in a city wasn't the same as it'd be on the battlefield, but the theory was still the same. The most deadly weapon ever invented, whether the battlefield was in Bumfuck, Afghanistan, or some pretty American city in the South, was a single well-aimed shot.

The key was to blend into your surroundings, to become part of the landscape. Which was why today his "hide" was a discreet brown—described by the salesman as "pebble beach"—Nissan Altima.

He'd done his research online before going shopping, and the 15.3 cubic feet of trunk space—even more when the split backseat was lowered—ranked among the best in its class. And in the event he did end up getting spotted, the 270 horses beneath the hood could come in handy in making his getaway.

Movement. Mobility. Aggressiveness. All were imperative in the sniper business.

He'd positioned himself in the parking lot of a Winn-Dixie, a convenient seventy-five yards from the Admiral Somersett Military Academy parade ground. Although those shit-ugly stone buildings surrounded the grassy square, from this vantage point he could sight in down the tree-lined Commander's Drive, past the uniformed guard at the gate, to focus on his target.

He knew that despite all the hedonistic temptations of the festivities taking place throughout the city, inside the walls of the two-hundred-year-old buildings, the mood would be grim and unrelentingly serious as one more class of college freshmen discovered that ASMA was to *Animal House* as the shooter's M16 was to a water pistol.

The rifle was a popular military weapon of choice for countries ranging from Australia to Cameroon to Ghana to Uganda to Vietnam.

The Colt name added cachet to its cold efficiency. If you were going to waste the enemy, it was a helluva lot cooler to go with the gun that won the American West.

Wild Bill Hickok had killed more than a hundred bad guys with his famous ivory-handled Colt revolvers; Doc Holliday and Wyatt Earp took Colts to the gunfight at the O.K. Corral; Patton had carried his Colt across Europe and Africa while defeating Nazis, and although John Wayne wasn't a real cowboy or soldier, his movies were practically a love story to the brand. More recently, American troops had carried variations of this Colt M16 from Vietnam to the Persian Gulf.

The shooter set up the weapon he'd named Thunderer—after Doc Holliday's favorite Colt—on a bipod set on the floor of the trunk. The two-legged stand would steady Thunderer, allowing for optimal "target acquisition," as the military euphemistically described a sniper's role.

"Target in view," his spotter's distant voice announced in his ear. "Drop the son of a bitch."

The crosshairs were jumping and the target in the shooter's scope seemed to pulse with the same cadence as the suddenly out-of-control beat of his heart.

He took a deep breath. Then another.

Forcing himself to focus on the task at hand, he used the screen of the optical gun sight to fix the man watching this year's class of cadets marching to a cadence the shooter was too far away to hear.

The Colt jumped. Added its loud crack to the roar of cannon fire from a mock sea battle on the harbor as it sent its copper-coated bullet flying toward the parade ground.

The acrid scent of burned gunpowder filled the steamy confines of the car trunk. The shooter watched as the bullet ripped through bone.

Pink mist filled his scope as the target dropped to the dark green grass.

A perfect, surgical strike.

He made another mark on the Colt's stock. "Two down," he said with the satisfaction of a job well done. There were more targets waiting. But this was a damn good start.

As the Altima pulled out of the parking lot, adrenaline, mixed with sweet, heady anticipation, surged through the shooter's veins.

5

It was funny how things worked out, Quinn McKade thought as he left his office in the academy's Admiral Hall. Mostly funny ironic, but occasionally he had to laugh at the twists and turns his life had taken.

There were times he wondered if his father, one of the country's most famous or, depending on your point of view, *infamous* war protesters, was able to watch his only son's strange journey. Was it even possible for atheists to end up in heaven? Or hell?

Or was Daniel McKade residing on some other plane, spending his eternity the same way he'd lived his life—challenging authority, creating unrest, and eventually proving himself an ultimate hypocrite, a pacifist who used violence as a weapon against war.

Those who live by the sword die by the sword.

And wasn't his old man proof of that? Though in reality, it'd been a perfectly aimed round from an FBI SWAT team sniper's rifle that had taken Quinn's father's life that long ago summer's evening.

Quinn, who was eight at the time, figured he'd be hearing the crack of that bullet until the day he himself died.

Now here he was, twenty-five years later, not only a decorated war vet but a writer-in-residence, teaching the occasional creative writing class at one of the nation's premier military academies.

"If you wanted to keep me out of uniform, you

should've stuck around, Pop," Quinn muttered as he walked past framed graduation photographs of cadets who'd been killed in various wars over ASMA's two-hundred-year history.

Too many were recent, making Quinn wonder what would happen when the academy ran out of walls. Because he'd bet any potential royalties on the book he was currently writing that the world wasn't ever going to run out of wars.

He hadn't realized he'd spoken out loud until he noticed that the kid he'd just passed, a wet-behind-the-ears cadet who didn't look old enough to shave, was looking at him funny, as if he was having a hard time picturing the guy in a plain white T-shirt, faded jeans, and sneaks belonging in these hallowed halls.

Heat hit like a sweaty fist as he left the building, headed toward the parking lot on the far side of the parade ground.

It was dog days in the Lowcountry, that steamy, somnolent time of year when any guy who had the sense God gave a gator would be kicking back in a Pawleys Island rope hammock beneath the spreading limbs of a moss-draped oak, a sweating glass of sweet tea or an icy brew on his bare stomach and a dog-eared paperback nearby.

Which was exactly what Quinn intended to do when he got home, where a bottle of Sam Adams and an unfinished James Lee Burke novel were waiting for him. Maybe he'd pick up some blue crabs on the way.

Unlike so many of the imitation antebellum structures that were so popular throughout the Lowcountry, there was nothing romantic or graceful about the buildings of ASMA. They were all gray stone—massive, imposing, fortresslike, without architectural adornment. Facing inward, they resolutely turned their backs to the three-hundred-year-old town framing the parade ground where, every Saturday afternoon for nine months of the year, cadets marched in full dress uniforms for an audience of locals and tourists.

The rest of the South may be in summer mode, but apparently the drill instructor hadn't gotten the memo that heat kills. An entire plebe class, currently 395 strong men and women (which attrition would narrow down to around 350 by graduation), was marching up and down the square green space in the staggering humidity, their ranks a little ragged but their shouted cadence strong and enthusiastic.

Pausing on the sidelines to watch, he was breathing in the scent of fresh-mown grass when the unmistakable sound of a rifle shot shattered air thick enough to drink.

Reacting on instinct, Quinn hit the ground just in time to hear the bullet whizzing past his head.

6

As Cait and Angetti walked through the gate toward the Admiral Somersett Military Academy's parade ground, it crossed her mind that the hulking gray stone buildings' architect must have designed fifteenth-century Spanish prisons in a former life.

When she saw the all-too-familiar man standing on the sidelines, towering over the pair of SPD uniforms who'd been first on the scene, Cait wondered what she could've done to so piss off the universe.

Emotions—tumultuous, complex, and humiliating—slammed into her. She rubbed her chest, which felt as if it'd been hit with a sledgehammer. Then, reminding herself that she'd come a long way since that December morning when she'd awakened, naked and hungover in Quinn McKade's hotel room, she squared her shoulders and marched toward the group.

At the same time he began walking toward her, his stride long and surprisingly easy for such a large man. Then again, he'd always had smooth moves. Both in and out of bed.

No! Do not go there!

"Well," he drawled, the deep bass voice delivering an instantaneous sexual punch, "isn't this turning out to be a day of surprises?"

She sure as hell couldn't argue that.

"McKade." Her tone was curt, her nod sharp.

"Nate Spencer told me you were working for the

feds." He skimmed a questioning glance over her, much as the cop had back at the scene of the first shooting. "FBI, right?"

"Right." No way was Cait going to explain to this man why she'd shown up at a crime scene in casual picnic attire. She glanced past him—no small feat—to the two cops still standing on the sidelines. "Since you're not wearing cuffs, I take it you're not my UNSUB."

He slipped his hands into the pockets of his jeans and rocked back on his heels. "If that's fed-speak for 'unknown subject,' the answer is nope. I'm not."

"And you're obviously not the vic."

Despite the seriousness of the situation, she thought his lips quirked, just a bit, at the corners, as if he were trying to hold in a grin. "You sound disappointed."

"What I sound is busy."

"Hey," Angetti said suddenly. "You're that writer guy. Quinn McKade."

"Guilty," Quinn said. "Only of publishing a book," he tacked on for Cait's benefit.

"I read *Kill Zone* last week." Cait had not seen her partner this animated over anything since the day they'd been assigned to check out coastal strip joints for a suspected would-be jihadist with a penchant for pole dancers. "It was one helluva story."

"Glad you enjoyed it."

"Not sure *enjoy*'s the word. More like it grabbed me by the balls on page one and never let go."

"If you have information pertinent to the murder, I'll need to hear it," Cait said as she resumed walking toward the body being guarded by the two uniforms. "Otherwise, Special Agent Angetti and I have work to do. Now," she stressed to Angetti. "While there's still an outside chance our shooter's close by."

"I wouldn't count on it." Quinn shortened his stride to keep pace with her. Which only annoyed her more. Then again, except for that one horrible lapse in judgment, everything about this man had always annoyed her.

"Why not?"

"Because he shot from seventy-five, maybe seventy-eight yards away. With an M16 or A-15 carbine. Or it could've been a Bushmaster XM15, which, as you undoubtedly learned during firearms training at the FBI academy, is essentially the civilian version of the A-15."

That got Cait's unwilling attention. She paused again and looked a long, long way up at him. "How would you know that?"

He shrugged. "I spent over a decade as a sniper. If there's one thing I know, it's guns."

"I heard about your part in that slasher case over on Swann Island."

Another shrug. "You know what they say. A man's gotta do—"

"What a man's gotta do." She'd never met a man who more personified that old axiom. "Meanwhile, this *woman*'s got a hot case."

She glanced over at the parking lot, where Briggs and Manning were getting out of an unmarked SPD vehicle, followed by all those damn news vans.

"Seems you beat everyone here," Quinn remarked.

"I knew a shortcut."

"I'm not surprised, given your penchant for speed." His wicked and, dammit, way sexy smile let her know that he hadn't forgotten their night together either. In fact, although she'd throw herself off the academy bell tower before admitting it, Cait suspected he remembered more than she did. "Nice to know some things—and some people—never change."

"Like I said, I caught a hot case." She rolled her shoulders to loosen them. "And since this is my second shooting today, I really don't have time to go strolling down memory lane."

That bit of information had him taking off his dark

glasses and hooking them in the neck of his snug white T-shirt. "You've had two sniper attacks? Today?"

"I believe that's what I said."

"Shit." His gunmetal gray eyes moved from the hoard of reporters to the uniformed body lying on the grass. "You, Special Agent, have landed yourself in one helluva shit sandwich."

"I'm beginning to figure that out for myself. But why would you think so?"

"Because your shooter missed me."

She frowned, resisting the knee-jerk response of *too bad.* Murder was too serious to allow any personal feelings about Quinn McKade to interfere with her investigation. "I'm not following."

"I'm six-five. Two-twenty-five. It's been called to my attention several times over the years that I make a fairly substantial target."

"So?"

"So, the bullet passed within six inches of me. Which means either your guy's one helluva lousy shot—"

"I don't think he is," Cait said, thinking back on the hole that had been drilled in the center of Jacob's forehead.

"Then you're dealing with a pro. Or at least former military."

Which they both knew, what with all the military bases in the Lowcountry, were about as plentiful as wannabe pirates during Buccaneer Days.

"Well, I guess I'd better check out the guest of honor at this party. The call I got said he was shot in the forehead."

"Dead on," he confirmed as they continued past the entire uniformed plebe class, standing by at parade rest, feet ten inches apart, hands clasped behind their backs and resting on their belts.

"Just like the first victim," she murmured as she took in the body, clad in the same kind of white uniform as the general had been wearing. But this victim's shirt had a lot fewer ribbons.

"Really?" Quinn slanted her a look. "Well. Obviously whoever smoke-checked your victims isn't a military sniper."

She hated having to ask. But, of course, she did. "Why?"

"Because a guy trained as a sniper would go for the chest shot. Because, though the single bullet smack in the middle of the head looks real cool in the movies, in real life a sniper always looks for the edge.

"A head makes too small a target, and if the target moves—like they usually do—or the wind does something weird after you pull the trigger, you can end up sailing a bullet over his head.

"Aim at the chest and if you hit high, you can nail the throat, or the head. Hit low and you've got the balls. Or even the thighs, which will bleed out like a stuck pig."

"Well."

Cait thought about that. And although it was an unpalatable thought, she also was forced to consider that the man she'd hoped never to see again might possibly be the most qualified to help her stop the UNSUB before he turned Somersett into his own personal shooting gallery.

"So, following your theory, why would this guy aim at his victims' heads?"

"Probably showing off. Could be he washed out of some program. Army sniper school, maybe. Or Air Force. Or, hell, even the Marines. They're lethal with their rifles."

"I can't help noticing you've left out the SEALs."

He'd put the shades back on, so she couldn't see his eyes, but from the way the muscle jerked in his cheek, Cait suspected he didn't much like that observation.

Tough.

"Or the SEALs," he allowed through set teeth, reminding her that he wasn't always as laid-back as he appeared. "Though this is where I feel the need to point out that you'd be hard-pressed to find a single incidence where a military-trained sniper from any of the services went bad and started shooting innocent people."

"What about those snipers in D.C.?" asked Angetti, who'd remained silent since the book discussion.

"One of them was a teenage kid," Quinn said. "The other, which you and your partner, being federal special agents and all, should know, might admittedly have qualified as an M16 marksman. But being able to blast away with an automatic rifle doesn't make a guy a sniper.

"John Williams, or John Allen Muhammad, or whatever the hell name he was using, would've washed out the first day of psych testing."

Although she hadn't joined the FBI yet at the time, like most Americans, Cait had been riveted on the chaos created by the Beltway snipers for more than three weeks back in 2002. The idea that Somersett might be facing such a threat made her blood run cold.

7

"San Diego PD got hold of Mrs. Jacob," said Briggs, who'd caught up with them. "She's on her way back here. If the airlines don't screw up the schedule, she should arrive early tomorrow morning."

"That's good to hear," Cait responded. "Especially since, with the general's car parked in the Hawthornes' driveway, some reporter's undoubtedly run the plates, which means his name's probably already hitting the airwaves.

"Meanwhile, we need to clamp down on this shooter. Set up roadblocks. Start checking vehicles."

"Do you have any idea how many cops that'll take? Especially with all the tourists in town?"

"Don't worry. I'll get you some FBI backup." She hoped. "And have your chief call ATF to see if they want to get in on the action."

Although she hoped she was wrong, Cait's spidey sense was telling her this could get a lot worse before it got better.

"One more thing you might want to keep in mind," Quinn offered. "Whatever the weapon turns out to be, it'll have been sawed down to make it more compact."

"Who the hell are you?" Briggs demanded.

"Quinn McKade," Quinn answered mildly.

"He's okay," Angetti assured the detective. "Guy's an ex-SEAL who wrote a book."

Which didn't seem to mean a thing to Briggs, who

Cait figured didn't read anything that didn't have a centerfold, but his partner, Manning, did a double take. She watched recognition dawn. "Hey. *Kill Zone*. I read that. Great story."

"Thanks," Quinn said simply. He shot a look Cait's way as if apologizing for the topic having turned toward him.

"You sure about the short barrel?" she asked, reclaiming the conversation.

"The sound was more of a boom than the usual crack," Quinn replied. "So, yeah. I'm sure."

"Well." She processed that information. "Thanks. That's very helpful."

She wasn't sure how yet, but that was the thing she'd always enjoyed about working homicide. You took all these seemingly unconnected little pieces of clues, put them together, and eventually, bingo, you were looking at the full picture.

As more detectives and uniformed cops arrived and started working their way outward from the crime scene, searching for evidence, Cait set about interviewing the faculty and staff.

The victim, Captain Will Davis, a former Air Force fighter pilot who'd served in both Desert Storm and the early days in Afghanistan after 9/11, was both respected and beloved at the academy. Not only was he the director of the academy's popular regimental bagpipe band, but he also played a mean sax in the commandant's faculty jazz quartet.

He'd just celebrated his first anniversary, and lived on tony Palmetto Drive, which had, since the city's founding, been home to Somersett's aristocrats. Having some idea of what her father, who'd been at the academy far longer and outranked Davis, earned, Cait wondered how a mere captain could afford the mortgage.

If he had any enemies, none of the witnesses or any of the staff who'd come running out when they'd heard of the shooting knew about them.

And even in broad daylight, with so many people on the scene, no one had seen anything that was helpful.

No witnesses. No evidence. And, dammit, the sun was setting.

"Might as well shut down for the night," Briggs said after he returned from questioning potential witnesses at the Winn-Dixie across the street. The body had been taken away in the medical examiner's van, and patrol cops were removing the crime scene tape from the supermarket parking lot. "Start fresh in the morning with new troops."

"We need to do more door-to-door questioning back at the first crime scene," Cait insisted.

"I'll call the chief," Manning offered. "Have him send some of the late-shift guys to help out."

"Thanks," Cait said. "Meanwhile, I'd better go break the news to Mrs. Davis before she turns on her TV and hears it on the six o'clock news."

Notifying families that a loved one would never be coming home had always been the least favorite part of her job. But it was also one of the most important duties a law enforcement officer ever performed, and it was one Joe had taught Cait never to leave to anyone else. Especially Briggs, who had the social skills of pond scum.

"Works for me," Manning agreed. "Also, I got a call from the uniform we left back at the Hawthornes'. The husband's back home."

"So, who gets to interview him?" Briggs asked.

From the edge in his voice, Cait could sense the turf battle brewing again.

"Since Manning caught the case, it makes sense that he does it." Briggs might be a scum idiot, but the other detective had always had decent interrogation skills. "But I'd like to sit in. If you don't mind," she tacked on with what she hoped was the proper deference.

Apparently she'd pulled it off.

"Sure," Manning agreed easily. "I want to keep the

captain away from his wife, just to make sure they don't compare stories, in case something is hinky. So I'll have a uniform bring him to the station and keep him on ice until you finish up with Davis's widow."

"Sounds good."

As soon as she reached the street where reporters were once again pressed against the barricades, Cait was hit with a barrage of questions.

One of the first things she'd learned in dealing with the media was that the best tack to take was maximum disclosure, minimum delay. Because if you didn't feed them at least some facts, they'd start making things up.

Not wanting to be responsible for erroneous or misleading information getting out, she shared as much as she could, holding back Quinn's take on the type of weapon used.

She announced that two faculty members from the Admiral Somersett Military Academy had been fatally shot in separate incidents. It was not yet known where the shots had come from. Or if they'd come from the same weapon. And no, she didn't know if they were looking for one shooter or two.

"You're on the JTTF force, right, Special Agent Cavanaugh?" Valentine Snow called out.

"That's right," Cait said, knowing full well that the newswoman had known the answer when she'd asked the question.

"Does your presence at the murder scenes mean the authorities believe that these shootings are terrorism-related?"

A wave of excited chatter moved through the press ranks at that idea.

"Special Agent Angetti and I were called in because the first victim had Pentagon ties," Cait explained. "While at this point in time we're consulting with the Somersett Police Department, nothing is pointing to terrorism."

"What's the name of the second victim?" a reporter from Charleston's WCIV asked.

Cait shook her head. "Somersett PD will be releasing that information after the next of kin is notified."

That said, she began walking away, thinking the impromptu press conference had gone well, all things considered.

Her momentary satisfaction evaporated like morning mist beneath a hot Lowcountry sun as she approached the SUV and saw Quinn McKade leaning against the front fender.

8

The moment Cait had met Quinn, when he'd shown up at the apartment she shared with a nursing student at St. Camillus, she'd known he was trouble. He had met her roommate at a Christmas party earlier that week, and although Cait had insisted she'd been looking forward to a sudsy evening watching *An Affair to Remember* on video, the other woman had flat out refused to leave her alone on New Year's Eve. So McKade had brought along a friend, Zach Tremayne, for her.

The two men had just completed SEAL training, which right away was a deterrent. And, although it was supposed to be the most glamorous night of the year, Cait hadn't bothered getting all dolled up because no way on God's green earth was she ever going to get seriously involved with a military man.

She knew some former service brats who actually claimed to have enjoyed the vagabond existence that was part and parcel of military life. They mentioned the fun of seeing the world—as if bases weren't pretty much identical wherever they were—of meeting new friends, of learning to fit in wherever their fathers (and in those days it was just the men dragging their families hither and yon) got posted.

But Cait had hated it. She'd longed for a room of her own that she could paint whatever colors she wanted; she didn't want to keep having to roll up her posters of Johnny Depp, 'N Sync, and Leonardo Di Caprio. By the time they'd finally settled down in Somersett, poor Justin Timberlake had suffered so many tack holes, his pretty face looked as if it'd been peppered with shotgun pellets.

By the time she finished the eighth grade, she'd attended nine different schools in nine different towns. And each time, when the teacher would announce the new student and she would stand there at the front of the room, with every other kid in the class staring at her, Cait had felt as if she'd had a big red target on her back. Or at least a KICK ME sign.

Not helping was her redhead's quick-fire temper. Oh, she'd learned to control it over the years, but when she'd been younger, playground fights—where she'd only been defending her own honor!—had landed her in the principal's office on a depressingly regular basis.

Her mother, she'd decided long ago, was a saint. Since Cait was about as far away as anyone could get from canonization, she'd sworn to avoid following her mother into that long-suffering-military-wives' club.

Which was why, when she came out of her bedroom on New Year's Eve and got her first glimpse of Quinn McKade taking up so much of the tiny apartment living room, she'd felt a frisson of unease.

First of all, he was huge, towering over her roommate and the other SEAL like Godzilla over Tokyo, making her feel small. And defenseless, a feeling she'd suffered too many times in her life. One that triggered fight over flight.

His face, even back then, was craggy. Too hard-edged to be conventionally handsome. Nothing like Johnny Depp's. And he looked to have been scalped; she could see nicks all over his shaved head.

Although he'd been smiling when she entered the room, his gunmetal gray eyes held a glint of hardness that told her this was not a man who could be manipulated.

Which was, again, totally different from the college boys she usually dated. Easygoing males who willingly let her call the shots. Guys who understood that she wasn't in a relationship for the long haul. She had plans. Goals. And none of them involved playing second fiddle to some soldier or sailor with plans and goals of his own.

Which was why when she practically saw the words "This Is the One!" flashing above his head in red neon letters, Cait truly understood fear for the first time in her life.

U.S. Navy SEAL Quinn McKade was dangerous. Dangerous to her future. And even more dangerous to her insane, mutinous heart—which, although he was her roommate's date, not hers, had suddenly taken a ride on a Tilt-A-Whirl.

Which was precisely why she had to hate him.

Which didn't explain how, eight years later, when they'd met at that damn wedding reception, she'd ended up in bed with him.

"I remembered something while you were doing that press thing," her partner—who looked even shorter than usual standing next to the former SEAL—said.

"Tell me it's something that'll close the case," Cait said, pointedly ignoring Quinn.

"Don't I wish. Sorry, but I'm supposed to meet the ball and chain at the Wingate Palace. It's her parents' anniversary, and there's this chichi family dinner thing in the restaurant. And I'm already twenty minutes late."

"So, we'll call you a cab. And I'll pick you up tomorrow morning at home."

"Or, as I've already suggested to Special Agent Angetti," Quinn said, breaking into the conversation, "rather than wait for a cab to show up, he could take the SUV. And I'll run you over to the widow's house."

"Thanks, but I wouldn't want to put you out," Cait said.

"No problem. All I had on tap for the evening was a beer and a book. Both of which can wait. Besides, I might be able to be some help."

"Oh?"

He'd taken his shades off in deference to the darkening sky. His eyes, in the whitish glow of the halogen parking-lot lamps, were the color of burnished pewter.

"I knew Davis. Personally. I also know his wife. If the lady falls apart, it might be helpful to have someone there with her."

Cait couldn't deny that. But still . . .

"Cait?" Angetti broke into her thoughts as she was going through all the reasons why she didn't want to collaborate in any way with the former SEAL. He tapped his index finger on the face of his watch.

Her partner might be a pain in the butt, but she had to give him points for worrying about ruining his in-laws' anniversary party. Though more likely he was concerned about pissing off his wife yet again. The long work hours were probably one of the many reasons FBI agents and cops shouldn't get married.

Maybe once he retired, he wouldn't be such a pain in the ass.

Deciding that the leopard down at the Somersett zoo suddenly sporting neon zebra stripes would be more likely than her partner doing a one-eighty personality change, Cait experienced a moment of pity for Mrs. Angetti, who would soon be stuck with her husband 24/7.

"Go." Cait waved him off. "Have a great time."

"Yeah, right. Like that's going to happen. We've been married twenty-five years, and my old bat of a mother-in-law still never misses an opportunity to catch Liles up on what her former boyfriend, aka 'the filthy rich dentist who has more money than God,' is up to."

"If you're trying to make points, you might want to stay away from the ball-and-chain analogy," Cait felt obliged to point out.

"Hell, it's not like I say it to her face," Angetti grumbled as he unlocked the SUV's driver's-side door.

"Sounds like a fun evening," Quinn said as they watched Angetti pull away from the curb.

"A root canal's undoubtedly more fun than an evening with that guy," Cait said. "Thanks for the offer for a ride to the Davis house, but I think I'll just snag a black-and-white and meet you there."

Ever since Nate Spencer, Swann Island's sheriff, had brought up Cait Cavanaugh's name during the slasher case, Quinn had been thinking about her. Too damn much.

From the first time they'd met on that long ago New Year's Eve, although he'd been dating her roommate and had set her up with Zach, she'd always been able to get into his head. Under his skin. Infiltrating his dreams so he'd wake up hard and horny.

He certainly hadn't planned to run into her today. But now that some psycho with an automatic weapon had thrown her into his lap—at least metaphorically—there was no way he was going to let her get away.

Not yet, at least.

"Taking a cruiser out of business will just cut into your resources," he said. "Which isn't a good move when you're trying to set up roadblocks."

"Good point."

She'd run out on him once before. From the obvious reluctance in her voice, Quinn suspected she would love to turn and walk away now. But he was counting—correctly, as it turned out—on her professionalism.

"One of the things you pick up right away when you're working with a team of five guys is that logistics is job one."

"I suppose so." She rubbed her fingers at the vertical lines carving their way between her eyes. "I have the horrible feeling this is going to get really ugly."

"It well could."

She shot him a look. "Excuse me if I'm underwhelmed by your support."

"I've never lied to you, Caitlin," he said, stressing the import of the claim by using the more formal version of her name. It had occurred to him on more than one occasion that if he had lied to her, just a little, until he'd maneuvered her where he wanted her, they might not have stayed strangers all these intervening years. "And there's no reason to start now."

"Everybody lies," she said as they began walking toward the faculty parking lot.

"That's a fun outlook on life."

"Hey, I'm a cop. I gave up my rose-colored glasses when I started carrying a badge and a gun."

"That's funny," he said as they passed the larger-than-life statue of Admiral Somersett in front of Buccaneer Hall.

It was a long-standing tradition that cadets piss on the admiral's boots sometime before graduation. Quinn idly wondered if that tradition had fallen by the wayside with the admission of women.

"What?"

"I never thought of you as being the kind to wear rose-colored glasses ever *before* you joined SPD."

"Something wrong with looking at life like it is? And not like you'd like it to be?"

"Not at all." Quinn clicked the remote to open the door on the BMW. "Gotta go with whatever works for you. I was just saying."

"In my business and, I suspect, your former one, pessimism can help keep you alive. Besides," she began to argue, in the way he remembered all too well, "just because—" She broke off when she noticed the car. "This is your vehicle?"

"Despite what you may think of me, I'm not stupid enough to boost a car in front of an FBI agent. Why? Something wrong with it?"

"Well, while it's the expected guy blind-your-eyeballs red, I would've figured you for something flashier. Like your buddy Zach Tremayne's ridiculously macho Viper. Or a Corvette. Maybe a Porsche."

"I'm six-five," he reminded her as he opened the passenger door before she could do it herself. "I'd have to leave the top off any of those. And it rains too much here for that. This baby gives me the five hundred horsepower and handling of a German sports car without making me lie flat on my back to drive it."

"Still, it's pricey," she said as she slid into the soft-as-a-glove leather seat. "The vice cops seized one from a drug dealer while I was on the force. Then, thanks to asset forfeiture laws, they turned around and sold it at auction for over seventy-five thousand bucks, which went to the SPD widows and orphans fund. I'd guess new ones cost more."

"A bit."

"You must have sold a *lot* of copies of that book."

"I'm no Grisham, but I'm doing okay. And while my advance was generous enough, thanks to Uncle Sam pretty much paying expenses all those years I was in the navy, I managed to put some money away.

"Plus I've got a gig on the side teaching the occasional creative writing class at the academy and I also do some work for Phoenix Team. That's an international private security firm—"

"On Swann Island. I know. I was offered a job with them."

"I suppose Phoenix Team's loss is the feds' gain."

She didn't respond, but being pretty good at reading people, Quinn sensed she appreciated the compliment.

9

They were two miles from the campus and she still hadn't spoken. Quinn figured she was thinking about the case, but then she said, "I can't get a handle on you."

"I'm not that complicated." That might not exactly be a lie. But if he were to be perfectly honest, it might be a bit of a hedge.

"Maybe. But how many SEALs end up novelists teaching creative writing? Which, no offense, isn't exactly a gung ho class."

"No offense taken. You've also been watching too many movies," he said mildly. "One of my classmates at BUD/S—that's basic underwater demolition SEAL training—had a Ph.D. in philosophy. And the class proctor was a rocket scientist."

She glanced over at him. "You're making that up."

"Swear to God." He lifted his right hand from the steering wheel. "He'd gone to USD in his spare time and graduated with a B.S. in aerospace engineering the week my class graduated from BUD/S."

"I'll bet they're the exception."

"You know what I think?"

"What?"

"That just maybe you took those profiling courses at the FBI Academy a little bit too literally. Because from what I've seen, people—even SEALs—don't fit all that well into tidy little niches."

"For your information, I happen to agree with you."

"Well." He flashed her a grin. "That's a start."

She didn't respond. Just folded her arms and directed her attention out the passenger window at the line of tall palm trees that had given Palmetto Drive its name.

"This is a pretty ritzy neighborhood for a captain," she murmured.

"Not when said captain's mother was a Hightower."

That got her attention. "Like *the* Hightowers? Hightower Oil, Hightower Shipyards, which just won a contract to build two atomic aircraft carriers? And then there's Hightower Bank and Trust, and God knows what else?"

"The *what else* including Hightower Library at the academy. According to Will, generations of male Hightowers were expected to attend ASMA, going back to its founding."

"Too bad for them. But we're talking serious family bucks."

"I'd say in the range of several billion," he agreed.

"The parents are dead, right?"

"Right. They died in a plane crash during a dust storm coming back from Dubai two years ago. But a board of directors is keeping the various companies going."

"So why was Captain Davis working as a teacher? Hell, why did he go into the military in the first place?"

"Maybe he liked it. Or thought it might be an adventure, a chance to see the world."

"Which he could've done first class."

"The guy never acted as if he came from money. As for teaching, some people find the career a calling."

"Some people aren't gazillionaires."

"Are you saying that if you won the lottery tomorrow—"

"I don't play the lottery."

"Hypothetically speaking. Let's say you were watching TV some Friday evening and saw that you'd just won Powerball, which would set you up for life. Would you actually show up for work the next morning?"

"Of course."

"You love being a special agent that much?"

"I can't imagine not working."

It wasn't a direct answer. Unusual for her. Quinn remembered her being unrelentingly direct.

"Well, I guess that's something else we can agree on."

She fell silent again, mulling his statement over. He could practically hear the wheels turning in her head.

"So you liked being a SEAL?"

"For the most part. A lot of the time it was like playing war when you were a kid. "

Not that he'd been allowed to when *he'd* been a kid. At least not at home, where he'd never been allowed to have friends over, anyway. But his parents hadn't been able to control what he did at recess on the school playground.

"The difference is, being in Special Operations, I got to play with the most expensive toys Uncle Sam could buy, which was cool. And it's true what they say about joining the navy and seeing the world. I liked going to lots of different countries, liked the adventure, the night runs, really liked the commitment and adrenaline rush of HALOing—that's high-altitude, low-opening parachute insertion—and I really enjoyed the camaraderie of being part of a team."

Actually, he'd freaking loved what had been the first real family he'd ever known.

"How about the fighting?"

"Yeah. That, too. There's one helluva rush to combat you can't get from anything else in life. At least nothing that's legal."

Whoa. Having grown up in the weird and solitary world of the Vietnam War protestors' underground, Quinn was an expert at keeping secrets. Which was why, he'd often thought, he'd been a natural to join a covert Spec Ops team.

The only people he'd ever shared anything the slightest bit personal with were Zach Tremayne and Shane Garrett. He'd certainly never spilled his guts to a woman. Most of whom, he'd realized early in his career, might really enjoy the idea of going to bed with a big, bad SEAL but didn't want to dwell on what, exactly, warriors did to earn their paycheck from Uncle Sam.

"Well." More turning of mental wheels. "That's not exactly a politically correct statement to share with a civilian."

He shrugged. "You're not exactly a civilian. You're a cop. A federal terrorist-fighting cop." Who knew the business end of a weapon and how to use it. "Besides, I've never been all that politically correct."

"Now there's a surprise," she murmured.

He didn't hear the edge to her voice that he would've expected. In fact, although it might just be hopeful thinking and although he couldn't see her face, because she was looking out the window again, Quinn thought he might just have heard a touch of a smile.

"It's become popular, especially these days, to admire the troops," Quinn said quietly. "For what's perceived as their innate toughness, courage, patriotism. But that image doesn't allow for the idea that anyone could actually, in some way, feel any exhilaration in combat. And if you do, you're damn well expected to keep it to yourself."

"Yet you just told me."

"Yeah. Must've fallen under the power of your excellent interrogation skills. I'll bet you busted a lot of balls in the box." In a stroke of lucky timing, he glanced over at her just as she looked back at him. "Isn't that what you cops call it? The box? Or is that just on TV?"

"Yeah." This time the smile in her voice was echoed

at the corners of her mouth. A mouth that, although it should have been impossible, he could still taste after all these years. She'd tasted like rum and sugar and mint and he could've drunk from those sweet lips forever. "That's what we call it. And, yeah, I was okay."

He suspected she'd been a lot better than okay. She'd always seemed driven to perfection. Something she probably, at least back then, never would've believed they had in common.

"I'd bet you played the good cop."

Quinn could easily visualize it, like a scene from a book. There'd be a small, stark, airless room with the requisite one-way mirror taking up most of one wall. Her partner would be seated in a straight-backed chair on one side of a narrow wooden table. Some low-life criminal would be seated on the other side.

He could imagine the partner grilling the perp, over and over, verbally pounding him, not letting him take a breath or gather his thoughts.

Then suddenly the steel door would swing open, and in would stroll a leggy redhead smelling as fresh as a spring garden, the scattering of freckles across the bridge of her nose giving her a look of innocence not often found in the testosterone-driven environs of the police department.

She'd be carrying coffee. Maybe an icy Coke from the machine if it was summer. As she ignored the county law against smoking in public places and offered a cigarette, her eyes, as blue as a County Kerry lake, would be warm and empathetic. Her smooth magnolia drawl would chide her partner for being too harsh. Too rigid.

Of course there'd be a way out of this mess, she'd say coaxingly. Then, leaning forward, perhaps even flashing a bit of lace in the open V neck of the silky blouse that clung to slender curves, she'd offer the lowlife a door out of the box.

Having fallen under her smooth, feminine spell, the

perp would leap for it. Only to find himself landing smack on his ass behind bars.

"You'd lose." Her words yanked him from the imaginary scene. The laughter he'd thought he saw hovering on her lips earlier had moved to those remarkable eyes. "I tended to play the bad cop. Perpetrators didn't expect it, so sometimes it caught them off balance."

"Makes sense to me. " She'd always, since the first moment they'd met, kept *him* off balance. "And did you just say 'perpetrators'?" He'd used the word once during a poker game conversation with Nate, who'd nearly laughed his ass off over what he'd insisted was a Hollywoodism.

"Yeah, I did." She folded her bare arms. "And if you tell anyone, I'll have to shoot you."

"Works for me," he said agreeably.

It occurred to Quinn as he pulled up in front of the nineteenth-century mansion, that as bad as it was that two men were dead at the hand of some psycho who was maybe planning to terrorize the town and smoke-check a lot more, for the first time in a very long while, he was actually enjoying himself.

10

Valentine was not in a good mood after her nightly newscast as she pulled into the parking lot of the gray stone building flying the orange, white, and green flag of Ireland next to the Stars and Stripes.

Having spent the past sixteen years cultivating sources all around the world, she was frustrated that that damn second shooting had thrown a monkey wrench into her broadcast schedule and she hadn't snagged an interview with FBI Special Agent Cait Cavanaugh.

That was the bad news. The good news was that no one else had either. So there was still a chance. Especially since she still had a kitten card up her sleeve.

It had begun to rain. She dashed across the cobblestones to the heavy oak door that had a sign stating, OPEN WHEN WE'RE HERE. CLOSED WHEN WE'RE GONE.

The Black Swan pub, decorated with yet more Irish flags and framed photographs of green hills, sparkling blue lakes, and castle ruins, was doing a standing-room-only business. The tall, dark-haired Irishman building pints behind the horseshoe-shaped wooden bar waved to her and pointed toward a two-top booth in the far corner of the room.

His welcoming smile smoothed her rough edges a bit. She waved back, then began making her way through the teeming throng of pirates and wenches. Fortunately, all were too busy partying and tossing back Guinness and Irish whiskey to pay her any notice.

Val wasn't going to lie; there were times she liked being recognized. When she'd first arrived in the Big Apple from that affiliate in Phoenix, she'd been jazzed at the idea of finally achieving her childhood goal of becoming famous.

That was then. This is now, she thought as she slid into the wooden booth. A hand-painted sign on the table stated RESERVED. The pub was essentially her home these days, since she was renting one of the two lofts upstairs. Brendan O'Neill, bartender and owner of the Black Swan, was not just her landlord, he was also her next-door neighbor. And, over the months she'd been in Somersett, he had become a friend.

Although having a reserved table in a bar wasn't as personal as having a husband greet you at the door with a hot kiss and a chilled glass of wine, Val liked the idea of someone waiting at home for her.

Taking in the broad shoulders stretching the seams of Brendan's green rugby shirt, narrow hips, and long legs as he deftly wove his way through the crowd, she wondered how the hell the Irishman had managed to stay single.

Or maybe he hadn't. Although they chatted each evening after she came home from the station and often in the morning, when he'd try to push breakfast on her, she realized that she didn't really know that many personal details about Brendan.

He'd been an attorney in Dublin. A barrister, she corrected herself. And had supposedly chosen family law because it had allowed him to avoid, in his words, "those frightful formal wigs and black robes" worn by lawyers in criminal or commercial law.

When she'd pressed a bit, the reporter in her wanting more facts, he'd admitted that the wardrobe hadn't been the sole factor. That standing up for the underdog had its appeal.

From the way his deep blue eyes had warmed at

the admission, Val had received the distinct impression that he'd enjoyed his work. Yet when his father had suffered a heart attack, Brendan had apparently given it all up to move back to a small town in the west to run the pub that had been in the O'Neill family for three generations.

A year ago she would have considered such a downwardly mobile career move odd. Even suspicious. Yet wasn't that exactly what she herself had done?

Of course, she'd had her reasons.

"What was the name of that town?" she asked, as he placed a glass of Chardonnay on the table.

"And what town would that be?" he asked, the lilt of Ireland singing in his deep voice.

"The one you came here from. Castleview? Castlelake? Something like that?"

"Castlelough. And why would you be asking that?"

"I was just pondering career choices." She picked up the glass, took a sip of the crisp, straw-colored wine, and eyed him over the rim of the glass. "How we all travel our own winding path."

" 'Tis true enough." Little lines crinkled outward from the corners of his eyes, adding not age but character. "I watched your report." His expression sobered. "It's a bad story, but you were excellent in the telling."

"Thanks." She wished she hadn't brought up work. It wasn't her favorite topic at the moment. "It should have been better."

"It will be."

"You're so sure of that, are you?"

"As sure as I am that the sun's going to rise out over the harbor tomorrow morning."

He skimmed a finger down her nose, the gesture casual, almost fraternal. Brendan, Val had discovered, was a toucher. She was not. Except in bed. From the time she'd shed her virginity with a cameraman at Northwestern's campus TV station, she'd always brought the same attention to detail to sex as she did to her work. Just as when she was doing a live broadcast in front of the camera, in bed Val knew exactly what to say, and how to move.

"Will you be having dinner? We've fresh oysters. And some soft-shell crabs."

He was always trying to feed her. Which, she had to admit, was rather sweet. Having lived a nomadic life the past years, using people and occasionally being used herself, Val couldn't remember the last time, before Brendan had come into her life, that anyone had simply wanted to take care of her without receiving something in return.

"I'm not that hungry. I think I'll just have a bowl of cereal and do some research on snipers."

She could tell he was inclined to argue. Appreciated when he didn't.

"A note was left for you. I found it on the counter, about ten minutes before you came in."

He reached into the front pocket of the half apron he was wearing and took out a plain white envelope with her name on it.

"That's odd."

"It's undoubtedly from a fan," he said. "Or a secret admirer."

"Those always come to the station." A little uneasy with any viewer knowing where she lived, she used a fingernail to open the envelope. Then felt her blood run cold as she viewed the two cards depicting a skeleton clad in a black suit of armor astride a white horse.

"What's wrong?" She could barely hear Brendan over the sound of her blood roaring in her ears. "You've gone as pale as Cromwell's ghost."

"They're death cards."

Without waiting for an invitation, and ignoring a call for a refill from across the room, he slid into the booth next to her. "They seem to be." He caught her wrist as she went to pull out the note accompanying the cards. "We'd best be leaving this for the police."

"You don't think . . . ?" Her eyes searched the

room wildly, skimming over the crowd, who were all currently clapping in time to the sprightly music accompanying two young girls step-dancing on a postage-stamp-sized dance floor.

"That it was left by the sniper?" His eyes turned as hard as flint. A muscle tensed in his cheek. "If not by him, perhaps by a compatriot. We'd best be calling the authorities."

11

Unlike its Tara-wannabe neighbors, the Davis house was two stories of imposing gray stone, not much different from that used to build the academy. A flagstone sidewalk, lined with precisely trimmed azaleas, cut across emerald grass that could have doubled as a putting green. A massive iron sculpture of an eagle took up the center of the lawn next to a towering flagpole from which an oversized American flag waved in the sea breeze blowing in from the harbor.

The double front doors were at least twelve feet tall and intricately carved. Cait suspected the work had been done by hand. A very long time ago. The doorbell tolled like she'd always figured Big Ben must sound.

One of the doors was opened by a fortysomething woman. Taking in the colorful turban and ebony complexion, Cait didn't need her detective skills to recognize Gullah roots.

"We're here for Mrs. Davis," she said.

"Mrs. Davis isn't at home."

And wasn't that always the case? Cait knew she was racing the local TV station and newspaper reports of the shooting. Although they hadn't released Captain Davis's name, she knew it was only a matter of time before some reporter dug it out.

"When do you expect her?"

Eyes the color of a raven's wing narrowed suspiciously.

"I'm FBI Special Agent Cait Cavanaugh." Thinking that she really needed to go home and change into something more professional, she flipped open her shield. "And this is . . ."

Cait paused, unsure what to call Quinn. He certainly wasn't a partner. Nor a friend. And no way was she going to refer to him as a former lover.

"Well, of course I know Mr. McKade." The housekeeper's gaze warmed considerably. "I'm sorry. But the captain isn't home yet, either."

"When do you expect Mrs. Davis home?" Cait asked.

"Anytime now. This is the day to volunteer at the library. But she's usually home in time to change for dinner."

Cait weighed the idea of calling the widow on her cell phone. But what if she were on the road? Learning in such a cold, impersonal way that her husband had been murdered could have fatal results. And weren't they dealing with enough dead bodies for one day?

"May we come in and wait?"

There was a moment's hesitation. Then, "I suppose that would be all right." The woman moved aside, allowing them into the mansion.

White marble flowed like a glacier beneath a massive chandelier dripping with crystal. Gilt-framed oil paintings hung on walls covered in burgundy silk, and in the center of the round foyer, a flower arrangement enormous enough for a Mafia funeral sat atop a heavy, lion-footed table. A flying staircase curved a long way upward, to the second-floor balcony.

They followed the housekeeper down what seemed to be miles of Oriental carpeting to the library, where leather-bound books filled the two-story mahogany bookcases on either side of a a black marble fireplace.

A Persian rug, so thin that Cait suspected it must be extremely valuable, glowed with muted colors.

After inquiring whether they'd like anything to eat or drink, an offer that both Cait and Quinn refused, the housekeeper left them alone.

"I've never been in a house like this that I didn't have to pay to visit," Cait murmured, looking up at the gilded mural of a race between two white paddleboats that had been painted on the plaster ceiling. She vaguely remembered hearing that the Hightower fortune had been made building paddle steamers to move cotton from the inland plantations down the Somersett River to the harbor.

"It's definitely not your average suburban tract house," Quinn agreed. "You should see the dining room. The table seats thirty."

"You're kidding."

"Nope."

"Wow."

Cait, whose dinner parties more often than not involved calling out for pizza, couldn't imagine the logistics of a sit-down meal for thirty of her best friends. Actually, thinking about it, she didn't think she *had* thirty friends. At least not close enough friends that she'd want to cook dinner for them.

"I guess it's true that the rich really are different," she decided.

"Maybe," Quinn said. "In some ways. But when F. Scott Fitzgerald said the same thing to Hemingway, Hemingway's response was, 'Yes, they have more money.' Still, I doubt money's going to make Kristin Davis's loss any easier."

"Probably not." Cait skimmed a fingertip over a black and white marble chessboard sitting atop the table in front of her. "This part of the job sucks."

"I imagine it would."

"So." She leaned back on the oxblood leather sofa and crossed her legs. "How well do you know the Davises?"

"Having spent the last six months playing on a basketball team with Will, I knew him better than I know Kristin." He paused.

"What?"

"I just realized that's probably how she met Mike."

"Mike?" Cait's cop senses went on full alert. Two sniper attacks in one day. What if both involved adultery?

"Mike Gannon. He's on the team, too. And no, to answer the question you're undoubtedly thinking, she wasn't romantically involved with him."

"Mike Gannon? Father Mike?" Who just happened to be the brother of her former partner. *Talk about your small world.* "And how did you know what I was thinking?"

"It was a logical enough assumption. But even if the lady did stray, which I've never gotten the impression she did, no way would Mike take up with a married woman. He might not be a priest any longer—"

"He's not?"

"He left the order after he got back from a sabbatical running a homeless shelter in post-Katrina New Orleans last year. He's set up a free clinic across from the church and is running a vets' PTSD group out of the basement of St. Brendan's. Kristin volunteers with the group. Mike says she's been a big help."

"She's a vet?"

"No, but she does have a degree in psychology, plus being a military wife gives her street cred with the vets."

"Maybe one of them got a little too interested in her?" Cait mulled that possibility over. "Decided to blow away the competition?"

"Just because a veteran is having a few problems—which shouldn't be surprising, given that going to war isn't exactly a normal life situation for anyone—doesn't mean he's a potential serial killer."

"I was just considering all the possible angles," Cait said. "Though that scenario gets tricky when you try to connect it to the first murder." The white queen was a little off center on its black square. She absently moved it back into place. "I wonder, since the parents are dead, who inherits in the event of Captain Davis's death."

"I imagine that would be Kristin. Unless she'd signed a prenup. But Will didn't seem at all concerned with his family's wealth, so I kinda doubt that."

"These are pretty snazzy digs for a guy who supposedly doesn't care about money."

"The place has been in the family since it was built." Quinn shrugged. "No point in not taking advantage of free housing."

"Convenient," Cait murmured.

"You don't suspect—"

"I never rule anyone or anything out," she said, cutting him off. "Besides, most homicides are personal."

They heard a door outside the library shut. There was an exchange of voices.

Then the paneled door opened and a willowy blonde entered the library. Her pale hair had been tucked into a French roll that was just messy enough to look retro rather than dated. At five-six and one-twenty, Cait had always rued her lack of curves. But she had a good ten or fifteen pounds on Kristin Davis, who looked as if the slightest wind might blow her away.

The widow was wearing a cream silk blouse, ivory slacks, and strappy sandals. A slender gold link belt circled the slacks' high waist.

The top two buttons of the blouse were unbuttoned, revealing a strand of what appeared to be very good pearls, which matched the pearls in her ears. Along with the pearls she wore a white-and-yellow-gold Rolex on her right wrist and an antique wedding band that Cait figured for an heirloom on the fourth finger of her left hand. The emerald-cut diamond in the center of the band, framed on either side with baguettes, was impressive, but not as gaudy as it might have been, given her deceased husband's bucks. Two carats, Cait decided. Of high enough quality to send off blue sparks beneath the light of the overhead chandelier.

"Quinn." Kristin Davis greeted him with a warm smile and an outstretched hand. "What a lovely surprise. I do hope you can stay for dinner."

Her hand disappeared between his two very much larger ones. "I'm afraid this isn't a social call, Kristin."

Her gaze moved to Cait. "Eugenia said something about the FBI?" A puzzled frown furrowed her brow.

"I'm Special Agent Caitlin Cavanaugh." Cait showed her shield, as she'd done with the housekeeper. "We're here about your husband, Mrs. Davis."

"Will?" Scandinavian blue eyes moved from Cait to Quinn. Then back again. "I'm afraid I don't understand."

"This is tough, Kristin," Quinn said soberly. "I'm afraid Will's dead."

"Dead?" She blanched, the color draining from her face. "That's impossible." She shook her head. "I was just talking with him a couple hours ago. He was finishing up tweaking this year's lesson plan. We were going to have a light supper in, then go out to watch the fireworks over the harbor." Her eyes welled with tears. "Was it an accident? I always warned him that stupid motorcycle was dangerous."

"He was fatally shot," Cait said gently. "At the academy."

"Shot?" Her beringed hand flew to her breast. Her startled, disbelieving gaze shot up to meet Quinn's. "That's impossible," she insisted yet again.

Then, before Quinn could catch her, Kristin Davis's knees buckled and she slipped bonelessly toward the floor.

"Damn." Cait dragged a hand down her face. "I hate it when that happens."

12

The Somersett police headquarters was housed in the courthouse, a Greek Revival building that would have looked right at home on MGM's backlot. There were times when Cait thought that the town where her family had finally settled was a Southern cliché. But that was partly what she loved about Somersett.

Although she was a realist through and through, sometimes, she considered as fireworks exploded over the harbor in a display of brilliant red, white, and blue, a little fantasy wasn't such a bad thing.

It was bedlam inside the stately building. Desks were crammed close enough to give a fire marshal apoplexy, phones were ringing off the hook, people were shouting back and forth across the room.

Ancient paddle-bladed fans creaked slowly overhead, struggling to churn moist air that smelled of mold, sweat, scorched coffee, chicken noodle Cup-a-Soup, and microwave popcorn.

Cait grinned at Manning, who had, as promised, waited for her. "God, I hadn't realized how much I've missed this."

"So, I guess it's not so colorful down at the FBI?" he asked, as they left the chaos and strode down the hallway to the relatively more quiet homicide bullpen.

"Hardly. We don't tend to get many transvestite hooker terrorists wearing fishnet stockings and five-inch Lucite heels with goldfish swimming around in them."

Although she would never claim to be an expert on style, even Cait could tell that the six-foot-tall prostitute with the prominent Adam's apple who was waiting to be booked could use a visit from the Fab Five; that silver-and-red lamé dress was totally wrong with the auburn wig.

"Your loss," Manning said.

Cait had begun thinking the same thing.

"Where's Briggs?" Cait asked as she looked in at the all-too-familiar man sitting alone in the interrogation room.

"He had a hot date."

"Guess he didn't notice that 'date' is out there in holding."

They both shared a laugh at that.

"So, where's McKade?"

"I assume he's at home." Though Cait hadn't asked Quinn's plans when he'd dropped her at the station, she'd refused to let him wait for her, figuring she could hitch a ride home in a cruiser.

She looked in at Captain Ryan Hawthorne.

"Well, I guess we'd better get to work," she said, her matter-of-fact tone meant to conceal her reluctance.

"Cait?" Ryan Hawthorne leaped up from the wooden chair as they entered the small room.

Despite his agitated demeanor, he still possessed the athletic golden-boy looks that had begun gracing the sports pages while he was still playing Pop Warner ball. Not only had he been the star quarterback of the high school football team, he'd also been president of the computer club and was voted class president two years in a row.

He'd also been prom king. Cait remembered that all too well, because, as embarrassing as she still found it, she'd been queen. Not that such rah-rah girlie stuff had been typical for her; she'd only run to please her mother, who'd been fighting non-Hodgkin's lymphoma at the time and had cared dearly about such things.

Not only had she been stunned to win—which she suspected had a great deal to do with her date being king—it was nothing she would ever want showing up on an FBI résumé.

"Thank God!" this blast from her past said. "Cait, you've no idea how glad I am to see you!"

Which was definitely a change. Cops didn't tend to be civilians' favorite people. During her three years in the Bureau, Cait had discovered that federal agents ranked even lower than local police in most people's personal hierarchy.

"Cait?" Manning shot her a look.

Cait shrugged. "We went to school together."

"Well, isn't that convenient?" He didn't bother keeping the sarcasm from his voice. "Makes this sorta like homecoming."

"It was a long time ago."

"I don't understand," Ryan Hawthorne said. "What's going on? Has something happened to Melanie? Is my wife all right?"

"She's fine," Cait assured him. "As for what's going on, that's what we're trying to find out, Ryan."

"Would you mind telling me where you were around five thirty, six p.m. today?" Manning asked.

"On the way back from Savannah. I was on a recruiting trip. There's this kid— But you probably don't need to know about that."

"You never know what might be relevant in an investigation," Manning said. "So, this kid's family, they can vouch for you?"

"Of course."

Since he hadn't been told about the general yet, he looked understandably confused. Cait hoped he hadn't become an expert liar in their years apart. As bad as having to interrogate an old boyfriend might be, putting him away for homicide would be a whole lot worse.

"We finished up around five. Right after he signed a letter of intent."

"Feather in your cap," Manning said.

"I feel good about it," he allowed. "The Citadel and VMI were both really pushing for him to sign with them. The general—that'd be my immediate superior, General John Jacob—assigned me to make sure they didn't get him." His stress seemed to ease slightly. "I think he'll be real pleased."

Cait and Manning exchanged a look, neither one missing his use of the present tense.

"Do you and the general have a relationship outside the academy?" Manning moved on.

"A relationship?" Confused blue eyes went to Cait, whose expression gave nothing away. "I don't understand. Are you asking if I'm gay?"

"No." Manning paused. Then asked, "Are you?"

"Of course not!" He dragged a hand over his close-cropped blond hair. "I mean, not that there's anything wrong with being gay," he said, addressing his words to Cait. "It's just that ASMA sends a lot of students to the military, so the administration tries to screen potential problems out in the recruitment process."

"Don't ask, don't tell," Manning said.

"That's pretty much it. But, like I said, I'm not gay. And while I know you can't be absolutely positive about anyone's sexual orientation, I'd bet the general isn't either."

Cait and Manning exchanged another look. She knew they were thinking the same thing. That if that red robe Melanie Hawthorne had been wearing was any indication, the general's orientation compass had definitely pointed in a hetero direction.

"Actually, I was asking if you were personal friends," Manning said. "You know, maybe you and your wife had the general and Mrs. Jacob over to dinner. Or you and he'd go out and get a beer sometimes after work, shoot some pool. That sort of thing?"

"No." He shook his head. "Mel and I have attended the annual department cocktail party that he and his wife host every year at the beginning of the school year. And we've run into each other at academy social functions. That sort of thing. But the general isn't one to make personal friends with junior officers."

"Yeah. I remember that separation from my days in the military," Manning said. "I was a sergeant. Armor."

"I always thought it'd be way cool to drive a tank."

"It was."

Despite the seriousness of the subject, Manning grinned.

Male bonding at work yet again. Cait understood it, on an intellectual level, but she also knew that, as good as she was at working in male environs, due to the lack of a penis she would never be quite as much a part of that macho world as these two former military guys.

Then again, she doubted that either Manning or Ryan could understand the pure hedonistic pleasure of indulging in a box of chocolate truffles while lounging in a scented bubble bath.

"So," Manning continued, getting back to work, "it wasn't usual behavior for the general to visit your house?"

"No. I can't remember him ever visiting." Intelligent eyes narrowed. Ryan Hawthorne might not be a cop, but he *had* been salutatorian of their high school graduating class. "Why?"

"Because General Jacob was killed this afternoon," Manning said.

"What?" His disbelieving gaze shot to Cait. "That can't be true."

"I'm afraid it is," Cait said. She glanced over at Manning, who nodded, giving her the go-ahead to reveal the details. "He was fatally shot once in the forehead by someone who appears to know what he was doing."

"Oh, my God."

His shock appeared genuine. Cait desperately hoped it was.

"There's more." She'd been standing against the door while Manning had sat opposite Hawthorne, conducting the interview. Now she crossed the small room and took the third chair. "He was shot in your driveway."

Beneath his athlete's tan Hawthorne went nearly as pale as his wife had. But then his eyes hardened and his jaw firmed as he morphed from a confused, stressed-out murder interrogation subject to the military man he'd once been.

"Cait?" His voice was steady. He was now a man in control. If not of the situation, of himself. "Will I be needing an attorney?"

13

"Well," Manning said as he and Cait watched Ryan Hawthorne leave the bullpen. "What do you think?"

"I think his wife's going to have to do some fast talking to explain that robe. But I also think he was telling the truth."

"Are you speaking as a former homicide detective turned FBI special agent? Or as the guy's high school squeeze?"

"I said we *knew* each other. I didn't say he was my boyfriend."

"You didn't have to. The way the guy was eating you up with his eyes when you came into the box, if you'd been a Big Mac and fries, you'd have been a goner."

"You know, Derek, I've always admired your way with words."

"What can I say?" He shrugged. "It's a gift."

"Look, I honestly don't think he had anything to do with the shootings."

"Neither do I. He may be on staff at the academy, but until that moment when he nearly lawyered up, I can't remember grilling a guy less likely to even own a gun, let alone know what to do with it."

"He worked the computers on the ship in the navy," she said. "I believed him when he said just about the only time he'd ever shot a gun was during basic training."

"Like I said, he doesn't fit."

"No." Cait rubbed her temple, where the headache that had been threatening earlier had hit with a vengeance. "Look, this probably doesn't have anything to do with anything—"

"But?"

"But when we ran into each other a couple weeks ago, he asked me out for a drink."

He rubbed his jaw. Narrowed his eyes as he considered that. "Could've just been one old friend catching up with another."

"Exactly." She was relieved he'd seen it her way.

"Or, he could've known his wife was getting it on with General Halftrack and since he doesn't have the cojones to blow the guy away, or even confront the guy, he decided to get himself a revenge fuck."

"Definitely a silver tongue," she muttered, echoing her earlier comment about his way with words.

"Or maybe *she* was the one getting back at him," Manning suggested. "Maybe the guy's a player. He was, after all, a sailor. And you know what they say about a girl in every port."

"He wasn't anything like that back in school."

"Yeah. Well, things—and people—change."

"True. But adultery doesn't necessarily lead to murder."

"Sometimes it does. Sometimes not." He rubbed the back of his neck and looked down at her.

"What?" she demanded as he dragged the silent study out.

"I don't make him for the shootings," he said finally.

"Neither do I," she said again.

"But no way am I giving him a get-out-of-jail-free card just because he's the guy who popped your cherry."

She kept her expression mild while inside she was screaming. "I don't remember mentioning anything about that."

"You didn't have to. Like I said—"

"Yeah. I know. French fries and all that." The maniac inside her head had moved on to pounding the back of her eyes with a sledgehammer. "And, although it's none of your business, he never got past second base."

"That's still personal," he countered. "So, this gonna be a problem for you? If he *does* end up high on the suspect list?"

"Not at all," Cait said quickly. Too quickly. "Okay," she allowed on an exhaled breath when he arched a brow. "Granted, it wouldn't be easy. I may have gone over to the dark side"—it was what he'd accused her of when she'd left SPD for the Bureau—"but I'm still a cop. I would never let any relationship I might have had with Hawthorne get in the way of doing my job."

He grinned. Ruffled her hair, patting her on the head like he might his favorite golden retriever. "I know that. Same way you never let the fact that you and I had that thing get in the way of us working together."

The *thing* in question had been a one-night stand during a time when she'd become unraveled after her divorce. A few weeks later, mired even more deeply in the pity party that had been her life back then, she'd gotten drunk and slept with Quinn McKade.

Cait had always been a control freak, and those had been the only two occasions in her life when she had gone slumming in "if-it-feels-good-do-it-ville." Both times, in the clear light of the following day, she'd felt anything but good. The difference was that she'd been able to brush off her night with Manning. While alcohol-blurred memories of Quinn had stuck like Krazy Glue.

Hell.

What were the chances of landing a case that forced her back into close proximity with not just a high school boyfriend but also the two coconspirators in her period of emotional insanity?

Suddenly patrolling the waterfront seemed vastly appealing.

14

As Cait was on her way out of the building with the uniformed cop who'd offered to run her by her house, Valentine Snow and Brendan O'Neill were coming in.

"Just the woman I wanted to see," Valentine said.

"Aw, jeez," Cait said. "Look, I'd love to get rid of another damn cat, and I'm sure you'd be a crackerjack kitty mommy, but right now I just don't have the time—"

"I think you'd best be making the time, Caitlin," Brendan said, his tone more serious than she'd ever heard it.

"It's important." Val seconded his quiet comment. "I think your sniper left me a letter."

Well, that certainly got her attention. And although she'd been feeling like a wrung-out dishrag only a moment earlier, a jolt of adrenaline came crashing through her system, bringing with it a second wind.

"I'm afraid I touched the cards," Val apologized as she, Brendan, Manning, who hadn't yet escaped, and Cait sat at his desk in the homicide bullpen. "But we left the note for you."

"Good thinking." Cait snapped on the latex gloves that the detective took from the box in his bottom drawer.

Next she took the tweezers he handed her and pulled out the note, which, dammit, had been printed on ordinary white copy paper.

" 'Dear Valentine Snow,' " she read aloud. " 'I've been a big fan of yours since you first appeared on network TV. You were—and still are—the perfect combination of beauty and brains, and I cannot understand why those idiots at the network would want to get rid of you and put that blond bimbo who couldn't find a news story if it bit her on her skinny, nonexistent ass in your place.' "

Looking up at Val, Cait said, "That would be Meredith Fuller."

"I suppose so," Val murmured. "Though she's no bimbo. And actually the decision to leave was mine."

"So I heard."

Cait had also read in *People* magazine, while waiting to get her teeth cleaned, that the network brass had ponied up another million to add to Valentine's current six-million-dollar-a-year salary if she would only agree to take over the anchor desk on the nightly news. Which, according to the article, she'd turned down flat.

"He does have one thing right," Brendan offered. "Your ass is decidedly finer."

His voice had turned as rich as cream over Irish whiskey.

Valentine flushed prettily.

Cait, who didn't need her detective skills to figure out that something was going on between the owner of the pub and television's former six-million-dollar woman, could practically see the birds and little hearts circling around Val's head.

The thing was, from the vibes she was getting, they hadn't figured it out yet, or acted on it.

She cleared her throat before everyone in the bullpen ended up getting pheromone poisoning.

"Getting back to the subject at hand." She returned to reading. " 'As your most faithful fan, I decided to do something to help you get your old job back. Trust me, Valentine, this is going to be the story of the year. Decade. Hell, it may even win you a Pulitzer.' "

"A Peabody," Val murmured.

Cait looked up.

"Pulitzers are for print, photography, and music. Peabodys are pretty much the equivalent, given in television and radio."

"Which you've already won," Brendan said. "For your Desert Storm reporting."

Val looked surprised by that. And more than a little pleased. "I'm amazed you know that."

"It was well deserved," he said. "I was still living in Ireland at the time, but the series ran on RTÉ. That's Irish national television," he informed Cait.

"I wasn't aware it went international," Val said.

"Aye, it did. In fact, when I started considering places to live in America, I kept thinking about Somersett, because of that interview you did with Michael Gannon, in the surgery."

"That was when he was a captain," she remembered. "And a doctor."

"He's lived a complex life, to be sure," Brendan agreed. "At the time, everyone in The Rose, which would be the pub I was running at the time, was glued to the set every night for a week. You even preempted a rugby match between Connacht and Munster."

"That's probably why you remembered," she demurred.

"Not at all," he said.

Jeez, Cait thought. Why didn't the two of them just get a room?

"That's very impressive," Cait said through set teeth. "But it's not to our point."

"It's still a clue," Manning said.

"Because whoever sent the note isn't up on broadcasting," Cait agreed.

"Obviously not," Val agreed, slipping from starry-eyed-teenager-hoping-to-be-asked-to-the-prom foolishness back into business newswoman mode.

" 'You did have one thing wrong,' " the printed note

continued. " 'When you suggested the sniper might be someone with a grudge against the academy.' "

Cait looked up again. "You *said* that? On the air?"

Val crossed her arms against the coral suit that was still amazingly free of wrinkles, making Cait wonder if she sprayed herself with Teflon every morning before leaving her apartment.

"Well, if you'd given me an interview, I just might have been able to share more actual facts with my viewers," Val said. A bit huffily, Cait thought.

"I happened to be a bit busy. What with the homicidal president of your fan club deciding to help your career out by killing people."

Cait went back to reading the note. " 'Thus David overcame the Philistine with sling and stone; he struck the Philistine and he did it mortally without a sword. One shot. One kill.

" 'The next target will definitely be a civilian. Stay tuned, as they say in the news biz.' "

"Christ." Dispensing with the on-air calm that had made her the go-to girl whenever tragedy struck anywhere in the country, the newscaster dragged a hand through her sleek dark hair. "This is a nightmare."

"I'm not going to argue that," Cait said. The maniac with the sledgehammer was now exploding grenades inside her head. "There's more: 'P.S. You probably don't recall, but we've met. You were even hotter in person than you appear on the air and it's a moment I'll never, as long as I live, forget. Love and kisses, your Best Fan Forever.' "

Cait carefully laid the note on the top of the desk. "I'm going to go out on a limb here and guess you don't remember meeting a guy who looked like Rambo."

"No." Val shook her head. "I'm sorry, but I'm thirty-nine years old, Cait, and I got into this business right out of college. Do you have any idea how many people I've met over the past eighteen years?"

"Well, maybe something will come to you," Cait said, not really believing it, but you never knew. Crazier things had happened. Like the Son of Sam getting caught on an outstanding parking warrant.

She studied the two cards. Although Val had already touched them, there was no point in risking smudging any latent prints with her own. Though she had a sinking feeling the shooter had been more careful than to touch them with his bare hands.

"This is the death card, right?"

"Right," Manning, who'd remained silent while Cait had been reading the note, said. Then his eyes widened. "Oh, shit," he said, his gaze colliding with Cait's as the thought struck them both at the same time. "It's just like in that book."

"Kill Zone," Cait said flatly. The idea had already occurred to her. After all, hadn't Quinn's book kept her up all night turning pages?

"That's right," Brendan said. "The shooter left it on the bodies of his targets."

"You don't think McKade—"

"He couldn't be our shooter." Cait cut Manning off. "The bullet that took out Davis nearly hit him."

Besides, as much as other things about him annoyed her, unless they were talking about the mother of all PTSD, Cait would bet her shield that Quinn McKade wasn't capable of cold-blooded murder.

"Guess you'd better go have a chat with McKade," Manning suggested.

As she left the station with the fresh-faced cop who'd waited to take her to her house, where she could pick up her own car, Cait decided that chatting with Quinn would come in at the very bottom of her to-do list.

Right below naked alligator wrestling.

15

The sun had come up bloodred and was moving across the sky as Quinn hunkered down with Zach and Lucas Chaffee a few yards from the downed copter. Their excuse, as they'd left the bunker, had been that they were going to retrieve some ammunition and equipment from the Chinook.

Which was partly true.

But the real reason was they needed to come up with a plan.

"Okay," Zach said. "If we hang around here, we're sitting ducks for any reinforcements those dead tangos might've called in."

"Roger that," Quinn said. "But won't we be risking Garrett dying of hypothermia if we take him out of the bunker into what's becoming a freaking blizzard?" he asked the medic.

"That's a distinct possibility," Lucas Chaffee allowed. "But here's the thing . . . I've done my best, conditions being what they are, but I'm not a surgeon."

"You saying his leg's gotta go?" Quinn asked, even as he dreaded the answer.

"I'm saying it's a possibility,*" Lucas sounded as grim as Quinn felt. "An even stronger possibility that if we don't get him to someone with more medical skills than mine, he might not make it until tonight."*

"Shit." Quinn dragged a hand down the black balaclava covering his face. The needles of ice were sting-

ing the skin around his eyes. He'd taken his goggles off, since unfortunately whoever had invented them hadn't thought to add wipers to clear off packed snow.

He exchanged a look with Zach, who shook his head, revealing his shared frustration with their situation.

"Why don't we just call 911," Quinn suggested. "Maybe the trauma center will send out an ambulance."

Frustrated, he glared at the CIA guy who'd left the bunker and was trudging through the deep snow toward them. Probably going to whine about conditions.

From what Quinn had witnessed over the years, spooks were more comfortable hanging around hotel bars and eavesdropping on drunken conversations than they were in actual battlefield conditions. He'd always figured if their asses were on the line more often, they might be more careful about getting their intel right.

"The pilot's in bad shape," the CIA guy announced, insinuating himself into their confab without an invitation.

"Now there's a news flash," Zach, who'd never been all that fond of the intelligence community himself, shot back. "Any other pertinent information you've picked up with your super-duper spook skills?"

"Actually, I do have some information that might prove helpful." The SEAL chief's sarcasm seemed to roll right off the guy's back. "There's a hospital we may be able to reach in time to keep your friend from dying."

"Sure," Lucas said. "And next you're going to tell us it's staffed with perky teenage candy stripers who'll kiss Garrett's boo-boo and make the hurt go away."

"There's no damn hospital in this region," Quinn said.

He might not have been in charge of this fucked-up mission, but since snipers were always looking for an edge, he'd gone over every square inch of the topo maps. A sniper's mind was packed with permutations, calculations, scraps of knowledge. Because you just never knew what you were going to need to know.

Or when you'd need to know it.

"There wasn't until last week," the spook said. "But the quake caused a lot of injuries and thousands of Afghanis and Pakistanis lost their homes. So various international relief agencies set up a camp—along with a reasonably staffed field medical unit—to treat the refugees."

"How far?" Zach asked.

He named a small village on the Pakistan side of the border.

"Shit. Even under perfect conditions, that'd be four and a half, maybe five hours," Zach said.

"Better than the eight plus you're looking at now, if we sit on our asses waiting for an evac copter," the CIA guy pointed out.

Quinn and Zach exchanged another look.

Quinn knew they were both thinking the same thing. If they took the Night Stalker pilot to the refugee camp, by crossing the border they'd be breaking not only their rules of engagement but international law.

"Odds are against keeping this secret." Lucas pointed out what they were all thinking. "If we do it, it's going to have to go into the report."

"Couldn't keep it out," Quinn agreed grimly. Can you say headlines, congressional hearings, and court-martials, boys and girls?

There was also the very real risk from al-Qaeda and Taliban who were holed up all over these mountains and weren't all that hospitable to strangers. Especially ones wearing the uniform of the U.S. military. By trying to save the life of the man who'd saved theirs with that un-fucking-believable landing, they could end up getting him—along with the rest of the survivors, including themselves—beheaded on Arab television.

And speaking of mountains, the goddamn village in question just happened to be straight up.

"The only easy day was yesterday," Zach said, quoting the BUD/S training slogan.

"Roger that," Lucas and Quinn agreed.

The spook didn't argue, which wasn't surprising, since it'd been his idea. Besides, the last time Quinn looked, the CIA guys didn't exactly play by anyone's book but their own.

So, with that it was settled.

They'd just returned to the bunker when what they'd been worried about all along happened.

The Chinook, which had been leaking fuel and smoldering since the crash, finally blew.

The earth rocked beneath Quinn's feet.

Rolling columns of blinding red and orange rose out of the wrecked metal.

The ammunition they hadn't yet had time to get off the copter—given that they'd been a little preoccupied with a firefight—exploded like fireworks.

"Damn it all to hell," Shane Garrett muttered, glaring up at the black smoke billowing into the sky. "I loved that bird."

His eyes, though laced with pain, hardened to brown flint. "Now those bastards are really going to have to pay."

Quinn hit SAVE, then leaned back in the desk chair and scrubbed at his face as he breathed in the acrid scent of aircraft fuel and smoke. Although the explosion had occurred eight months ago and more than six thousand miles away, while he'd been writing the scene he'd been right back there, reliving that never-ending day in the Hindu Kush.

He knew that most people, not just civilians but those in the military as well, thought of snipers as being coldhearted killers who'd been trained not to let emotion get in the way of their jobs. He suspected there were even those who didn't think they even *had* human emotions.

But they did. They just didn't show them to anyone.

The thing was, on the battlefield, you needed to be coolheaded and coldhearted, and you had to be able to control yourself, no matter what was going on. But, dammit, you were still human. If you didn't hang on to those feelings, you could step over the line and become some crazed, homicidal maniac, like whoever the hell had shot those victims today.

It wasn't an easy balancing act. Which was why his team had always been important. Quinn had never allowed anyone inside his head while he was shooting, but sometimes a guy had to let his guard down. And that was where Zach and Shane had come in. They'd never judged him, which had allowed him to expose his personal feelings, which—in turn, he'd always thought—had kept him human.

Eight months ago, Quinn's power had come out of the barrel of the gun. Now, having sold the novel he'd written while still in the SEALs, it came from his computer keys. He didn't expect the novel he was currently writing based on his experiences to change the world. But just maybe it might help some people understand that war wasn't something you watched on TV or in movies. Or even read about in books, like his.

It was all too real. Which he was discovering all over again. He'd originally planned this book as a novel, believing that sometimes more truth could be told as fiction. But the words that kept showing up on his computer monitor weren't merely reality-based products of his imagination. They were a blow-by-blow account of those long, cold, deadly hours that had changed all their lives.

The doorbell rang. Glancing down at his watch, he realized that more than two hours had passed since he'd sat down at the computer to write that scene, which would forever be burned onto his memory.

Emotions still raw, he got up to answer the door. Quinn had stopped being surprised by life a very long time ago. But when he saw Cait Cavanaugh standing on his porch, he felt as if he'd been hit in the solar plexus with a Louisville slugger.

One thing for sure—life had been easier, and definitely less complex, back when Quinn's view had been narrowed to what he could see through his sniper's scope.

16

"You're being ridiculous." Valentine continued the argument that had been going on since she and Brendan had left the police station.

"Is it that American mothers haven't taught their daughters about the fragility of the male ego?" he asked mildly. "Or is it just that you'd be choosing to ignore the warning? Because being referred to as *ridiculous* might possibly take the winds out of a lesser man's sails. So to speak."

Reaching into the front pocket of his jeans, he pulled out the key to unlock the pub's heavy door. Although there'd been a howl of complaint among his customers, he'd shut down early in order to take the letter to the authorities.

"But you're not one of those," she allowed as they entered the building. Everything was just as they'd left it—glasses, some not yet empty, sitting on tables, giving the pub the air of a party interrupted. "A lesser man."

"I like to think not."

He'd always kept a tidy establishment, which was why it pained him to walk past all those cluttered tables to the door leading to the stairway at the back of the room. But Caitlin had said she'd be sending a crime lab team over in the morning to check all those glasses for fingerprints, so he'd have to be waiting to clean up.

She'd admitted she wasn't expecting to find anything useful, but had hoped perhaps they'd get lucky and at least discover that one of the would-be pirates had served in the military. Even better would be if they'd find themselves a sniper.

"I'll be perfectly safe," Val insisted yet again as she walked up the stairs in front of him.

Despite the seriousness of their situation, what he'd told her in the police station was absolutely true. Valentine Snow did, indeed, have a very fine ass. World class, in Brendan's opinion.

"Of course you'll be safe," he agreed. And wasn't he going to make sure of that?

"I meant alone."

"You won't even know I'm around," he said yet again.

"Yeah. Right."

Her dark hair fanned out as she shook her head with seething frustration. It was not the first time he'd imagined it spread across his pillow. His chest. His thighs.

With a sigh of resignation, Brendan knew it wouldn't be the last.

"You're not that easy to ignore," she said.

"Am I not?" he asked as they stopped at the top of the stairs.

There were two doors—one leading to his loft apartment, the other to hers. He thought about asking, "Your place or mine?" but decided the American cliché wouldn't help him make his case.

"Any male as good-looking as you has got to know he's a woman magnet," she said. "Or do you actually expect me to believe that you haven't noticed that a good two-thirds of your clientele on any given night is of the female persuasion?"

He *had* noticed. It would have been difficult not to when he often found telephone numbers written on the small paper napkins when he'd clear the tables. He wondered what Valentine would say if he told her the truth—that there was only one woman he wanted to attract. And she was currently standing right in front of him.

Another image popped unbidden into his sex-starved brain. One of cutting off the argument by taking her mouth, pressing her against either one of those two doors, lifting up her snug skirt, and—

"Well?"

Her annoyed voice shattered the sexual fantasy just as she'd been wrapping those long, tan legs around his hips.

"Well?" His brain had gone to mush. Which, Brendan supposed, made sense, given that all the blood in his head had shot south below his waist.

"You're not going to deny you've noticed all those females who want to get into your pants."

"Perhaps they frequent the Swan because they enjoy the step dancing," he suggested.

Did *she* want to get into his pants? And wouldn't he be glad to help her with that? Starting now.

The frustrated sound deep in her throat sounded a great deal like a growl. Which he found inordinately sexy. Then again, Valentine could turn him on by reading the fecking IRS code.

"Which apartment?" he asked, getting back to the initial argument, since this second, sexual one was threatening to undermine all his good intentions to protect her.

"You're not going to give up, are you?"

"I'm Irish. We're a people known for our tenacity."

"Hardheadedness, you mean."

"Aye, that too."

Unfortunately, his head wasn't the only thing that was hard. Which he'd grown accustomed to. Ever since the newscaster had arrived in the city and moved into his vacant apartment, he'd been walking around semi-aroused.

"Mine," she decided on a huff of breath. "At least I'll have all my things."

"You certainly seem cool-minded about all this," he said as they walked into the apartment on the left.

She'd made some changes—painted the beige walls a soft blue gray, exchanged the heavy leather furniture for a floral blue, yellow, and white sofa and coordinating striped wing chair. Framed gardens bloomed on walls that, he noticed, were lacking any plaques or trophy photos of her with all the famous people she'd interviewed over her career.

"It's something you develop early in this business," she said as she went around turning on lamps. "Never let them see you sweat."

And she'd never seemed to. Not even during that interview in the scorchingly hot Afghan mountains with bin Laden. Of course that had been when he'd been just a run-of-the-mill terrorist. A month later to the day of that August interview the man had hit the Top Ten list.

She went around a half wall separating the living room from the kitchen, opened the refrigerator, and took out a green bottle of Chardonnay. "Would you like some wine?"

"Thank you, but I believe I'll pass." There was no way he'd risk dulling his reflexes with alcohol.

She poured the wine into a stemmed glass. "I'm sorry I don't have any beer."

He smiled at that. "If I were to want a beer, I have a great deal on tap downstairs."

"Of course you do." She didn't physically slap her forehead, but her tone suggested the gesture. "Stupid," she muttered as she walked over to the huge window, which during the day flooded the loft with sunlight.

One of the reasons Brendan had bought this building was for the stunning view. Tonight, through the rain-streaked glass, the lights on the bridge looked like blurred stars.

"You shouldn't be so hard on yourself." He went to stand behind her and, as he breathed in the herbal scent of her shampoo, began massaging the knots in her shoulders.

Seeming to understand that the gesture was that of a friend, not an attempt at seduction, she leaned back against him as she sipped her wine. A comfortable silence settled over them, and though she'd had him nearly as knotted up as her slender shoulders since she'd moved into his building, Brendan almost felt himself beginning to relax.

"That feels good," she murmured.

"We aim to please." It was all he could do not to pull her even tighter and bury his lips in the fragrant dark silk of her hair.

"You do." She sighed. Took another sip. "And it's not that I'm not grateful—"

She glanced back up at him, and when he felt her tense beneath his palms Brendan realized she'd seen the raw desire he knew must be written all over his face.

"It's been a long day." She sounded guarded. Emotions as tangled as the renewed knots in her shoulders swirled in her dark eyes.

"Aye, it has, indeed," he agreed.

Nine years he'd lived in this country, and he still—especially when his feelings were involved, as they were now—slid into the language and cadence of his native County Clare.

She moved away. "I believe I'll go to bed."

Jesus, Mary, and Joseph save him, wasn't that idea tempting?

Obviously a reporter didn't achieve the level of success Valentine had without becoming very good at reading people. As she read his thoughts, her own expression closed up.

"Alone."

And didn't he deserve that edge in her voice? "I wouldn't be in the habit of joining any woman in bed without an invitation."

"Well, that's reassuring." She forced a smile they

both knew she didn't mean. "Where will you be sleeping?"

"The sofa will do."

It was nearly a foot too short, but the length didn't matter, given that he had no intention of sleeping anyway.

Much, much later, as he sat in the wing chair, staring out the rain-streaked window, listening to the sound of the rain on the roof, Brendan tried, with scant success, to put the idea of the delectable Valentine Snow sleeping just a few feet away out of his mind.

It wasn't as if he didn't have enough other things to ponder.

Such as how he was going to keep the woman he'd fallen in love with safe.

17

Cait had spent the first twelve years of her life traveling the world as a navy brat, but the moment her father first drove the family past the sweeps of blinding spring-green spartina grass and still, black waters reflecting stark gray cypress, she'd felt an inner click.

As if she'd finally come home.

She'd been so happy when they'd moved into the sprawling white house on Officers Drive—so named because it had originally been settled by officers from the fort that had been built in the harbor to defend Somersett against a British sea invasion. Cait was one of five children, and this was the first time she'd had her own bedroom. And, better yet, the first time she wouldn't have to wait in line for her morning shower.

Proving that life was often a trade-off between bitter and sweet, she'd also understood that the only reason Vice Admiral Michael Cavanaugh had resigned his commission and taken the teaching position at the Admiral Somersett Military Academy was because of his wife's cancer.

Fortunately, Cait's mother had won her valiantly fought battle with lymphoma soon after Cait entered the University of South Carolina. But the Cavanaughs had stayed in Somersett, sinking their roots deep into the southern Lowcountry.

Except for the insanity of Buccaneer Days, life in Somersett was certainly nowhere near as fast-paced as in a lot of cities where Cait's father had been posted. It was certainly slower-paced than Virginia Beach, where she'd spent the sixth grade, San Diego, or even nearby Charleston. Whenever she drove past St. Brendan's Cathedral and over the bridge into the marsh, Cait could feel her mind and body relax.

Usually.

But, of course, usually she wasn't trying to apprehend a serial sniper.

Using her handheld GPS, after two wrong turns and forty-five minutes after she'd left Somersett, the two-lane road dead-ended in front of an old house.

As she climbed the steps, she noticed that someone had done an admirable job of restoring the tabby foundation—that once-popular Lowcountry building material made up of easily accessible broken oyster shells, lime, sand, and water. The roof, which she suspected had once been tin, was now copper, and hung over a long screened-in porch. Black storm shutters added hurricane protection and provided an attractive contrast to the sand-hued outer walls.

Quinn answered the door on the second ring. And although she'd prepared herself for this meeting, there was no way she could have anticipated that the only thing he'd be wearing would be a pair of khaki cargo shorts.

Heaven help her, he looked like some Renaissance marble statue of a Greek god.

No.

Not marble. Marble was too smooth. Too cold. And way too finished.

The man who was currently making her damn knees weak could have been hewn from an enormous piece of rough-textured granite.

And was that a bullet he was wearing around his neck?

She wasn't sure how long they stood there, her looking up at Quinn, him looking down at her. Time seemed oddly suspended.

"Well, hello," he said finally. He glanced past her, looking, she suspected, for her partner. "Did you come all the way out here alone?"

"I did." What? Did he think she was a fraidycat girl who needed a male bodyguard to venture into the marsh at night? "And we need to talk."

"Sure."

He moved aside, making room for her to enter the house. Which was a direct contrast to the restored outside.

"I like to think of it as a work in progress," he said as she looked around at the buckets of paint, sawhorses, and stacks of lumber.

"So I see."

"The termites had been using it as their own personal smorgasbord," he explained. "Even after I had the place fumigated—twice. I decided it'd be easier just to gut the interior and start over from scratch."

"Well. That's certainly an ambitious project." So far he'd managed to get some interior framing done and some Sheetrock up, but that seemed about it.

"I like a challenge."

"Lucky thing. Because this definitely fits the definition."

The only furniture appeared to be an oversized couch, a chest of drawers, a desk on which his laptop sat, four wooden chairs, a table that was home to a Mr. Coffee and a microwave, and an admittedly impressive stainless-steel and black Sub-Zero refrigerator against a back wall.

"I'm enjoying the work," he said. "Gets the kinks out after sitting at a desk all day. Though John Tremayne, Zach's dad, is acting as the general contractor. And Zach's come over from the island and helped out some."

He looked around with what actually appeared to be pride. Obviously whatever vision of a completed home he had in his mind was a long way from what Cait was seeing.

"I've never owned a house before," he said.

"No offense, McKade, but you don't exactly own one now."

Though now that she looked more closely, she could appreciate the outer walls, which appeared to be local Somersett brick. And the hand-hewn cypress ceiling beams were wonderful.

A deep laugh came rumbling up from his remarkably cut dark chest. "Ah, ye of little faith. Now you're stuck."

She lifted a brow.

"You're going to have the honor of being my first dinner guest. So I can show the place off to you."

"Great. I'll bring my grandchildren to your housewarming party. And although I hate to rain on your HGTV parade, I feel the need to point out that unless you plan to nuke a stack of Hungry Man chicken potpies, you'll need an actual kitchen in order to cook that dinner."

"The range is on order—ETA, if all goes according to plan, next Wednesday. Meanwhile, we could always send out for pizza."

Oh, hell. She wondered if he was remembering that room-service pizza they'd shared in bed, amid those tangled sheets, at some point during that sex-filled night.

He was. Cait could see it in the way his eyes darkened as they roamed her face for an unnervingly long time before settling on her lips. She could feel it in the dangerous sexuality radiating from him, like the hum of the ground beneath your feet just before lightning strikes.

"We need to talk," she repeated.

"I thought that's what we were doing."

"This is law enforcement business."

"Why does that not surprise me? Especially since you seem to have changed into your official special agent uniform."

The suit was the first she'd bought when she'd come to work at the Bureau. Both the severe cut and the color—known around the bureau as "Hoover blue"—were designed to give the wearer a no-nonsense image.

"I *am* a special agent," she reminded him.

"So you keep telling me." He sighed, plucked a T-shirt off the back of one of the chairs and pulled it over his head. "Since I seem to be lacking proper guest furniture, let me get you something to drink and we can go sit out on the porch."

"I don't need anything to drink," she said. "This won't take long."

"Efficient as always, I see," he murmured. "How about some water?"

"That'd be nice." It was hot as a sauna outside. Despite the open windows, even hotter inside. She hoped, for Quinn's sake, that he was planning to install central air-conditioning. "Thanks."

"My pleasure," he said dryly, as he took a plastic bottle from the refrigerator and snagged a beer for himself.

When he laced the fingers of his left hand with hers, Cait remembered, all too well, him doing the same thing as he'd led her into the Wingate Palace Hotel elevator. The elevator where, as soon as the door had closed, he'd pressed her against the mirrored wall, taken her mouth, and kissed her senseless.

Not wanting to reveal that the casual touch had her reliving that scene in full Technicolor detail, Cait resisted the urge to tug her hand free.

There was a traditional rope hammock at one end of the covered porch, a wooden glider at the other. Cait chose the glider.

"I need to know everything about snipers," she said.

"Do you own your own home?" he asked.

"I have a year's lease on my apartment," she said, not understanding the non sequitur. "Why?"

"Because you might want to call up your landlord and see about breaking that lease. Because you're going to be out here for a long time."

"All right." She exhaled a frustrated breath. "Perhaps that was a bit of a sweeping statement. I need to know what makes someone who'd hunt human beings for sport tick."

"I see." Instead of sitting down beside her, he leaned back against the porch railing and folded his arms. "And you believe I'd know that why?"

It had begun to rain. Cait was grateful for the clouds that had moved in from the coast to cover the full moon that had been hanging low in the sky while she'd driven out here. They kept him from seeing the flush darkening her cheeks.

"I'm sorry. Bad choice of words again. Of course I understand that you didn't shoot the enemy for sport, but . . ."

She dragged her hand through her hair. It was not often that Cait felt flustered. She didn't like it. She especially didn't like it that Quinn McKade was the one making her feel that way. But she was admittedly grateful when he seemed willing to help her out.

"You want to know what makes a man be able to put another human being in his rifle's crosshairs and squeeze the trigger without remorse."

"That's it exactly. And the reason I'm asking you is because I suspect my sniper is using your book as a how-to guide."

Cait had never known it was possible for anyone to go absolutely still. Once again the statue image came to mind.

"Why would you think that?"

"Because he sent Valentine Snow a pair of tarot death cards. The same as the sniper in *Kill Zone*."

"You read my book?"

He seemed surprised by that revelation. And, Cait thought, a little pleased.

"Is there anyone on the planet who hasn't?" Damn. That came off as too defensive.

Despite the seriousness of the topic, his harshly cut lips quirked, just a bit, at the corners. "I suspect a few."

If it had been anyone else asking him about this, Quinn wasn't sure he'd have been willing to share his feelings. But this was Cait. And he realized that the shooter might have just supplied him with the golden opportunity to overcome the animosity she'd inexplicably had for him since they'd first met.

He'd been going out over the holidays with her roommate at the time, who'd refused to leave Cait alone on New Year's Eve, so since he and Zach had both been in town on leave after completing BUD/S training together, he'd talked his best friend into taking her out on a double date.

Zach and Cait had gotten along just dandy. While it had been more than a little obvious that she'd hated Quinn's guts.

Which shouldn't have pissed him off, since her roommate was not only nice but really, really hot to boot. But, dammit, it had.

A few years later, when they'd coincidentally met again at that same roommate's wedding reception, she'd proven a whole lot friendlier. Until she'd run out on him the next morning.

"Just because he's tossing around tarot cards doesn't necessarily mean he's using my book as a murder manual." Christ, that was not a fun thought. "It's not like it's a brilliantly original idea. There've been other killers who used death cards as a symbol. The Zodiac Killer, for one. And didn't those D.C. snipers leave one behind?"

Quinn might have been out of the country during that time, but he would've had to have been on Mars not to read about the two men who'd terrorized Washington for so many weeks.

"Hell, the military itself came up with those Deck of Death playing cards of wanted terrorists in Iraq. In fact, I saw a Marine sniper wearing a patch with a picture of Saddam as the king of spades card in the crosshairs."

"So, the sniper in your story isn't a real person?"

"The book's fiction." Quinn had lost count, during the promo tour the publisher had sent him on, of how many times he'd had to explain that. "Did some of the events portrayed actually happen? Sure. There were also lots of stories about snipers in Vietnam leaving tarot death cards behind on their victims. Maybe your guy's heard some of them."

"Maybe he was *one* of them."

"I suppose anything's possible. Though it seems odd that he'd wait all these years to go off the deep end."

"I'd agree if I hadn't read that news reports of the current Iraq war have begun triggering some deep-seated PTSD issues among Vietnam vets."

"Yeah, I've heard the same thing," Quinn allowed. "But I still don't believe you're looking for an actual sniper."

"Maybe not. But maybe the guy's a wannabe sniper. Or a wannabe SEAL."

"Yeah." He'd certainly met a lot of those over the years. In fact, an organization committed to exposing fake SEALs had even put up a Wall of Shame on the Internet outing impostors. "I suppose that could be."

"But what are the chances of the quote?"

"What quote?"

"The Bible quote he ended his letter to Val with." She took a notebook out of her purse, flipped it open, and read the David versus Goliath line, including the "one shot, one kill" ending.

Damn. Quinn blew out a breath. Took a long pull from the brown beer bottle as he considered that perhaps the shooter *had* taken inspiration from his novel.

"Okay. This isn't good."

"Murder never is." She turned to a clean page in the notebook. "So. Tell me about snipers."

It was not his favorite subject. He especially wasn't wild about discussing battlefield death with a woman he still wanted, after all these years, to get horizontal with.

Putting aside the fantasy of making love to her on that hammock he'd been using for a bed, he took another drink.

Then got down to business.

18

Tyler Long couldn't sleep. It was the night before his first day in a new school and his mind was spinning with possibilities.

Would he like his teacher? He'd really liked Miss Cunningham, the teacher at his old school last year, who'd smelled like flowers and always greeted her second-grade class with a smile.

Would the other kids laugh at him when he stuttered?

Well, duh.

Tyler hated stuttering, which he'd only begun doing last year when his mom and dad split up and he and his mom had to move into this apartment from their house on Swann Island, with the swimming pool and the cool tree fort his dad had built for him.

The first time he couldn't get the words out, he'd felt as if an alien had come down from outer space and stuffed his throat with rocks. He still felt that way, but things were getting a little bit better since the speech doctor his mom had taken him to had taught him to take a deep breath, then stretch his words out. Which helped him spit those rocks right out of his throat.

"It-t-t's going to be okay."

So long as he used the speech utensils he'd been practicing every day. That was what he needed to remember. Instead of getting so nervous the nasty old alien would be able to sneak up on him and shove more of those rocks into his mouth.

He hugged his stuffed Dalmatian, Spots, to his chest and buried his face in its soft black and white fur. The stuffed dog looked just like the real dog he'd had to give away when they'd moved to the mainland. Their landlord didn't allow pets. His mom had said that it wouldn't have been fair to keep Spots locked up in an apartment all day, but as soon as she saved up some money, they'd get a place with a backyard. Then they could go to the shelter together and pick out a new dog.

Meanwhile, he had a goldfish in a bowl on his dresser. Which was okay, but you couldn't take a fish to bed with you. And a fish mostly just swam around in circles or hid behind the plastic bush. It didn't really want to listen to your problems, like Spots always did. Then lick your face when you cried.

His mother was a cocktail waitress at the Wingate Palace hotel. Because she had to work past midnight, she slept in a lot. Afraid that she'd sleep through the alarm and cause him to be late on this super-important first day, Tyler crept out of bed and went over to where his new uniform was hanging on the closet door.

Some of the other kids in the building had teased him because he was going to St. Brendan's School and wouldn't be able to wear cool Spider-Man T-shirts and regular clothes like they did at public school. But Tyler liked the idea of having a uniform to wear. It made him feel like he was going to fit in. Because if everyone was dressed the same, it'd be like he was one of the gang, right?

A normal kid. Not a stutter-mouth.

He put on the white shirt and navy blue pants. Then his socks and the black dress shoes, which he had to admit were dorky. But all the boys had to wear them, so it wasn't like he was going to stick out or anything.

Returning to the bed, Tyler lay on his back, arms

stiff at his sides, being careful not to wrinkle his new clothes. He reminded himself what his speech doctor had taught him about James Earl Jones, whose stuttering hadn't stopped him from growing up to be Darth Vader's voice in all those *Star Wars* movies.

And there was always Kenyon Martin, a pro basketball player, who was also on that "people who stutter" poster hanging on his wall next to all his drawings of concept cars. He'd planned on becoming a car designer when he grew up, but after hearing about Darth Vader, he'd been thinking maybe it'd be cool to be an actor and get to dress up and pretend to be someone else.

Someone who didn't stutter.

19

"So, are we gonna blow their fucking minds tomorrow, or what?"

"We'll definitely get their attention," the shooter said for the umpteenth time.

He was beginning to consider just putting a bullet into the guy's mouth to shut him up.

"Maybe you might want to slow down on that," he said as he looked up from cleaning his rifle.

A rifle was a sniper's most treasured possession. Any sniper worth his salt—and he was—became so intimate with his rifle that he could take it apart and put it together blindfolded. Which the shooter wasn't doing tonight. But he could, if need be.

"You need to be sharp tomorrow. Which you're not going to be, if you're nursing the mother of all hangovers."

"You sayin' I can't handle my liquor?"

That was exactly what he was saying. Christ, what had he been thinking, hooking up with a damn alkie?

Corporal Charles Jensen had been one of the boots on the ground in Iraq when he'd gotten shot in the head by friendly fire during Shock and Awe. The bullet that had crashed through his skull—moments after he'd lost his helmet to a mortar attack—had rewired his brain.

And not in a good way.

Jensen was about as dependable as the weather during

hurricane season. Problem was, there weren't a lot of guys around who were willing to take on what could, if he screwed up, end up being a suicide mission.

"I'm just saying we both need to be sharp," he repeated. His tone was mild, but he had to struggle to fight off the temper he felt beginning to boil.

He reached up and took hold of the bullet he wore on a chain around his neck and reminded himself that losing his temper wouldn't achieve his objective.

"Sharp as fucking tacks," Jensen promised as he poured another shot of his best friend, Jim Beam.

The shooter decided he was going to have to change tactics. Because his spotter had goatfuck written all over him. The problem was that the plan, as he'd originally conceived it, beginning at St. Brendan's and ending up at the far opposite end of the city, involved moving fast. Which meant he needed someone to drive the car.

So, he'd work on logistics. After tomorrow's mission.

Which was, he thought with a burst of anticipation, going to blow their fucking minds.

20

"Okay," Quinn said. "The thing is, high-tech military machinery is way cool and it can assist the troops, but what people don't understand is that even in these days of modern warfare, it can never replace them.

"Sooner or later, although it might not be pretty to think so, the ultimate weapon is the guy on the ground with a gun. Like Theodore Roosevelt said, the only bullet that counts is the one that hits. Which is why snipers are a cost-effective force multiplier—they're cheap to train, cheap to equip, and cheap to deploy."

"They're also human beings," Cait pointed out. "With, hopefully, human emotions."

"Sure. And the trick is being able to keep in touch with those emotions, while doing your job."

Quinn paused, trying to figure out how to describe something he'd never talked about with anyone except his teammates.

"Look," he said, "snipers aren't anything new. Even cavemen realized that being able to kill at the farthest possible range gave them one helluva advantage over their enemy.

"Over time, primitive man's stones became replaced by spears, which in turn were replaced by arrows."

"In your book you mentioned Attila the Hun conquering much of Europe and threatening the Roman Empire with horse-mounted archers."

Maybe it was foolish, but Quinn really, really liked

the idea of Cait having read *Kill Zone*. "Those archers were capable of shooting their arrows beyond one hundred yards, which at the time was unheard of. And Leonardo da Vinci picked off enemy soldiers at the siege of Florence at three hundred yards with a rifle he'd designed himself."

"Is that true?" He wasn't surprised that she questioned everything. That was probably part of what made her a great cop.

"Hey, I learned it in BUD/S training." He flashed her his best grin, welcoming the light moment in what was a decidedly grim topic. "It must be."

A rich laugh bubbled out of her. It was the first time, outside of that night, he'd ever heard her laugh. Quinn decided he liked the sound. A lot.

"A sniper shot Admiral Horatio Nelson at the Battle of Trafalgar," he said, reluctantly returning to the topic of killing. "And during the Second Battle of Freeman's Farm, in 1777, Private Timothy Murphy climbed a tree and drilled a British general with a single shot, which forced the British to break off their offensive and retreat to Saratoga, where their surrender was the turning point of the war."

She raised her tawny eyebrows. "I grew up in a navy family. My father even teaches military history at ASMA, but I never heard those stories."

"That's because they're not real popular. The idea of snipers violates the sense of fair play we're all brought up to believe in," he admitted. "Other soldiers kill so they won't be killed, often up close and personal in hand-to-hand combat, which, as stupidly risky as it might be, is still regarded as a noble necessity.

"But since a sniper coldly and calculatedly chooses a target from a long distance away, public attitude—hell, even the attitude from a lot of the military—is, 'Okay, we need to use the sniper. But let's not tell anyone about him. Then, after the war's over, we can put him back into his bottle until we need him again.' "

"That's harsh."

He shrugged. "War's no cakewalk, Cait. And I can't speak for every sniper in the military, but it's a helluva lot different when you can view another human being as a target through your scope, without any personal attachment, rather than taking a life in the heat of battle."

"No personal attachment at all?"

It would've been easier to lie. But Quinn decided she needed to know the truth. Not just to possibly get a handle on her serial shooter, but because if he was going to win her over—and he fully intended to—she also deserved to know the truth about him.

"Kill them all and let God sort them out might make for a snappy bumper sticker, but professional snipers can't work that way. A sniper has to be certain that a target is a legitimate threat, which means you may spend a long time watching him.

"Okay, which, yeah, does make it personal. Maybe you watch him eating dinner, taking a piss, smoking a cigarette. Maybe even kicking a soccer ball with his kid. And all the time he has no idea that you're holding his life in your hands."

"I never discharged my weapon in the line of duty," she volunteered.

"You were lucky."

"I know. But to tell the truth, that, along with making sure victims received justice, was one of the big appeals of homicide. Homicide cops tend to come in after the bullets stop flying, which makes it a lot safer occupation than, say, vice or narcotics. But I always knew if someone was shooting at me, or my partner, or an innocent civilian, I wouldn't hesitate to pull the trigger."

"And, being the kind of person you are, you'd never forget having killed another human being."

"No." She was looking at him more closely now. Looking hard. Looking deep. Quinn wished he didn't give a damn about what she might be seeing.

"I can still remember each of my targets," he was surprised to hear himself admitting. "I can still see their expressions in that last instant of their lives."

He could see her thinking about that. "That has to change a person," she said carefully.

"Sure." He knew he'd been forever altered by the job he'd done so well and for so long. And the eyes he could still see through his scope.

"Was there a very strong part of me that might've hated what I did when I pulled the trigger? Absolutely. But I also understood I was involved in something a helluva lot larger than myself.

" 'Thou shalt not kill' is an admirable commandment to live by. But in battle, even more important is 'Thou shalt not kill my teammates.' The men I killed were trying to kill American soldiers. Which meant my job was to keep the enemy from doing theirs."

"I can understand that."

She took a long drink of water, and once again the silence spun out. Somewhere out in the marsh a bullfrog was calling to its mate and an owl hooted.

"Still," she murmured, "it's not something that just anyone—even every soldier—could do. At least not on a regular basis."

"A sniper can't have any compunction against killing. But he has to have compassion. A conscience."

Watching her carefully, he could practically see the lightbulb go on in her head. "Unlike someone who can shoot innocent civilians from a distance."

"Absofuckinglutely unlike that," he replied. Giving in to temptation, just a little, he took the two steps from the railing to the glider and sat down beside her, encouraged when she didn't move away. "You don't necessarily have to be a religious person, not in the sense of attending church, and you don't even need to believe in a higher power."

He gave the glider a little push. Forward. Back. Forward again.

"But you have to be able to justify what you do

when you pull that trigger. Some take shots to save lives—"

"Which would be you."

"Yeah." Her lips were just inches from his. It'd be so easy just to duck his head and . . .

"Which would be me." He wondered if there was a male anywhere on the planet who'd want to talk about deadly missions in the past while sitting so close to such a sexy, sweet-smelling woman.

"Others shoot because they hate the enemy. Some, because for them, it's their job. But the important thing to know is that a sniper never, ever kills for the sake of killing. The military doesn't want any nutcase who gets his rocks off by wanton killing."

"You mentioned a rigid selection process."

"Yeah. It's tough. Selection boards look for good markmanship, natch. And good physical condition. Hearing, vision, have to be excellent. You have to be intelligent. But if those were the only criteria, most of the guys—and women—in the military could be snipers.

"They're also looking for intangibles. Initiative, common sense, an even temperament, above-average observational skills, the ability to get along with team members, and a mature personality that allows you to cope with the stress of calculated, deliberate killing.

"Along with all that, you need patience. You've got to be willing and able to endure lying in the jungle, or the sand, hour after hour, hell, day after day, with bugs crawling all over you, biting the hell out of you, the sun baking your skin, the rain pouring on your head, remaining absolutely focused, no matter what.

"Because the one thing for sure is that the bad guy's coming. And when he does, you're going to kill him."

Cait shivered at that. Oh, she covered it up quickly enough, but like he said, a sniper needed good observational skills. And his had always been excellent.

He was also getting damn sick of the subject. "You smell like a piña colada."

"It's my shampoo."

"I like it." Taking a risk, he skimmed a hand over the bright curls that were soft as silk and misted from the fog rising from the marsh surrounding the house. "It reminds me of that song."

"What song?"

"The one about piña coladas. Getting caught in the rain." Which was currently tapping on the copper roof that extended over the porch. "The feel of the ocean." His caressing touch moved down her sleeve. Over the back of her hand. "And champagne, and—"

"I know it," she said, cutting him off before he got to the best part, about making love at midnight. "So, is that all?"

He wasn't surprised when she stood up. Disappointed, but not surprised.

"Pretty much." He stood up as well. "At least about snipers, but like I keep telling you—"

"I know." She exhaled a frustrated sigh that ruffled her bangs. "You don't believe he's a sniper."

"No. I don't. But you'd better hope I'm wrong."

"Why?"

"Because that weapon I told you he's using?"

She nodded. "The M16 or AR-15. Or Bushmaster XM15."

"That's it." He wasn't surprised she remembered. She'd always been, to his mind, the perfect combination of beauty and brains. "It may just be the best assault rifle ever invented, though admittedly some advocates of the M4 carbine might disagree. It's got a thirty-round magazine, a muzzle velocity of 948 meters per second, and an effective range of 800 meters."

Quinn figured that despite her familiarity with handguns, those numbers might not mean all that much to her. But, God help them all, there was more.

"With a rate of fire, depending on the guy pulling the trigger, of 700 to 950 rounds a minute."

She stared at him. Although he couldn't tell for certain, with those rain clouds having covered up the rising moon, he thought her already fair skin paled.

"Oh, shit," she said.

"I'd say that about covers it," he said.

21

Quinn remained on the porch, watching Cait drive away until her taillights finally disappeared in the rain. He knew she would accuse him of being sexist—and maybe he was—but he had to force himself not to go after her. To protect her.

"She's an FBI special agent, for Chrissakes," he reminded himself. "She's been trained to handle terrorists." Including the domestic types, which he feared this madman was going to turn out to be.

Although Phoenix Team took on bodyguard assignments, Quinn had never been interested in that kind of gig.

Until now.

The problem was, if he *had* offered his professional services, she'd have laughed in his face. Then probably drop-kicked his ass all the way back to Afghanistan.

Which meant he was going to have to find some other way to get involved.

He went back into the house, seeing it for the first time through someone else's eyes. "I guess it could use some work," he allowed.

The studs were up for the drywall; that'd be a start. Not that he wanted to cut the place into little boxes, but a separate bedroom might be an idea. While he didn't mind racking out in the hammock—which was a helluva lot more comfortable than most of the places he'd slept over the past dozen years—or the sleeping bag he'd been throwing on the floor, he suspected the lady would probably prefer an actual bed. And a door that'd actually lock.

Over the years he'd never given a lot of thought to such things; the apartment back on Coronado where he used to crash between missions was as stark as he imagined a monk's cell must be. He'd grown up traveling light, a behavior that fit right in with being a SEAL, and if women were put off by the lack of pictures on the walls, or pretty pastel towels and dishes of smelly wood chips in the bathroom, none had ever mentioned it.

Then again, most of the women he spent time with weren't exactly into conversation. Which, again, was just how he'd always preferred it. If there was one thing life had taught him it was that very few things were permanent. Besides, while he'd never been afraid of hard work, long-term relationships just involved too much heavy lifting.

There was also the fact that, as one of the instructors in BUD/S had told the class when one of the guys had rung out of training because his fiancée wanted him home watching reality TV with her in the evenings, if the navy wanted a SEAL to have a wife, they'd issue him one.

Quinn could just picture it, like a scene from some black-and-white fifties sitcom on TVLand.

"Hi, honey," he'd say as he came in the door smelling of blood after returning from battle in some godforsaken Third World hellhole. "I'm home."

"Hello, darling." His beloved wife, inexplicably clad in a dress, high heels, and pearls, would greet her grizzled warrior at the door with a perky smile, an adoring gaze, and an icy martini. "How was your day?"

"Just fine and dandy." He'd toss back the drink and hold the glass out for a refill. "I killed a whole bunch of guys. So, how was *your* day?"

Nope. While he knew SEALs who'd gotten married, that scenario had never worked for Quinn.

Until that night when he and Cait had found themselves together at that wedding reception. Of course, she'd been busily trying to drink her former husband out of her life when she'd literally thrown herself at him.

He shouldn't have even been there. Ever since getting out of BUD/S, he'd taken to spending a couple weeks a year in Somersett with Zach and his old man, a former SEAL who'd done three tours in Vietnam. Quinn had always liked John Tremayne, who'd become sort of a surrogate father.

The problem was, the Southern city wasn't the most exciting place on the planet, and since they'd come straight off a mission in Central America, both Zach and Quinn had been feeling antsy. Which was when, after reading in the paper that Cait's former roommate was getting married, Zach got the idea to crash the reception at the Wingate Palace hotel.

"Never met a woman yet who could resist the whites," Quinn remembered Zach saying. Quinn's own personal experience had proven those words to be true. So they'd put on their U.S. Navy dress white uniforms, which they'd brought along for some dog and pony show they'd agreed to do at the academy (which Zach had attended for a time before dropping out and becoming a SEAL), borrowed John's F-350, and driven down to the hotel, where they breezed into the ballroom as if they had every right to be there.

The moment he'd walked into the gilded and ornately decorated room, Quinn's eyes had immediately gone to the head table, where Cait Cavanaugh, wearing the most god-awful dress he'd ever seen, with her bright hair in some sort of fancy upsweep, was making a toast to the new bride and groom.

Her words were a mere buzz in his ears, drowned out by the jolt of testosterone flooding his system.

Later, looking back on it, he'd think it sappy, but he'd walked straight toward that long, white-draped table. Later, Zach told him that a buzz of interested murmurs had followed him, but looking neither left nor right, every atom of his body focused on her, Quinn hadn't noticed.

Maybe she'd heard it. Or maybe it had been the same instinct he'd felt, because suddenly her gaze had shifted from the smiling bride and groom to where he was standing, just a few feet away.

Oh, she was good, even then. Her only outward response was a blink. And a slight stain on those cut-crystal cheekbones. Then she'd finished her toast, which must've gone over well enough, because Quinn was vaguely aware of a ripple of applause behind him.

Another clue that he wasn't alone in his feelings was the way the lady tossed back the champagne, swallowing it in one long gulp, as if she needed the dulling effects of the alcohol.

As a sniper, Quinn knew that timing was everything. And it was definitely working in his favor when the wedding singer called for the bride and groom's first dance.

The newlyweds, who'd obviously been taking lessons, did a few impressive turns and spins, ending in a deep dip that drew yet more applause.

Then the bride danced briefly with her father, the groom with his mother, after which the singer, a Tony Bennett wannabe, called for the wedding party to take to the floor.

Which was when Quinn made his move.

He stepped in front of his target, effectively blocking her way.

"Sorry," he informed the tuxedo-clad usher, "but this dance is mine."

The guy stopped in his tracks. Confusion clouded his expression as his gaze went from Quinn to his appointed partner.

"Cait?"

She rolled her eyes. Watching her, he could practically see the wheels turning in her head.

"It's Heather and Danny's day," she said. "I don't want to do anything to cause a problem."

Although Quinn towered over the guy by a good eight inches and was radiating his best don't-mess-with-the-big-bad-SEAL attitude, he had to give the kid credit.

"But if this guy's bothering you—" he started to say.

"It's okay." Cait put a hand on his arm. "I know him."

As they'd stepped onto the wood parquet, her back couldn't have been any stiffer if she'd had his sniper rifle strapped to her body beneath the fugly Pepto-Bismol-pink dress.

"Small world," he said.

"I refuse to believe Heather invited you." Her arms remained stiff at her sides.

"She probably would've if she'd known I was in town." The dress crackled like cellophane as he drew her into his arms while the singer suggested flying to the moon on gossamer wings. "*She* always liked me."

Cait glanced over at the couple who were so engrossed in each other, they could've flown off to their very own planet. In the galaxy lovey-dovey. "Her taste has obviously improved."

"Ouch." Fortunately Quinn had always enjoyed a challenge. "Actually, this wedding-crashing thing was Zach's idea." He splayed his hand against her back, pressed her a little closer. "But I'm damn glad he had it."

She sighed dramatically. "You realize I'm only dancing with you because I didn't want to risk you causing a scene."

"You want to believe that, go right ahead." He lowered his head, nuzzling her neck, which was bared by her gravity-defying hairstyle. "Damn, you smell good. Same as you did that New Year's Eve."

"You were Heather's date. Which meant you had no business smelling another woman." Even as her tone was sharp, Quinn was encouraged when she lifted her bare arms and twined them around his neck. "And for the record, I don't wear perfume."

"I know." Deciding that dragging her to the floor and lifting all those crinolines she was wearing beneath the Southern belle skirt would definitely cause a scene, he contented himself with brushing his lips against her temple. "Which, of course, made you even more dangerous."

She lifted her head at that. Looked him straight in the eye. "Good line. But there's no way I'm going to believe a SEAL can be afraid of a mere woman."

"Believe me, Cupcake, some women—of which you'd be at the top of the list—can be a helluva lot more dangerous than a nest of terrorists."

She slitted her eyes. Studied him as they swayed back and forth to the music, all those petticoats hopefully keeping her from realizing that he was rapidly getting a redwood-sized boner.

"Am I supposed to take that as a compliment?" she asked.

"I guess that's up to you. What it is, however, is the truth. I knew you were trouble the minute you came out of that bedroom that New Year's Eve."

She surprised him by laughing at that. A rich, deep sound Quinn decided was even sexier than her scent. "*You're* the one who was trouble, McKade."

Although being a sniper required a great deal of patience, sometimes you had to act on instinct. Which Quinn did now.

"I've got an idea."

"What's that?"

"How about we spend the rest of the evening getting into trouble together?"

She stopped moving. Stood there on the floor, looking up at him. And, hoo-yah, actually seemed to be considering his suggestion.

He knew that the saying about time standing still was a cliché. But Quinn would've sworn on his life that it did at that moment.

"Okay," she said after what seemed an eternity.

22

Quinn had let out a breath he'd been unaware of holding.

Then bent his head and touched his mouth to hers.

She tasted of champagne. Of temptation. And, as she tightened her arms around his neck and clung, of sex.

He might not have the moves of, say, George Clooney, or Brad Pitt, but Quinn did know that immediately dragging a woman you hardly knew out of a wedding reception to have monkey sex with her was perhaps over the line. Even for a U.S. Navy SEAL.

So, utilizing the same patience required in his work, he'd spent the next couple of hours making nice, chatting with folks at the open bar—including Heather, who'd looked surprised but not offended to see him—and watching Cait Cavanaugh toss back mojitos as if CNN Headline News had just reported that rum was going to be declared illegal come midnight.

"You know," he suggested, "if you have to get drunk to hang with me, maybe we ought to rethink this trouble thing."

They were back on the dance floor, swaying to another slow tune, and he was beginning to get the impression that part of the reason she was twined around him like a python was to stay upright on a floor he suspected must've begun spinning on her.

"Isn't that just like a man?" she muttered, tilting

her head back to look up at him. "Losing interest just when you've finally got a woman on the line."

"You'd have to do a lot more than down some drinks to get me to lose interest." It was the absolute truth. "I'm just trying to be a gentleman here."

She stared long and hard at him. At least, as hard as she could with her unfocused lake blue eyes. "What would be the fun in that?" She lowered her arm and laced her fingers through his. "Let's go."

"Where did you have in mind?"

"Somewhere private." She skimmed a pink-tinted nail down the front of his uniform. "Where I can have my wicked way with you."

The smile she gave him would've tempted a saint. Having never claimed to be bucking for sainthood, Quinn reminded himself he'd been straight with her from the start. Even before she'd started on all those drinks.

He glanced across the ballroom at Zach, who seemed to have hit it off with a brunette wearing a purple minidress that fit her very fine curves like a second skin.

"Let me just take care of a little business first."

"That's fine with me. Since I need to make a little stop in the ladies' room." She did another of those skimming things, this time going a bit lower on the front of his tunic, stopping just short of where his body, which had been in a perpetual state of arousal for the past two-plus hours, was pressing against his white uniform trousers. "I'll meet you in the lobby. Lucky for us, it's not high-tourist season, so you should be able to get a room without any trouble."

Roger that.

Quinn watched her weaving her way through the tables and decided that she didn't appear *that* unsteady. Sure, she was looser than she'd been that New Year's Eve, but it wasn't as if she was falling-down-drunk or anything.

After telling Zach he wouldn't be needing a ride

back to the Tremayne house, he went to the front desk, where he learned that while it might not be high tourist season in Somersett, the hotel was booked. Except, the clerk told him with a sly glance toward Cait—who was sitting on a brocade couch across the lobby, legs crossed, impatiently swinging one pink satin–clad foot—the Presidential Suite.

The nightly rate came to nearly what Quinn made in a month of fighting terrorism around the world. Still, he didn't hesitate to book the suite. Because the lady was definitely worth it.

As soon as they entered the elevator, the tight rein he'd been keeping on his libido snapped. He claimed her mouth, fast and hard. Grasping his hair, she kissed him back. Just as fast. And just as hard.

Her taste—of rum, and sugar, and mint—was as potent as his passion. He could have drunk from her sexy, wet mouth forever.

More wildly wanton than he'd imagined in his hottest fantasies, she wrapped her legs around his. Crushing the stiff, crackly layers of bridesmaid dress in his hands, he cupped her butt and pressed her up against the mirrored elevator wall.

He'd miscalculated, Quinn realized, as her hair tumbled free from the pins that had been holding it in that upsweep and turned into a sexy silk tangle around her face. Just thinking about those fiery strands draped across his naked thighs had Quinn nearly losing it on the spot.

A distant ding managed to make itself heard through the pounding of hot blood in his ears. The elevator slowed. Then stopped.

Quinn was damning himself for not pushing the button to keep the door closed, when Cait, apparently also aware of what was going on, slid down his body, and was back on those skyscraper heels, smoothing down the wrinkled pink skirt as the metal door opened.

A middle-aged couple, dressed for the evening, entered from the floor that featured a revolving restaurant. Although he was no expert on menswear, even Quinn could recognize the man's suit as custom-tailored; the woman was wearing some sort of silk cocktail suit with fancy jeweled buttons. Diamonds winked at her ears and throat. Her scent, as heavily applied as her makeup, was thick and cloying.

They both skimmed an appraising glance over Quinn and Cait. Although the woman's face appeared to have been Botoxed into an expressionless mask, it would have been impossible to miss the disapproval in her heavily lined eyes.

The man, on the other hand, after focusing a bit too long on Cait's flushed breasts, which rose appealing above the deeply cut neckline, flashed Quinn a quick grin of approval. One that was laced, Quinn thought, with a touch of envy.

Then the couple's eyes rose and stayed glued to the lighted numbers above the door as the elevator continued its ascent to the top floor, which housed the Presidential, Ambassador, and Honeymoon suites.

Cait and Quinn were watching the floors flash by as well, though a sideways glance revealed her white teeth biting her kiss-swollen lips.

The elevator stopped again. The door opened. The couple exited first, turning left. Cait and Quinn followed, headed in the opposite direction.

Neither spoke as he pulled the keycard from his pocket and opened one of the two ornately carved doors.

They were no sooner in the suite than Cait's fought-for composure collapsed in laughter.

"I think we scandalized them," she said, pressing a hand against her breasts.

"Maybe her," he allowed. "But he would've given anything to be in my shoes."

She glanced down at the white patent leather shoes in question. "I don't get it."

"What?"

"You should look like a Good Humor man in that getup."

Since it was, ironically, the first thought he'd had when he'd bought it at the San Diego uniform store so many years ago, Quinn didn't take offense. Instead he grinned leeringly.

"Want a treat, little girl?"

Her eyes lit up with a knee-weakening mixture of laughter and lust. "Absolutely." Her gaze moved over him, lingering on the erection he was no longer even trying to hide. "And I want it supersized."

Which, of course, only caused another surge of heat through his penis, stiffening it so he wouldn't have been surprised if it had burst right out of his pants.

"The problem," she said, "as I see it, is we're both wearing too many clothes." She reached behind her back. "Unfortunately, whoever designed this nightmare of a dress was also a sadist."

Grasping her shoulders, he turned her around, intending to take care of the row of tiny satin-covered buttons. "Let me help."

"It's okay." Before he could stop her, she'd ripped the dress open, sending buttons flying across the room. "I can handle it."

Deciding that she was, indeed, handling things just fine, Quinn stood back and watched as she pushed the dress, petticoats, and hoopskirt over her hips, then stepped out of them, leaving them lying on the plush white carpeting.

Which left her standing in a beaded white corset that plunged to her waist and displayed her breasts in a mouthwatering way, a garter belt, white stockings, a pair of lacy white panties so skimpy she may as well have been going commando, and those pink stilettos, which had looked overdone with the dress, but now, with the rest of that Victoria's Secret underwear, looked damn hot.

"Well?" When she folded her arms beneath her

breasts, lifting them even higher over the top of the corset, Quinn realized that while he'd been eating her up with his eyes, she'd been waiting for some sort of response.

He cleared his throat. "It's a little difficult for a guy to talk," he said in a voice rough with need, "when he's just swallowed his tongue."

The explanation, which was the absolute truth, appeared to work. Her remarkably kissable lips twitched.

Then she said, "Your turn."

He'd never stripped out of a uniform so fast.

And then, although he'd stuck to beer and wasn't anywhere near as drunk as he suspected she must be after all those mojitos downstairs, the next hours passed in a sex-hazed blur.

He recalled retrieving the condom from his wallet, sweeping her up and carrying her into the bedroom.

She'd laughed as she'd bounced on the mattress. Then shimmied out of the panties, bent her knees, crooked her finger, and said, "Hey, Sailor. Wanna get lucky?"

Which pushed his last button. He'd barely managed to get suited up before plunging deep and hard, which immediately had him shuddering with an orgasm that seemed to go on and on forever.

"Christ, I'm sorry," he said against her neck, when he could speak again. "Believe it or not, I have heard of the concept of foreplay."

He'd collapsed on her, and realizing how heavy he must feel, he started to roll away, when her hands caught him and skimmed down his damp back.

"Don't apologize." She turned her head and kissed him again, a long, slow, deep kiss that involved a lot of clever tangling of tongues. "I figure your line of work has you having to be like me in some ways. A control freak."

"Roger that," he said as lust rose again to steamroller over his humiliation.

"Well, then, I like the idea of making you lose control." She slid her hand between them and danced her fingers down his chest. "Besides, we've got all night." Her caress went lower. "And I'm not nearly through with you yet."

She hadn't been kidding. Fortunately, between the both of them, they'd had enough rubbers on hand to last until sometime just before dawn. With a short time-out for pizza he'd ordered from room service. While claiming he'd needed it to keep his strength up, he'd also figured that after all those drinks she could use something in her stomach.

After a brief combat nap, he'd taken a shower and left her sleeping—or at least appearing to sleep—while he went out to round up breakfast.

When he returned, she was gone, without so much as a note.

Okay, so maybe she didn't have to tell him that he'd been the best she'd ever had, but at least she could've used the gilt-edged pad by the phone to let him know she'd had a fun time, and hey, have a good life.

Wondering what the chances were of feeding the lady mojitos until he broke down the barricades she'd built up around herself again, Quinn put aside the memory, took his laptop out of sleep mode, went online, and wrote an e-mail to another former SEAL who'd not only kept in touch with each and every one of his own BUD/S classmates but seemed to have his fingers in all sorts of clandestine pies.

The rest of the world might believe in six degrees of separation, but in the Spec Ops business, you'd be hard-pressed to find four.

After sending off the message asking what the guy might know about rogue snipers, he pulled his cell phone out of his pocket and scrolled through the names and numbers.

Quinn figured Cait would probably show up at the free clinic Mike Gannon had established across the street at St. Brendan's first thing tomorrow morning.

He also suspected she wouldn't be willing to share everything she knew with him.

Which meant he was going to have to beat her to the punch.

The voice mail on the priest's home and cell phones announced the same message: "You've reached Mike Gannon. I'm currently at a conference in Baltimore, but I'll be back in Somersett first thing tomorrow morning. If you'd like to leave a message, you know what to do."

Although it wasn't his first choice, Quinn left a message for Mike to call him ASAP.

Then, deciding that other than chasing Cait down and sticking to her like glue, there wasn't much he could do until morning, Quinn returned his mind to the Afghan mountains.

23

The U.S. Army Night Stalkers might be in charge when the Special Forces were in the air. But since they were all now on the ground, it was the SEALs' ball game.

"Okay," Zach said. "This might not be the best day we've ever had."

"Not the worst, either," Quinn said. "At least no one's freaked out."

Which was true. Despite the earlier bloodbath, not a single one of the survivors was curled up in a fetal position, crying for his mama.

"We're risking a court-martial by going into Pakistan," Zach reminded him, as if giving him one more chance to cast a vote against the plan.

"Beats waiting around here for more tangos to show up and start firing off more mortar rounds," Quinn said as they stood there, side by side, staring up at the mountains looming over them. "If those REMFs hadn't wanted us to cross the border, they should've sent in another bird to evac us out of here."

"Roger that," Zach agreed.

They'd managed to get a red rolled-up Sked—which looked like a kid's sled—for Shane and some stretchers for the injured Marines and Rangers from the Chinook before it had blown.

It wasn't going to be easy, even with four men assigned to each stretcher. But it wasn't as if they had a whole lot of choices.

"We're not going to leave our buddies behind," one of the Rangers said, folding his arms.

The kid didn't look old enough to drive. Hell, Quinn bet that just a few months ago his biggest problem was what kind of corsage to get his girlfriend for the prom. This was probably his first battle experience that didn't involve paintballs.

"This is war," Zach reminded the kid. "And war doesn't stop just because people die."

"We don't leave our buddies," another baby-faced Ranger said.

Quinn and Zach exchanged a look. A mutiny was all they needed to cap off a really lousy day.

"Look," Quinn said, "it's not going to help your buddies if you get blown away by crazy radical terrorists because you didn't use your Ranger training. CENTCOM's got our bearings. They're sending an evac copter as soon as the sun goes down. Hell, your buddies will be back home before you are."

Not that they'd know it, being dead and all. But still . . .

Quinn could tell it wasn't their first choice. But they fell in.

It turned out to be just as difficult as Quinn had figured it would be. They were seemingly taking one step forward only to fall two steps back.

Having trained to plan for the worst, hope for the best, and accept whatever happens, the SEALs had brought along their snowshoes. The Rangers and Marines, who hadn't, kept sinking into the deep drifts. Sometimes they were reduced to crawling on the icy scree.

But still they continued to move. Doggedly, pausing every hundred meters to allow the slower men to catch up.

"This sure as hell isn't anyplace a guy'd want to be alone," one of the Marines muttered under his breath as he dragged himself up over an ice-clad boulder nearly as tall as he was.

Quinn wasn't going to argue that.

Realizing that they looked like a line of ducks in a carnival shooting gallery against the sunlit fields of snow, he also missed his ghillie suit.

The camouflage trick had originated with Scots gamekeepers who'd invented them to make catching poachers easier. Pushing grass and branches from local plants into burlap netting sewn into an old fatigue uniform broke up the human form, helping a sniper to vanish into the background.

Although you could buy them for all seasons, Quinn had made his own winter one with strips of white canvas, which made him invisible by allowing him to blend into the snow. Unfortunately, since this clusterfuck had originally been planned as a night mission and weight had been an issue, he'd left the suit back at the base.

"I've never seen snow before," one of the baby-faced Rangers said.

"Well, now you have, son," Quinn said. Personally, if he never saw the damn stuff again, it'd be too soon. "And, hey, lucky you, soldier, Uncle Sam's picking up the tab."

They'd been trudging along for about an hour, struggling up the steep mountain slope, when one of the Marines stumbled, letting go of his corner of the Sked carrying the Chinook's wounded pilot.

Which, in turn, caused another Marine to fall.

A third.

Then, shit, the fourth landed on his back, disappearing into a drift.

To Quinn's horror, the Sked carrying the wounded pilot took off down the mountain, racing like a bobsled down a double diamond run.

Quinn took off running.

As always, Zach was right with him.

24

The Somersett resident FBI office didn't look anything like the headquarters that movie and television viewers were accustomed to. Located in the basement of the courthouse, it resembled Mulder's office from *The X-Files*. Though decidedly tidier, which was some small comfort.

Wood-framed photos of the FBI director and the U.S. president shared space with a rogues' gallery of fugitives—two armed bank robbers, a carjacking murderer, another male wanted for assault and battery with intent to kill, and a pedophile playground recreational director who, so far as they knew, had committed sexual conduct with sixteen minors.

Not that any of those fugitives were guilty until proven so in a court of law.

Yeah, right, Cait thought, hoping they caught up with the pervert before the members of the neighborhood watch group—who were in danger of turning into vigilantes—found him.

Adding to the decor were the United States flag and the blue FBI flag on either side of the president's photo, plus a pitifully weeping ficus. Cait didn't need her detective skills to realize that the lack of daylight had more than a little something to do with the leaves scattered all over the industrial blue carpeting.

Before being moved to St. Camillus Hospital, the

morgue had been located in this basement. Which explained the lingering odor of formaldehyde.

She'd been keeping in touch with the Columbia field office, and as soon as she'd reported the note Valentine Snow had received, her superior, Special Agent in Charge Brooke Davidson, had instructed her to start setting up the office to make room for a joint task force.

Every available agent in the region had been called in on the case, and they were working the phones and the computers. SAC Davidson had requested assistance from the ATF, who would be arriving first thing in the morning from their nearby office in Florence. Fortunately, while local police might get pissed off about FBI arriving on their crime scenes, there wasn't a cop in the country who didn't do a happy dance when told the ATF would be showing up. There flat out wasn't anybody better than their forensic lab guys when it came to tricky ballistics and multiple shootings.

Not that her own Bureau didn't have something going for it, Cait thought as she left Angetti—who, when she'd called him at the restaurant, had leaped at the chance to escape his in-laws' anniversary party—arranging for extra desks, phones, and computers while she drove to the morgue.

The FBI Rapid Start program—occasionally called Rapid Stall by its detractors—had been used in every major investigation from the Oklahoma bombing to the twin towers and Pentagon bombings to the D.C. snipers. It might not be perfect, but the computer system was, hands down, the best computer software program available for managing multiple leads in a complex investigation.

Also a plus for their side was that the medical examiner wasn't your typical small-town coroner. Son and grandson of plastic surgeons to generations of Southern belles, rather than using his talents with a scalpel to pretty people up, Drew Sloan had sent shock waves through the Sloan family by leveraging his Duke medical degree into a job where he cut up dead people.

His near-genius IQ and his ability to make the complexities of forensic medicine understandable to laymen, along with his movie star looks, had earned him a regular guest spot on Court TV. It had also created a demand for his expert testimony among both prosecutors and defense attorneys.

And if all that weren't enough, he'd written three books profiling a few of his more gruesome cases, all of which had hit the best-seller lists, which, in turn, explained his designer duds and the Porsche that pulled into the hospital parking lot of St. Camillus right behind hers.

For Dr. Drew Sloan, crime not only paid, it paid handsomely.

"Hey, darlin'," he called out as he climbed out of the Batmobile-like black sports car. "Fancy meeting you here."

She'd caught him on his cell and he'd promised to come right over to the hospital. What she hadn't realized was that he hadn't been at home.

"I'm sorry," she said, taking in the tuxedo that fit so fantastically that even Cait, who knew nothing about fashion, guessed it must have been custom tailored. "I didn't realize you had something important going."

"No big deal." He shrugged. "I was at the theater."

She suspected he wasn't referring to the Palmetto multiplex down on the harbor.

"What's playing?"

"What else?" He flashed the dazzling smile that would have undoubtedly, had he followed in his family's Gucci-clad footsteps, had every woman in the Lowcountry standing in line for Botox, boob jobs, and face-lifts. "*The Pirate Queen.*"

She'd needed that laugh. Ever since she left Quinn's house, her mind had been swirling like a leaf caught in a whirlpool. This case was already loaded with potential problems. The last thing she'd needed was the former U.S. Navy SEAL entering into the mix.

"Guess it's bad, huh?" Drew asked as they walked toward the sleek modern building located on the verdant banks of the Somersett River.

"Yeah. And I'm afraid it's going to get worse. Which is why I called."

"No problem," he said as the sliding glass doors gave way to a lobby that was both open and inviting.

During the day natural light from the towering windows and glass canopy of the atrium flooded the space. Tonight, glancing up, Cait could see only darkness. Which wasn't the most promising of metaphors.

"I live to serve," he said with his trademark smile. "Especially beautiful women."

The doctor had always been a charmer. Having worked with him on several homicides over the years, Cait knew Drew was one of those men who truly liked and appreciated women. And, unsurprisingly, women all seemed to like and appreciate him right back.

"I don't need full service tonight," she said, wondering how on earth all those trees managed to thrive when the poor ficus in her office was in dire need of life support. Maybe she ought to throw it in the SUV and bring it down here for resuscitation. "I just need you to check out a couple victims. I need to know if their wounds were made from the same weapon."

He glanced over at her as they passed the gift shop, its windows filled with bright balloons, stuffed animals, and pyramids of paperback novels with glossy covers featuring vampires, running women in jeopardy, or bloody daggers.

"They're not from the same incident?" he asked.

"No." The cobalt blue elevator doors opened. "Haven't you heard the news?"

"I was at the theater," he reminded her. "With an early dinner beforehand."

"I've got two vics," she said as the elevator took them down to the basement morgue.

St. Camillus seemed to have purchased a seventies Muzak disco package, which was annoying enough by itself, but "Stayin' Alive" playing through the speakers seemed a particularly ironic choice for a hospital.

"Both shot by what I'm ninety-nine-point-ninety-nine percent sure is the same guy," she said. "A sniper who wrote Valentine Snow a note promising more."

"Damn. That's not good."

"You are, yet again, the master of understatement."

Icy air blew through the vents of the morgue, making it probably the only place in town that was cold.

When Cait had first joined SPD, the morgue had been a gathering place for cops to hang out. The equivalent of a corner doughnut shop or cop bar where uniforms and detectives all stood around, shooting the breeze, drinking coffee out of 7-Eleven cups, smoking cigarettes, and wolfing down Krispy Kremes.

Then Drew Sloan had come on board with what more than one of the old-timer detractors had regarded as a quaint notion—that people should be accorded the same respect in death as they were entitled to in life.

Quicker than you could say Jack the Ripper, he'd banned the cigarettes, coffee, and doughnuts. And, although there was a lot of grumbling down at the cop shop, he'd gone on to limit witnesses to his autopsies to his assistant, the detectives who'd caught the case, and the occasional street cop who may have worked the scene. The prosecutors were also given an open invitation, though very few ever bothered to show up.

He went into the annex where the bodies of the two former military men had been tucked away in drawers. Rolled up his sleeves and snapped on a pair of latex gloves.

"Let's see what we've got here."

Less than an hour later, Cait had her answer.

Quinn had been right. Which is exactly what she'd been afraid of.

"Funny choice for a sniper," he murmured. "Most,

at least the ones I've read about, go for a bolt-action rifle. Why would he need an automatic, unless . . ."

Cait had known Drew Sloan for nearly ten years. And he'd always looked as if he'd just stepped off the cover of *GQ* or returned from sailing off Cape Cod with the Kennedys. Cool and unflappable, he'd never seemed the least bit unnerved about anything.

Until now.

"Unless he's planning one helluva finale," she answered the dread she viewed in his dark eyes.

A dread that had had its icy fingers wrapped around her own heart ever since Quinn had told her about the weapon's deadly capabilities.

25

Cait's cell phone rang as she left the hospital. The display read UNAVAILABLE, but she had a feeling she knew who it was.

"Cavanaugh."

"Hey." Frank Angetti's voice confirmed her guess. "The place is all set up, ATF will be here at nine in the a.m.—"

"Nine? They keep bankers' hours?"

"Hey, don't jump on my ass. I'm just the messenger."

"They're going to miss morning drive time."

"Yeah, but you asked for their forensic guys," he reminded her. "Which means you won't need them until the guy shoots someone else."

"*Unless* he shoots someone else." Although it was overly optimistic, especially for her, Cait was hoping that letter to Valentine Snow had just been bravado.

"You don't really figure we're done with the wacko? Or him with us?"

Her partner might make her want to scream on an often daily basis, but he *had* gone through the academy. He wasn't stupid. And he'd been an FBI agent a lot more years than she had. Like he was always saying, he'd seen it all and had the ulcers and the bald head to prove it.

"No." She told him what she'd learned about the UNSUB's weapon.

"Christ."

"Yeah. Which is why we've got to get this guy. Like yesterday."

"No shit, Skippy. But unless you've got a secret decoder ring you've been keeping from me, we're not going to break the case tonight. So I'm going home and hitting the sack."

"Might as well. Since I have the feeling it might be the last sleep you get for a while."

She knew she should take her own advice, but she was so wired, she figured it was going to be one of those nights she spent staring up at the ceiling with her mind in hyperdrive.

"We need to talk to Michael Gannon first thing in the morning," she said.

"Father Mike?"

"He's not a priest anymore."

"He's not? Jeez, I guess that shows how long it's been since I've been to Mass."

Finally something they had in common. "I don't know the particulars, but he's running a free clinic now. And he's got some veterans' PTSD group."

"You think our UNSUB's one of 'em?"

"I don't know. Maybe. Or maybe one of them might know someone he thinks could be capable of going postal and blowing people away. Or have a handle on where our guy could get his hands on a weapon like that."

"Even if one of the group's vets suspected one of their own, why would they tell us? Semper Fi and all that."

"I thought about that. A vet turning in one of his own would have to be one of those major decisions of conscience. Especially in a culture where troops are fighting for the guy in the foxhole next to them. But how does keeping silent about a killer protect your fellow soldier? Wouldn't you be risking all vets being painted with that same wide murderous brush?"

"Beats me."

The shrug in his voice had her grinding her teeth. He might be senior, he might have graduated from the academy, but thank God he was so close to retirement, because if she was stuck with Angetti as a partner much longer, she wouldn't have any molars left.

"My brother's a career Marine," he said. "I've never gotten why he'd drop out of college to go fight in Desert Storm. No way am I going to try to understand the military mind-set."

That attitude sure wasn't going to help get the vets to open up.

"Look, I've got an idea," Cait said, deciding there was no way she could take her partner to the group with her. "We need all the manpower we can get, so it doesn't make any sense us running around together. Drew Sloan's doing the autopsies tomorrow. Why don't you cover them, and I'll go talk to Gannon. Besides, I know him. He's my former partner's brother."

"Just how I wanted to spend the day," he grumbled. "With a double-feature slice and dice."

"Let's just hope that's the worst thing that happens tomorrow," she said. "So, does that work for you?"

"Yeah. Good luck with the priest. We break this before the guy decides to get up in a tower and start blasting away at all the tourists in town, and we'll probably get ourselves some shiny medals from the mayor."

Cait didn't want a medal. What she wanted was to catch her sniper before he could shoot again. As she drove through the streets, which on any normal night would be dark and silent but tonight were still packed with drunken party animals, she was hoping Michael Gannon could provide a key.

Not only did the widow of one of the victims volunteer with his group, but given that he was a former vet himself, he might just have another viewpoint.

She wondered about confidentiality. If he'd still been a priest, any confession could have been protected by the seal of the confessional, which bound a priest to silence under Church law.

But he was no longer a priest, she reminded herself as she pulled into the parking garage of her apartment. And, knowing him as she did, she knew that if anyone of his group were actually to confess to such a crime, he would do the right thing—if he couldn't get the guy to turn himself in, he'd report it himself.

But what if the vet didn't actually confess?

She climbed the three flights of stairs to her apartment, which, unfortunately hadn't been built with Buccaneer Days in mind. The pirates belting out "Louie, Louie" on the street below sounded as if they were in her living room.

Focus.

Okay, so, what if, perhaps, a vet was just giving off bad, even dangerous vibes? Like he might be thinking about blowing people away. Or having flashbacks. Could having the FBI suddenly show up at his door be the final straw?

Which wouldn't be the end of the world if he was her sniper.

But what if he was some innocent guy who'd done his duty for flag and country and come home understandably messed up?

Cops and FBI agents weren't superhero crime fighters. They were human. They made mistakes. But Cait knew she'd never forgive herself if she fucked this up and sent an innocent person over the edge.

Deciding she'd better get up to speed on PTSD, she took a bag of coffee out of her freezer, spooned a heaping measure into her coffeemaker, filled the reservoir with water, and turned on the switch.

By the time she'd taken a shower to wash the stench of the morgue out of her hair and changed into a pair of boxers and a T-shirt, the coffee was done. She filled a dark blue FBI mug and turned on her laptop. It took Google .13 seconds to kick up 5,000,310 Web sites.

Which meant she was looking at a very long night.

26

"This is so fucking cool!" Charlie Jensen said, stroking the black silencer on the Russian sniper rifle with the same expression other men might have while stroking a beautiful woman's naked breasts. "So, it's really silent, huh?"

"At the range I'm going to be using it," the shooter said.

It was a risk, shooting from a mere fifty yards from the front of the cathedral at one of the busiest times of the day, but he figured all those feds and cops who were undoubtedly spending the night setting up their command post would shit bricks when they realized they were up against a guy with solid brass balls.

"Fucking cool," Jensen repeated as he popped the top on another bottle of Bud. His second this morning.

Which was just as well. Although the alcoholic vet wouldn't have been his first choice, like a former defense secretary once said, "You've got to go to war with the army you have."

Now the shooter just hoped they could get through the day without his army of one getting a PTSD flashback. Which was why he was letting him drink. Hopefully the beer would work as a tranquilizer.

"I'll bet it cost a fucking arm and leg, huh?" Jensen asked for about the tenth time in the last ten minutes.

"It wasn't cheap," the shooter agreed as he finished filing the serial number off a Steyr GB.

He held it up. Pointed it at the TV—where some guy was explaining isobars on a big weather map studded with smiling cartoon suns—and pulled the trigger.

The big black automatic was a Special Forces favorite. If everything went according to plan, he'd need only a single round, but after reassuring himself that the freshly oiled mechanism worked perfectly, he filled the magazine to its eighteen-shell capacity.

"So, whatcha gonna do with that anyway? Can't shoot long range with a nine-millimeter," the guy said, demonstrating that he did have some functioning gray cells.

"It's a backup piece."

That was the truth, so far as it went. It wasn't the whole truth and nothing but the truth, but hell, the shooter and veracity had never exactly been on speaking terms.

"Fucking cool." That seemed to be the phrase of the day. "Maybe I should keep it up front with me," he suggested. "Since you'll be in the back with the rifle."

"No." He stuck the pistol into a black leather gym bag. "Your job is to drive." He stood up. "Soldier."

He used his best military tone. The guy, who, according to what he'd shared at the whiny vets group, had been a more gung ho soldier than the shooter, apparently recognized the tone of authority when he heard it.

He pushed himself up from the couch.

"Yes, sir," he said.

His salute was sloppy. The shooter hoped his driving would be better. The last thing they needed was for him to get pulled over for a DUI.

The shooter picked up the rifle and stuck it into the golf bag he'd gotten at a pawnshop in Georgetown.

"Okay," he said. "Let's get this show on the road."

27

"Mom?"

"Yes, darling?" Dara Long asked her son absently as she drove across the Somersett bridge, maneuvering her ancient Honda into the right lane and trying not to see the blue smoke billowing up from the Civic's tailpipe.

Of all the changes in her life since her husband had decided to trade her in for the bottle-blond so-called physical trainer with the bought boobs who'd supposedly been helping him rehabilitate his knee after arthroscopic surgery, one of the things she missed most about her marriage was her ice white Volvo V50. Although she'd never, in a million years, ever thought she would end up driving a station wagon, having a child had changed her.

Gone was the fast-living baseball Annie who'd nabbed the sexy shortstop every sports reporter in the South said was on the fast track to New York City and Yankees pinstripes. In her place was a stereotypical soccer mom who would do anything to keep her child safe. Including buying that Volvo she'd ended up having to sell to pay the lawyer bills.

Not that Chad had ever really wanted custody of their son—a son who was happier drawing pictures of cars than swinging a bat and had pretty much flunked out of T-ball because he'd been too small. Too slow. And, well, to her mind, too sweet.

But Bimbo Barbie was high maintenance, and if there was one thing her former husband knew, it was how to play hardball. Which was why, when his new trophy girlfriend—and Dara *knew* it was her idea—suggested it, he threatened to use that bout of depression she'd suffered through after Tyler was born as a reason why she wasn't a responsible mother and shouldn't be awarded custody of their son.

And if that hadn't been bad enough, he'd also brought in her hard-drinking, hard-partying days—never mind that *he'd* been the one she'd been drinking and partying with.

She'd known Chad and Barbie didn't really want Tyler living with them in their little love nest. What they did want was to put her in a position where she'd be willing to negotiate away any divorce settlement.

In the end, she'd won custody. But not before it had cost her the pretty little Craftsman bungalow, her car, and seventy percent of the child support any family court judge in the country would've considered acceptable. As it was—surprise, surprise—eighteen months later, Chad still hadn't come up with a single payment.

She'd watched him strutting out of the courtroom with the bimbo and known he believed he'd won the long, drawn-out battle. Which just went to show that not only was he an adulterer, but he was a stupid one.

Because the son they'd created together that day when he'd gotten called up from Charleston, where he'd been playing for the A-level Devil Dogs, was a prize more valuable than any house, or car, or wide-screen high-definition TV—which Chad had also ended up with.

"Did you know that Somersett wasn't really founded by a pirate?" Tyler asked.

"It wasn't?" She turned onto a wide street shaded by magnificent old oaks. Maybe someone ought to inform the tourism bureau. Or, maybe not, she thought, as she braked for a crowd of colorfully dressed jaywalkers. Given how many bucks the wannabe Blackbeards and wenches poured into the town's coffers.

"Admiral Somersett wasn't a pirate. He was a privateer."

"What's the difference?"

"A pirate is a guy who commits robbery on the sea. Privateers had official government papers, called letters of marque. That's French, I think."

"I'm pretty sure it is," she agreed.

"The papers were given to them by kings and queens so they could attack enemy ships. Then they got a percentage of the booty."

"Sounds a lot like piracy to me."

"But it wasn't. Because it was official."

His earnest tone had her fighting a smile. "Well, I suppose that does make all the difference."

"It does. Even our country had privateers working for them during the Revolution and the War of 1812. Congress said the president could use privateers during the Civil War, but President Lincoln never did it."

"I had no idea."

"It's true."

"If you say it, Tyler, I believe it."

"Admiral Somersett was one of the bravest of all the privateers. Even better than Sir Francis Drake. He even had a battle with Blackbeard in the harbor."

"Did he now?"

It had been a long time since she'd heard him so excited about anything. Which gave Dara's heart a lift and made up for the traffic and the bad muffler she couldn't afford to replace.

"Yeah. I guess it was a really big deal. And the admiral won. And took all the gold that Blackbeard had on his ship and gave it to the king. Who rewarded the admiral by giving him Somersett. But it wasn't a town yet. It was just a swamp. But Admiral Somersett could see its potential."

"A farsighted man, the admiral."

"And really, really rich." He sighed as they approached the twin towers of St. Brendan's Cathedral. "I wish there were privateers these days."

"Why is that?" After braking to allow a flame red BMW to cross in front of her, she pulled over to the curb, getting in line with the other parents delivering their children on this first day of the new school year.

"Because then I could grow up to become one and get lots of gold and silver and rubies and buy you a new house. And a new car. And anything else you want."

"Oh, darling."

Dara was grateful for the sunglasses she'd put on against the bright morning glare, since they kept him from seeing the tears welling up in her eyes. She leaned across the space between them and ruffled his carrot-colored hair. Which was, she feared, something else that probably acted as a red flag to childish tormentors.

"I don't need rubies. Because I have you."

"I love you, Mom." His freckled face was too serious for his age.

"I love you, too, sport." The moment the doctor had put him into her arms in the delivery room, she'd been flooded by so much love she'd been afraid her heart might explode in her chest. "And thanks for the history lesson. Where did you learn all that, anyway?"

They'd been to the library just last week and she couldn't remember him checking out any books on pirates or local history.

"I looked it up online while you were sleeping," he said.

"Clever."

She made a mental note to make sure her parental controls were set up. Not that she thought he'd go looking for trouble, but these days there were so many more things endangering children than when she'd been her son's age.

"I guess you were interested because of Buccaneer Days?" She reached behind the seat and retrieved his Spider-Man lunch box.

"Sorta." He glanced up as a group of boys walked past the car, laughing and punching each other on the arms. "Mostly I wanted to be prepared for school."

How on earth had she and Chad the jock created this serious, intelligent child? There were times she wondered if he could have been accidentally switched with another baby in the hospital nursery.

"I'm sure your teacher won't expect you to know all that history the first day of school," she assured him.

"It's not for class. It's for recess."

"Recess?"

"I've been practicing what to say. So I can use my speech utensils and not s-s-stutter so the other kids won't laugh at me."

The tears threatened anew. She wanted to tell him that he needn't worry. But she'd never lied to him and had no intention of beginning now.

"Good plan," she said, forcing optimism into her voice. "So." She took a deep breath. "Want me to walk with you?"

"Mom!" She'd have never thought she'd be thrilled to have him suddenly turn into an average eight-year-old in danger of being embarrassed by his mom. "I'm not a little kid anymore."

"True." She didn't have to fake this smile. "So, have a super day."

"Okay." He squared his thin shoulders. As he reached for the door handle, she kissed him on top of the head, and refused to have her feelings hurt when he rubbed at his hair.

As she watched him, looking heartbreakingly small and vulnerable as he made his way all alone toward a plump, snowy-haired crossing guard who was shepherding a flock of uniformed children across the street, Dara Long said the small, silent prayer she'd been saying every day of his young life.

Please, God, keep my child safe.

28

Quinn parked in the clinic lot across the street from St. Brendan's, jockeying for position with all the soccer moms delivering their children to their first day of school. A pretty blonde in an old beater Honda Civic that stood out like a sore thumb among the shiny SUVs and crossovers, stopped to let him cut across the long line.

Mike's Taurus was already in the lot. When he'd returned the call last night, after Quinn had explained the situation, he hadn't hesitated to agree to the early-morning meeting. Unsurprisingly, he revealed he was also expecting a visit from Special Agent Cait Cavanaugh.

Who, talk about your timing, was pulling into a spot six cars down from Quinn.

"Fancy meeting you here," she said as she climbed out of the black sedan. It wasn't quite as noticeable as the SUV he guessed her partner was still driving, but the whip antennas screamed "federal government agent car."

She'd been pretty at nineteen. Prettier, even, despite being tanked, the next time they'd hooked up. But as she walked toward him on those long legs, the slanting morning sun making her red hair gleam, he decided the aura of confidence and determination she wore so well had caused her to grow into a beauty since the last time fate had thrown them together.

"Something wrong with me dropping by to catch up with an old friend?" he asked.

"Nothing at all. The timing's just a little coincidental."

"Caught me," he said easily, falling in beside her as they walked toward the clinic door. She looked lean, lithe, and strong. Smelled damn good, too. And although she had fabulously long legs, the difference in their height still had him shortening his stride to match hers.

"You're a civilian. This isn't any of your business."

"The hell it isn't."

The harshness of his tone got her attention. She stopped. Took her shades off and looked up at him, her blue eyes narrowed.

"Excuse me?" There was enough ice in her tone to cover Jupiter several times over.

"You can get up on that federal high horse of yours all you want," he said, deciding she needed to understand right off the bat that just because he might appear more low-key than some of the guys she'd been with, he was no pushover. "But that's not going to change the fact that you've got a whacked-out shooter running around town who apparently wants the public and the authorities to think he's a sniper. Which makes every guy who's ever picked up a rifle in the line of duty a suspect."

"That's an overstatement. I certainly would never imagine you doing such a thing."

"Thanks for the vote of confidence." His tone, as they began walking again, was a great deal drier than the weather, which, although it was only eight o'clock, was already thick enough to drink. "But if you weren't already thinking along those lines, why do you want to talk with Mike?"

"I'm here for the same reason you are. To see if anyone in that group of his might stand out as particularly unstable."

"Ever think you might run into a confidentiality problem?"

"It occurred to me. But he's not a priest any longer."

"But he's a vet. One running a counseling group."

"So, you're saying he'd risk innocent people being gunned down in the street to protect a killer?"

"Hell, no. I am suggesting that if you go in there like Joe Friday or Eliot Ness, you might run into problems."

She stopped again. She'd put the dark glasses back on, but he didn't have to see her eyes to sense the glare.

"I'm just saying."

"And you're also implying that if you're with me, he'll be more cooperative?"

Quinn shrugged. "Maybe. Maybe not. But if you hadn't already considered you might have problems, you would've brought your partner along."

"He's supervising setting up the task force room."

"Good for him."

Cait could tell she wasn't fooling him for a minute. Which wasn't anything new. She'd always gotten the feeling that Quinn knew things about her. Things she might not even know herself. It was a sixth-sense thing that had probably made him a good sniper. She also suspected that if he hadn't entered the military, he would've made one hell of a detective.

"Did you ever think about being a cop?"

He threw back his head and laughed. A nurse clad in blue Bart Simpson scrubs who'd just opened the clinic door turned around to see the source of the deep, rumbling, sexy-as-hell sound. Cait watched as the nurse stood up a little straighter. Smoothed an absent hand over her hair. No doubt about it, the man had always been a chick magnet.

"I hadn't realized that choosing law enforcement as a career was so funny."

"Not funny." He was struggling with the smile as

he held the glass door open for her. "It's just, well, ironic. But no, that thought never occurred to me."

There was something else going on. Something she couldn't quite get a handle on. She had no time to think about it, though, because Michael Gannon was standing at the front reception counter, as if waiting for their arrival.

The first time she'd met her former partner's brother, Cait had nearly swallowed her tongue. In contrast to his brother Joe's golden athleticism, the priest named for an archangel could have been a fallen angel, washed off the nave ceiling of a cathedral.

Lush black hair—longer now than when he'd been a priest—framed a narrow, aesthetic face. His eyes, set above high, slashing cheekbones, were a riveting neon blue. Was it any wonder that women all over Somersett had referred to the priest as Father What-a-Waste?

Rather than the starched and stiff traditional white doctor's coat, he was wearing a white T-shirt that read, "Air goes in and out; blood goes round and round; any variation on this is a bad thing."

No, there was nothing traditional about doctor-turned-priest-turned-doctor-again Michael Gannon.

"Cait." Beautifully sculptured lips, designed to tempt both sinner and saint, curved into a warm smile. "It's been way too long."

"I know." What with his brother quitting the force, getting married, and moving to Swann Island, her joining the FBI, and Michael having been off in New Orleans post-Katrina, those casual days of the three of them getting together over a pint at the Black Swan had become too few and too far between. "I'd use work as an excuse, but . . ."

She shrugged, thinking that life was becoming pretty pitiful when work trumped friendships.

"Keeping the country free from terrorism is important," he said. "I imagine it's also a 24/7 job." He was, hands down, the most unjudgmental person she'd ever met. Which was why, she supposed, the lines had always been longer when Father Mike was handing out absolution.

"It can become one."

She glanced around at the cheery posters on the crayon-colored walls. The furniture was wood, painted in equally bright hues. There were baskets of toys, and shelves of books. A sign invited patients to take a book home with them and bring a replacement the next time they visited.

"This is a nice place." And much different from what she'd imagined a free clinic would look like.

"Being sick is no fun, even when you're well-off," he said. "More difficult when you don't have health insurance and you're worried about how you're going to feed your babies. It's our goal to make the experience as pleasant as possible."

Michael Gannon was a good man. A nice man. Now that he wasn't a priest any longer, he'd probably make a terrific husband. Cait bet that since leaving the Church, he'd jumped to the top of the Lowcountry's Most Eligible Bachelors List.

Not that she would be joining the women who were undoubtedly swarming around him like piranhas; although they'd always shared a mutual affection, even since his vow of celibacy had stopped being an issue, there'd never been any sparks.

Nothing like the ones that flared through her system every time she got anywhere close to Quinn.

"I'd love to give you the grand tour," he said, "but I suspect you need to get down to business."

"Yes, I'm afraid so."

"Another time, then."

"Absolutely."

Since she'd left only a sketchy message on his voice mail, she filled him in on the details, such as she knew them, of the crimes.

"I'm sorry." He shook his head, his gaze echoing his words. "You know I'd love to help you, Cait. But even if I had an official group membership roster with addresses and phone numbers, I couldn't give it to you without a court order."

Damn. This was exactly what she'd been afraid of.

"But you're not a priest anymore."

"No. But I am a physician, which brings up the subject of patient-doctor confidentiality."

Cait wasn't sure that would hold up in court, since, after all, it was merely a volunteer support group, but keeping in mind that what she needed was his cooperation, not a legal battle, she tried a different approach.

"When's your next meeting?"

"As a matter of fact, it's this evening."

"May I sit in?"

He lifted a jet brow. "I didn't realize you were a veteran."

Of course they both knew she wasn't. "Okay." She folded her arms, going into negotiation mode. "May I speak to the group?"

He exchanged a look with Quinn. Something passed between them, but Quinn's expression was totally unreadable.

"I'll have to ask them," he said. "I'm not trying to be difficult," he added when she couldn't help huffing out a frustrated breath. "You have to realize that you're talking about a group of men who, under usual conditions, do not open up to anyone. They've always seen themselves as Superman. No way are they going to want their wives, lovers, parents, friends, employers, or even their doctors to know that a lot of days they feel more like Jimmy Olsen.

"They certainly, most of them, would never be caught dead joining a support group. But once we get someone here, the chance to listen to brothers who've gone through the same things is the first time they've been able to experience authentic camaraderie and kinship since the combat that landed them in the group.

"It's also the first place they can openly share

locked-up experiences with other vets who understand and listen without judgment and who also validate their own feelings. It's a delicate balance, Caitlin. I wouldn't want to risk that."

"It won't help for civilians to think all PTSD sufferers are going to pick up an automatic weapon and open up in some shopping mall," Quinn said. It was the first comment he'd made since they'd all exchanged greetings.

"Point taken," Mike said. He gave Quinn another one of those looks Cait couldn't quite read.

As if sensing her frustration at those silent messages zapping back and forth over her head, Quinn said, "I'll talk with them. Hopefully make them see how important it is that they cooperate."

Mike nodded. "I'd appreciate that. I know they listen to you." He turned to Cait. "We usually start the pre-meeting coffee and conversation around seven. Why don't you stop back around seven fifteen and Quinn and I'll see what we can do to win the troops over."

"Thanks. I'd really appreciate it." What she'd prefer was a list of names and addresses that she could start checking out immediately, but meanwhile she'd have to try a different tack.

Beginning with the second thing on her to-do list. Tracking down the gun.

"Well, hello." The crossing guard, who was holding the kids back on the sidewalk, smiled down at Tyler. "How are you this grand and sunny morning?"

"Just f-f-f-fine, ma'am."

"Well, I'm glad to hear that," she answered cheerfully, ignoring his stammer. "You're new to St. Brendan's, aren't you?"

"Yes, ma'am."

She tipped down her sunglasses and skimmed a look over him. "Well, you certainly look sharp in your uniform."

Color rose in his cheeks as he felt the other kids, who so far had ignored him, checking him out. "T-t-thank you, ma'am."

"Okay." She shoved the glasses back up, lifted her sign, and stepped off the curb into the middle of the street, stopping the traffic. "Let's everyone keep together now."

29

"Well," Cait said, as she and Quinn walked back out into the blindingly bright summer sun, "that was enlightening." She shielded her eyes with a hand and looked a long, long way up at him. "Why didn't you tell me that you're a member of the group?"

"I'm not really, though I do drop in from time to time. Would it have made a difference last night?"

"No, but—"

"So now you know."

She wanted to ask if he was suffering from PTSD. But wasn't that a given? Why would he belong to a support group if he wasn't?

Unless he was just getting fodder for his next book?

No. There were many things about Quinn that unraveled her last nerve, but unless he'd changed one hundred and eighty degrees from the man she'd known, there was no way he would ever profit off another person's misery.

There was an awkward little silence. At least awkward on her part. Once again, she had not a single clue as to his feelings.

"Well," she said on an exhaled breath, "I appreciate your agreeing to help with the group."

"No problem."

"But other than that, you really can't get involved in a federal investigation."

"Sorry. Too late. I'm already involved."

"It's against policy."

"Like the FBI doesn't use civilians? What about snitches? And stings? And witness protection?"

"Witness protection falls under the jurisdiction of the U.S. Marshals."

His flash of grin surprised her. And sent an unwanted little zing through her.

"What?" she demanded.

He hesitated. Laughter and what impossibly seemed to be affection lit up his eyes. "It's just that you're really hot when you talk like a special agent."

Cait refused to let the chauvinistic comment, which he apparently took as a compliment, give her any pleasure. "I *am* a special agent."

"And a crackerjack one, too, I'll bet," he replied. "But being smart and good at your work doesn't preclude you being hot."

The conversation was getting decidedly uncomfortable. Cait figured if she didn't leave now, he'd start strolling down memory lane back to that night. Which, if she were to be perfectly honest, she thankfully couldn't entirely remember.

"This is a ridiculous conversation." Could she sound any more uptight? Why was it that she seemed to swing to extremes where this man was concerned? "I've got work to do."

"Then I'll let you get to it. I'll see you tonight."

"Tonight," she agreed. She started to walk to her car, then turned back. "And I need you to stay out of my case."

"No, you don't. Not really."

"And why is that?"

"Because I know guns."

"So does ATF. They've joined the investigation."

"Good call. Their forensics department's top-notch. But they're still feds."

"Surely you're not suggesting using the local police lab?"

"No. What I'm suggesting is that although I've not

a single doubt you're damn good at your job, you've still been trained at the academy."

"That's standard procedure. For an FBI agent."

"Well, sure. And you've probably learned the latest ways to eavesdrop on terrorists. But the bureau's undoubtedly like every other agency in the government. Including ATF. And even the Pentagon. People tend to think inside the box."

"And you don't?" She knew the answer to that before she asked it.

"Sweetheart, a SEAL sniper survives and keeps his team safe by thinking *outside* the box. Now, granted, I still don't think your UNSUB is a legitimate sniper. But a buck gets ten I'd be better at locating potential places for him to shoot from than anyone you've got on your team. Which could be really important given that having your two victims lying in state is probably going to draw one helluva crowd."

"What are you talking about?"

"You haven't heard?"

"If I'd heard, I wouldn't be asking."

"Right. I guess I got notified because as a writer-in-residence, I'm sorta very loosely, on staff. But the powers that be at ASMA decided it would be fitting to have a public memorial service while Jacob and Davis lie in state in the academy rotunda."

Just what she needed. "When?"

"Tomorrow. Beginning at zero ten hundred. That's—"

"Ten a.m." She did, at least, know that much. "Shit."

They could end up with a crowd in the thousands. One attractive target for a guy with a gun that could shoot nearly a thousand rounds a minute!

Cait's mind was spinning with logistics when she heard a distant *pop!* over the laughter of children lining up in double rows in front of St. Brendan's School.

Reacting faster than she'd known it was even possible for a human being to move, especially one as large as he was, Quinn dragged her to the ground.

The force caused her bones to rattle. Lifting her head, Cait felt her heart hitch as she saw the body lying in the crosswalk in the middle of the street.

30

Emily Davenport was not dead.

The bullet, which had done exactly what Quinn had described was a possibility when aiming for a head shot, had grazed the crossing guard's forehead, singeing her tightly permed white curls.

The shot had, unfortunately, either knocked the elderly woman to the ground or caused her to fall, resulting in what Mike Gannon, who'd made it to the scene moments after the shooting, had diagnosed as a cracked rib, and perhaps a broken hip as well.

"All those kids," Cait murmured, feeling as shocky as the crossing guard, who'd been taken to St. Camillus by ambulance, had looked.

It was bedlam. Helicopters—police and TV news ones—were noisily circling overhead. Cops—local and federal—had arrived and begun to swarm over the crime scene.

The children in question were currently safely locked up inside the school. Which some might feel was a bit like closing the barn door after the horse was gone, but Cait was worried the shooter might use the chaos as an opportunity to get more shots off.

Unfortunately, those parents who'd still been parked outside the church school when the shooting had taken place, which may have made them potential witnesses, had scooped up their children and rushed off—Cait guessed they were taking the children back home where they would be safe.

Good luck. If an elderly woman could be shot leading a clutch of elementary school children across a city street, was there any place in Somersett that was truly safe?

"God." She pressed her fingertips against her forehead. "He could have killed them all."

"But he didn't," Quinn said. "We got lucky."

She looked up at him in disbelief. "Try telling that to today's victim."

"Who's still alive," he pointed out. "You told me the note he wrote Val said that he had something big planned. This isn't exactly on a par with blowing away a couple of former military guys at the academy."

"No." Cait was a little surprised to find the two of them thinking the exact same thing. Then the idea hit, like a lightning bolt from a clear blue sky. "He's not finished. Is he?"

"No." Quinn's expression was set, his flinty eyes harder than she'd ever seen them. "He's damn sure not."

The joint operational task force was faced with its first challenge before the main players could even arrive at those desks Angetti had been arranging for them. Being the sole fed on the scene, Cait instructed the uniforms to shut down all the intersections around the cathedral. Then she got on the phone and asked the highway patrol to cut off access to the bridge.

As more detectives and cops flooded the scene—no one wanted to miss *this* party—she sent them into the neighborhood to find witnesses.

Quinn, who continued to ignore her instructions about not getting involved, had wandered off on his own. She'd lost track of him, but caught up in trying to herd cats, she decided he must have taken off on his self-assigned task of locating potential sites for the sniper to use.

He surprised her yet again by showing up in front of her as she was on the phone trying to find someone with the authority to restrict the airspace over the scene to get those news copters out of the sky before they crashed into one another. Or, worse yet, into one of the police copters.

"Come over here," he said.

Getting nowhere, she slammed the phone shut. "This better be good."

"It's interesting, at any rate."

She followed him across the cobblestone sidewalk and up the steps of the church to the center of three arched doorways.

"I left this for you," he said.

The wood had been splintered. She leaned forward, saw the bullet, and called to the ATF crime lab investigator who had appeared on the scene.

"Check this out," she instructed.

The woman pulled out a Swiss Army knife and chipped the bullet out of the doorframe.

"Wow," she murmured. "Isn't this a lifer?"

"A lifer?" Cait asked as the woman looked down at the copper cartridge she was holding in her gloved palm with the same look a religious zealot might have when looking into the face of her god.

"I'm a birder in my free time," the ATF special agent said. "A lifer is a bird you've never seen before. Once you see one, it can be added to your life list."

"And you've never seen this before?"

"If it's what I think it is, I doubt many people outside the former Soviet Union have."

"It's an SP-5," Quinn said. "A full-metal-jacket 9 mm with a small steel core and lead behind it."

"But the M16 uses a 5.56 x 45 mm," Cait said. She'd spent part of her computer time last night looking the gun up so she would know better what they were dealing with.

Quinn nodded. "You've done your homework."

"I always do."

"The SP is a subsonic bullet, designed as a sniper load for the Russian 9 mm VSS silent sniper rifle."

"Which is why we didn't hear the crack, just that faint pop."

"Exactly. The most common cartridges used in silenced guns are the 9 mm NATO and the .45 ACP. This baby has twice as much muzzle energy as those and at least three times the range."

"It's capable of piercing eight millimeters of steel at a hundred and ten yards," the ATF agent said, dropping the spent copper cartridge into a plastic bottle and labeling it.

They'd been more than lucky. As had the crossing guard.

"So," Cait wondered out loud, "are we dealing with different snipers? Or a guy with one helluva arsenal?"

"It'd be my guess you're talking about a single shooter," Quinn said. "One who wants to show off."

For Valentine Snow? Cait wondered as she glanced at the reporter in question, standing behind the yellow police tape stretched between light poles surrounding the scene.

"I guess you weren't kidding when you said you knew about guns," she said.

"I never kid about deadly weapons. And, yeah, the VSS is pretty rare outside Russia. They were originally adopted by units of the Soviet Union Internal Affairs Ministry forces. Then the Soviet Army Spetsnaz, which are sort of equivalent to our SEALs and Delta Force guys, started to use them. I've heard the Russian Special Ops guys are still using them.

"One of their advantages, along with being silenced—though it's possible to silence just about any rifle if you know what you're doing—is that they can be stripped down to fit into a briefcase."

Cait so didn't need to hear that. "You know," she muttered, "you are one fun guy, McKade."

"It's the circumstances," he argued. "Once you nab your bad guy, you and I'll go out dancing and I'll show you exactly how much fun I can be."

She blinked.

Was he actually asking her out on a date?

In the middle of a crime scene with about a gazillion law enforcement types buzzing around them like worker bees around a hive?

"In your dreams."

His grin was slow, totally inappropriate to their circumstances, and sexy as hell. "Well, you know, now that you bring it up, Special Agent," he drawled, "I've gone that route. A lot lately, and it isn't really working for me anymore."

Not a date. Along with the humor, his eyes gleamed with something far more deadly than the Glock 9 mm she was wearing beneath her jacket. A glint that suggested a lot more than dancing.

More like the mattress mambo.

She supposed that macho come-on might work with a lot of women.

But not her.

Definitely not her.

"Look, you might be used to women throwing themselves at your feet." Or, more likely another part of his anatomy. "But I'm not most women."

"You don't have to remind me of that." His voice was deep and rough.

He was doing it again. Bringing up that damn night of the wedding. Although she still couldn't remember whether it had been Quinn or her—or perhaps both of them—ripping off her pink taffeta Southern belle bridesmaid dress, they were going to have to deal with it.

But not here.

And not now.

"I've got to go," she said briskly. "I'll meet you at the clinic. At seven."

He snapped a brief salute. "Roger that."

Although she refused to look back as she walked away, she could feel him watching her all the way to her car.

31

"We need a sexy name."

Cait had just walked into the JOC—joint operations center —which, if anything, was even more hectic than the crime scene she'd just left. The desks were jammed so close together it was nearly impossible to move.

A team of technicians from BellSouth were crawling around beneath the desks installing additional phones. The conversations were so loud she could barely hear herself think. Let alone hear her partner.

"A sexy name?"

"We're going to need more phone lines to handle tips," Angetti said. "Gotta pay for the pizza and burgers. And if this guy keeps shooting, we may even need to call in more troops, which means we'll have to go out and find us more office space to rent, which isn't cheap."

"We're going to catch him before that." Cait hoped that was true, even as she secretly admitted she would love just about any excuse to get them out of this dark basement.

"We're still going to need more bucks in the meantime. I just got back from Staples. We needed bulletin boards to put maps and names of suspects and shit on. Do you have any idea how much those suckers cost?"

"No."

"Well, they weren't cheap. At least, the good ones that'll stand up to this kind of case aren't. And they damn well don't grow on trees."

She was tempted to state that nothing—including leaves—grew on trees in this office, but she didn't want to risk sounding flip.

"And a projector. We're gonna need one of those. And a larger screen for the PowerPoint presentations."

"PowerPoint?"

"Gotta have PowerPoint," he said. "And a reward for tips leading to an arrest. The public loves those. And let's not forget what all this is going to cost in motel rooms for the troops. Unless you intend to invite everyone to crash at your place."

"Hosting a murder slumber party isn't on my to-do list."

"Well, in order to get funding from headquarters, we need to get this declared a major case," he informed her. "Which means we need to come up with a sexy name."

She'd never worked a major case before. Sure, she'd consulted on the Swann Island Slasher case, but that had been on an unofficial basis, and the island's sheriff hadn't tagged it with that tacky tabloid-type name. The local paper had.

"Surely you jest."

"Surely I freaking don't. Look, kid," he said, "you may be the hot new agent on the block, but you don't know jack about how to get a case through the system."

She wasn't going to argue that.

"Isn't that what the SAC does?" The special agent in charge was, after all, at the top of the state's FBI pyramid.

"Sure. But the more help we can give her, the more help we get back from her. It's a quid pro quo situation. It's just too bad the guy had to shoot that old lady."

"That stinks." There wasn't much she and her partner could agree on, but Cait wasn't going to argue that point. "At least she's alive." And hopefully would be okay, though at her age that hip could be a problem.

"Well, yeah. But the problem is, before she entered into the equation, we had a good thing going."

"Excuse me?" She pushed her hair back from her forehead. "Maybe I'm a little slow on the uptake, but how is having two men shot in cold blood a good thing?"

"Well, we all were tossing ideas around"—he waved around at force members currently manning the phones—"and kinda liked SNIPEASMA. You know, for 'sniper' and the academy initials?"

"Shouldn't it be SNIPERASMA?" Cait asked.

"Leaving the *R* out gives it a better ring," Angetti said. "But now that he's branched out from nailing military guys, it's lost its relevance."

Cait was beginning to feel as if she'd fallen down a rabbit hole. "Are you positive we need a name?"

"Hey, call the SAC if you don't believe me."

"It's true," volunteered an African American who'd just walked in with a twenty-ounce cup of coffee. "It's the same deal we've got over at ATF. If you want Uncle Sam to open up his checkbook, you gotta be classified as a major crime. Want to be a major crime, you gotta come up with a sexy name."

"How about SNIPESOM?" she suggested, just tossing something out there so they could move on to fighting crime. "For 'sniper' and 'Somersett.' "

The two men exchanged a glance. The ATF agent nodded. "Works for me."

"That'll do it," Angetti agreed. "I'll call the SAC and get the ball rolling."

"Good idea."

He'd just headed off to make the call when Derek Manning walked into the crowded office and came over to her.

"I just interviewed Mrs. Jacob."

"And?" Cait pulled open a drawer of one of the black metal filing cabinets and began leafing through manila folders.

"She says that to her knowledge, in thirty years of marriage, the general never strayed."

"Admirable man, the general."

"Indeed."

Cait glanced up at him. "But you don't believe her."

"Do gators shit in the swamp? Hell, no. The lady's tough, though. She swore in no uncertain terms that if her husband was over at Captain Hawthorne's house, he was only there to discuss their recruiting efforts."

Cait went back to the files. "Which you also don't believe."

"Hey, I interviewed your friend's wifey, remember? Her excuse for wearing that short robe in the middle of the afternoon was that she'd just taken a shower. To get ready to go out to dinner and watch the fireworks with her husband."

"That's always a possibility."

"Maybe. But that sure as hell wasn't Palmolive I smelled on her. It was sex."

She wasn't going to question the detective's nose. Not when his nickname around the precinct had always been Bloodhound.

"There's something else we need to talk about."

"Okay."

"It's about that jerk-off partner of yours."

Cait sighed. On a scale of one to ten, Angetti would rate at least an eleven on her list of least favorite things to discuss. "Okay."

"This is important."

"I can multitask." There it was. The list of county gun dealers. "Shoot."

"If you don't do something about that guy, you're going to end up spending all your time putting out fires."

"I know he can be obnoxious, but—"

"Obnoxious I can deal with. Hell, I've got idiot Briggs for a damn partner. But this guy's a loose cannon. Did you hear his press conference?"

That got her attention. Cait stopped flipping through the papers.

"Frank called a press conference?" On whose authority, she wanted to ask, but didn't.

"Well, it might not have exactly been an official conference. But a reporter staking out the courthouse stuck a mike in front of his face, and it was like Angetti suddenly got hit with a case of diarrhea of the mouth. He gave a profile of the killer."

"Oh, no."

Cait would bet a month's pay that she wasn't the only FBI agent who rued the day Frank Angetti had gotten tapped to attend that class he'd taken from the Behavioral Science Unit. He'd latched on to the idea of profiling like it was the Holy Grail.

"What did he say?" she asked, bracing herself for the detective's response.

"He said he was most likely a white male between the ages of twenty and thirty-five. A loner."

"That's what he always says." Cait sighed. It wasn't good. But it wasn't a disaster, either. "What else?"

"That he probably has a military background and a familiarity with weapons."

"I'd say that speaks for itself. He *has* shot three people in two days."

"He also said that he probably frequents gun shows."

"Again, a given." She told him what the ATF agent had said about the weapon used to shoot the crossing guard.

"That he's addicted to magazines, books, and movies about guns and the military, and takes pride in his prowess with firearms."

"Quinn McKade said pretty much the same thing. He said an actual sniper would go for a body shot. That a head shot was showing off."

"Well, it's not surprising that the jerk-off got those right, since it's the same thing your own people came up with."

"They've already done a profile?" That was news to her.

"A sketchy one came in from Columbia while you were interviewing the doc, but the chief wanted to keep it under wraps."

Add another thing to her to-do list. As the only person in the room who'd worked for both SPD and the FBI, Cait was the logical choice to smooth over intra-agency conflict.

"Like I said, once your partner got started, it was as if he couldn't shut up. He told the reporter that our UNSUB could be a guy who's angry with how the government runs the war and has targeted anyone wearing a uniform."

"What?"

"There's more."

Detective Derek Manning's expression was as grim as she'd ever seen it. And that was saying something, given that they'd worked a lot of homicide cases together, including the Flamemaster, a serial arsonist who'd terrorized the city.

"An alternative idea is that he's a whacked-out, hypersensitive, suspicious head case who can't get it up with a woman and who, maybe when he got to Iraq, figured out that he really likes shooting people. So, now that he's back stateside, he's trying to turn Somersett into Fallujah."

"Oh, my God."

Didn't he understand that if their UNSUB *was* unstable—which, odds were, he was, because, let's face it, shooting civilians who posed no threat to anyone wasn't exactly normal behavior—being called a head case on television could drive him around the bend? Or make him lose his temper, provoking more killings?

"He also, after comparing him to the Unabomber,

which I suspect our UNSUB would probably take as high praise, said the profile suggests the guy won't be confrontational—"

"What?" And wasn't that all she needed? Citizens thinking they could catch the bad guy themselves and win the reward?

"It gets worse."

Cait couldn't see how.

"Speaking directly to the shooter, he advised against suicide by cop and suggested that he turn himself in to authorities. The authority in question, natch, being Special Agent Frank Angetti."

It was true, Cait discovered. You really did see little white spots when your head went light.

"You gotta muzzle the guy, Cait," Manning said grimly.

"I don't have the authority to do that."

Fortunately she knew someone who did.

Five minutes later, after being assured that an FBI media expert was on the way from Columbia to handle the press briefings, Cait headed back out to start checking gun dealers.

Her partner was on the phone. From the set expression on his face and the fiery flush in his cheeks, Cait could only hope he was getting a new one reamed by Special Agent in Charge Brooke Davidson.

32

Door knocking on every gun dealer in the county was admittedly a shot in the dark. But sometimes you got lucky.

And although they were all cooperative enough, Cait was also subjected to a Second Amendment lecture at each and every one of them. She'd also had pointed out to her what she already knew: Since the federal statute against semiautomatic weapons hadn't been renewed, it was no longer illegal to sell, buy, or shoot the weapon her UNSUB had used for the first two killings.

Unless he'd altered it to make it fully automatic, which, of course, each and every one of those gun shop owners felt the need to remind her needlessly, *was* illegal.

Like a guy who was okay with blowing people away in the street would be bothered by that little detail? Cait didn't think so.

She didn't find anyone who'd ever seen the Russian sniper rifle in question. Though, unsurprisingly, everyone asked to get an up-close-and-personal look at it if she got her hands on it.

"When," Cait had repeatedly corrected them. "We'll get him. And his stash."

Three of the twenty dealers she questioned had asked to be notified if the feds decided to put the 9 mm VSS silent sniper rifle up for auction.

It was like looking for a needle in a haystack. No, not a haystack, Cait decided as she headed toward the bridge out of town. There were even more dealers in the more rural part of the county, where bumper stickers reading GOD, GUNS, AND GUTS MADE AMERICA GREAT were particularly popular.

"It's like looking for a needle in a damn hay*field*."

Her phone trilled. Cait looked at the caller ID screen. Rolled her eyes. She was beginning to understand that Valentine Snow hadn't made it to the top of the TV news business on her looks. She was as tenacious as a pit bull.

"Cavanaugh," she answered.

"Cait." The reporter's usually perfectly modulated voice had a shaky tone Cait had never heard in it before. "I received another letter. Here at the station."

Damn. Cait turned on the red flashers behind the grille of the sedan, then punched the gas.

"I'll be right there."

33

She made it to the station in five minutes flat. Partly because the streets weren't nearly as crowded as they'd been just yesterday. Or even last night. A serial sniper, it seemed, was not very good for tourism.

The TV station, coincidentally kitty-corner from St. Brendan's and down a few doors from Michael Gannon's free clinic, was well secured. The receptionist sat behind a glass window, and the double glass doors leading from the lobby into the back offices and studios were kept locked, opened by a button beneath the receptionist's desk.

The vanilla bean ice cream–colored walls of the narrow hallway were brightened by posters in narrow black frames. While many of the posters featured the network's most popular shows, it seemed that Valentine Snow smiled down at visitors from at least every third one.

The main newsroom reminded Cait of the police station: all the desks together, phones jangling, computer keys tapping, the scent of burned coffee lingering in the air, the buzz of conversation that abruptly stopped the moment she entered the room.

Valentine was not smiling when Cait entered the station owner's office.

The walls in this expansive office, which overlooked the harbor, had been faux-painted to look like dark brown leather. Rather than colorful posters, the trophy walls were covered with photographs of the station owner, Talmadge Townsend IV, doing the "grip and grin" with various politicians, including, she noticed, both state senators and three former presidents.

The third person in the room was introduced as the station's attorney. Not surprised to see him and thinking that this must be Constitutional Awareness Day, Cait prepared herself for an argument promoting the First Amendment.

"The mail room already opened the envelope," Val said apologetically.

"We're going to have to start making sure we get to it first," Cait said, even as she hated the idea that this case would drag on long enough for them to even be concerned about another letter. "All mail to Valentine needs to be set aside the minute it arrives. And I need to be notified."

"You were the first person we called," Val pointed out.

"Good."

Cait reached into the evidence case she'd retrieved from the trunk of the bureau sedan, pulled on the latex gloves, and, using a pair of tweezers, plucked out a tarot card showing Adam and Eve in the Garden of Eden. Complete with the snake and a winged angel hovering overhead.

"Do you know anything about this stuff?"

"Sorry." Val shook her head. As did Townsend and, unsurprisingly, the lawyer.

Deciding that they would have to check out a New Age store, she next pulled out the single piece of folded paper from the envelope.

"Dear Valentine. You looked especially lovely in that red suit. I look forward to seeing what you'll be wearing on tonight's newscast. While I approve of the power color, I'd strongly advise you to consider something a bit more somber, which will give you more gravitas. More like the way you looked when you broadcast during those early days of Shock and Awe. *Because we*

certainly wouldn't want viewers, or even more importantly, those executives at the network, to think you take multiple homicides lightly. Love always, your most loyal fan."

"Oh, God. He's not done," Valentine said.

"No."

Cait slipped the card, letter, and envelope into a glassine pouch. She was going to send them to the crime lab, but she had the sinking feeling that they wouldn't find anything. Her shooter was both evil and cunning. Not at all what she'd expect from someone with PTSD.

She didn't know much about the disorder, but from what she'd Googled last night, she would've expected someone who suffered from the syndrome to be more scattered, less able to focus. Yet the envelope to this latest note bore a Charleston postmark, demonstrating that not only had he been confident enough to mail it before today's shooting but he'd planned ahead.

"Maybe I can send him a message on the air," the newswoman suggested. "Make him think I'm on his side. Arrange a private interview."

"Right," Cait said. "And turn him into a sick celebrity like Son of Sam or the Zodiac Killer."

"He's already becoming a celebrity," Townsend argued. His Scotch-Irish heritage had given him a head of hair that looked like a rusty Brillo pad. The same heredity was responsible for his ruddy complexion.

"Celebrity is exactly what he wants. No point in giving it to him."

"You could risk angering him," Valentine warned.

Unlike her boss, Val seemed more willing to look at the big picture than to zero in on how this shooter gaining nationwide publicity could benefit her career. Then again, she *had* walked away from a multimillion-dollar New York gig.

"So we piss him off," Cait said. "What's he going to do? Shoot someone?" She shook her head. Held her ground. "For now, we just need you to stick to the facts of the case," she said. "No personal messages."

"I don't exactly see how you can legally put a gag order on this station." The lawyer now entered the conversation. "Given how that other FBI agent has already given an interview to Charleston's Channel 4."

"That was inappropriate." Cait hated to criticize another FBI agent, but no way was she going to allow Frank Angetti to set the standard for press coverage of this situation.

"That reporter who interviewed that agent's real cute," Townsend drawled. "Little gal probably used her feminine charms."

"That little *gal* just happens to have a degree in broadcast journalism from the University of Georgia," Val said through gritted teeth.

"Wonder if she was a Daawgs cheerleader," Townsend mused. "She's sure got the looks for it."

"Look." Cait wanted to cut this conversation off before the reporter shattered those perfect white teeth. "The FBI is sending in a media spokesperson. He should be here within the next few hours."

She turned toward Valentine. "Meanwhile, I want to ask you some questions about the time you spent reporting in Iraq. And just to show my appreciation for your discretion, I'll tell you what I can. And give you an exclusive when we nail this guy."

"*If* you nail him," Townsend said.

If looks could kill, the one Cait shot him would've put him six feet under in Somersett's Queen of Angels Cemetery. For her part, Val looked equally annoyed. Even the station lawyer looked uncomfortable.

"Nailing the lowlife's a given," Cait said.

Failure was not an option.

Unfortunately, the opening days of Operation Iraqi Freedom had been hectic for Valentine, who'd been embedded with the Marines' Charlie Company. She admitted that her memories of racing toward Baghdad, and the battle that would be remembered as one of the most savage of the war, were all pretty much a blur.

"Except the faces of the dead and wounded," she said. "I'll never forget them."

Which was much the same thing Quinn had said.

Wondering how she could get the records of any Marines from that campaign who might now be living in or around Somersett, Cait told Val what she could, leaving out any possible theories on motive.

She did not share what type of weapons the sniper had used because she didn't want to tip her hand to any gun dealer or private trader who might have sold it to her UNSUB.

She did give Val the joint task force phone numbers so she could put them on the air, asking anyone who might know anything to call in.

She was leaving the station, intending to take the note back to the JOC, when out of the corner of her eye she caught a glint of something in the cathedral's bell tower.

She looked up. Every muscle in her body tensed when she saw the male form cast into silhouette by the early-afternoon sun.

34

Magdalena Mendez Henriques was running late. Her day had begun badly when her bus broke down and she was forced to wait by the side of the road with the other passengers—most of them wearing the pink or black uniforms of domestic workers—for the twenty minutes it took for the company to send a replacement.

That delay had caused her to arrive late at her employer's house on Officers' Drive, which in turn had earned her a lecture on punctuality. Including several not-so-veiled references to the stereotypical Latino laziness.

As far as Magdalena could tell, all Mrs. Stockton did was spend the morning on the phone before heading off to the gym and day spa, after which she would have lunch—and several martinis—with friends. Or, according to Carlos, her driver, a noontime rendezvous at a motel across the river with a light colonel from the military academy.

She'd make it back to the house approximately an hour before her husband—a former two-star general on staff at ASMA—returned home. She'd bathe, change her clothes, and be downstairs to greet her husband with a phony smile and the first of several glasses of scotch.

They would share a silent dinner, which Magdalena

both cooked and served, neither seeming the least bit interested in each other.

Having lost her own husband, a newspaper publisher, to death squads in her native Central American country of Monteleón more than fifteen years ago, Magdalena couldn't imagine living in such a cold, detached relationship.

Her own marriage had not been easy. The civil war had been raging the entire time they were married, and Diego's insistence on writing editorials calling for basic human rights and dignity of the peasants had landed him in prison several times, causing extended separations.

And when he was home, they'd often argued about the dangers of her own work. As a social worker in the slums, she had drawn the unwanted attention of government troops, who routinely made sweeps of the ramshackle buildings, kidnapping young boys and conscripting them into the army.

Diego worried about her.

Magdalena worried about him.

But neither of them could surrender the work of their heart. Even at the risk of death.

Still, they'd loved each other deeply, passionately, with their entire hearts and souls, and even now, with the twenty-fifth anniversary of their marriage approaching, not a day passed that Magdalena didn't miss Diego. Not a day that she didn't feel as if she were merely passing time, waiting until the day when they could finally be reunited.

After making two bag lunches for the children, she'd put the Stocktons' Tibetan terrier into his carrier, which she strapped down in the backseat of the family Lexus with the seat belt. The pampered Mrs. Stockton seldom used the car, preferring to be driven, which, considering her afternoon drinking, was probably a good thing.

Magdalena exceeded the speed limit by five miles an hour to make up the time the bus breakdown had cost her, her heart beating like a rabbit with fear of being pulled over by a Somersett policeman. Like all people who'd suffered under violent regimes, she was terrified of the police, which in her country had not been someone that you would ever go to for help, but someone you tried to avoid at all costs.

She was even more terrified that the authorities would discover that she was illegal and deport her.

A fact that her employer not only knew very well but also used to her advantage, working Magdalena as many as eighteen hours some days and paying her far less than the minimum wage—something she'd been getting away with for the past three years, since they both knew there was no way Magdalena could complain to the authorities.

Her first stop after dropping the children off at the school, just as the bell rang, was the dry cleaners, where she left the general's shirts and two green dress uniforms that he would be using as soon as the semester began.

Unfortunately, her bad day was continuing when she was forced to wait five minutes for the counter clerk to locate the black silk dress Mrs. Stockton planned to wear to the memorial service at the academy.

The shootings had shaken Magdalena. She knew that there was no place in the world that was truly safe, but one of the reasons she put up with her employer was that Somersett seemed to be one of those towns that she would see in the old black-and-white TV shows she watched on TVLand back in her apartment at night. The ones she'd used to teach herself English.

Like Mayberry.

Or Mayfield, where the Beaver lived with his mother and father and his brother, Wally.

Or Springfield, where Betty, Bud, and Kathy's father always knew best.

She couldn't imagine anyone shooting off rifles in

any of those towns. She still couldn't quite accept that a killer had come to Somersett. The idea had kept her awake most of the night, and when she had slept, fitfully, she'd dreamed of death squads and gunfire, and bodies of innocent women and children lying in the street.

Assuring herself that this was not Monteleón, that no one would have any reason to want to shoot her, she hung the dress on the hook in the backseat, then headed to the groomers, where she dropped off the dog with instructions to change the terrier's toenail polish from Sunset Coral to Platinum.

She moved on to the Piggly Wiggly to buy the ingredients for the buffet for high-profile guests who'd been invited to the house after the memorial service. General Stockton had been vying with General Jacob for the position of commander, and now that his rival was conveniently out of the picture, his wife—who'd already been going through stacks of fabric samples with a mind toward changing the window treatments in the commander's house—had kicked up her lobbying efforts to get him appointed to the post.

Racing through the aisles at the supermarket, Magdalena managed to make up fifteen minutes, hopefully giving her time, she hoped, to stop by the cathedral and light a candle for those unfortunate victims of the shootings.

And, of course, she'd light another one for Diego. She'd kept a light burning for her deceased husband all the years she'd been in this country and when she'd been to Mass on Sunday, the current one had been burning low.

She pushed her loaded cart across the asphalt lot to the Lexus parked in the far corner. Mrs. Stockton had warned her against allowing the paint to be chipped, so, even in the worst rainstorm, Magdalena never parked anywhere near another car.

Magdalena Mendez Henriques never heard the shot that took her life.

Later, witnesses to the murder would tell Special Agent Cait Cavanaugh that there'd been no sound.

One minute the fiftysomething Hispanic woman wearing a pink uniform and heavy black rubber-soled shoes was loading groceries from her cart into the trunk of the car.

The next minute a mist exploded from her head, glowing crimson in the bright summer sun.

35

Just as Cait reached for her Glock, the figure in the bell tower waved. And moved forward and a bit to the left, which allowed her to see him more clearly.

"What are you doing up there?" she shouted, her heart beating jackhammer hard, jackhammer fast in her chest.

"Come on up and I'll show you," Quinn McKade shouted back.

She should've shot him just on principle, Cait thought furiously as she marched across the street and yanked open the huge oak door.

St. Brendan's Cathedral had been built in the Gothic style, of pinkish-gray bricks made from local clay. Inside, the ceiling was vaulted with heavy timbers, and benevolent angels and cherubs smiled down from the fresco in the nave. A sanctuary lamp glowed dimly in front of the tabernacle, votive candles flickered in red glass holders, and the sun shone warmly through the stained-glass windows that depicted tableaus of the saint's life.

Cait's thoughts were far from saintly as she marched furiously past the softly varnished pews, her heels ringing on the stone floor.

She climbed a narrow, twisting stairway that led to yet another door. Just as she reached for it, it opened.

"What the hell do you think you're doing?" she demanded as she burst into the bell chamber.

"I told you—I'm checking out sites your shooter might use."

Although women had remained a mystery to him for all thirty-three years of his life, Quinn realized she would not be flattered by his observation that she really was flat-out gorgeous when riled up. It brought a bright flush, not unlike that during sex, to her cheeks, and her eyes flamed a brilliant cobalt blue. She'd looked at him like that once before. Right before she'd taken him inside her.

"Did it ever occur to you that I might have shot you?"

"Never happen. You said you'd never used your weapon in the line of duty before."

"Just because I haven't in the past doesn't mean I wouldn't have today."

"Nah. You're too good a cop. You'd never go off half cocked." His lips quirked at his unintentional pun. "So to speak."

"What if someone had called the cops? And one of them got a little trigger-happy? SEALs might think of themselves as Superman, but I've never heard of one yet who can actually outrun a bullet."

That scenario, as unlikely as Quinn believed it to be, was admittedly a bit sobering.

"Okay. Maybe I should've notified the cops ahead of time."

"Well, duh." She dragged a hand—a surprisingly unsteady hand—through her wild mass of red hair.

"Better be careful, Special Agent," he said. "If I didn't know better, I might get the idea you actually care whether I live or die."

"Of course I do." Before he could take satisfaction in that, she just had to tack on the qualifier. "I joined the cops to protect and to serve the citizens of Somersett. Which, as it turns out, includes you."

"Ouch. And here I thought maybe you'd decided to drop the grudge."

"I don't know what you're talking about."

But she did. He could tell it in the way she squared her shoulders. Lifted her chin. And in the quick flare of color on those high cheekbones that could cut diamonds.

"You know, if we're going to work together, we're going to have to put it behind us," he said.

"We're not really working together. And there's nothing to put behind us."

Quinn rubbed his chin and decided that he had her right where he wanted her. Well, actually, he'd prefer her in bed. Or in his hammock. Or in his shower, with water streaming down her slick, wet, naked body.

But since that wasn't likely to happen in the next ten minutes, he'd settle for right here, where the only way she would be able to escape the overdue conversation would be to jump off the roof.

"So, I guess what you're saying is that having wild, chandelier-swinging sex with a guy in his hotel room, then taking off before he can get back with breakfast and refusing to ever speak to him again is standard behavior for you?"

"Of course not."

"Better be careful, sweetheart," he said. "If you clench your jaw any tighter, you're going to shatter those pretty white teeth."

"I'm not your sweetheart. And this entire conversation is inappropriate while innocent people are getting shot. If you want to talk about snipers, I'll be more than happy to listen. Anything else is off the table."

Actually, he wouldn't mind having the luscious FBI special agent *on* a table.

"You're a tough cookie, Cait. But okay. Here's the deal. There's no way the guy's just picking sites on a whim."

"Why not? If you factor in the crossing guard, he certainly seems to be shooting people at random."

"I'm not so sure about that. Think about it. What's more likely to boost him from a local crazy blowing away former military guys to leading all the national newscasts? How about killing someone surrounded by kids on the way to the first day of school? And hey, those little blue, green, and white plaid uniforms make an even better picture on TV."

"You know," she said slowly, thoughtfully, "that's not such a bad point."

He slapped a hand against his chest. "Damn."

"What?"

"I think you just gave me a heart attack. Maybe all the years being around gunfire have left me hearing-impaired, but I thought for sure you just agreed with me about something."

"Ha. Ha. Ha." Because the small chamber was taken up mainly with three iron bells hanging mute on their thick ropes, Cait put the briefcase on the wooden floor, opened it, and showed him the note, which was visible through the clear envelope.

"So this is all about Valentine Snow?"

"I can't discount it. Not when it could be like John Hinckley shooting Reagan to get Jodie Foster's attention."

She glanced around, as if really taking note of her surroundings for the first time since she'd come storming into the bell tower to confront him.

"This isn't good."

"Depends on your point of view. To a would-be shooter, it's one of the best places in town."

She shielded her eyes with a hand to the forehead and made a slow circle. The bell tower was the highest point in the city, offering panoramic views for miles.

To the east was the harbor, leading out to the sea. While some of the harbor-front development was still necessarily industrial, more and more of the area was being gentrified, with the old warehouses turned into trendy restaurants, shops, and loft apartments.

Normally, especially during Buccaneer Days, the cobblestone streets would be packed with tourists. The shooter—and Quinn continued to refuse to refer to him as a sniper—had definitely taken a bite out of the shopkeepers' profits.

To the south was the river, its banks having recently been turned into a greenbelt. On weekends locals would flock to the grassy expanse for picnics. Today, it too was largely deserted. Beyond the river, the marsh spread out over the land, the still, black waters reflecting stark gray cypress.

Admirals' Park, with its formal gardens, Spanish moss–festooned ancient oaks, and lacy white Victorian bandstand, was to the west. As was the military academy.

Whatever sprawl the city was experiencing was to the northeast, where new subdivisions, featuring leafy green parks, playgrounds, tennis courts, and swimming pools, were being established for young, growing families.

"He could shoot right down into the parade ground of the academy," she said.

"He could. Actually, from here he could shoot just about anywhere he wanted."

"But he'd have to get off the roof without being noticed."

"There's an alley right behind the building," Quinn pointed out. "Wouldn't be that difficult to tie a line around one of these steel beams, then rappel down. Especially now that he's switched to a silencer. If he sticks to a single target, he could be gone before anyone realizes there's been a shooting."

"Damn." She briefly squeezed her eyes shut, as if wanting to rid her mind of possible images, none of them pretty. "You know what I hate about this? Other than innocent people being killed?"

"You're playing catch-up. You're on defense, while he's on offense."

"Exactly." She didn't look as surprised as she might have last night that he'd known what she was thinking.

"There's no way of knowing where he's going to be. Or when. We're getting a lot of help from a lot of different agencies, but even if we called in the entire U.S. military, there wouldn't be enough personnel to protect everyone in the city. We've probably got a one in one hundred gazillion chance of catching him in the act."

"There you go, being pessimistic again," he said. "We're not talking New York City here. I've come up with a few other hides, like this one. Station some plainclothes guys at them, and odds drop to maybe one in a thousand."

"Well, that's encouraging."

"It's a start. He's also making it easier by moving from place to place."

She cocked her head. Gave him a hard look. "Why would that make it easier? Seems like with him being on the run the way he is, it's only going to make it more difficult."

"You'd think that. Which is yet more proof that he's a shooter, not a sniper. A sniper's main role is to dominate the battle by removing the threat."

"The threat being the bad guy."

"Sure. A lot of militia, which are big on strutting around and acting like big shots, have a top-down leadership structure. Which means the grunt on the ground isn't trained to take command. So if you kill the officer, the troops'll scatter like cockroaches.

"But it's other things, too. Communication is key on a battlefield, and someone not trained to think about the big picture might think the best idea, when you spot a radio guy, is to shoot him."

It took her only a split second. "Better to shoot the radio. If you kill the operator, anyone else can pick up the radio."

"Roger that. You've wiped out a major threat. The thing about being in the middle of a firefight is that your entire focus is on what you're seeing in your sniper scope. Which means you want to stay put and let the other guys protect you from additional firepower."

"Our guy isn't in a firefight. And he doesn't exactly need protection," she pointed out dryly. "Since we can't find him."

Quinn wondered if she realized she'd gone from talking about the shooter as *her* guy to speaking of him as *our* guy. He liked the idea of her thinking of them as a team, even though she might not be willing to admit it yet. Even to herself.

"True. But again, he's demonstrating he doesn't have true sniper skills. Or a sniper mind-set. Moving from place to place is going to make him vulnerable. Someone's going to spot him. Or at least his vehicle. Then we've got him."

He could read the skepticism on her face. But there was determination there as well. The odds might be against them, but he could tell that she wasn't going to let them get her down.

A zephyr of wind blowing off the nearby water slipped into the chamber, picked up the ends of her hair, and blew a few random curls in her eyes. She was just about to push them away when he caught hold of her wrist and took care of it himself.

The red curls were soft as silk. Memories of that bright, fragrant silk spread over his chest were all it took to make thoughts of snipers and death leave his mind.

"Do you ever think about that night?" he asked as he trailed his fingers down the side of a face that was as smooth and pale as porcelain, but much, much softer. And warmer. "Not New Year's. The second one."

"No."

Her own memory, which flashed in her eyes, came and went so quickly that a lesser man might have missed it.

Quinn did not.

She was a liar. A lovely one, but a liar just the same.

"I do."

Emboldened despite her insistence that she only wanted to talk about the case, he allowed his caressing touch to follow the arched line of her upper lip. That night, after he'd called her beautiful, she'd felt the need to point out flaws that were imperfections only in her own mind. Like her slight overbite, which had her bemoaning years of braces that hadn't achieved perfection but which Quinn had assured her was sexy as hell.

"I remember a lot of things. Like the way you tasted." He stroked her bottom lip. From the way her lips parted, ever so slightly, Quinn knew he wasn't the only one thinking about hot, sweaty sex. "And the way that god-awful dress crackled like cellophane—"

She lowered her eyes, just for an instant. She'd darkened the tips of her lashes, but they gleamed gold at the lids. "It was taffeta."

"It was ugly as homemade sin."

She'd regained her composure. Met his gaze again as a hint of a smile teased at the corner of those lips he'd spent a great deal too much time in the long dark hours of last night thinking about.

"It was a bridemaid's dress. They're supposed to be ugly so the bride can shine."

"The only way any woman could outshine you, Cupcake, would be if you took to wearing a brown paper bag over your head and a pair of camouflage BDUs. But I'm not even sure that'd work. Because you'd still be radiating sex from every fragrant pore."

"I don't recall you being such a sweet talker."

"That's because you were pretty much wasted."

"So were you."

He really hadn't been, given that he'd stuck to beer. She'd switched to rum after the obligatory champagne toast, then gone on to outdrink him. But since he'd known at the time that he was breaking all the rules about not making love to a woman who'd drunk too much, Quinn had let her think so.

He slipped an arm around her waist and drew closer. Close enough that he could feel the heat of her body. The weight of her sidearm against his thigh should've splashed cold water on his libido, but Quinn figured it'd take a lot more than a Glock 9 mm to make him stop wanting her.

"This isn't going to happen," she warned.

"Want to bet?" He bent his head until his lips were a whisper from hers. "I don't remember you being a coward, Cait."

She went rigid. Tossed up her chin, bringing her tightly drawn mouth even closer. "I'm not."

"Then kiss me." He splayed his hand against her back. "One kiss." He could feel her draw in a breath as his lips lightly touched hers. "Then, if you can honestly tell me you don't want to explore this a little deeper—"

"Even if there was anything to explore—which there isn't—I couldn't. Because I've got a killer out there." She pressed her hand between them. Against his chest. " I have to stay focused."

"Try focusing on this," Quinn suggested.

Then took her mouth. And ravished.

36

Cait had been married. She'd had lovers, and had even experienced a few reasonably lengthy relationships. It wasn't as if she was some inexperienced virgin who'd get all starry-eyed and weak in the knees just because some hot guy kissed her.

But, dammit, the problem was no man had ever made her feel as desirable as Quinn did. With a simple look. Or touch. And, heaven help her, as a liquid heat began to pool in the lower part of her body, she'd never wanted a man as much as she wanted—needed—this one.

She *wasn't* a coward. But she *was* afraid. Not of Quinn, but of this dizzying, out-of-control way he made her feel.

Then there was the fact that the timing was all wrong. She couldn't go falling into bed with the former SEAL while some maniac was running around Somersett with an arsenal of weapons, gunning people down.

But oh, God, he tasted so good. Like black coffee, cinnamon gum, and lust.

"This is so not a good idea," she managed to say right before he sucked her tongue into his mouth, kissing her so hard he drew the air right out of her lungs.

The hell with it. It was only a kiss. No big deal, right?

She grabbed his hair in her hands and, arching

against him, kissed him back, a damn-the-torpedoes, full-steam-ahead, hard, vicious kiss that set off explosions inside her.

Hooking one strong arm around her waist, he lifted her off her feet.

They knocked against the largest of the three bells, setting off a deafening clanging that shattered the silence.

And the mood.

"Well." Quinn took his time, sliding her down his body in a way she was surprised didn't cause sparks. "I suppose it'd be a cliché to ask if you heard bells."

"I think I'll be hearing them in my sleep for the next ten years."

As if on cue, the phone she was wearing on her belt rang.

With her sixth sense sounding nearly as loud as those damn church bells, she flipped it open.

The message, from Angetti at the JOC, was short and to the point.

The shooter had struck again.

37

Although once again the shooter had managed to disappear seemingly without a trace, no one on the task force doubted they were dealing with the same guy.

In contrast to the smaller force that had shown up at the first shooting, hundreds of local, state, and federal officers descended on the supermarket parking lot. Along with the various cops, ATF brought in a yellow Lab.

"Our dogs never eat from a bowl," the handler, who despite the heat was wearing a black ATF raid jacket, informed Cait. "They're trained to sniff for gunpowder and when they find it, they get fed. It makes for one motivated dog."

Unfortunately, they were getting this down to a science. The dragnet went out. The dog walked back and forth across the lot, nose to the asphalt. Two police helicopters circled overhead.

Cait couldn't allow herself to think their efforts would be futile, but in her heart she was worried, because the shootings didn't seem to fit any known pattern. They were too random, too geographically scattered.

A check of the license plate had shown the car belonging to a General Stockton, who was—no surprise—on staff at ASMA. According to the general, who'd been contacted at the academy, he and his wife had employed the victim as a domestic.

Coincidence? Or some connection?

But if they *were* connected, then where did the elderly crossing guard fit into the picture? So far, other than the fact that she had a grandchild enrolled in Air Force ROTC at Clemson, investigators hadn't been able to find a military link.

"How long has it been since you've had anything to eat?"

Cait looked up at Quinn. They'd arrived at the crime scene two hours earlier, and she'd been so caught up in the investigation that she hadn't noticed the time passing.

"I've no idea. In case you haven't noticed, I've been a little busy."

"Gotta keep fuel in the engine," he said. "We've still got that vets meeting to go to."

"That's hours from now."

She glanced down at her watch. Three hours, anyway. She wondered if they'd be able to get through rush hour without another demonstration of firepower.

"We need to talk."

"I'm busy."

"Don't look now, Special Agent, but your crime scene is shutting down. I've got some thoughts I want to run by you. And since I'm hungry, I figure we might as well talk over burgers."

The search crews were wrapping up. The dog had come up empty, which had her worrying he might not get fed. Witnesses had not seen anything overtly significant. Oh, they'd gotten some descriptions of vehicles seen leaving the lot right after the housekeeper had been shot, but it was one of the busiest grocery stores in Somersett. Open twenty-four hours a day, with people coming and going all the time.

And then there was always the chance that he was using multiple vehicles. Perhaps even stealing them, then discarding them later.

She made a mental note to start running checks on all cars reported stolen.

Yet another needle in their hayfield.

"Twenty minutes," she decided.

"Thirty," Quinn countered.

Not wanting to waste any time arguing, she gave him his ten additional minutes.

38

The Black Swan, always popular, should have been packed. But even though it had been cleaned up after having been gone over by the lab, nearly half the tables were empty.

Quinn was surprised to see Joe Gannon sitting at the bar, a glass of iced Coke in front of him. He was even more surprised, and decidedly not pleased, to see the warmth with which Cait greeted her former partner.

"So," Joe said, after a hug that went on, to Quinn's mind, too long. "Just think, if you'd come to work for Phoenix Team, you'd be missing out on one of the hottest events to hit the Lowcountry since Sherman's boys rode through with their torches."

"Lucky me," she said. She glanced up at Quinn. "I guess since you both work for Phoenix Team, you two know each other."

He nodded. "Sure. What brings you off-island?"

The former cop exchanged a glance with the Irish proprietor, who nodded.

"Brendan here hired me."

Cait glanced pointedly around the nearly deserted pub. "It's not as if you're in dire need of an armed bouncer."

"I hired Gannon as a bodyguard," Brendan O'Neill revealed. "For Valentine."

"That's not such a bad idea," Cait said. "I would've

loved to have offered her protection, but it's not as if we have a lot of extra resources."

"Exactly." Brendan nodded. "Which is why I took matters into my own hands."

"Does she know yet?" Cait asked.

"No."

"She may not like you taking responsibility. It's not like she's never been in danger before, given all her war coverage."

"She's an intelligent woman. I believe she'll see the light," Brendan said with absolute confidence. "I'd be watching over her myself, but even though business is still down, I've still a pub to run. There's also the little matter about me not being licensed to carry a firearm."

And Gannon was. Having shot on Phoenix Team's firing range with the former homicide detective, Quinn knew him to be good. Not sniper good, but still good enough to give Quinn a run for his money once they'd switched from rifles to handguns.

Quinn could only hope Gannon wouldn't need that Glock he knew the Phoenix Team agent had holstered it in the back of his jeans, beneath the navy blue polo shirt.

After placing an order for two cheeseburgers—one topped with chili—and fries, with coffee, Cait and Quinn chose a table in the corner. There was a little jockeying for position, as both of them automatically picked the seat that would put their backs to the wall, allowing them to view the entire room.

"Old habits," he murmured, leading her to a booth instead, where they could sit side by side.

"Die hard," she finished. "So." She leaned her elbows on the table, linked her fingers, and rested her chin on them. "Shoot."

"My guess is you're looking for two guys."

"Yeah, I know that's how it worked in D.C.," she agreed. "But the profilers are saying one. Or if there's a second one, he's subordinate."

"Yeah. Exactly. The thing about being a sniper is that you get so your eyes magnify things even without the scope. Everything's intensified. Your sense of smell, your hearing—your brain filters out the noise and turns down the volume until all you hear is silence. Or white noise, like the sound machines you can buy in those yuppie stores."

"But you keep insisting he's not a sniper."

"True. But he's still got to be concentrating on what he's doing."

"Which he can't do if he's also worrying about driving the car."

"Yeah. There's also the fact that if he had any sniper training at all he knows snipers all have spotters. Which means he'd want one just to feel more like the real deal. So, when we're at that meeting tonight, you might want to keep that in mind. Don't just be watching for a vet you think capable of blowing people away without a qualm."

"I should also be looking for a guy willing to play second fiddle." She took a drink of coffee, then shook her head. "I have to believe we're responding as well as we can, given the circumstances of the case. We've even been in touch with the guys who worked the D.C. sniper case, and some of them are coming in to assist. But we need more evidence, dammit."

"Which means more shootings."

"Yeah." She managed a faint smile, thanks to Brendan, who delivered their burgers and sweet potato fries, refilled their thick white coffee mugs, and returned behind the bar to continue setting his own strategy with Joe Gannon. "Talk about your catch-22. We really, really want this psycho to stop. But the longer he keeps on killing, the better our odds of catching him."

As serious as the topic was, when she bit into a crisp golden fry, Quinn felt a jolt, like lightning, shooting straight to his groin.

He was concentrating on keeping his expression from revealing the slap of lust when Joe Gannon ambled over, turned a wooden chair around, and straddled it.

"So," he said to Cait, "tell me what you know about this guy."

"Not a helluva lot, unfortunately."

She filled him in, including, Quinn noticed, what weapons the guy had used. He'd learned early in his work for Phoenix Team that local authorities didn't like to share with private cops, which made it more difficult to do their job.

"I just keep thinking how, when I first made the move from street patrol, you taught me that the most important thing a detective had to keep in mind was *who benefits,*" Cait said.

"That's pretty much it," the former detective agreed. "Figure that out, nine times out of ten you'll close the case."

"Also, murders are more often committed by individuals the victim knows. Most often family members."

He nodded. "Spouses are always the first place to look."

"So, I can see Jacob's wife wanting to get rid of a cheating spouse."

Sure, divorce was easier, but she'd also checked out the Jacobs and discovered that the general's widow had inherited a tidy sum from her grandfather, a former WWII general who'd come back from the war and parlayed his service into a cushy seat on Wall Street. Maybe she hadn't wanted to waste any of that money on lawyers when she could get rid of the guy—or pay to have him exterminated—herself.

"And, although I don't like to think it, since I used to know the guy and liked him a lot, maybe Ryan Hawthorne's wife had a rosy scenario about a future with Jacob and decided her husband was in the way of her own happily-ever-after."

"That's not an impossible leap." He paused. "Just like it's not impossible that Hawthorne decided to pay the guy back for sleeping with his wife."

"True," she allowed. Quinn could tell she hated that idea. "Though it's even harder to stomach than Ryan's wife being a serious suspect, we both sure saw worse things during our days on the force."

"The second murder somewhat lets them off the hook," Joe said.

"Yeah. Kristin Davis stands to inherit big bucks. Also, she volunteers with your brother's PTSD group. It's not impossible she could've found herself a shooter."

"I think this is where I point out that not all vets with PTSD are candidates to become serial killers," Quinn said, breaking into the conversation. "And taking advantage of some vet with problems that Kristin's supposed to be helping would be damn cold."

Though he, too, had seen worse.

"That's probably why it's called cold-blooded murder," Cait suggested.

"Kristin doesn't seem the type."

"Says the guy who pointed out that it's often hard to tell the good guys from the bad guys," Cait said.

"Touché."

"One problem with either of those who-benefits scenarios is, the murders aren't connected," Joe pointed out.

"They could be if one was done to throw us off track," Cait said.

"That's a stretch."

"But not impossible. But, damn. Shooting the crossing guard." She bit into another fry and chewed thoughtfully. "That doesn't make any sense. Unless it was a meant to be sleight of hand."

"To take the focus off the real motive," Quinn said.

She nodded. "Exactly."

"Or the guy's a wacko." Joe snagged a fry from Quinn's plate. "Who just likes smoking people."

"I'm trying not to go there," Cait said. "Because if

that's true, then we're going to have to hope like hell we get lucky and the shooter screws up, because it's the only way we're going to catch him."

"Like the truck driver spotting the D.C. shooters at that rest stop," Joe mused.

"The main problem is that they don't fit any identifiable patterns," she complained. "Most homicides are about greed. Or revenge. Or hate."

"Or love. Or at least a twisted version of it," Brendan, who'd come over to refill their coffee mugs, offered. "Where I guess Valentine would come in."

"It's always a possibility. And one we're taking seriously, though I'm glad you hired Joe as backup," Cait said.

"It's best someone apprehend him quickly," the pub owner said.

"Well, we're all in agreement with that."

"Because if the bastard were to harm one hair on Valentine Snow's head, I'd have no choice but to tear off his bloody arms and legs and beat him to death with them."

Silence dropped like a stone over the table. Quinn figured he wasn't alone in thinking that the threatening words sounded even more deadly for having been uttered in such a calm, matter-of-fact tone.

"Works for me," Quinn said.

Cait's gaze went back and forth between the two men, reading intent. "If either one of you goes cowboy on me, believe me, you'll be wearing cuffs and eating dinner on an aluminum tray behind bars."

She clearly meant it. But, interestingly, O'Neill seemed less than impressed by the threat.

"Then you'd best be apprehending the shooter," he said mildly. "Sooner, rather than later."

Cait's eyes turned as hard as O'Neill's, the clash of stone on stone almost audible.

"She's important to me," the man finally said. And in the confessing of it, he revealed a weakness that felt all too familiar.

One of the reasons Quinn had never allowed himself to get emotionally involved with any woman while he'd been in the SEALs was that as soon as you cared about someone, you risked becoming weak. It would take only a split second, while you worried about leaving behind a widow and kids, for the enemy to gain an advantage. Which could end up costing not just your own life but your team members' as well.

Spending his first eight years constantly on the move and then the next eight in the revolving door of foster care had taught Quinn that relationships were as ephemeral as the morning mist floating over the marsh.

But that hadn't stopped him from thinking about Cait Cavanaugh over the years. Too much. And too damn often.

"Nothing's going to happen to Val," the woman in question was assuring him as Quinn dragged his uncharacteristically wandering mind back to the conversation. "Especially since the love connection thing doesn't feel quite right to me, because it brings us back to a Hinckley-type shooter. Or even that guy Chapman, who shot John Lennon. Which this guy isn't."

"Because he doesn't stand around and wait to get arrested," Quinn said.

"Yeah. I'm not even going to try to get into the legal definition of insanity, but Hinckley had to know that Reagan was surrounded by Secret Service agents, and John Chapman just stood there after killing Lennon at point-blank range and handed his weapon over to the Dakota's doorman . . .

"This guy has an agenda. And I have this horrible feeling that he's got a cat-and-mouse game going."

"That definitely gets my vote," Joe agreed.

"The thing is," Cait said, clearly on a roll, "with most crimes, the victim and the perpetrator are either related or know each other. And, like Joe always says, the answer comes down to who benefits."

"Which, as you already pointed out," Quinn said, "gives you quite a few suspects with the first two shootings."

The burger was medium rare, the chili topping it hot enough to set off the smoke detectors. Just the way Quinn liked it.

"Yeah. But none of the dots connect them."

"At least not yet." Quinn didn't envy her. "But you'll get him."

"Damn right I will. I just need to get him yesterday." Cait balled up her paper napkin. "Right now I need to run by the JOC. See if the media guy's arrived yet. And see if Drew Sloan has turned in the paperwork on the first two autopsies. Maybe something will show up that'll connect them. Maybe something in their systems."

"You're thinking something like drugs?" Joe asked.

"Not really. But sure as hell the one thread we don't pull will be the one that's connected to the motive."

"There's something else you need to do," Quinn said.

"What's that?"

"Run a check of all the military guys who've washed out with undesirable or bad conduct, or dishonorable discharges."

"Talk about needles in haystacks," Cait muttered.

"Hey, you're the feds. Use that FBI badge for something other than intimidating local cops and law-abiding citizens. While it's true the military might not be real fond of the bureau, one thing the brass does care a helluva lot about is negative publicity.

"The National Personnel Records Center in St. Louis has all the military records of discharged and deceased vets of all services after World War I. NPRC also stores medical treatment records of retirees from all services, as well as records for dependents and other persons treated at naval medical facilities.

"If I were you, along with those who didn't have honorable or general discharges, I'd have them run a computer search for any vets who'd gotten DD458s or Article 15s in the last few years."

"I realize the military lives on numbers and acronyms," Cait said. "Which, granted, the Bureau does too. But would you mind spelling that out for us civilians?"

"Sorry. It gets to be ingrained after a few years. A DD458 is a Court-Martial Charge Sheet. An Article 15 is a nonjudicial punishment imposed by a field grade officer. Normally a battalion commander."

"But if it's nonjudicial, would it even be in the records?"

"A formal grade article is permanent. A lesser, summarized one that's not placed in a 201 file remains at the unit level."

"But that still represents a helluva lot of information," Joe said.

"Yeah. I thought it was silly, naming the case," Cait said. "But since it looks as if we're going to need a lot of money for additional personnel to sift through all this, if the military does come through—"

"They will," Quinn assured her.

Cait shot him a look. "And you know this how?"

"The guy currently in charge is a three-star who transferred in from Armor. Tossing out my name should be like saying 'Open Sesame.' "

"You're that good friends?"

"No. Only met the guy once."

"Wow." Cait cocked her head. "You must have made one helluva impression."

"Probably more so on his kid. Who was taken hostage in Iraq."

"And whom your SEAL team rescued," Joe guessed.

"Got it in one," Quinn confirmed.

"Well." She blew out a breath. "Seems like you might just be a handy guy to have around, McKade."

He flashed a grin. He was getting to her. She might not want to admit it, but those razor-band-topped barricades she'd erected around herself were beginning to crumble. The bitch was, his situation was a lot like what she'd said about getting more clues the longer the shooter stayed out there.

If some bad guy hadn't started targeting Somersett residents, he doubted she'd even be speaking to him. Which meant that the longer the wannabe sniper kept treating the town like his own private shooting gallery, the better chance Quinn had of getting the luscious special agent into his bed.

If he *had* a bed.

Definitely getting a decent rack had to be moved to the top of his to-do list.

Cait stood up and gave Joe another hug. Quinn respected the former murder cop, who was hugging her again. Liked him a lot, actually.

He also wished he'd keep his damn hands off the woman.

Mine.

The thought struck with the force and power of that RPG that had brought down the team's helo in those Afghan mountains.

Fast, hard, and every bit as dangerous.

He suddenly realized Joe Gannon was looking at him over the top of Cait's head. With, damn it all to hell, laughter in his cop eyes.

You can run, that look said, *but you cannot hide.*

39

Although the shootings of the crossing guard and the maid pretty much took terrorism off the table, the Somersett PD chief was more than happy to keep the feds and their deep crime-fighting pockets around. Which was why, when Special Agent in Charge Brooke Davidson arrived from the FBI field office in Columbia, Chief Billy Ray Carter ceded command and control of the operation.

While interagency rivalries were a normal occurrence, since this was a far from normal situation, everyone seemed willing to put competition and long-held resentments aside. At least until the guy was behind bars. Which not a single task force member was willing to think wasn't going to happen. Hopefully sooner rather than later.

Every detective on the Somersett force was ordered to report for duty. As were the county sheriff's deputies. The U.S. Marshals Service arrived to increase the federal force on the scene and even the Secret Service sent an officer from each of the Savannah, Charleston, and Columbia field offices. In addition, operators began having to handle calls from police departments as far away as Seattle, offering officers. It seemed everyone wanted to get in on the hunt.

Carter went on TV, asking citizens to go on about their lives but stay vigilant. Easier said than done. Although many residents called for the schools to be closed, most administrators instead went to a "code blue" alert, keeping the children indoors.

The streets became so deserted that had they not been so neat and tidy, the city would have looked like a scene from one of those end-of-the-world movies. A deluge of calls overwhelmed 911 operators as people reported such benign things as car backfires and turned in suspicious-seeming neighbors.

Unsurprisingly, there were the usual crackpot calls, none of which could be dismissed out of hand.

The Somersett Buccaneers baseball team was forced to cancel a game when its opponents decided not to bring their guys into the city from Rhode Island. The road over the bridge became a parking lot as cops with sniffer dogs searched each and every car.

"Somebody saw something," Cait complained to Angetti, who was stuck on the phones again. "This guy isn't the Invisible Man. We've got four separate crime scenes scattered across the city. Someone, somewhere, had to have witnessed something unusual."

As if on cue, one of the patrol cops brought in to man the citizen call-in line came up to her.

"I think you need to talk to this one," he said. "It's a woman who was dropping her kid off at school this morning when the guard got hit."

Cait exchanged an *I told you so* look with Angetti. "She saw the shooter?"

"No. But she says her son claims to have seen him."

Not as good. But not impossible, either. "How old is the kid?"

"He started third grade today."

Terrific. Not exactly the gold standard of witnesses. But as she left the basement office, Cait told herself that it was at least more than she'd had five minutes ago.

Valentine Snow was as furious as Brendan had ever seen her. She stormed into the pub, flags flying in her cheeks, eyes blazing.

"What the hell do you think you're doing?"

Brendan swished a pint glass in the sudsy water at the bar sink. "It would seem I'm washing glasses."

"Don't be a smart-ass. I want to know why you felt the need to hire"—she waved a manicured hand toward Joe Gannon, who, having predicted this reaction, was right behind her—"this man."

"You don't care for him? If you'd like me to call Phoenix Team and ask for a replacement—"

"I like him just fine," she snapped, her usually perfectly modulated voice sharper than the crystal wineglass he began drying with a white linen towel. "I just don't need anyone hovering over me like some sort of damn rottweiler guard dog."

"That's your opinion." Brendan hung the glass by the stem in the rack over the bar. "I'd be having an entirely different one."

"Excuse me." She folded her arms. Tapped a toe clad in an alligator high-heeled shoe that he suspected cost more than his entire inventory of stemware. "Since when do you have an opinion concerning my life?"

"Since I began falling in love with you," he responded.

"What?" Her eyes widened and she shot a look at Joe Gannon, whose shrug said, *Don't ask me.*

"I said, I'm falling in love with you." He held up a hand. "Now, whether that's wise or not, under the circumstances, I can't say. But since I didn't seem to have a choice about that, I'm not going to question it, but merely go with the flow, as you Americans are fond of saying. There is also no way that I'm willing to stand by and watch while your life is in danger."

"I don't believe this."

"Believe it."

"You can't be serious."

"On the contrary. I've never been more serious in my life. Now, I understand how it might be coming as a bit of a surprise to you—"

"Talk about your Irish understatement." She splayed her hands on her hips. "You can't be in love with me."

"And why not? Surely you know that you're a very appealing woman."

"You just want to get me in bed."

"Aye," he agreed easily. "But didn't I want to do that from the moment you first walked into the pub carrying that newspaper ad for the apartment?" He swished another pint glass in the sink. "The other, the love, came more gradually."

She was clearly thunderstruck. Having watched her for years on television, and more closely these past months, with the both of them living beneath the same roof, Brendan had come to the conclusion that very few things unsettled the coolly sexy newscaster. He also decided that, as bad as the timing might admittedly be, he liked being one of them.

"I can't deal with this right now," she insisted on a flare of heat. "I have a stand-up to do at the supermarket where that latest shooting occurred."

"Then I'd suggest you be doing it," he said. "I'll be here when you return."

He wanted to go with her. To hover over her, to protect her, as he was paying Joe Gannon to do. But, as he'd told Cait, he didn't own a weapon. He also knew there were limits to what the sexy reporter would stand for. And he was already pushing them.

She stared at him for another long moment. Then shook her head.

"I so don't need this right now."

Brendan watched her march back out of the pub, perversely, despite the circumstances, enjoying the way her hips swayed in that short bright red skirt.

Then as Gannon followed her, Brendan sighed and went back to work, wondering how in bloody hell his life had gotten so complicated.

40

Tyler Long was an eight-year-old redhead, with a sprinkling of freckles across a pug nose and too-serious-for-his-age brown eyes behind round-lensed Harry Potter glasses.

"I like cars," he explained to Cait. "I like to draw them. And put together models." He'd shown her several of the plastic models when she first arrived at the Longs' apartment. "For a while, when I was just a little kid, I thought maybe I'd be a car designer when I grew up."

"Well," Cait said, looking up at the pictures he'd tacked up all over his bedroom wall, "I think you'd certainly be a good one."

"Maybe." His small brow furrowed. "But I mostly outgrew that. These days I'm thinking about becoming an actor. Or maybe an animator. For some place like Pixar. And make movies."

"That'd be way cool." It also worried her. "I wonder if people who create stories for movies and books ever get fiction and reality confused."

Her attempt at subtlety was not lost on him. "I know the difference between make-believe and real life."

"That's good to know." She was not going to lie and tell him she wasn't concerned about that. "Because this is a very serious situation."

"I know." The forehead furrows deepened. "That lady's not going to die, is she?"

"No. The doctor says she should be able to go home tomorrow."

"That's good news. She seemed really nice."

"That's what people say," Cait agreed. "So, your mom called and said you saw a car that caught your attention?"

"Yeah. A Nissan Altima. It drove by just before I got out of the car. I noticed the taillights right away. They were inspired by fighter jets, and are really, really cool. They wrap all the way from the back to the C-pillar."

"The C-pillar?"

"That's the roof support between the back side window and the back window. Most taillights aren't so radical."

"I guess not. What color was it? And did you notice anything else that stood out?"

"Pebble Beach. That's sorta a boring brown color."

Boring being all the better to blend into the surroundings, Cait considered.

"Did you happen to see the license plate?"

"Yeah. That was one of the weird things. It was muddy. But the rest of the car was clean."

The better to conceal the numbers. Cait felt a little spurt of excitement.

"And it had a decal on the back." He furrowed his brow as he tried to picture it. "It was white. And in cursive, but I can read that too. It said SANDMAN'S SOMERSETT NISSAN. I didn't think that much about it, because I was concentrating on what I was going to say at school," he said. "I kinda have this stutter that makes kids laugh at me."

"I never would've realized that. You're not stuttering now," Cait said.

"Yeah." He looked surprised at that idea. Exchanged a look with his mother. "I guess those speech utilities are working."

"I guess so," Dara Long agreed with an encouraging smile.

"Do you think that was the shooter's car?" he asked Cait.

"It could be." Mindful of the way all the D.C. task force had gotten sidetracked by looking for a white van, Cait was determined not to jump to any conclusions.

"Because, if I was a bad guy looking to shoot people and drive away, I'd pick the Altima," the kid said.

"Why is that?"

"Because it's got the biggest trunk in its class. Plenty of room for a guy to set up a rifle." He frowned thoughtfully. "But he'd probably need another guy to drive it so he could make a quick getaway."

Which was exactly what Quinn had suggested.

"Well, thank you," Cait said. "You've been very helpful."

"We're supposed to help the police," he said. "That's what Officer Friendly said when he came to my school on Swann Island last year. He said it's part of being a good citizen."

"Officer Friendly's right." Because he seemed so much older than his years, she extended a hand. "I appreciate you being such a good citizen. Maybe, after we apprehend the shooter you'd like a tour of the police station." She figured he'd enjoy that a lot more than her dark and dingy basement FBI office.

"Wow. That'd be cool." He beamed, his grin lighting up his freckled face.

"That's quite a kid you've got there," Cait said to his mother as she left the apartment.

"He's a joy," Dara said. "Smart as a whip, but sweet, too. May I ask a question?"

"Sure."

"You're not going to put his name out there in public, are you? Because if the shooter knew there was a witness—"

"No." Cait had already made that decision. "I'm

going to keep him a confidential source. At least until we get this guy behind bars. He may be called as a witness in the trial, but I'm going to try to gather enough other evidence we won't need him."

She absolutely believed the boy, but knew a jury might not be so open minded. Then there was the fact that she didn't want to submit him to cross-examination by a pit-bull defense attorney unless absolutely necessary.

"Thank you." The woman's relief was palpable.

Cait had never given much thought to having kids, other than thinking about all the sacrifices her mother had made for her family, which didn't make the idea all that appealing, but as she drove away from the apartment building, she decided that if she could have a son like Tyler Long, it might just be kind of cool.

41

The shack, tucked into a narrow bend on the Somersett River, resembled a toolshed kept afloat by fifty-five-gallon oil drums. Locals had been plunking the river shacks—used for hunting, fishing, and vacations—down on Lowcountry marshes since before anyone could remember, and although a recent law made them illegal, the authorities didn't exactly appear to be out there beating the bushes looking for them.

Not that the shooter planned to stay here much longer. The trick, he'd decided, was to keep moving. After all, a moving target was harder to hit.

The outside of the ramshackle wooden building sported a corrugated tin roof, a broken window, and a toilet bolted to the deck. A johnboat was tied to the dock's pilings.

The inside of the shack wasn't much better, though. Along with a pair of army green canvas cots, an uneven wooden table, two chairs, a sofa with the stuffing falling out of it, and a kerosene stove, it also boasted a thirteen-inch television powered by a gas generator. The signal was plucked out of the humid air by a pizza-sized satellite dish atop the rusting roof.

"Would you look at that!" his spotter crowed. "That Valentine Snow is talking about us."

The reporter was, indeed, standing in the parking lot of the Harborview Piggly Wiggly, her expression sober as she reported on yet another shooting. Her red suit was the color of fresh blood, much brighter than the splotch darkening the asphalt near where she was doing her stand-up.

"We are fucking famous!" The spotter strutted around the cramped interior like a banty rooster. "Cheee-rist, wouldn't all those vets down at the center shit a brick if they knew it was us making all these headlines?"

"Yeah. And then, once they were done shitting, they'd pick up the phone and call the cops," the shooter pointed out as he cleaned and oiled a Glock 17 he'd bought on the Internet.

He liked the Glock, which was the most popular police weapon going. When it had first come out, there'd been a misconception that the bad guys would be able to sneak it past security onto planes because of its plastic frame. That fear was quickly put to rest because the slide, barrel, and other internal parts were metal, easily caught by metal detectors. Which, to the shooter's mind, was too bad.

Still, he appreciated its light weight and the fact that it consisted of only thirty-three parts, including the magazine, which made it easy to take apart.

"Well, sure. It wasn't like I was gonna tell anyone," the other man said. "But you gotta admit it sounds like fun. Just to see the look on their faces."

Once again proving he had nothing in common with this loser, the shooter shared no such temptation.

"Wait till they see what we've got planned for tonight," the spotter said as he took a long pull from the bottle of Jim Beam. "We will blow their freaking minds!"

Speaking of blowing minds . . .

The shooter pointed the black pistol at his soon-to-be former partner's face. "Sit down."

He got a goggle-eyed look in return to the quietly issued command. "What?"

"I said, Sit. The. Fuck. Down. And shut the hell up."

"Hey!" The spotter didn't argue, but quickly plunked his bony butt on the wooden chair. "I didn't mean to piss you off. I was just saying—"

"You talk too damn much."

"Well, yeah, sometimes. I mean, that's what all my ex-wives used to say, but—"

"See. There you go again. Rattling on about nothing of any importance."

The guy may have been an alcoholic loser, but apparently he hadn't pickled every gray cell, because some distant, primal lizard part of his brain got the message.

He slammed his cigarette-yellowed teeth together. And shut the hell up.

"That's better." The shooter stood up from the rickety old table that bore the cigarette burns and carved initials of previous residents. It took him two strides to cross the single room. "Now, why don't you have a drink?" he said pleasantly.

The other man licked his lips. "I wouldn't turn one down," he said. Then, belatedly remembering the shooter's instructions, shut up. And took a long swallow.

"Another," the shooter said.

The man drank.

"Another."

They kept that up until the bottle was empty.

Most normal people would probably be passed out from that much bourbon. Or at least puked their guts out. Years of excessive drinking had given Charlie Jensen an increased tolerance to alcohol. The only sign that he'd just polished off 1.75 liters of Kentucky bourbon was the fact that his red-rimmed eyes looked a bit blurrier than usual.

"Next step." The shooter took the gun from the towel he'd used to clean the Glock. Picked up Jensen's right hand and wrapped his fingers around the stock.

"Hey." The single word was slurred. "Whatcha thin' you're doin?"

"Ensuring you your own spot on the nightly news."

Using the towel to prevent his fingerprints from getting onto the pistol, he flicked off the safety lock and curled his latest victim's index finger around the trigger.

Then pulled.

The sound rang out over the marsh. Outside the shack, a blue heron took to the sky. Inside, what was left of Corporal Charles Jensen's brains joined the blood, bone, and fish guts on the rotting plank floor.

One shot. One kill.

42

James "Sandy" Sandman was somewhere in his mid-fifties, graying at the temples, and sporting a mahogany tan that Cait figured he'd acquired on the golf course. Or maybe sailing in the harbor.

He was wearing a blinding Hawaiian shirt covered with purple hibiscus, a pair of khakis, and white shoes. Although Cait would have trouble taking him seriously, it was impossible to turn on the TV without seeing one of his commercials, and if the ads could be believed, he was the top Nissan dealer in the Lowcountry.

"We sell a lot of cars here, Special Agent," he said. "It's hard to remember everyone who drives out with one."

"Yet you offer small-town Southern friendliness at big-city discount prices." She quoted his slogan.

"Well, that's true enough." He frowned. "You don't really believe the sniper's using one of my vehicles to do his killing from?"

Cait thought he seemed more upset by that possibility than by the idea of the murders.

"I don't know," she said honestly. "But a suspicious car with your dealership decal on it was seen in the vicinity of the school shooting. So of course we have to check everything out."

"Well, anything I can do to help," he said. He reached into the pocket of the hibiscus shirt and pulled out an embossed white business card. "You might want to tell your superiors that we offer special fleet discounts to law enforcement."

"I'll pass it on." Like she was going to interrupt a manhunt to pimp for this Somersett Don Ho.

She was surprised to discover that he actually did sell a lot of cars. Even more surprised by how many brown Altimas hadn't been financed.

"We've got a lot of retirees settling down here," he said. "When you're in your eighties, you're not all that likely to be taking on more payments."

Cait supposed that was so. Although she didn't want to rule out anything, she'd also guess that her shooter wasn't going to turn out to be a grumpy old man.

Despite his claim of personalized small-town service, Sandy Sandman hadn't actually shaken the hand of every customer who'd driven off the lot. But Cait did leave with a list of names and addresses.

She strongly doubted that her shooter, who'd proven himself fairly clever so far, would have been stupid enough to hand out factual information. Then again, shake enough trees and something may fall out.

She was driving back to the JOC, planning to turn the list over to one of the desk guys to check out while she went to the PTSD meeting with Quinn, when she automatically slowed down as she approached an intersection two blocks south of the cathedral. Although she'd really, really tried to cut back on her speeding, ever since the city had installed that traffic camera—

"Shit!"

How could she not have thought of that? The first camera had only taken shots of license plates—which wouldn't be useful in this situation, given what the kid said about the mud—but the cops had quickly discovered that quite a few normally law-abiding people were more than willing to lie through their teeth and swear they weren't driving the car when the photo was taken of their car going over the speed limit.

Which was when the city council ponied up the additional bucks to buy the upgraded camera that not only shot the plate but took a photo of the driver as well.

With any luck, their shooter might just have been caught on Somersett's very own candid camera.

43

One of the skills of a sniper was an ability to put himself into the head of your enemy. So, as Quinn drove around the city, searching out possible hides, he also thought about where, if he'd been the guy, he'd hang out when he wasn't terrorizing innocent citizens.

When a possible answer came to him, he'd called John and Zach Tremayne over from Swann Island.

"Okay," he told the men, "I think he might be hiding out in the marsh."

"Makes sense to me," John said. Like his son, Zach, he was a former SEAL and kept his hand in the Special Ops world by doing tactical work for Phoenix Team. "Got a lot of miles out there. Some too shallow for the Coast Guard to get into."

"That's why I thought you and Zach could take out your johnboat. Unless," Quinn said to Zach, "you're too caught up in wedding plans."

John roared at that idea, while Zach rolled his eyes. "It hasn't been that bad."

"Sure, that's what you say now," his father said. "But I seem to remember a lot of bitching like a girl about some fool groom's gift during last week's poker game."

"Got me." Zach shook his head. "Who the hell makes up all these rules anyway? I swear it was easier humping through minefields than maneuvering through all this matrimonial stuff."

"Not that I'd know," Quinn said, "but my guess would be that the best way to handle the situation would be to go along with whatever the bride wants. Especially since Sabrina probably used to plan stuff like this for a living."

Zach's fiancée had just been promoted to manager of a luxury international hotel chain when a terrorist bomb had literally blown the building out from under her. Which was how she'd landed back on nearby Swann Island and gotten hooked up with Zach, who'd also come home after that debacle in Afghanistan.

It hadn't been easy for either of them, and just as they'd begun to learn to love and trust again, a stone-cold serial killer had nearly destroyed everything they'd fought so hard to rebuild.

They were good people, good friends, and Quinn was damn happy for both of them. He was also glad that afterward, along with working on the remodeling of Sabrina Swann's antebellum family home, the man who was like a brother to him had joined him at the private security firm.

Along with Shane Garrett, who was still at Walter Reed Army Hospital in D.C., there was no one Quinn would rather work with; their shared battlefield experiences had forged a stronger, closer bond than blood ties ever could have.

"Going along with the program is pretty much what I've been trying to do," Zach said. "I've been looking at it like BUD/S training. I just show up and do whatever the hell I'm told. At least I've got it luckier than Nate. He's on his way back from a trip to Charleston with Titania, on a mission to choose a flatware pattern."

"Do me a favor?" John said.

"What?" Zach asked his father.

"Don't let anyone know that my son not only knows the word 'flatware' but just used it in a sentence."

"Roger that," Zach agreed with a grin that told Quinn that as much a pain as all the wedding preparations were, his bride-to-be was well worth the trouble.

"Fortunately, Swannsea's loaded with china and silverware, so since Sabrina's set there, I escaped that part of the exercise."

Swann Island sheriff and former Marine Nate Spencer was marrying Sabrina's best friend in a double ceremony. It was, according to local papers, going to be the highlight of the Swann Island social season. Which Quinn figured just showed how much in love both men were, since he suspected they'd rather have a case of the clap than go through any dog and pony show that involved formal attire.

"Speaking of Swannsea, do you think you can spare some construction crews from the remodeling over there to get going on this place?" Quinn asked.

"Sure," John said. "If you recall, I mentioned that we could move a little faster, but you kept saying you weren't in any hurry. So, hell, figuring you were busy on your book, I didn't want to push."

"Well, now I'm in a hurry."

"This sudden need for a proper house wouldn't have anything to do with Cait Cavanaugh, would it?" Zach asked.

"Negative," Quinn lied.

Zach's laugh was short and satisfied. "Damned if you're not nest building."

"The hell I am. And if you don't mind, can we get back to the reason I called you both over here?"

"Sure," Zach said agreeably. "Better begin with the bedroom," he told his father.

"Roger that," John replied.

Quinn blew out a frustrated breath between his teeth. "I told Cait the guy's not a sniper."

"I gotta agree," John said.

"Me, too," Zach concurred. "Any sniper worth his salt wouldn't go risking a head shot. But it sounds like he's got himself an arsenal."

"Yeah," Quinn said grimly. "Along with a mission."

Since she hadn't sworn him to secrecy, and he knew they would keep it to themselves, he told the two men about the letters Valentine Snow had received. Which it turned out they already knew about, given that Joe Gannon had taken on the bodyguard job.

"Think he's really obsessed with the woman?" Zach asked. "Or are the letters and the tarot cards merely a smoke screen?"

"To get everyone chasing their tails." Quinn nodded. "I've considered that. So has Cait. But sure as hell the one thing that gets ignored is going to be the thing that could crack the case. Meanwhile, while you and your dad check out the marsh, Cait and I are going to go to Mike Gannon's PTSD group meeting tonight."

"I went to a couple of those," Zach revealed.

His dad shot him a look. "You didn't tell me about that."

Zach shrugged. "It wasn't that big a deal. The shrink the VA sent me to suggested it. But spilling my guts to strangers, even guys who were going through the same thing, just felt too weird."

Quinn knew that of the three of them, Zach had suffered the most emotionally after that clusterfuck in the Kush. He suspected that guilt had played a major part in the former SEAL's problems. Which, he'd always known, was why his former teammate avoided visiting Shane at Walter Reed as often as Quinn himself had.

"I was in Washington this past weekend," Zach said. Quinn wasn't surprised his friend was on the same wavelength. The ability to read one another's minds had proven valuable during all their years of covert missions.

"And how did that go?" he asked with studied casualness.

"Pretty good, actually. I was surprised at all the programs they have there. When I got there he was on the FATS shooting range."

"They've got a shooting range at the hospital?" John asked.

"Across the street. The Firearms Training System is

a pretty cool setup. A computer system runs simulated battlefield scenarios, and you can shoot a bunch of electronically integrated weapons at this huge screen. They start with basic marksmanship stuff, then move on to close three-round shot grouping, then finally the pop-up target lanes like we did in BUD/S and video combat scenarios.

"A computer keeps track of the results. Shane managed to requalify in the first five sessions. By fifteen, he actually topped what he was shooting when the helo went down."

"Good for him," John said approvingly.

"Yeah. He said it makes him feel like a soldier again. He's also like a damn monkey on the rock wall they've got him climbing."

"That's a lot different PT than guys had when we got back from 'Nam," John said.

"Yeah. Well, to hear vets tell it, your generation got the shaft," Quinn said. "But this is great news. So, when does he think he's going to get sprung from there?"

"He could probably leave now, but he signed up to be part of a test group for this new bionic leg, so it looks as if it's going to be a couple more months at least. But he assured me he'd be back to stand up for me when I get hitched. Which reminds me," he said, turning back to his father, "I've been meaning to ask you to be my best man."

Quinn figured John Tremayne would swear it was a trick of the light, but there was no mistaking the sudden sheen of moisture the request brought to the older man's eyes.

"You sure about that? Because I figured you'd want guys your own age."

"Quinn and Shane have already agreed to be ushers. But, hey, since grooms don't have their fathers walk them down the aisle like brides do, I figured the next best thing would be to have you standing beside me. Like you always have."

He left unsaid what Quinn knew all three men in the room were thinking. That it had been John who'd dragged his son back into the real world when PTSD had Zach trying to drink the state of South Carolina dry.

"Well, if we're going to capture this guy, we'd better get a move on," the older man said gruffly.

"Roger that," Zach said.

He stayed behind a moment after his father left the house. "Interesting, you and Cait Cavanaugh working together," he said.

" 'Interesting' is one word for it, I suppose."

"So, I guess she's put behind her whatever the hell it was you did to piss her off?"

"I didn't do anything, dammit," Quinn said the same thing he always had whenever the redhead's name had come up over the years. "Unless you know something I don't?"

"I haven't a clue. Women are fabulous creatures, and I thank God for them every day, but hell, any man who pretends to know what goes through their minds is flat-out lying. Though," he tacked on, "there was that little matter of you taking advantage of her inebriated condition to sleep with her."

"Hey, she was the one who jumped me," Quinn complained. And they certainly hadn't done that much sleeping. "The next thing I knew, she'd shed that damn Pepto-Bismol-pink dress and was twining herself around me like a goddamn python, and . . ."

Although Quinn had never been one to kiss and tell, he'd shared the story in the Kush, when it looked as if none of them would get out of those mountains alive. The idea that he would die without ever knowing what the hell he'd done to so piss Cait Cavanaugh off had been one of the few regrets of his life.

"Well, I guess you just needed to be there," he muttered.

"I'm just as glad I wasn't. Since she still likes me."

"Rub it in, why don't you?" Quinn plowed a hand

through his hair. "At least I'm making some progress. She doesn't look like she wants to shoot me whenever she sees me anymore."

"Well, I guess that's a start."

"Yeah. That's kinda how I see it."

Cait was, hands down, the most frustrating, hard-headed, exasperating person—male or female—he'd ever met.

She was also the most compelling.

She'd gotten into his system like a damn virus years ago, and as much as he tried to convince himself that an intelligent, sane man would stay clear of anything or anyone who could so mess with his head the way that woman could without even trying, he'd never been able to quite shake loose of her.

And if that wasn't bad enough, since the shooter had forced them back together again, Quinn wasn't real sure he wanted to be loose of Special Agent Caitlin Cavanaugh.

44

"This just in," Valentine Snow announced on the television as the retort from the shot was still reverberating inside the shack.

From the way she tilted her dark head, the shooter suspected she was listening to a voice in her earphone. "Authorities are seeking a brown 2008 Nissan Altima in connection with the recent shootings. The license plate may be unreadable due to mud. If you spot such a car, call police right away. Do not attempt to approach, as the occupants are considered armed and dangerous. Stay tuned for more details, and you can always receive up-to-the-minute updates from our Web site."

Shit. How the hell had that happened? He'd purposely chosen the Pebble Beach color to blend in.

The plan had been to make Jensen's death look like nothing more than an alkie suicide. He hadn't intended to get rid of the car. At least not yet. But no way was he going to risk driving it around town now that the police had everybody in the damn Lowcountry out looking for it.

Painting it wasn't an option, since not only did he not want to risk driving the Altima back into the city to buy the damn paint but it had begun to rain again.

He checked Jensen's clothes, retrieved a pocketknife, a rumpled card offering a free meal at the Redemption Mission, and ten bucks, partly in change, partly in the kind of folded-up dollar bills people give to panhandlers.

He stripped the clothes from the corpse, dragged it out of the shack, lifted it into the trunk, then doused both the body and the car with gasoline from the five-gallon jerrican the owner of the shack had left behind for the generator.

He shut the trunk, locked it with the remote, and used the knife to cut Jensen's pants and shirt into long strips, which he tied together, then soaked in kerosene from a second can intended for the stove. Lucky for him, the fool owner of the shack had left behind enough fuel to blow the place up several times over.

He opened the gas cap of the Altima, stuck one end of the cloth strip, which was now about twelve feet long, down into the tank.

Then, after stretching the rest the length of the dock, he climbed into the johnboat, took out a plastic cigarette lighter, and lit the cloth, which flared nicely, yet more slowly than the hotter-burning gasoline would, giving him sufficient time to get away.

The shooter was about a hundred yards from the shack when the car went up in flames. Satisfied, he disappeared like a shadow into the darkened marsh.

The JOC, which had been buzzing like a beehive, suddenly went still. All heads turned toward the two women standing in the doorway.

Sabrina Swann, dressed in snug white jeans and a bright blue T-shirt beneath her shiny yellow slicker, was carrying a large cardboard box. Her companion, Titania Davis, was clad in a scarlet-as-sin dress that fit like a second skin beneath her red hooded slicker and skyscraper-high sandals, which, impractical as they were for the rain that had begun to fall, made her legs look a mile long. The wicker basket, its handle looped over her arm, added to the impression of a very sexy Little Red Riding Hood.

"We figured you could use some food that didn't

come from a vending machine or a fast-food restaurant," Sabrina said in greeting to Cait. "I come bearing rosemary egg salad croissants, smoked-chicken salad on twelve-grain bread, ham and pear salad with blue cheese on a sourdough baguette, and Vietnamese rolls with mint soy dipping sauce."

"And I brought the sweet stuff," Titania said, lifting her basket. "Chocolate chip, oatmeal, and vanilla drop cookies, along with Swann Tea's scrumptious signature chocolate mint brownies."

As everyone surged forward for the free food, Sabrina took Cait aside.

"So, how's it going?" she asked, her brow furrowed with concern beneath her smooth blond bangs.

They'd met during the Swann Island Slasher case and had become friends afterward.

"There's not much to tell," Cait said. "We're working some leads, but the guy's pretty much a ghost."

"Well, hopefully Zach and John will be able to be of some help."

"Zach and John Tremayne? What do they have to do with my sniper case?"

"Oops." Sabrina grimaced. "I guess Quinn didn't tell you?"

"I guess not." Cait crossed her arms. "So, why don't you fill me in?"

"He had some ideas he thought they could help with. Both of them being former SEALs and all." She looked honestly chagrined that she'd unwittingly let Quinn's damn cat out of the bag.

"I don't suppose you'd know what those ideas might be?"

Sabrina shrugged her slicker-clad shoulders. "Sorry. I didn't talk with Zach in person. I was on the phone with the people who are designing the furniture for the new teahouse when he called, so he just left a message that he and his dad were coming over from the island to help Quinn out."

"How nice of him to let me know," Cait said through gritted teeth.

"I'm sure he's just trying to help."

"Look around. If we had any more help, we'd have to start moving desks out into the parking lot. One thing I don't need is a civilian playing Lone Ranger and screwing up my investigation."

"Quinn may be a civilian, but his military training does give him a skill set that the average guy on the street doesn't have."

"I wouldn't want the average guy on the street instigating himself into the damn case, either." Realizing that she'd drawn attention to them, Cait lowered her voice. "Look, he was admittedly helpful on sharing the sniper mind-set. And he's agreed to come to a vets' PTSD meeting that Mike Gannon's holding tonight, which I appreciate, because I doubt any of those guys would talk to me on their own. But he doesn't have any right to start bringing in other people."

"Other *SEALs*. Who have done a lot of black ops missions," Sabrina said.

"If he misses that world so much, I don't see anything stopping him from going back to it. Otherwise, he ought to just stick to making a gazillion bucks writing his books."

It was Sabrina's turn to blow out a breath. "Look, I'm getting the feeling that there's something else going on here, but that's between you and Quinn. I don't want to be telling tales out of school, and no way am I going to betray a confidence, but I do think you need to be aware that Quinn might have more complex reasons for leaving the service. Other than making money."

Her tone was calm. Collected. But having spent so many years as a cop, Cait had learned to listen not so much to what people were saying as to what they weren't. And there was something there, something to do with Quinn, and, she suspected, perhaps Zach, that the other woman wasn't prepared to share.

"Well." She tipped her head in a nod. "Thanks for the heads-up. I guess I'll give him a chance to explain before I shoot him."

Sabrina's smile was dazzling enough to brighten the dreary day. "I appreciate that. Since I'd really like him to stay alive long enough to usher at my wedding." Her eyes narrowed speculatively. "You know, Titania and I were just saying on the drive over here, that we could use another bridesmaid, to even things out. I don't suppose—"

"No." Cait's response was quick, sharp, and final. "I've done the pink taffeta thing."

"Well, we weren't going with taffeta. And pink's definitely out, though the right shade could look fabulous on you. We've been thinking black and white. Which would also work with your coloring. So, if you change your mind—"

"Thanks. But I think I'd better pass."

Her last stint as a bridesmaid had ended up being one of the worst nights of her life. Even worse, though she wouldn't have thought it beforehand, than the day her divorce had become final. No way was she going to relive it. Especially with the man who'd played a starring role in the debacle.

"Of course." Intelligent blue eyes swept over Cait's set face. "It was just a thought. I didn't mean to upset you."

"You didn't." Cait dragged a hand through the red hair that definitely hadn't gone with the bubblegum pink dress she could vaguely, just barely, remember peeling out of before jumping Quinn McKade's studly bones. "It's just that I've been having a really lousy couple of days."

"And of course you have far more important things to worry about than Titania's and my wedding," Sabrina said soothingly. "So, we'll get out of here and let you get back to work."

"Thanks. And thanks for the food. It smells delicious." She also wished she'd snagged a sandwich before having this conversation, since the members of the task force were swarming over the food like ants at a picnic.

"Titania's a super cook. I count myself lucky every day that she agreed to come work at Swannsea Tearoom."

As she returned to the computerized DMV base, Cait considered that Sabrina Swann had a lot more to be grateful for than that. If it hadn't been for Zach and John Tremayne, and yes, undeniably Quinn, neither woman would be alive to be planning a wedding.

Cait had certainly used the hottie Navy SEAL once before.

Of course, that had definitely not proven to be her best idea.

Still, she considered, her fingers tapping unnecessarily hard on the keyboard, given that some maniac was out there running around Somersett shooting innocent people, perhaps she should go ahead and take what Quinn McKade was offering.

So long as this time they both kept their clothes on.

45

One of the advantages of living in the South was you couldn't throw a stick without hitting a military base. Which meant if you were hitchhiking in Marine BDUs, you were pretty sure to get picked up in no time at all.

After ditching the boat on the bank, the shooter had been walking along the marsh road for about five minutes when a white van with CAPTAIN JACK'S LUCKY STRIKE CHARTERS painted on the side pulled over onto the crushed-shell shoulder lining the asphalt.

There was a slight grinding noise as the passenger window rolled down.

"Where you headed, son?" asked the driver, a guy in his forties wearing aviator shades and a blue and white ball cap with a fish leaping at a line on it. His skin was deeply tanned and lined with wrinkles.

"Somersett."

"Well, this here's your lucky day. I'm on my way to visit my sister in Fort Lauderdale, so I'll be goin' right through Somersett. Toss your gear in the back and hop in."

The shooter didn't hesitate.

"Name's Jack." The driver introduced himself. "Jack Slater, but most people just call me Captain."

"Pete Webb." The shooter had come up with the new name while steering the johnboat through the marsh.

"So." Eyes shielded against the early-evening glare

gave him a quick, decisive once-over, sizing him up. "You're in the Second MAW."

"Yes, sir. From up in Cherry Point."

The one thing about the Marines is that every goddamn thing you ever did was sewn onto your uniform, which was why he'd chosen a MAW band patch from the Internet supply site. No way did he want to get into any discussions about logistics some witness might remember later, so he'd decided to put himself in the Marine Air Wing band.

"What do you play?"

"The trombone." He flashed a grin. "Chose it because it puts me at the front of the parade. Sir."

"You don't have to call me sir, son. I'm not active military anymore, and the 'captain' I go by these days sure as hell isn't the saluting kind."

"So, you served?" the shooter asked. One of the problems with hitching was the people who'd pick up a stranger were usually lonely and prone to conversation.

"I was a Checkerboard, out of Fightertown." Which, decoded into civilian-speak, meant he'd been a member of the 312th VMFA—Marine Fighter Attack Squadron—out of nearby Beaufort.

"Guess you saw some action."

"A few missions back in the day flying Hornets," he said around a fat cigar that was stinking up the inside of the truck. Not that the shooter minded; he figured it'd mask any odor of gas or kerosene lingering in his clothes or hair.

Although the Marine's tone was casual enough, pride for the corps and his unit rang clear in his voice. For the next forty minutes the shooter was subjected to an account of a dozen or so years of Checkerboard history: Desert Shield, Desert Storm, Provide Promise, Sharp Guard, Desert Fox, Deny Flight, Southern Watch, Deliberate Force, Deliberate Guard, Deliberate Forge—who the hell thought up those names, anyway?

But, again, the shooter damn well wasn't going to bitch. The longer the Marine talked, the fewer questions he might have to answer.

It crossed his mind that they'd both find out exactly how lucky Captain Jack really was, because if the talkative jarhead asked something the shooter couldn't answer, well, he just might not have any choice but to kill him, right here and now.

Which wouldn't be the end of the world. Since it'd give him a van to use for his next mission.

"Guess I'm boring the friggin' socks off you," Captain Jack said.

"No, sir. I mean, no, it's really interesting," the shooter lied. "Though it does make me wish I'd seen more action."

"If you had, you might choose a different wish," the Marine said with a shrug.

His compact frame looked custom-designed to fit in a fighter jet's cramped cockpit, but his broad shoulders and square jaw shouted out a flyboy's overload of testosterone, making the shooter hope he wouldn't have to go one-on-one with the guy.

"Besides, being in the band's good for morale. Not to mention being a cool recruiting tool. I took my kids to Disneyland for the Fourth of July last year when you guys performed there. Hearing all those people lined up on Main Street screaming—in a good way—made me real proud to be a Marine."

"Yeah, it was cool." The shooter had never been to Disneyland. Didn't plan to ever go there. But from the way the guy paused, he figured he was supposed to say something.

"And, I gotta admit, I kinda teared up when y'all played the Marine Hymn."

"They always do."

"Yeah. I guess so." The blue cap nodded. "So, like I said, you MAW band guys have your own mission. Which is, in its way, just as important as dropping ordnance over Yugoslavia or some damn desert."

"Yeah, but I'll bet doing bombing runs is more of a rush." Though not as much of one as lining someone up in your scope and blowing them away, the shooter bet.

"Nothing like it," the Marine admitted, a bit reluctantly. "But hell, there's a lot to be said for hauling in a fifty-pound barracuda. You do any sea fishing?"

"Never got into it."

"You should. Golf's not a bad game," he said, nodding toward the backseat, where the golf bag holding the shooter's rifles lay, "but there's nothin' better to clear a guy's head than getting out on the water."

He reached into the pocket of the T-shirt and pulled out a white card with a blue logo matching the one on the truck and the cap. "We offer the full service, from a few hours to overnight, family trips, or party boats, or serious fishing. We've got all forty different kinds of fish in these waters covered: trigger, sea bass, snapper, wahoo, king mackerel, barracuda, tuna, grouper, sharks. You want it, we'll find it for you. Then all you have to do is—oorah—haul the suckers in."

"I'll keep that in mind," the shooter said.

"You do that," the Marine said as he slowed for the traffic stopped up on the approach of the bridge leading into town. Red and blue bar lights atop cruisers flashed bright in the golden summer dusk. "Looks like the cops have set up a roadblock. Guess they're lookin' to catch that sniper."

"Looks like it," the shooter said as he reached beneath his shirt for the Sig he'd replaced the Glock with.

He had no intention of being captured. But if the cops did try to take him down, he damn sure wasn't going alone.

46

Quinn answered his cell phone on the second ring. "What can I do for you, Special Agent?"

"How did you know it was me?" Cait asked. "The caller ID was blocked."

"Let's just say, since we're due to meet in forty minutes, I took a wild guess."

"We need to talk."

"Isn't that what we're doing?"

"This line's not secure," she said, telling him nothing he didn't already know about cell phones. "We need to meet somewhere private."

"Name the place."

"My apartment. I have to run home and feed cats."

She was obviously impatient, which he could understand. But he also thought he heard an underlying anger in her tone as she rattled off the address he already knew. Because, as pitiful as he knew such behavior to be, he'd driven by the building several times.

"I'll meet you there in ten."

Quinn had always been able to compartmentalize. It was a vital skill in his line of work, but in his case he'd always figured it was a gift. Maybe one he'd developed when he'd been too young to realize it was happening, or perhaps it was a talent he'd been born with, a gift from an omnipresent God who knew the baby boy born to Julia Van Pelt and Daniel McKade would need all the help he could get.

He'd never cried. Not even when he'd watched his father die. Not at the funeral home, where he'd stood beside the plain wooden casket, staring at his old man's body for a long, long time, imprinting every feature onto his memory, trying to understand the inexplicable, while the woman from Social Services kept impatiently glancing at her watch, trying to hurry him along.

He'd never allowed himself to wallow in grief over all the fathers and sons whose lives he'd taken, either. It wasn't that he was callous. It was just that life could get messy if you didn't keep your feelings separate. Such ability, he'd often thought, was how he was able to leave the military without any outward sign of the PTSD he knew Zach had suffered.

Maybe it was because he'd been reliving that last mission in the writing of this book, or the shooter could've triggered—no pun intended—deep-seated emotions about life and death that seemed out of place in this tidy Southern town.

Or perhaps it was because Cait Cavanaugh had him thinking about what-ifs. About how his life might have changed if things had gone differently between them in the past. Would they have gotten married? Had themselves a passel of curtain-climbers?

Which was, truth be told, an even scarier prospect than having tangos shooting at you. Because how the hell was a guy like him supposed to know how to be a father?

"Yeah, like the lady seems real eager to have your babies," he muttered as he pulled into the parking lot of the three-story clapboard building across the street from the harbor.

Just two nights ago, the sidewalk—hell, the street—would've been packed with partygoers. Tonight the scene was as quiet as a graveyard.

The stairs were on the outside of the building. Her apartment was a corner unit, on the top floor. Although some people might get tired of climbing three flights of stairs at the end of a long workday, he figured others would consider the view worth the forced exercise.

There was only the slightest pause after he rang the bell; he could feel her looking at him through the peephole and then the door swung open.

"What the hell do you think you're doing?" she demanded.

"You said we needed to talk. Named the place. So"—he spread his arms out—"here I am, as ordered."

"That's not what I mean." She moved aside, allowing him to enter. "What I want to know is why you felt the need to go bringing other people—civilians—into this case."

"Ah, I see," he murmured as he glanced around.

The living room was as tidy and spare and lacking of clutter as his own might have been. Would eventually be, once Tremayne Construction finished the renovation.

The colors, however, might have been a surprise to anyone who'd only seen the tough, just-the-facts-ma'am special agent. The walls were painted the pale green of sea glass, the wooden coffee and end tables were bright white, and blue-and-white-striped pillows scattered over the white slipcovered furniture echoed the misty seascapes on the wall. The room was casual, inviting, and revealed a softer, more feminine side that he suspected she didn't show to that many people.

"I take it you heard about Zach and John."

"Sabrina let the cat out of the bag," Cait confirmed. "It appears you big, manly SEALs forgot to tell the little woman it was a secret mission."

"I was going to tell you," he said as a gray striped kitten jumped off a chair it'd been sharing with two apparent littermates and began weaving figure eights through Quinn's legs.

Cait folded her arms, which lifted her breasts in a really interesting way. When she caught him looking at them, her glare darkened, annoyed energy vibrating from every pore. "When?"

"I called your office, but the guy who answered the phone told me you were tied up."

Which had conjured up some appealing kinky mental images and reminded him all too painfully how long it'd been since he'd had sex.

The kitten began sharpening its claws on his jeans. When it dug in, attempting to climb his leg like a SEAL would a rock wall, Quinn bent down and scooped it up. " So, since I knew your task force was overextended—"

"We happen to have team members from every local and federal force out there beating the bushes and taking calls."

"True. But how many do you have trolling the marsh?"

"The sheriff's department's got deputies doing drive-bys."

The kitten was purring like a small motor. Quinn had never been a cat person. While his lifestyle had precluded having a pet, given his druthers, he would've preferred a dog. And not one of those little foo-foo girlie ones that needed regular grooming, wore cute little outfits, and had their toenails painted, but a real guy mutt that'd shed on the furniture, bury bones in the yard, and like to ride in cars with its head sticking out the window, floppy ears blowing in the wind.

Still, he admitted, as he looked into a pair of gold crossed eyes, while it was a long way from the dog he'd dreamed about when he was a kid, this ball of gray and white fur was cute. In a feline sort of way.

"Lot of marsh out there," he said. "I figured you could use some extra eyes."

"You're a civilian," she reminded him yet again.

"So, you've never heard of a concept called Neighborhood Watch?"

Her lips quirked, just a little. "Dammit. I really, really don't want to like you, McKade."

"Why don't you tell me something I haven't figured out for myself?" he said. "Though since I've been thinking back on it a lot lately, I feel the need to point out that there was that one time when you seemed to like me well enough. That night you nearly fucked me blind."

"I'd been drinking."

"Yeah. We both had. That's what people do at wedding receptions. I've always figured it's out of relief at not being the one who got caught."

"Finally. Something we can agree on."

"Really." And wasn't that progress? "Here I thought all women want to get caught. Or at least let some clueless guy think he's the one doing the catching."

"Well, you'd be wrong. I, for one, definitely prefer my freedom to captivity."

Too late, he remembered she'd been fresh off a divorce that night. And still stinging from the failure of it.

Deciding that any attempt to backtrack and apologize would only dig the hole deeper, he decided to forge on. "The thing is, I knew exactly what I was doing." He'd also known it was a mistake, but at the time he'd been thinking with his cock and his head hadn't been fully engaged. "And so did you."

"Like I said, I was drunk."

Remembering all too well the way that crackly pink skirt had been crushed against his thighs, and how her nipples had felt like two little stones as she'd twined around him on the hotel dance floor, Quinn wondered which of them she was trying to convince.

His gaze dropped to her lips. "Are you drunk now?"

"Of course not."

"Well, then." He put the kitten back on the chair. It mewed a momentary complaint, then set about licking its paws.

Quinn pressed his palm against her cheek. Encouraged when she didn't bat his hand away, or worse yet, use one of those martial arts moves he had no doubt she'd learned at Quantico to throw him on the floor, he slid it beneath her piña colada–scented hair, cupping the back of her neck.

"So," he asked, tormenting himself by nibbling on her earlobe rather than ravishing her mouth again the way he was dying to do, "exactly how much about that night do you remember, anyway?"

"I remember the endless toasts, the too sweet cake, and the maid of honor and the bride's cousin getting into a tug-of-war over the bouquet," she said on an exhaled breath that was just raggedy enough to assure him that he wasn't the only one beginning to heat up here. "After that it's pretty much of a blur."

"Too bad. But maybe I can refresh your memory." Using his free hand against her back to press her closer, he brushed his lips down her throat and felt her swallow. "Do you remember slow-dancing to that wannabe Tony Bennett wedding singer?"

"Not really."

Quinn sensed the lie. But what the hell. He was still on his feet, and she was still pressed against him the same way she'd been that night.

"Maybe if you put your arms around my neck, the way you did that night, it'll ring a bell."

"What if I don't want my bell rung?"

But she did. He could hear it in her husky voice, see it in the heat warming her eyes.

He brushed his lips against hers. Gently. Teasingly. "Humor me."

"I don't want this."

"Sure you do." He took hold of her wrist and lifted her arm up over his shoulder. Then did the same thing with the other. "Same as I do. You just don't *want* to want it."

He skimmed the tip of his tongue over the tightly set seam of her mouth. "Now, link your fingers together behind my neck. Same way you did that night."

"I'm supposed to be yelling at you." But even as she said it, he felt those long, slender fingers lace together.

"You yelled that night." A deep moan vibrated in his chest at the memory of her calling out his name as she bucked beneath him. He began to move. Back and forth, dancing in place. "Actually, it was more of a scream."

"Hah." She leaned into him as he spun her around, moving to the music he could still hear. "Now I know you're lying. Because I never, ever scream."

"You sure as hell did that night." He began to hum "Fly Me to the Moon," which was what the band had been playing the first time they'd kissed, on the dance floor.

"Three times." He brought her closer, pressing her breasts tight against his chest as a raw ache of lust tangled in his groin. He was desperate to touch her. Taste her. All over. "Or was it four?"

"What it was was a mistake. One I don't want to talk about," she insisted, even as she moaned beneath his mouth.

"Fine." He tugged her white blouse free of the waistband of the gray slacks, so he could touch her. Quinn didn't want to talk about it either. He wanted to freaking *do* it before his body took off all on its own like a Patriot missile. "How about we table the conversation?"

One hand fisted in her hair while the other deliberately cupped her breast. She could deny wanting him until doomsday, but the way her nipple puckered against the lacy cup of her bra gave her away.

"And move on to the good stuff."

"Dammit, it's not that easy."

Was that a tremor he heard in her voice?

Nah. Couldn't be. Not from law-and-order, I-eat-terrorists-for-breakfast Special Agent Cait Cavanaugh. He drew his head back. Her eyes were dark and clouded, swirling with the same lust that was ripping at him.

"I want you to let go of me," she insisted. "Now. Because, in case you haven't noticed, I'm armed."

And damn dangerous, Quinn thought.

He could take her. Here and now, and not only would it be a piece of cake, because he knew she wouldn't fight him, but he also suspected she'd be every bit as hot and eager as she'd been that night.

The difference was that this time he'd make damn sure she remembered every damn thing he did to her. Every single thing she did to him.

And then what?

Where the hell would they go from there?

Because he couldn't answer that question to his own satisfaction, Quinn dropped his hands to his sides.

"You're right," he said. "It's not easy. You'd think it should be, given that we're both past the age of consent and sex is a normal adult activity, but maybe it's because we got off on the wrong foot back in the beginning that screwed things up, because it sure as hell seems complicated now."

"Which is why we should just stay clear of each other."

"Yeah. Like that's going to happen."

He'd never been one to obsess over any woman. But from the way he'd been thinking about her, too much, lately, Quinn figured she represented trouble with a capital T.

The thing was, he wanted her. And from the way she'd stuck her tongue down his throat up there in the bell tower, she wanted him, too.

So, what the hell was the problem?

"We're adults," she repeated what he'd just pointed out. "Which means that unlike hormone-driven teenagers, we don't have to give in to every sexual urge we might be feeling."

Hooyah. At least he now had her admitting he

wasn't the only one feeling too damn horny for his boxers.

"That's one way of looking at it," he said. "Of course, since we're both adults, we don't have to go mistaking sexual urges for anything other than what they are, prettying them up with all sorts of hearts and flowers and forever-after kinds of stuff . . .

"But here's the thing. You might not remember burning up the sheets, but I sure as hell do and that night was, hands down, the hottest, most mind-blowing sex I've ever had. The problem, as I see it, was you sneaking off the next morning while I was out scrounging up breakfast."

"How was I supposed to know you were coming back?"

"One clue might've been my shaving kit I'd left sitting on the bathroom counter," he suggested dryly. "If you'd stuck around, we'd have just kept fucking like rabbits until we'd probably have gotten tired of each other before the weekend was over."

She tilted her head. Narrowed her Kerry blue eyes. "As much as I hate to admit it, you may have yet another point. It could be the expectation of sex that's turning out to be the problem now. Especially since there's undoubtedly no way the actual event could possibly live up to the fantasy."

"You've fantasized about having sex with me?"

"Maybe. A time or two."

"Was it good for you?"

"It was okay." She shrugged. "But don't let it go to your head, because I've also fantasized about a three-way with George Clooney and Denzel Washington."

"Well, I'm glad you left me out of that one, because I don't like to share. So, what you're saying is that it took two movie stars to equal one of me?"

"What I'm saying is just about any guy in dress whites, which is what you had on, is hot. Which, thinking about it, Denzel was wearing, too. For a very short time."

"Ouch. Bull's-eye. That sound you hear is my ego deflating."

"Ha. Like your ego could be dented with an Abrams tank," Cait countered with a toss of her bright head. "So, getting back to the topic at hand and following your line of reasoning," she continued briskly, "the only logical thing is to just go ahead and get it over with."

It was, to Quinn's mind, the absolutely logical thing to do. But he didn't exactly appreciate the way she made it sound like something to be endured. Like a yearly gynecological exam.

"That isn't exactly how I would've put it. But, yeah. Especially if your joint task force doesn't catch this guy right away and we're stuck with each other for a while. All this pent-up lust could risk complicating an already stressful situation."

"Are you actually suggesting sex as a stress reliever?"

Though he wasn't prepared to admit it, the line sounded just as lame to him as soon as he'd heard it leaving his mouth.

"Hey, it's a lot better than trying to zone out with booze and drugs," he said. "But the thing is, when I do take you to bed again, Cupcake, I want to take my time to do it right. So you'll be sure to remember afterward." He glanced down at his watch. "Time we don't have if we want to make that meeting."

"No way am I going to miss it." She tucked her blouse back into her slacks. "And if you call me Cupcake again, I'm going to have no choice but to shoot you."

"I'll consider myself duly warned."

"You are," she complained, as they left the apartment, "the last man on the planet I should be having sex with."

"Don't feel like the Lone Ranger, because you're probably the last woman in the galaxy *I* should be having sex with."

While he appreciated the irony of spending so many years earning a living doing exactly what had earned his parents infamy for protesting against, Quinn was still having trouble wrapping his mind around having hot, chandelier-swinging monkey sex with an FBI agent.

"But that doesn't seem to matter a helluva lot, does it?"

She didn't answer. But Quinn suspected that once again, although she hated to admit it, they were on the exact same wavelength.

Game on.

47

At first glance, someone stumbling into the PTSD support group meeting in the basement of St. Brendan's might have mistaken it for any other 12-step program. Having attended a few Al-Anon meetings herself during the final, dying days of her marriage when her former husband had become too fond of the bottle, Cait recognized the slogans on the hand-painted signs on the wall: RECOVERY IS AN INSIDE JOB. IF IT IS TO BE, IT IS UP TO ME. THE WAY TO GET ANYWHERE IS TO START FROM WHERE YOU ARE. IF YOU FIND YOURSELF IN A RUT, STOP DIGGING.

One she could definitely identify with after having spent so much time in close proximity to Quinn McKade read: NEVER WALK UNESCORTED THROUGH YOUR OWN MIND—IT CAN BE A DANGEROUS NEIGHBORHOOD.

Although she suspected there was no reason female soldiers hadn't come back from wars suffering from PTSD, this group was all men. Those who weren't wearing cammies were decked out in leather. Most wore insignias symbolizing their units and military history. Even Quinn, she noticed, had pulled the chain out from beneath his olive drab T-shirt, revealing the copper-clad bullet she'd noticed last night when she'd driven out to his house.

There was a bit of time for pre-meeting mingling and coffee, and although she stayed on the sidelines, from the curious but not overly resentful looks shot her way, Cait could tell Quinn was telling people about her.

After ten minutes or so, the group all staked out chairs and stood for the Serenity Prayer, asking God to grant them the serenity to accept the things they could not change, the courage to change the things they could, and the wisdom to know the difference. Which, Cait thought, wasn't bad advice for anyone, not just 12-steppers.

A new member stood, introduced himself as a former Marine, and was greeted with the standard "Hi, John" from the others. Other than revealing that he'd opted out of the military after his third Iraq rotation, he didn't seem prepared to share any more information. Nor did anyone ask.

"So," Mike Gannon said, after an initial silence settled over the group. "Anyone have something good happen?"

He did not, Cait noticed, use the typical word "share," which she suspected might be too touchy-feely for this group.

One guy, who from his gray hair and furrows on either side of his mouth looked to be in his late fifties, early sixties, stood up.

"I went to my grandson's birthday party. He just turned ten last Saturday and had a bunch of friends over for pizza and to swim in my daughter's backyard."

"Sounds nice," the former priest said.

"Yeah." The guy shrugged. "At least until they started unwrapping presents."

"The kid got a toy gun," one of the vets jumped in to suggest.

"Hell, at that age, I already had a Red Ryder BB gun," another scoffed.

"Which was probably responsible for you ending up in the army and coming home whacked out," a third suggested.

"It wasn't a damn gun, okay?" The older vet struggled to regain the floor. "In fact, the kid's father wanted to get him a Nerf gun, but my daughter nixed the idea. So, it was the usual stuff—Legos, some new video games, and a basketball hoop that fit on the side of the pool. But my son-in-law didn't have time to put the hoop together ahead of time, so he and I were doing it, and it had come all taped up in bubble wrap. Which didn't seem like such a big deal—until one of the kids got the cool idea to jump on it. Then all the others started in."

"Oh, shit," Quinn, who was sitting beside Cait, murmured. "I can see this one coming."

"As soon as I heard that popping sound, I grabbed my grandson and hit the deck," the vet said. "I dragged him under the patio table and covered him with my body to protect him from gunfire. My daughter tells me that all the time I was screaming, 'Incoming!' "

When he pulled a hand down his face, Cait recognized the ASMA ring on his index finger. "Needless to say, that sort of put the kibosh on the party. Especially since I'd managed to knock the table over. Which sent the Star Wars ice cream birthday cake smashing to smithereens on the deck."

"That must have been embarrassing," Mike suggested.

"As hell," the man allowed. "Most of the kids looked scared to death, my grandson looked like he couldn't decide whether to cry or just throw himself into the pool and stay down at the bottom until he drowned, and my daughter was trying to split herself between calming the kids down and making sure I wasn't going to go all the rest of the way postal on her."

He cursed. Shook his head and looked both bleak and bewildered. "I had some troubles after I got back from 'Nam. But shit, that was decades ago. I got my head on straight, started up my contracting business, joined the Chamber of Commerce. People respect me, ya know?"

"We respect you," several of the men assured him.

"Yeah. Easy to say. You weren't there. You didn't see my daughter's face. Hell, I was supposed to babysit the kids while she and her husband go away for the weekend next month. Wanna bet that's going to happen?"

"It might not," Mike surprised Cait by saying. "But maybe if you go in for some one-on-one counseling—"

"I showed up at the VA first thing the next morning," the obviously depressed vet said. "Asked to see the shrink I'd started working with when I first started getting the flashbacks after watching the damn news about this war."

"Which you've quit doing, right?" Quinn asked.

"Yeah. But that doesn't stop the flashbacks. My wife says I'm back to talking all the time in my sleep. And I'm sleeping on my stomach."

"To protect vital organs," Quinn murmured to Cait.

"Well, anyway," the Vietnam vet continued, as if once he'd opened the floodgates, he was determined to get his entire story out, "it turns out the first appointment I can get is six weeks from now."

Cait was wondering if that was because the Veterans Department was so overwhelmed with PTSD patients, when he answered the question she hadn't intended to ask.

"Turns out they had to send a lot of shrinks to Iraq. So there aren't enough to take care of vets here at home."

"That's probably helpful for the troops downrange," Mike began. "I'll make some calls tomorrow and see if I can find someone willing to talk with you sooner, but meanwhile, I think it's important to keep in mind that what happened at the party, as stressful and embarrassing as it was, is still just one incident. Not a crisis."

"What the fuck is it with you, Gannon?" one of the

other vets, a man in his mid-thirties, ground out. "Guys come here and spill their guts, and all you can do is offer platitudes. Hell, were you even in the service?"

"I was in the army," Mike answered.

"Like a chaplain knows what it is to be in a firefight," the guy scoffed.

"Chaplains experience everything soldiers feel in a war zone," Mike countered. "The constant fear of being killed by an IED, or mortar fire that can take out your tent, or the risk of being shot out of the air by antiaircraft fire. They don't know if they're going to come back alive, and one of the hardest things to handle, on a personal basis, is that too many of them get really, really good at memorial services.

"But as it happens, I wasn't a chaplain. I was a doctor. A surgeon, actually."

A surprised murmur rippled through the crowd.

"Yeah. Big deal. So I've seen *MASH*," the guy pressed on. "Just because you went to medical school and stayed safe by doing appendectomies and C-sections on a base hospital, that still doesn't give you any cred for running this group."

"Like you even belong here?" one of the vets sitting in the back of the circle shouted out. "Hell, you're just using this group to slide through that court-ordered anger-management class the judge forced on you after you tried to kill some guy with your fists at the Stewed Clam over on the island."

The guy's eyes narrowed, but even so, in them Cait could see the barely repressed rage that had, if the accusing vet could be believed, landed the alleged attacker in jail.

"I don't recall you being there that night."

"I wasn't, but—"

"Then shut your pie hole because you don't know what the fuck you're talking about."

He sat back in the metal chair and folded his arms over his chest. Cait, who'd been taught to watch for signs of impending trouble, noticed that his fingers were digging into his arms, as if he was trying to hold the building rage in.

"I try to keep this as rule-free a zone as possible," Mike said mildly. "Given how most of us had our fill of regs in the military. But personal attacks are off-limits. As it happens, I've been where most of you are. Working in a medical unit during Desert Storm."

"Where he won the combat medical badge, for taking enemy fire," Quinn said. His own eyes, as they narrowed in on the troublemaker, were flint.

No stranger to men acting badly, Cait watched the barely reined-in aggression emanating from both males. She hadn't been all that happy when Quinn had made her leave her sidearm in the car, but now she was grateful for the groups' "no weapons inside the building" rule.

Of course, given that they didn't have to go through a metal detector to enter the church basement, it was always possible that one, if not more, of the vets in the room was carrying concealed.

"Is that true?" asked a kid who looked as if he should be on his way to the prom, not spending his evening in a PTSD group. "You got a medal?"

"It wasn't any big deal," the former priest said, shooting a look toward Quinn that suggested he wished the former SEAL had just left him to deal with the situation on his own. "People get shot at in a war. Some die quick. I nearly lost one of my closest friends, another military doctor, when a SCUD hit her barracks. She came close to dying on the operating table, so, yeah, I know damn well how you don't always get over things that happen in a war zone. But you can learn to live with them."

"My wife says she doesn't know me anymore," the kid volunteered. His eyes swam, causing a tug at some deep-seated emotional center inside her that Cait had tried—with varying success—to wall off when she'd become a cop.

"When Odysseus finally made it back home to Ithaca from the wars, no one except his old nurse and his dog recognized him," Mike said.

"And then the dog died," the troublemaker broke in. "Proving yet again that shit happens."

"According to the legend, the dog died," Mike agreed through set teeth. Cait wondered if he'd learned to rein in his impatience during all those years listening to confessions.

"That sucks," the kid said. "My wife says if we break up, she's keeping my dog."

"Yet another reason to keep working on your marriage," Mike suggested. "But my point, and I do have one, is that war had changed Odysseus. Yet eventually Penelope recognized him. It just took time."

"And afterward Odysseus and his sons killed all her lovers."

Yet more helpful input from the alleged brawler. Cait suspected Mike was beginning to wish that judge had just thrown the guy in the slammer instead of trying the counseling route.

"A solution I wouldn't recommend," Mike said. "Given that murder's against the law and modern times call for modern solutions. You're doing the right thing, coming here, Corporal. As opposed to trying to use violence to solve your problems."

He shot a challenging glare at the troublemaker, who glared back but kept his mouth shut.

The exchange, as heated as it had been, seemed to open people up. Cait spent the next hour listening to how nightmares could be a good thing, since they were an improvement over night terrors, which remained after awakening, and how some men were struggling with having lost their fight-or-flight reflex and being left only with the fight. It turned out the troublemaker wasn't the only vet here for court-appointed reasons.

Others, due to so much of their lives having been out of control for so long, seemed to have taken on a kind of fatalism, a what-the-fuck attitude that caused them to take dangerous risks. Risks that created problems within their families, who, unsurprisingly, were concerned about them.

Two others had taken to staying up all night, patrolling their neighborhoods. Which might not have been such a bad thing had they not been wearing full battle gear and carrying semiautomatic weapons at the time the cruising cops had spotted them.

Even as all the stories touched her, in some cases deeply, given that their pain was so obvious, Cait managed to distance herself, studying each vet in turn, listening to him, watching for signs, wondering, *Is this the one? Is this my shooter?*

"Where's Miz Davis?" one soldier suddenly asked.

"I imagine she's at home," Mike said. "Given her loss."

"What loss?" the guy asked.

"Christ on a crutch," another muttered, "her husband just got whacked."

The questioner's eyes widened. His jaw dropped. "You're shitting me."

"Captain Davis was fatally shot yesterday evening," Mike confirmed.

"By his wife?"

"No. By some unknown assailant."

"Who's also been smoke-checking people all over town," the new member of the group, the Marine, spoke up for the first time since introducing himself by his first name at the beginning of the meeting.

"Shit." The guy dragged an unsteady hand through long, unkempt, shoulder-length hair that didn't look as if it had been washed anytime in the past month. "I didn't hear anything about that."

"Hard to watch Fox News when you're living under the Somersett bridge," the troublemaker pointed out.

"Okay, dammit, that's enough."

Mike Gannon's sharp tone slashed like a bayonet. His jaw was granite. No longer looking like the softspoken former doctor who'd so recently worn a Roman collar, before everyone's eyes he morphed into

Captain Gannon, a military man who'd won a medal for bravery under enemy fire.

"One of the few rules of any 12-step group is that cross talk isn't encouraged, since everyone's supposed to address the meeting as a whole. Now, I'm willing to let that slide from time to time in order to keep a dialogue going, but one more negative word from you and I'm getting on the phone to the judge who decided it'd be a great idea to send you here, and believe me, this time tomorrow, your ass is going to be grass."

There was a stunned silence. Then, to Cait's surprise, while color stained the troublemaker's cheeks, the Vietnam vet began to clap. Followed by the kid whose wife claimed to no longer recognize him. One by one, the sound spread around the circle.

Until Mike held up a hand, the simple gesture abruptly cutting off the applause, like water turned off at the tap.

Cait admired his control of the group. And the way he smoothly moved on to a discussion of this week's step, which was led by one of the vets who, like the newcomer, had remained silent during the sharing part of the meeting. Perhaps, she thought, because he was busy concentrating on his presentation about continuing to take personal inventory and learning to admit when you were wrong.

Although the vet wasn't going to be elected president of Toastmasters anytime soon, his speech seemed to be well received by everyone in the room.

Speaking in public was one of the things Cait didn't like about her job. Another reason she'd been dodging Valentine's interview.

"One last story," Mike said, as the vet sat back down to another strong round of applause. "This is a legend I learned during a summer spent working on a reservation in Arizona. About an elder Apache teaching the young people of his tribe about life.

"He sat them down in a circle around the fire one night, and said to them, 'There is a fight going on inside me. Right now, as I speak. It is a terrible, deadly battle, between two wolves. One wolf represents fear, anger, envy, regret, greed, arrogance, self-pity, guilt, resentment, lies, false pride, and ego. The other stands for peace, love, hope, serenity, humility, kindness, friendship, generosity, truth, and faith. This same fight is going on inside you. And every other person, too.'

"As the sparks flew up from the fire into the night sky, the young boys thought about the elder's words.

"Then one asked the old man, 'Which wolf will win?'

"The elder replied simply, 'The one you feed.' "

With the same excellent timing that had packed the cathedral on those Sunday mornings when Father Mike was scheduled to give the weekly homily, he paused, allowing that message to sink in.

"Some of you may have noticed we have another guest who hasn't spoken," he said after a long moment, his tone shifting gears. "She's a friend of Quinn McKade, who many of you know well. And trust."

He nodded at Quinn, who nodded back.

"Which is why," Mike continued, "I also ask you to trust Special Agent Caitlin Cavanaugh, who's part of the task force trying to apprehend this person who's already taken three lives and sent a much beloved elderly crossing guard, who was doing her job protecting children crossing the street right outside this building, to the hospital."

He turned to Cait, whose palms had gone moist. God, she hated public speaking. "Cait. Would you like the floor?"

Actually, she'd like to escape this room, which seemed to be getting smaller by the moment. And something was sucking all the air out of it.

Quinn leaned toward her. "You'll be great."

"Yeah. That's probably what Butch Cassidy told the Sundance Kid just before they got the not-so-nifty idea to face down the Bolivian military," she muttered.

48

Screwing up her courage, Cait stood and walked to the podium, all too aware of twenty-five pairs of male eyes focused on her butt.

She gave the spiel, telling the group what she could without going into detail, including why the task force thought they were dealing with a vet. From the stony faces and crossed arms, she could tell that idea didn't go over real well.

When her eyes drifted to Quinn, he actually winked, as if she was doing great. She wished.

"I understand that's an unpopular idea," she pressed on, "because it means that every man and woman who has worn or is wearing the uniform gets painted with that same wide brush. Which is unfair. But, as I suspect you all know all too well firsthand, life isn't always fair.

"So, the best way to change the perception that everyone who's experiencing PTSD is a potential mass murderer is to stop this guy. Now."

She took a stack of cards from her suit jacket pocket and placed them on the corner of the table beside the podium. "The task force is, unsurprisingly, being inundated with phone calls. Some tips may prove helpful. Most probably won't."

She couldn't quite hold back a faint smile at the thought of Angetti, who'd landed in the FBI doghouse after that impromptu television interview, currently being stuck on phone duty. Her partner definitely hadn't been happy about that assignment. *Tough.*

She went on, "I've lived in Somersett since high school, and I never had any idea so many neighbors left their trash cans out at the curb past the pickup day."

It was, the members handling the phones had discovered, one of the top three complaints. Along with barking dogs and loud outdoor speakers blasting music all over the neighborhood.

That drew a ripple of laughter. Which was encouraging. If only one person in the room knew something, and felt more likely to call in with information because she'd come here tonight, the time spent away from the field investigation would be worthwhile.

"I've written my cell phone number on these cards," she said. "So if any of you think of anything which might prove helpful, you can bypass all the phone hoops and call me directly.

"I can't stress the importance of this," she said, her tone cracking a bit from the stress that was grinding away at her gut and head. "Because one thing I'm positive about is that this guy isn't going away. He's going to kill more people. The other thing I'm equally sure about is we're going to catch him. I'd just prefer it to be sooner rather than later."

She let out a breath, immensely grateful that she was now coming down the home stretch. "Thank you. Both for hearing me out this evening and for your service."

She didn't receive any applause, but as she returned to her seat, more than one vet met her gaze, and in those eyes she thought she saw if not friendship, which she wouldn't have expected, at least acceptance.

"You did good," Quinn said as she sat down beside him. He reached over, took her hand in his, and briefly squeezed her fingers.

"Let's just hope someone knows something they're willing to tell," she murmured back.

"I echo Special Agent Cavanaugh's statement," Mike was saying. "It's in all our interests for this evil to be stopped.

"I'd like to remind everyone that in order to preserve every member's anonymity, we ask that all you see and hear here stays here. Remember, opinions expressed are personal ones. Please take whatever you find helpful, and leave the rest.

"In closing, let's all remember that no matter how deep-rooted or hopeless life's problems may seem, we all start from where we are. By working the program one day at a time, we'll begin to reclaim the freedom and happiness we once experienced. What may seem impossible will become a reality, and we'll find our lives—as well as the lives of those around us—becoming richer and more joyful."

After the majority of group members repeated the closing Unity Prayer, the meeting broke up.

Many of the men gathered around Quinn carrying his book. Appearing a bit uncomfortable as he signed his name on the title page, he chatted briefly with each person.

"He's uneasy with the fame aspect of this new life he's chosen," Mike said as he and Cait watched the scene.

"His choice," she pointed out.

"Some vets deal with what they've seen and done by coming to meetings like this. Others choose methods that work for them. Quinn McKade's method of coming to terms with his former life is with the written word."

"Yet the book's fiction."

He gave her a "what turnip truck did you just fall off of?" look. "So it says on the cover."

In truth, she'd wondered about some of the scenes as she stayed up all night reading the gripping but violent page-turner. If Quinn had experienced even a quarter of the story he'd written, she was surprised he was as centered as he appeared to be.

After chatting with Mike a bit longer, catching up on his brother Joe's life and pleased to learn that her former partner and Val's current bodyguard was going to become a father in the new year, Cait was making her way through the dwindling crowd back to Quinn when a vet stepped in front of her, blocking her way, her white card in his hand.

"You're making a big mistake, Special Agent," the Marine said. His tone was rough, the animosity emanating from him as dangerous as his dark, deadly empty eyes.

"And how is that?" Cait asked. She had seen stone-cold killers demonstrate more emotion than this guy.

"No one in the room's gonna share any information with you. Even if they do know the guy you're looking for."

"Do you? Know the guy I'm looking for?"

"Good try." His lips quirked, just a little at the corner, drawing her attention to a scar that went from his mouth up his right cheek. *From a knife,* she thought. "But here's the thing. The reason no one's going to tell you anything is because I'll goddamn guarantee it that everyone here already knows about the snitches."

"And what snitches would that be?" Cait could feel Quinn glance over at her, but kept her attention directed toward the Marine.

"The ones who try to get you to share stuff." He shrugged. "Nightmares, feelings, things you might've done out on patrol. Always supposedly to cleanse the bad stuff." He heaped an extra helping of scorn on the word "cleanse." "Like it's not all bad stuff. But here's the deal. As soon as you admit to anything, the next thing you know, you're separated on an OTH discharge."

"OTH?"

"Other than honorable discharge. And you know what that gets you."

"What?" she asked, thinking back on what Quinn had suggested about the shooter.

"Squat." His hands, she noticed, had curled into fists at his sides. "Depending on how the VA decides to clear the case, you can end up risking your life for goddamn Uncle Sam only to get all your benefits stripped away."

"Is that what happened to you?"

The flash of fury faded from his eyes. His face was still stone, but he'd gone somewhere inside himself, revealing nothing of what he was feeling.

"We weren't talking about me. I was just saying, hypothetically, why you're wasting your time. Instead of trying to get guys who in no way are going to talk to you to spill their guts, you ought to be out there combing the streets and the marsh, looking for these guys."

The plural did not escape her notice. "What makes you think there's more than one?"

Again that little quirk of the lips. "Maybe, since the two of you seem so friendly, you ought to read McKade's book. Because, if you had, you'd know that snipers need spotters. Which means, Special Agent, you're talking about two guys."

Apparently deciding he'd shared enough, he did a military pivot turn and marched away, passing Quinn, who was headed toward Cait. But not looking at him, she noted. Instead, his eyes stayed directed straight ahead, a little above the rest of the men, who were gathered around the coffeemaker.

49

"You okay?" Quinn asked.

"Sure." Cait rubbed her arms, which had gone all goose-bumpy. "That is one unhappy Marine."

"I doubt you'll find that many guys in this room who aren't."

"True. But he sort of creeped me out, which isn't easy to do after all my years on the force. It was as if he could explode at any minute. I also think he had an OTH discharge."

"Not surprising. It's a handy way to keep veterans costs down."

She looked up at him. "You don't mean that."

He shrugged. "Hell, I gave up a long time ago trying to figure out government-think. But I do know that there are a lot of vets, including those who came back from 'Nam suffering from the effects of Agent Orange and or the Desert Storm vets who spent years trying to get the government to admit to Gulf War Syndrome, who don't exactly trust the people in control of the system."

"You realize, of course, that you're not being real encouraging here."

"Just telling it like it is," he said with a shrug.

"He also said that no one here will tell me anything about my shooter. Even if they know."

"Yeah. The snitch thing."

"You knew about that?"

"Sure."

"Then why didn't you say anything beforehand?"

"Would it have changed your mind about coming here?"

"No, but—"

"That's one reason why I didn't. The other reason is that just maybe, if you turn over enough rocks, you'll find the guy. This was one more logical place to try."

"I was thinking he might be in the room."

"Could've been."

"Because if he didn't show up for this meeting, wouldn't people notice?"

"Not at all," said Mike, who'd come over to them. "There's a reason we keep things anonymous. We're not the only PTSD group in the Lowcountry. People tend to go to the one that's most convenient, or where they feel most at home. Like that Marine you were talking with. He might come back. He might not. Maybe he'll get some help somewhere else, maybe he won't."

"Wow." Cait blew out a frustrated breath. "You two are sure a bundle of optimism."

"That day-at-a-time thing isn't just a cliché," the former priest said, sounding a bit as if he knew something about the subject firsthand. Which, given the brief story he'd told about his own battlefield experience, Cait suspected he did. "We can help people work the system, and we're finding that cognitive therapy, which is what Kristin Davis has been doing with group members, guiding them through the events they've experienced, can take them to a safer place, but in the end, recovery, such as it is, is up to the individual."

"I think that guy is a long way from getting over whatever's made him so angry," Cait murmured, watching through the window as the Marine climbed into a white van.

"You never really get over war," Mike said.

"But you can learn to live with it," Quinn said as

he took his cell phone, which had just buzzed, out of the pocket of his jeans.

"Hey, Zach," he said, after a glance at the caller ID. "What's up?" He listened for a moment. "Roger that." He picked up one of the cards Cait had left on the table and scribbled some numbers on the back. "We're on our way." He snapped the phone shut again and turned to Cait.

"They think they found the Altima."

"Where?"

"Out in the swamp."

"Is there anyone with it? Or was it ditched?"

"Since it's been burned, I'd say ditched. As for anyone being with it, they're leaving that for the authorities to check out." He handed her the card. "Here's the GPS coordinates."

Cait pulled out her own phone, called the location in, and said she was on her way to the scene.

"Dammit, that was the only thing we knew about him. Now we're back to zero."

"You never know," Quinn said, "Bad guys are like everyone else. They screw up. Maybe you'll find something he left behind."

"Maybe." She did not feel all that optimistic.

"I'm sorry I couldn't have been more help," Mike said as he walked them toward the door.

"Well, you can't tell what's going to turn out to be helpful," Cait said. "I didn't really expect anyone to raise their hand and volunteer in front of everyone. Maybe I'll still get a call."

"I'll pray that's so," Mike said. "Meanwhile, I'll probably see you tomorrow at the memorial at ASMA. Kristin has asked me to speak. And, of course, there's your niece's baptism day after tomorrow."

"Oh, shit." Cait slapped her hand over her mouth. Too late.

Her youngest sister, the one with the new Orphan Annie curls, had nearly died. As had the baby, who'd been born by C-section nearly two months early. This upcoming ceremony was an official reason for the entire family to celebrate. There was also the little fact that Cait had agreed to be her niece's godmother.

"Sorry," she said automatically, inwardly cringing at having cursed in front of a priest. Even a former priest.

"I've heard a lot worse," Mike said with a quick, sexy grin that had been a large part of the reason for his Father What-a-Waste nickname. "Said worse, too. You know, your mother will probably understand if you can't make it."

"No." She shook her head. "My mother will so *not* understand." Not after all Megan had been through. "I'll make it." Somehow.

"It'll be good for you," Mike suggested. "A moment of optimism during a difficult time."

And couldn't she definitely use that, Cait thought as she walked with Quinn out to his car.

The shooter had parked the van at the back of the lot, far from the glare of the lights. He sat behind the wheel, watching as the pair came out of the cathedral. There was a connection there that was more than professional. They were comfortable in each other's space. Yet at the same time he sensed a tension that suggested they hadn't yet acted on the chemistry sparking between them.

Special Agent Cait Cavanaugh was driven. That was damn sure. He suspected that, like the Tommy Lee Jones character in *The Fugitive,* the woman wouldn't stop until she got her man.

Which meant that he'd have to get her first.

50

"You knew the prayer," Quinn said as they drove out of town into the marsh.

Cait didn't ask what prayer he was referring to.

"I guess I failed to mention while I was drunkenly bemoaning my newly divorced state that I'd gone to some Al-Anon meetings. My ex was an alcoholic."

"That's tough." He also suspected it might have had something to do with why she'd been in such an uncharacteristically fragile state that night when she'd been fresh off the official end of her marriage.

"It wasn't easy. The irony that I went through a brief stint of overdrinking myself after the breakup has, by the way, not escaped me," she said, confirming his suspicions. "And, although I know we all have to take responsibility for our own actions, it wasn't entirely his fault. He was a nice guy—when he wasn't drinking—and a good person, who also happened to be a vice cop."

"Who, let me guess, stayed too long on the job."

"Yeah. He's in burglary and arson now. Which, although it's not exactly Disney World, is a lot better than hanging out in the vice sewer. He's been sober going on four years."

"Good for him."

"He remarried a couple years ago. They've got a toddler and another one on the way. They seem really happy." She paused. "Happier, I think, than he would've been with me."

"Don't you think that's being a little hard on yourself?"

"Not so much on myself, but I do think our situation contributed to our problems. His new wife's a kindergarten teacher. She reminds me a bit of Mary Poppins, which is probably just what he needs in his life. Murder," she said dryly, "doesn't make for the best pillow talk."

"Probably not. Yet I know this SEAL, Nick Broussard, who works for Phoenix Team. So does his wife, who used to be a Chicago homicide detective. They seem to be making it work."

"Good for them." She shrugged and pretended intense interest in the scene outside the passenger window.

"Sounds as if you're not a real fan of matrimony."

"I'm sure it's a fine institution. For people who want to spend their life in an institution," she said. Then sighed. "I'm sorry. That sounded really negative."

"You've had a rough couple of days."

"That's still no excuse to be so snarky. Especially since I've seen marriages work. My parents have been married thirty-six years."

"That's admirable."

"Yeah. How about yours?"

He paused. How much to tell? Obviously she'd been too busy with her shooter case to run a background check on him. Or maybe she just wasn't interested.

He was going to have to come clean. But, telling himself that she already had a lot on her mind, Quinn decided to hedge.

"My dad died when I was eight."

"That's too bad." She glanced back toward him. "He must have been fairly young. Was it an accident?"

"No." Not unless you considered it an accident that

had taken ten years to finally happen. Like a runaway freight train racing without brakes down the side of Mount Everest. "Actually, it was suicide."

Suicide by cop. Specifically FBI.

"I'm sorry."

She touched a hand to his arm, her fair skin a contrast to his dark. Although he knew it was only his imagination, Quinn imagined he could feel her touch, which was meant to soothe, branding his flesh.

"So was I."

"But your mother's still alive?"

"Yeah."

"Where does she live?"

Jesus. Cait Cavanaugh was obviously a detective all the way to the bone. The need to question everyone about every little thing was probably woven into her DNA, along with her blue eyes and bright hair.

"West Virginia."

"I've never been there. But I've heard it's beautiful country."

"So I hear."

"This is admittedly none of my business, but you haven't visited her?"

"She only moved there recently."

Which was the truth, since his sources had informed him she'd been transferred from the federal prison in Phoenix. Which he'd never visited either, because she'd insisted, from the day the FBI had taken her away in handcuffs, that she wanted him to forget she existed.

Like that was ever going to happen. Though he did quit writing to her the summer he turned eleven, after three years of weekly letters being returned to sender. A guy can take only so much rejection, after all.

Even from his mother.

Especially from his mother.

"Oh." She seemed to accept that. "I guess that's why you don't have an accent."

"Yeah. We moved around a lot while I was a kid."

"Well, I can certainly identify with that. Personally, I know people who like a constant change of scenery and lifestyle. But I hated it. How about you?"

"Like the plague," he agreed.

Then, deciding it was time to drop the subject before he found himself in over his head, he said, "You did good back there at the meeting."

"You couldn't tell my knees were shaking?"

"Not at all. I wouldn't hold my breath, but it's possible you might get some calls."

"I sure hope so. Oh, since you seemed to have assigned yourself to the role of my unofficial partner, you might as well know about a few other avenues I'm checking out."

Quinn knew that given her druthers, Cait would rather that the shooter had never shown up in Somersett. He could tell that she regretted the loss of life and was concerned about the little boy who'd given her the possible vehicle ID, and he agreed with her conclusion that so long as the kid's name didn't get out, he was probably not in any immediate danger. Especially since she'd said he hadn't seemed like the type to feel the need to brag about his part in the investigation all over his new school.

He could also tell that there was a part of Cait that was jazzed about being back in the action. Which made him wonder what his chances would be of recruiting her to work for Phoenix Team.

She might not have wanted to admit it, but they worked well together. Quinn sure wouldn't mind making their partnership official.

"May I ask a question?"

"Sure," he said, bracing himself for something personal.

"That bullet you wear around your neck? I assume there's a story behind it?"

"Yeah. Sorta. It started back in 'Nam with Marine scout snipers. The other troops in-country started calling the snipers pigs, because they ran around half shaven, with camouflage paint all over their faces, and their eyes perpetually bloodshot from lack of sleep. Instead of being insulted, they decided to claim the title, and since snipers never wear insignias on their uniforms, they started wearing a bullet on a chain around their necks as a badge of the profession."

"Snipers don't wear insignias?"

"No. Because they don't need that kind of recognition."

"Another reason my shooter might not be an actual sniper," she mused. "Given that he's obviously looking for notoriety."

"Exactly. It's a sniper's duty to work behind the scenes. And unlike a uniform ribbon or badge, you can decide whether or not you show a bullet."

"Like you did today. As a way of letting the other vets know your credentials without actually having to talk about them."

"Got it in one."

"But you're not a Marine."

"Thank God." He grinned. As grim as the subject was, Quinn realized he was actually enjoying himself. Enjoying being with her, whatever the circumstances that had brought them together. "Although the SEALs didn't pick up the practice, the army snipers eventually did."

He reached up and fingered the copper-clad bullet. "This belonged to a Marine who was on a mission with our team in Afghanistan. He gave it to me right before he died."

"That's nice, I guess. In a sad way."

And wasn't that an understatement? He'd only taken to wearing the bullet from the kid Zach had nicknamed Opie when he'd started writing the book based on the battle that had taken the young Marine's life. It kept him in the scene, which might be helpful for the writing but sure as hell hadn't done a lot for his peace of mind.

"He must have thought a lot of you," she said quietly. "To want you to have it."

Quinn wasn't sure, but he had the feeling that the story—which he hadn't intended to share with her, at least not until they nabbed this shooter and could move on to the personal aspect of their relationship—had softened whatever animosity she'd been hanging on to.

Which was, he decided, perhaps one positive thing to come out of that deadly clusterfuck in Afghanistan.

51

The crime scene, which was quickly becoming dotted with orange evidence flags, was lit up like Christmas. Along with the flashing red, white, and blue lights atop the various vehicles, ATF had brought out some klieg lights so bright Cait felt as if she was looking into the sun.

"The kid was right," she murmured, looking down at the charred corpse inside the burning hulk of galvanized steel. "It actually was an Altima."

"Not that we know yet that this vehicle has any connection to our shooter," the ever pessimistic Angetti, who'd somehow escaped phone duty and shown up from the JOC, pointed out.

"True. But it's one helluva coincidence if it doesn't."

"You can see the bullet hole," Drew Sloan pointed out. "In the right temple."

"An execution," Cait said.

"Obviously, despite all the evidence, I'm not about to officially call it as a homicide until I can get the guy into the morgue," the medical examiner said. "But it sure as hell would've been a tricky way to pull off a suicide."

"Light a fuse, climb inside the truck, and shoot yourself before the car catches on fire isn't exactly the easiest way to off yourself," John Tremayne said.

"He got rid of his spotter," Quinn murmured.

"From the bottles of liquor in the ashes of the

shack, the guy had probably become a liability," the ATF agent said.

"Probably went over the tipping point," Zach agreed. "Where he became more trouble than he was worth."

Cait shielded her eyes against the glare and turned to Sloan. "You can't get DNA from charred bones, can you?"

"Not usually from the bones themselves," he said. "But occasionally it's possible to extract it from marrow or connective muscle. But I doubt that'll be necessary in this case."

"Why not?"

He snapped on some latex gloves and tossed a second pair to the ATF guy standing next to the smoldering car. "Help me turn him over."

Cait watched as together they carefully lifted the body onto its left side.

"Wow." She stared down into the trunk. Not only was the carpet still unsinged, but the entire back of the dead man's naked body was intact. "How did you know that?"

The doctor grinned. "Saw it on *CSI.*"

"No shit?" Angetti asked.

"Actually, I picked it up during a class put on by the University of Tennessee's body farm and Oak Ridge National Lab."

"Cool," Quinn said. "Gross. But cool."

"We needed the guy to make a mistake," Cait said. "And lucky for us, it looks as if he may have just screwed up."

52

Although the Home Handi-Man parking lot, like most of the others in Somersett, was nearly deserted, the shooter parked the van far enough away from the automatic doors to stay out of the glare of the halogen lights.

He would have preferred for the store to be busier, which would've allowed him to blend into the crowd, but beggars couldn't be choosers, and besides, since the lack of customers in the building supply store was his fault, it wasn't like he had any right to bitch about the situation.

He strolled through the aisles, picking up several cans of white spray paint, a one-hundred-gallon heavy-duty plastic storage box with a tight-seal lid, a box of black industrial-strength trash bags, a hacksaw with a locking screw design for jab sawing, and three carbide grit blades. He doubted he'd need that many, since bone was a lot easier to saw through than steel, but like that drill instructor had kept screaming at him during boot camp, failure to prepare was preparing for failure.

He paid cash for his purchases, then drove to the same harbor-front Piggly Wiggly where he'd blown away that spic maid. Unsurprisingly, this store was even emptier than the Home Handi-Man had been. He picked up some bleach, a bottle of hydrogen peroxide, some sterile gauze, and tape. Then, as the manager went into the back to get the dry ice the shooter claimed to need for a Buccaneer Days party, he was treated to a breathless, play-by-play account of the shooting from the cashier.

"I just cannot believe such an evil thing happening right here in Somersett," she said. "Maybe New York City. Or Chicago. Or one of those other Northern cities." Her gray hair, sprayed to steel-helmet consistency, didn't move as she shook her head and clucked her tongue. "But this has always been such a safe, peaceful, family town."

She glanced around as if expecting to see armed assassins leaping up from behind a nearby larger-than-life cardboard cutout of a leering pirate.

"It's like nobody's safe anywhere, anymore."

"Unfortunately, I'm afraid you're right," the shooter said.

"Well." Her plump pigeon bosom puffed out as she drew in a deep breath. "Like I told my daughter, Brenda, this morning, when you've got serial killers on Swann Island, and snipers in Somersett, it's a sure sign of the Apocalypse."

"Next we'll be seeing four horsemen riding down Harbor Boulevard," the shooter agreed.

She nodded vigorously as the manager returned. "That's the very same thing I told Brenda."

He paid for the purchases and left the grocery store. He'd been a little bummed by having his schedule screwed up, first by Valentine Snow's report about the Altima, and second by Captain Jack, who hadn't gone easily, which was the reason for the first-aid supplies, to deal with the damn bullet wound in his shoulder.

But the idea that he'd had such an effect on an entire town lifted the shooter's spirits considerably.

Just wait, he thought, as he opened the back door of the white van, until they saw what he had planned for his next act.

53

"So, do you have time for that interview now?" Valentine approached Cait, microphone in hand and a cameraman in tow. "I figure this latest twist is really going to start freaking people out, so if you'd like to go on the air and reassure people that they should continue living their lives, we can make the eleven o'clock news."

As much as she hated interviews—Joe had always handled those when they'd partnered at SPD—Cait had to give credit to the newswoman for seeming to take a charred corpse in stride.

Plus, she did have a point. If they didn't handle this carefully, people could begin to panic. And the last thing any of them needed was for citizens to start arming themselves for protection. That was a sure way to end up with accidental shootings.

"You've got it," she agreed. "You've also got yourself a kitten."

The smile Val flashed was nearly as bright as the ATF's klieg lights. "Lucky for me my landlord allows pets."

Cait had the feeling the hunky pub owner would allow his tenant any little thing her heart desired.

"So, how's it going?" she asked, glancing over at Joe Gannon, who was standing nearby. His posture, as he leaned against the fender of the news van seemed casual enough, but she noticed that his eyes were constantly scanning the group, watching for anything that might pose a threat to his client. "With Joe?"

"He's very sweet. And very hot. If he wasn't already married, and I wasn't, well"—she paused, as if seeking the right word—"somewhat involved, I might consider hitting on him."

"You wouldn't be the first," Cait said.

And probably not the last, since Valentine was definitely right about him being hot. Cait figured a good percentage of the female population had gone into mourning when the former cop was taken off the marriage market.

The cameraman set Cait up far enough away from the car that late-night viewers wouldn't be subjected to the sight of a charred corpse right before bed. But he also allowed for a shot of the task force team swarming over the site and a long shot of the burned vehicle.

"Your nose is shiny," Valentine said.

"That's probably from the Vicks," Cait said. She'd learned the trick of rubbing VapoRub above her upper lip to mask the smell of death during her homicide days.

"Well, it'll look like hell on TV."

Valentine held out a tissue.

Cait sighed, obediently wiped it off, then, aware of Quinn watching her, felt like a fool as the newswoman swept some powder over her nose, chin, and cheeks with a soft black brush.

"I'm not trying out for *America's Next Top Model,*" she grumbled.

"You also want to get your message across. Which you can't do nearly as well if viewers are distracted by your glowing face," Valentine countered.

The newswoman swept a brush through her long dark hair, touched up her red lipstick, did a voice check for the cameraman, and began the interview.

"An unidentified victim has been found in the trunk of a burned car out in the marsh not far from Somersett," she informed the viewers, her expression appropriately serious. "Although members of the joint task force are still in the process of conducting an investigation, the car is thought to possibly have been used in the recent shootings in our city.

"I'm here with FBI Special Agent Caitlin Cavanaugh." The camera lens widened to include Cait. "Special Agent, I know from the calls and e-mails we've been receiving that people are concerned about their safety while this sniper is on the loose. We reported on our six o'clock newscast about a run on firearms and Tasers at local gun stores. What advice can you give our viewers?"

"The first is to remain calm," Cait responded. "The second is that more citizens carrying around guns on our city streets, or even in their homes, is not the answer. It's much more likely for someone to mistake a family member or other innocent person for a threat, which could result in a tragedy none of us want.

"For those viewers who've bought guns and have children in the homes, I'd remind them to make sure they use trigger locks. Which, if they didn't purchase with their weapon, they can pick up for free, without any required paperwork, at the Somersett Police Department."

The Program Child Safe was something Joe had lobbied the city council for funds for while he'd been on the force, and although there was no way to prove its effectiveness, there hadn't been a single accidental shooting in Somersett since its inception.

"Do you advise staying indoors until this shooter is apprehended?"

Cait welcomed the softball question that allowed her to address people's fears.

"I understand how some people might consider that an option, but it's extreme. And a difficult way to live. Obviously we have a situation right now where any public venue risks becoming a potential shooting event. One of the safest things people can do is to go about their normal lives, while thinking about shaving minutes from the time they're exposed in any target zone."

"And how would you suggest doing that?"

"Well, for instance, instead of buying an entire week's worth of groceries, which involves time putting several bags into your car, park close to the store and buy just what you need for that day."

"The snipers in Washington, D.C., shot several victims at gas stations," Valentine said. "I've spoken with service station operators who say their business is down seventy-five to ninety percent over the last twenty-four hours."

"I'm not surprised, but there are some methods for handling that as well. Rather than stand next to your car while pumping the gas, lock in the hands-free mechanism on the nozzle. Then go into the store to pay, rather than using the credit card option at the pump. This should cut your exposure time from five or six minutes to a minute and a half."

"And every minute saved is a minute tipped in your favor," Val said.

"Exactly."

"What do you advise people to do if they happen to be somewhere a shooting event happens?"

"If they happen to be by a car, duck down in the front, beside the tire."

"It seems there'd be more coverage behind the middle of the car."

"The front is better, because of the heaviness of the engine block, which makes it more difficult for a bullet to penetrate," Cait said. "Be patient. Resist the urge to look up, because all you'll do is garner attention.

"Also, it's important for everyone to be proactive. If you see something suspicious, make a note of it right away. Because if events do suddenly unfold, you won't have time to document details, and you may, in the heat of the moment, forget what you've seen.

"We're definitely not advising citizens to risk their lives attempting to capture this shooter or shooters.

Just the opposite. But we do need everyone to be thinking about not just his or her own safety, but being a good witness as well. So we can apprehend this suspect and we can all get back to living our normal, everyday lives."

"Thank you, Special Agent Cavanaugh, for that helpful advice."

Valentine turned her most serious look to the lens as the camera moved in for a close-up. "This is Valentine Snow, for WBUC, reminding viewers to stay alert. And stay alive."

As the camera lights switched off, Val groaned. "God, that sounded so corny."

"Well, it's not a bad thought," Cait said, even though she somewhat agreed that it sounded a bit over the top.

"Well, if it manages to save even a single life, it'll be worth sounding like a small-market moron," Val decided.

They didn't speak much on the way back to town. Quinn figured Cait was thinking about the grisly crime scene, which had reminded him of too many of the things he'd witnessed during his years in the military.

Amazingly, even through the odor of death that they were both carrying on their clothes, he could smell her piña colada hair.

"Something funny?" she asked, making him realize he'd been smiling. Which, under the circumstances, was undoubtedly inappropriate.

"It's your hair."

"My hair?" She might be a tough-as-nails special agent, but she still possessed enough feminine vanity to lift a hand to the red spiral curls.

"It still smells great."

"Well." She lifted her arm and sniffed at her jacket sleeve. "If that's truly the case, it's probably the only part of me that doesn't stink. I can't wait to get into the shower."

The mental image of her wet, naked, and slick with soap created a spike of lust. "That makes two of us."

The only light was the soft glow from the dashboard, but that didn't keep him from noticing the way she narrowed her eyes at that, as if wondering exactly how he meant the murmured comment.

"We should have taken two cars," she said. "So you wouldn't have to drive all the way back out to the marsh again tonight."

"As it happens, I'm staying in the city."

"Really? Why?"

"Because my house is going to be overrun with Tremayne Construction crews."

"Ah. About time."

"I just needed the right motivation." Like the thought of getting Cait into a real bed beneath the skylight John Tremayne was going to cut into the bedroom roof.

"Hmm." She didn't say anything, but he could tell when she was thinking, and he suspected her thoughts had moved from that dead body and burned car.

"Will you be able to get a hotel room? This time of year?"

"Look around." Harbor View, which was one of the busiest streets in the city on any night, but more so during Buccaneer Days, was so deserted Quinn figured it'd be possible to shoot a cannon down the street without hitting anyone. "Seems the town's pretty much emptied out."

"Worrying about getting shot tends to take some of the fun out of partying," she muttered as he pulled up in front of her apartment building and cut the engine.

She turned toward him.

"You know, there's no point in your wasting your money on a hotel room."

He paused as he pulled the key out of the ignition. *Don't screw this up.*

"Is that an invitation?"

She shrugged. "It's been a stressful couple of days. You're the one who suggested a remedy."

"Yeah. I seem to recall saying something like that." Although it had been only a few hours ago, it seemed like a lifetime.

The thing to do, he decided, was just to lay his cards out on the table. She might shoot him down, but hey, no risk, no reward.

Got any more clichés, McKade? he asked himself.

"But here's the deal. I think I've sorta changed my mind," he heard himself saying.

"Oh." Her entire body stiffened. "Well, that's certainly your privilege."

"It's not that I don't still want you," he said.

"And here's where I admit I want you," she said. "So, what's changed?"

"I've waited a long time for a rematch," he said. "And I came to the conclusion, driving out to the marsh, that if we're going to have a round two, I want a commitment."

"A commitment?" She looked at him as if he'd admitted to being her sniper. "What, like you want to go steady? Maybe have me wear your SEAL class pin on my cheerleader sweater?"

"That wasn't what I had in mind." Though the idea of Cait in a short, tight, midriff-baring cheerleader outfit definitely caused another spike of lust. "I probably do have my trident stashed away somewhere, if you'd like it. But I've decided I don't want to just be the guy you fuck as a brief escape from this case. If we go to bed, I want some intimacy."

Her expression revealed the same surprise he would have felt if someone had suggested this situation to him only two days ago.

"Granted, it's been a while since I've had sex," she said. "But unless things have suddenly changed, getting naked usually means intimacy."

"True. But there are different kinds of intimacy. I'm talking about the whole ball of wax."

She tilted her head. Studied him with serious, guarded eyes. "Actually, it sounds a lot more like a ball of strings."

"Use whatever metaphor you want." A muscle ticked in his jaw. "But if you want my body, Special Agent, you're going to have to take the entire package."

She skimmed a long, slow look over him.

"It's not a bad package, so, sure, I can live with that."

"I'm not just talking about my body or what fits where." Though he remembered them fitting together really, really well.

"What? Like a relationship?"

Why was it that a word that had always given him hives suddenly seemed unreasonably attractive?

"Something like that, I guess. Like I said earlier, I've never been real big on sharing, and I damn well refuse to share you."

"Well." She glanced out the passenger-side door window at the empty sidewalk. "I suppose that means I'll have to send that long line of would-be suitors extending down the block home."

"I'm not joking."

"No." Cait blew out a long, labored sigh, turned back toward him, and subjected him to a searching look. "I can see you're not. The thing is, I don't understand."

"Join the club."

"As you said earlier, I'm probably the last woman on the planet you should go to bed with."

There was an underlying hurt in her tone that once again told Quinn he was going to have to come clean with her. Because it appeared she'd taken his words personally. And why shouldn't she have? Since she had no way of knowing his checkered past.

"Though it really doesn't have all that much to do with you, but with some stuff in my past, that's what I said, all right."

"Then why—?"

"I don't fucking know, okay?" He swiped a hand through his hair. "What I do know is that there probably isn't a guy on this planet who wouldn't run over his dog for some hot, uncomplicated sex with you."

She arched a brow. At the same time a slight smile curved her lips. "That's a vast overstatement, but the idea works for me. Except for the running-over-the-dog part."

"Okay. That was a bad analogy. And if someone had told me even last week that you were up for some hot, mindless sex, I would've been fighting off every guy in the Lowcountry to make sure I was at the front of the line."

Quinn was confused. And he didn't like the feeling. He also decided that if Zach or Shane ever found out about this idiotic need for honesty, when nirvana was waiting for him right upstairs in Cait's apartment, he'd never live it down.

"But something's changed, and no, I don't know why it did, or what the hell we're going to do about it, but I figure the only right thing to do is to let you know where I stand."

"Well." She glanced down at her hands. Began twisting a knotted silver ring she wore on the index finger of her right hand. "Thanks. I think."

"Do you have any idea how many women I've slept with trying to get over you?"

Her eyes met his. "No."

"Neither do I." And wasn't that the truth? "But here's another thing, since I seem to be determined to make a damn fool out of myself. It didn't work."

"Well," she said again. Quinn figured there weren't that many times Caitlin Cavanaugh had been at a loss for words.

As the sexually charged silence spun around them, and his body shouted at him to just shut up and grab the woman and do what they both wanted to do, she finally said, "It appears we have two choices."

"I guess so."

What the hell had he been thinking?

Her eyes gleamed like blue neon as they swept over his face, moving down his body, lingering for a moment on the boner that was pressing painfully against the damn metal buttons of his 501s, which was one of the downsides of going commando.

Then her gaze returned to his.

"We can risk getting arrested by ripping each other's clothes off right here and now. Or we can try to summon enough restraint to hold off until we get upstairs."

When she touched a finger to the tip of her tongue and trailed it around his mouth, Quinn was amazed his skin didn't sizzle.

"Where," she said, as she continued the stroking touch, down his chest, then, Sweet Jesus, lower, "I intend to have my way with you. And this time I'm going to remember every dirty detail."

His lungs clogged. His hands, which could take a rifle apart and put it back together again in seconds, began to sweat. He wouldn't have been surprised to see his palms grow hair.

She lifted both her hands, framing his face. Her smile somehow managed to be both sweet and incredibly hot at the same time. "And I promise to respect you in the morning."

When she pulled his suddenly dry mouth down to hers, Quinn was lost.

54

Quinn wanted to carry Cait up the stairs to her apartment like a conquering warrior. No, he thought, as he felt his heart tumble, then soften, he wanted to lift her into his arms, as he had that first night, when, over her breathless, laughing protests, he'd carried her down the long hallway to his hotel room.

He settled instead for merely keeping his hand on her slender hip as they climbed the stairs together. In his other hand he carried his rucksack and a garment bag with the dress uniform he'd picked up from that very same Vietnamese dry cleaner where the Stocktons' maid had retrieved her employer's uniform before continuing to the fatal encounter at the Piggly Wiggly.

He'd also brought along his laptop, though she suggested that with all she had in mind for him, he wouldn't have a whole lot of time for writing.

Every atom in his body was up—literally—for whatever plans she could come up with.

And this time there'd be no drinking to cloud her mind and his judgment.

No sooner were they in the pretty living room than he cupped her chin in his palm. His thumb brushed her lips. "I want you to be very sure about this."

Her lips parted at his stroking touch. "Yes," she said, the word expelled on a breath of ragged need.

He needed no further invitation. His mouth captured hers, crushing, conquering, as he pulled her tight against him.

His teeth, scraping over her lower lip, dazed her. His mouth, as he drank deeply from hers, stole the breath from her lungs.

Cait swayed as her body softened, fitting her curves to the rigid lines of his body. Her nipples pressed against his chest; his stony erection was huge against her belly.

Her body came alive as never before; her nerves sparked, her blood ran hot in her veins, her temperature rose, heating her flesh.

Even as she tried to tell herself that it was only raw chemistry that had her responding to him, deep down inside she knew it was something much more elemental.

Even more than the irresistible pull of a female to a male, more than the need to have him inside her, as much as she'd fought it, from that first moment she'd seen him, looking too large, and too hot, and way too dangerous to her mind and her future, Cait had felt herself engulfed in a flood of acceptance.

Not just acceptance that she was about to fall off the celibacy wagon. But acceptance of the knowledge that once she had sex with Quinn, her life would inexorably, forever change.

"I was in Central America a few years ago," he murmured against her hair. "On an undercover mission."

As his hands cupped her breasts, his thumbs brushing against her painfully taut nipples, Cait's mind was screaming for him to just shut up and *do* it.

"There was this woman—Svetlana—who ran a beachfront cantina where all the Special Forces guys who were down there training rebel troops used to hang out. We had U.S. teams there, and the Russians had their Spetsnaz guys. That's their version of Spec Ops.

"There was even a handful of British SAS agents around. Svetlana was a real friendly woman. To everyone. I doubt there was a guy in uniform she wasn't more than happy to go to bed with. I also doubt there was anyone who didn't know she was a Russian secret agent."

"That didn't bother you? Sleeping with the enemy, so to speak?"

He shrugged. "Sex was sex. I knew she was working me. She knew I was working her. Besides, she was giving us as much information as she was Ivan."

"She was a double agent?"

"Hell, Svetlana would do double, triple, whoever paid her. In U.S. dollars."

"Which meant her information probably wasn't very reliable," Cait guessed, wondering if he was using the terminology to describe her spying. Or her screwing around.

Had Quinn been involved in a sexual double? Maybe with one of Svetlana's friends? A tall, slinky, double-jointed blonde named Anastasia?

He'd said he refused to share. Suddenly Cait understood the feeling—she hated the idea of him having sex with any other woman. Even if had been for flag and country.

Yeah. Right. He'd obviously forced himself to get it up in the name of patriotism. To keep people like her safe on the homefront.

And she was Lara Croft, Tomb Raider.

"We were drinking in this cantina on the oceanfront. I stuck to tequila, but she was drinking frozen piña coladas. And even though I kept trying to focus on the mission, which was to infiltrate a terrorist cell, all I could think about was you."

Her breath caught. If it had been any other man telling her this, she would have thought he was feeding her a line. But she knew Quinn was telling the truth.

"Maybe you've been hanging out with SEALs too long," she said, as he pulled her blouse free and bunched it in his fist, "if you consider telling one woman you're about to get naked with a story about you getting drunk and having hot beach sex with another to be foreplay."

"That's my point." His fingers splayed across her bare abdomen while his thumbs brushed against ultra-sensitive nipples. "I blew the mission because I couldn't get it up."

Revealing a familiarity with female clothing, he unfastened the front closure of her bra with a deft click of the wrist, while the tip of his tongue skimmed a hot, damp trail around her ear.

"Well, that's encouraging."

He surprised her by laughing at that. Then his long fingers caught her wrist and pressed her palm against the front of his jeans. He was hot and hard and huge. It was all she could do not to drop to her knees right there on her living-room floor and rip open those metal buttons and take him in her hands, and her mouth, and . . .

"I think you can tell that isn't going to be a problem tonight." He pinched a nipple between the thumb and fingers of his free hand, making her go all liquid inside. "The thing is, the minute the bartender delivered that damn drink with the umbrella in it, all I could think about was you. How your hair smelled. How you turned me inside out. And how I wanted to track you down and have you again."

He shoved his hand into the waistband of her slacks, between her panties and her hot flesh and pushed a finger deep inside her. "And again."

Cait's head fell back as her body clutched at him. She heard a ragged moan and realized it had come from her own suddenly parched throat.

"I need a shower," she managed.

Maybe her hair smelled like a tropical drink, but she feared the rest of her smelled of smoke and burned flesh. And since this time she planned to remember every moment of the night, she wanted it to be perfect.

"Works for me," he said agreeably, scooping her up into his arms. "So, where's the bathroom?"

55

He stood her up again on a plush rug the color of ripe grapes. Reached behind her, opened the glass door, and turned on the tap.

Flashes of the last time they'd been together suddenly sparked in Cait's mind, and she realized that it had indeed been she who'd ripped off the dress, peeled down the pantyhose, taking her panties with them, and, wearing only the strapless corset with the painful boning that had been digging into her skin for the previous eight hours, literally leaped into his arms, wrapping her legs around his waist as she'd practically raped him.

She also remembered him trying to turn her down as her mouth had eaten into his. But she'd been drunk and determined to get laid, and he'd been, after all, a SEAL. And not only that, a SEAL who'd slept with a Russian spy named Svetlana.

Because, after all, as he'd said, sex was sex.

Which was why it hadn't taken him that long to throw in the towel. So to speak.

"It's not," she murmured as he unbuttoned the blouse that was clinging to her too hot skin.

"What's not?" Since her bra was still unfastened, he was able to slide them both off her shoulders and down her arms, where they pooled on the floor at her feet.

"Sex." She sucked in a breath as his hands got busy on her belt, unfastening it and pulling it slowly, insinuatingly, through the loops, in a way that had it been any other man but Quinn, Cait might have found a bit threatening. "It's not just sex."

The sound of the zipper on her slacks lowering was unnaturally loud. So loud she could hear it over the rush of the water flowing behind her in the shower.

"At least, not all the time."

"No." His thumbs snagged the low waistband of her panties. "Definitely not this time." She leaned her head back and closed her eyes as he drew the slacks and panties down her legs.

The crotch of the panties was soaked. She wondered if he'd notice.

He did.

"Do you have any idea," he said as his mouth touched hers, holding back his need to take, keeping the kiss gentle. Tender. "What it does to me to know that you want me as much as I want you?"

She laughed softly, the sound a sexy blend of humor, surrender, and pleasure. "Unless you've taken to wearing your weapon in the front of your jeans instead of the back, I have a clue." She skimmed her fingertips over the raging hard-on, the same way she had in the car. "As a detective, I'm very good at reading clues."

"Not that I doubt your skills, having seen you in action, but I believe even Inspector Clouseau could read that one."

"Well." She unfastened the first metal button. Then the second. The third. "I suppose it is a bit more noticeable." The fourth. "And substantial." Thank the good Lord, she finished with the fifth. And he wasn't wearing anything beneath the jeans.

Slipping free of his arms, she went down on her knees on the rug and slowly drew the jeans down over Quinn's bare hips.

"And ever so much larger than your average"—her fingers curled around his length and she began stroking him, from root to painfully swollen tip—"clue."

He sucked in a harsh breath when she leaned forward and gathered in a drop of moisture from the cleft with a swirl of her tongue.

"You make me want things." His voice was rough, more groan than words as he swelled in her hand. "Hot things." He cupped her butt with his hands and squeezed. "Pelvis-grinding, dirty, blow-your-mind things."

"Well." He nearly wept when she leaned back on her heels, breaking the glorious contact of her mouth on his cock. "Don't let me stop you."

He grabbed her hair, urging her back to her feet. They kicked off shoes, and later, although he wouldn't remember how, the socks went flying, too. One of them landed in the sink. The other he wouldn't find until the next morning, behind the toilet.

Pausing just long enough to pull out one of the rubbers he'd stuck in the pocket of his jeans, he yanked her beneath the stream of hot water. Or maybe she pulled him. More likely, he thought, as he crushed his mouth to hers, hot and hungry and hurried, they pulled each other.

Quinn had never used his superior strength on a woman before. But, after tossing the condom packet onto the rack next to a white bottle of that shampoo he'd never been able to get out of his mind, he used it now to press her against the tile at the back of the stall, while his thumbs traced the fold between her smooth thighs and her crotch.

"Oh, God," she managed, her voice as slurred as it had been that night. But this time it wasn't alcohol making her nearly incoherent. It was desire. For him.

He pressed his palm against her pubis. Drew a long, shuddering sigh from her lips as she arched her back, beyond words now, but urging him to take more.

Which he did.

He lowered her to the tile seat built into the corner

of the stall, then knelt in front of her, just as she'd done to him. He used his palms to spread her legs apart, then bit the inside of her smooth, wet thigh—just hard enough to make her tremble.

Then, parting the slick pink folds with his fingers, he clamped his mouth onto her.

He brought her to a peak, with lips and teeth and tongue. She cried out, bucked against him, then went so limp, if he hadn't been holding her, she might have slid bonelessly to the floor.

"Wow. When you're right, you're right," she said. Her head was back against the tile, her eyes closed, her lips parted.

"About what?" He stroked her thighs, frowned a bit as he noticed the bruise. But at the same time he couldn't feel all that guilty about having marked her.

Branded her. And wouldn't that get her temper up if she knew that thought had just flashed through his brain?

"About sex being a good stress reliever." She grinned and combed her fingers through his wet hair as the water continued to pelt down on them. "I'm feeling better already."

"Told you." He grinned back.

Quinn decided that watching Cait as she watched him roll the thin latex over his penis was one of the sexiest things he'd ever seen. Her eyes gleamed, and when she unconsciously licked her bottom lip with the tip of her tongue, he felt himself on the verge of losing it.

"I wanted to take my time," he said, even as he lifted her off her feet.

"Next time." She scissored her long legs around his hips. "Right now I think I'm going to die if I can't feel you inside me." Despite their difference in height, they were crotch to crotch.

"Roger that." Because the need to be inside her had become unbearable for him, he gripped her hips and surged into her, filling her with one deep stroke.

Then paused. Partly to let her become accustomed to his size, but mostly because the shock of pleasure was so hard and so strong, it almost knocked him off his feet.

Lowering his head, his mouth found her wet breast. He suckled deeply, feeling the convulsions surrounding him as she lifted her hips with each downstroke, meeting him thrust for thrust, and this time, when she climaxed around him, her inner muscles clutching at him like a greedy fist, rather than holding back as he'd planned, Quinn surrendered, giving in to his own release.

56

The shooter had gotten the idea from the episode of *The Sopranos* where, after Tony had whacked Ralphie, he and his nephew had cut the mobster's head and hands off to prevent identification if the body washed up.

Not that he intended to get rid of Captain Jack's body quite yet, because he still had tomorrow's bloodfest to plan for, but anything that would cause the cops to divide their forces was, in his view, a good thing.

Fortunately, the town had emptied out, making it easy to rent a motel room in one of the hot-sheet places across the county line. The V in the VACANCY sign had burned out, but it still managed to get the point across.

One major advantage to the place was that the desk clerk, a kid with piercings in his nose and eyebrows, was too busy blowing people away on his PSP to pay all that much attention.

"Fifty bucks for a hour," he said. His acne-pitted face didn't glance up from the *Grand Theft Auto* mayhem taking place on the small black rectangular screen. "Two Ben Franklins for the night."

Irritation spiked. The shooter knew that lack of control was both a regrettable and an often risky flaw in his personality, but that didn't stop him from arguing the price. "Last time I was here it was one."

The kid shrugged bony shoulders draped in an oversized black Megadeth T-shirt depicting a shark rising out of the flames of hell. "It's Buccaneer Days." On the screen a gangbanger had just shot a cop in the head and stolen a police car. "You never hear of supply and demand?"

The shooter refrained, just barely, from pointing out that if there'd been any demand, the parking lot wouldn't be nearly deserted and there wouldn't be any goddamn room to rent out in the first place. Then he reminded himself that the desk clerk's lack of interest tended to be run-of-the-mill for such hooker havens, which is why the shooter had chosen it. Like it wasn't as if he could drag a body unnoticed through the gilt lobby of the Wingate Palace.

He handed over the money in exchange for a pair of thin, yellowed sheets and a single equally threadbare towel that might once have been white but was now a dingy shade of gray.

He chose a room at the far end of the row of outer blue doors, then, after dragging the dead Marine out of the van, he held him upright, making it appear, if anyone did happen to glance out a window, that a queer guy on a bender had gone shopping for some back-door sex.

He carried the captain into the bathroom, stripped off his clothes, and dumped him in the bathtub, just as Tony had done with Ralphie.

Not wanting to get an infection, he took some time to clean the wound from the graze he'd gotten when the Marine, who'd caught on to the fact that he was about to lose his van, and maybe his life, had grabbed hold of the KA-BAR knife just before it had plunged into his heart.

The shooter sucked in a sharp breath as the peroxide bubbled and stung. Then after taping the gauze over the cut, he stripped off his own clothes, got out his bloodied KA-BAR again and the hacksaw and had just started when a loud banging interrupted his work.

At first he thought it was the cops at the door. Fuck. He'd known it'd been a mistake to go to that meeting at the church. But he'd have risked more trouble taking the chance on being missed. He'd been between a fucking rock and a hard place and, as he had his entire life, he'd taken the hard.

But the banging wasn't on the door. It was the bed in the room next door slamming against the wall to the accompaniment of bedsprings and the sound of a man shouting, "Ride the Blackbeard's sword, you fucking cock-sucking wench!"

From the giggle high enough to shatter glass, the shooter guessed that the sword-riding wench wasn't insulted by the description.

A shouted, "Aaaagh!" signaled the pirate's release.

There was the sound of a toilet flushing. One that continued to run long after the bowl would've emptied. Despite the city's no-smoking-in-indoor-places law, the shooter heard a match strike.

Then the TV came on, with the unmistakable bass beat of a porn flick. Obviously Blackbeard and his rent-by-the-hour wench were taking an intermission before getting on to the next round.

Which left the shooter free to go back to work.

Thanks to the carbide blade, which cut through flesh as if it were butter, it didn't take that long. The job was bloody, but that was why Captain Jack was in the tub.

Once he finished, he stuffed the head and hands into separate trash bags, then loaded them, along with the torso, arms, and legs, into the container, surrounding it with the dry ice.

The plan was to dump the body in the marsh. The head and hands in the ocean. That way, even if the various parts did escape getting eaten by gators, sharks, and fish, good luck on the cops' ever managing to put the pieces of Humpty Dumpty together again.

"Meanwhile," he said, chuckling at his own cleverness, "I'll keep the captain on ice."

He drained the tub, ran the shower into it, watching the blood swirl down the drain. Then he took a shower himself, making sure to scrub between his toes, and rubbing the bar of soap against his chest, where droplets of blood might have been caught.

As the pair next door began doing it again—with Blackbeard assuring the wench that she could suck the white off rice—he splashed the bleach over the tub, the same way Tony had instructed Christopher to do after they'd dismembered that poor fuck Ralphie, and sent it, too, washing away.

After getting dressed again, he dragged the container back into the van. Then drove off to the oversized storage locker he'd rented to keep his guns in.

He pulled into the locker, took out the cans of spray paint, and within fifteen minutes, had covered up the jumping fish logo on the van.

With his mission accomplished, the shooter was smiling as he loaded his cache of weapons into the now plain white van.

57

Quinn was not an inflexible guy. Hell, that's what he'd always liked about being a SEAL; as carefully as you might plan a mission, something always happened that required you to change.

The ability to adapt was what made a SEAL different from the pack. It was what he'd always prided himself on.

So. Thanks to those tangos' RPG, the team now had a change of mission. No sweat.

Except, humping up a two-thousand-meter climb in what was rapidly becoming a whiteout definitely was living up to the SEAL motto that the only easy day was yesterday.

The high elevation was searing the men's lungs. Others were throwing up, which only added to their dehydration.

But they continued on, snow and sleet stinging their faces, forging their way up the mountain, every man aware that a single misstep could send him tumbling hundreds of feet into the dark crevasses below.

And then things got worse.

The snow stopped falling. The sun came out, blindingly bright, and before long they were literally baking inside their ceramic bulletproof vests.

"We've got to dump some of the weight," Zach said.

"A few of the Rangers have asked permission to take their backplates out," Quinn said.

"Shit." Zach glared up at the sun. "I knew this was going to be a clusterfuck from the get-go." He yanked off his helmet and dragged his hand through the hair he'd kept long to blend into the population.

He stopped, held up a hand. Since he was the most senior officer still alive, the responsibility for getting the men who'd survived the initial crash and battle out of here alive fell on his shoulders.

"Okay," Zach said. "Here's the deal. Those who want to take your backplates out, do it now."

One of the young soldiers didn't hesitate. He pulled off his vest, took out the backplate, and hurled it down the mountainside.

The others followed suit.

"Those are the most expensive damn Frisbees they'll ever throw," Quinn said to his friend.

"And watch us get our ass chewed for losing them," Zach said.

With the loads lessened, they continued on, reaching a grouping of mud huts. The population of the small village had evacuated so suddenly that many of the residents had left their small stoves burning. Shifting columns of dark smoke rose into the morning sky.

"This isn't good," Quinn said, scanning the village and the mountains beyond.

"Why don't you tell me something I don't know?" Zach countered.

He instructed the troops to go through the huts and gather as many weapons as they could find. Though this was the most heavily armed region in the world, there weren't as many as he'd hoped, but both men figured that any gun that wasn't going to be aimed at them could only be a good thing.

"We've got something," Sax Douchett, Quinn's longtime spotter, said. He'd always had the best eyes on the team, able to see like a hawk even without a scope. "I just saw the sun glinting off an object at two o'clock."

Quinn turned slowly, appearing not to be zeroing in on any one particular spot. He also began moving around, just in case he happened to be in any enemy sniper's spot.

"Could be binoculars," Sax said.

"Or a rifle barrel." Which Quinn figured was more likely, given their circumstances.

"Well, we can wait to find out," Sax said.

"Or we can go after the guy before he comes after us," Quinn said.

"Roger that," Sax said.

One problem with being taller than your average SEAL was that it was really hard to just disappear into the landscape. Especially a landscape as bleak and empty as this one.

Strolling with apparent nonchalance in case he was being observed, he went into one of the huts, where he found a pair of the baggy trousers and shirts men in this part of the mountains wore.

Since the owner had to have been a good foot shorter, and fifty pounds lighter, there was no way they'd fit Quinn. But he didn't plan on wearing them anyway. Using his KA-BAR, he cut them into strips. Then took a second pair and did the same thing.

SEALs might be prepared for anything, but they didn't tend to carry sewing kits with them.

No problem, though, since Lucas Chaffee did.

Using a pair of needle holders and gut suture—fortunately the always overprepared medic had brought along a shitload of the stuff—and some superglue, he created ghillie suits for both himself and Sax.

Needing a distraction, Zach instructed the Rangers to torch two of the huts. On one level Quinn regretted destroying anyone's home, but the cache of AK-47s, grenades, and handguns left behind suggested that these weren't exactly the homes of the local Welcome Wagon greeters.

Using the distraction, he and Sax slipped out of the village, their white suits blending into the sun-glistening snowfields. Although both men were wearing their blue shades, Quinn could only hope that the sun was proving as much of a distraction for the tangos as it was for him.

Unfortunately, the bad guys not only knew this terrain a lot better than Quinn did, but they also had a head start.

Quinn and Sax humped up the mountain, the frigid air still and silent except for the crunch of their snowshoes on the ice and snow and the sound of their breathing, which, despite all the hours of PT that had them in beyond excellent aerobic condition, still wasn't easy at this elevation.

Although he never would have made the mistake of saying it out loud, Quinn had just thought So far, so good, *when bullets began pinging off rocks and kicking up snow.*

He and Sax hit the ground as one. Crawled on their bellies, more bullets hitting all around them, behind a boulder.

Quinn lifted his rifle and scanned the area above them in a long sweep, found the guy hidden behind some trees that had fallen behind a snowdrift.

Obviously the shooter thought he was invisible to the naked eye. Which he was, but he'd made the common mistake of confusing concealment with cover, assuming that being hidden would protect him.

Like a bullet couldn't slice through some damn tree branches and snow?

"Give me a check," he said to Sax.

The spotter shot the laser. "Thirteen hundred and fifty-seven yards. Wind's north, northeast about three miles per hour. Five minutes to the left."

Which made it no factor.

There were all sorts of intricate formulas Quinn kept in the journal he never went on a mission without. But any sniper worth his rifle could do the equations in his head.

Motion. Distance. Weather. Angle and speed of the bullet.

All flashed instantaneously through his mind as he

braced against the boulder, leaned into the stock of the rifle, looking through the scope with his right eye and dialing in the focus ring until the guy and his trees stood out in sharp relief.

He could've been starring on Quinn's own personal HDTV.

He locked the crosshairs on the guy.

Time slowed. Quinn's eyesight sharpened. He could hear the faint sound of the wind in the top of the few trees that managed to grow this high up in the mountains, imagined he could even hear some distant conversations, but tuned them out. They weren't important.

Even his sense of smell became heightened as he inhaled the tang of fir and a cigarette and wood smoke on the wind.

The five S's of the sniper's mantra, which he'd repeated a thousand times in training, in real life echoed in his mind: slow, smooth, straight, steady squeeze.

He took a breath. Partially exhaled.

Then gently, with the same practiced skill he would use to bring a woman to climax, Quinn pulled the trigger.

The bullet exploded from the rifle with a muzzle velocity of more than 2,550 feet per second. Although he knew there were those who'd say it was impossible, Quinn's senses were so heightened he could actually see the vapor trail of the bullet leaving the rifle.

An instant later it exploded the guy's chest, spinning him around.

"Got him," Sax said.

"There'll be another."

Without lowering the rifle, Quinn worked the bolt with the thumb and two fingers, ejected the spent cartridge, and loaded a fresh round.

Sure as hell, a guy came out from what appeared to be a cave cut into the side of the mountain and stared down at the dead shooter.

"He's dead," Sax said.

"Just doesn't know it yet," Quinn agreed, even as

the guy raised his own rifle, scanning the snowfields in their direction.

Inhale. Exhale.

Count it out.

One.

Two.

Three pounds of pressure on the trigger.

Through the scope he saw his target's black eyes locked on him.

The brief flicker of surprise that showed on the craggy, weather-hewn face cost the tango his life as Quinn eased back on the trigger, then nailed him where he stood.

Before Sax had time to congratulate him on the hit, at least a dozen men came tearing out of the cave, AK-47s blazing, looking as crazy as a swarm of mosquitoes kamikazing around a bug zapper.

58

Just as had happened the last time they'd been together, Cait woke up alone. But this time, rather than needing to escape, she would've preferred to have Quinn sprawled beside her, his leg heavy over hers.

There was a strange, soft clicking she wasn't used to hearing coming from the next room. She paused a moment, then realized that it was the sound of a computer keyboard.

She climbed out of bed, snagged her terry robe from the back of the closet door, and went out into the living room, where, in the reflected lights from the Somersett bridge and the illumination from his computer monitor, she saw Quinn, clad only in the jeans they'd ripped off him earlier, sitting alone in the dark.

Surprisingly, given what she'd learned about a sniper's heightened senses, he didn't seem to realize she'd come into the room. She padded barefoot over to the table where he'd set up his laptop, touched a hand to his shoulder, and jumped back when he leaped up, knocking over the chair.

"Shit." He dragged that wide hand that earlier had created such glorious havoc on her body down his face. "I'm sorry."

"I'm the one who should apologize. Sneaking up on you that way."

"I'm a SEAL." He bent down and picked up the

chair. "No one's supposed to be able to sneak up on me."

"A former SEAL," she reminded him. "Who seemed to be somewhere else."

"Yeah. Try hell."

"I'm sorry."

She was not going to press. Nor was she going to allow herself to so much as peek at that screen to see what he'd been writing. But she was curious as hell.

"You know those guys? The ones at the meeting."

"Sure. Since it was only a few hours ago."

"Yeah." He managed a faint, crooked smile. "Seems like a lifetime ago. While other things"—he shut the laptop's lid—"seem like yesterday."

"Other things like the war?" she asked carefully.

He didn't give her a direct answer. "Those guys talk about it. Zach had to work it out in his own way, which involved some therapy, wearing himself out by pounding a hammer all day for his dad so he could fall asleep." This time the smile brightened his eyes. Just a little. "And apparently the love of a good woman."

"And you write about it."

"Yeah."

"But that's not enough to let you sleep."

"It appears not."

She could feel the tension radiating off him in waves. And, for the first time, she realized that the big strong SEAL could be as vulnerable as she herself was. And as reluctant to admit it.

In that moment came understanding.

And, she realized, without as much surprise—or fear—as she would have expected to feel, love.

"When was the last time you slept all night?"

He shrugged his bare shoulders, which she took to mean so long ago he no longer remembered.

Cait's heart went out to him. But she also knew that sympathy was the last thing he needed.

"Well, then." She went up on her bare toes and twined her arms around his neck. "Did I mention I woke up feeling sexy as sin?"

"I don't recall that. Then again, I didn't exactly give you a chance."

"Well, I did. But there was a problem."

She ran her hands over his shoulders. They were broad, amazingly muscled, capable of carrying heavy burdens. Too heavy, she suspected. And for too long.

"What problem is that?" His voice was deep and rough and irresistibly sexy. Of course, she'd always found everything about Quinn irresistibly sexy. Which is why she'd had to work overtime to resist.

What a waste of time and effort.

Refusing to allow regrets for time lost, Cait trailed her palms down his chest, loving the way his heart, strong and hard against her stroking fingers, picked up its beat. And, she hoped, began to be soothed.

"I was all alone." She could also feel the tension starting to leave his body. Replaced by an entirely different kind of pressure against her stomach. "Seems my lover left me in the lurch, so to speak."

He bent his head. Nuzzled her neck. "I should be keelhauled."

"That's one suggestion."

Cait pulled just far enough away to untie her robe's belt, letting it slide onto the floor. Then, without even the slightest bit of self-consciousness, stood naked in front of him.

"Or you could just come back to bed and let me use your fabulously buff SEAL body."

"Typical female trick," he scoffed. "Offering sex to make her man feel better."

She was not going to challenge his chauvinistic statement. He *was* her man. As she was his woman. And as ridiculously caveman as that sounded, even ringing in her own mind, Cait couldn't deny it also sounded absolutely, positively right.

"I'm told it's a tried-and-true method."

"And was this feminine trickery passed down from mother to daughter?"

"Hardly."

Cait could more easily envision Quinn in a loincloth, throwing her over that massive shoulder and carrying her back to his cave than imagine her mother ever actually discussing sex.

"I seem to recall reading it last month in *Cosmo.* At the dentist's office, while waiting to get my teeth cleaned."

He threw back his head, a rich, deep laugh rumbling up from that ripped dark chest.

Then he kissed her. A long, slow, deep kiss that had her blood pounding in her veins from the sheer, unspeakable pleasure of it.

They walked, hand in hand, fingers laced, back to the bed, where she pleased him, and herself, for a long time, again and again, until her own body was finally sated and his had gone lax with release.

And finally, wrapped in her arms, as the rain tapped on the roof and the moon rode across the midnight sky, Quinn slept.

59

Although classes had not yet started, due to the solemnity of the occasion the decision was made by the governing board of the academy to switch from the summer white uniform to the winter "salt and pepper" —Confederate gray tunics with three rows of shiny brass buttons over white pants with a gray stripe down the side of the legs. The accompanying gloves were white, the covers—hats—black, as were the shoes, which were spit-polished to a mirror shine.

"It's true," Cait murmured as she drank in the sight of Quinn, dressed in the uniform he'd brought from his house.

"What's that?" he asked as he rinsed his coffee mug and put it in the dishwasher. They'd agreed that since each of them had a different duty to perform at the memorial, it only made sense to take separate cars.

"That there's just something damn sexy about a man in a uniform."

"You continue to surprise me," he murmured. "Because I was in uniform the night we met and I could've sworn you hated me at first sight."

"You scared me," she admitted. It was the first time she'd said the words out loud.

Quinn could not have been more surprised by that admission. He remembered every detail about that blind date, and she damn well hadn't looked scared.

"Me?" He slammed a hand against his chest, which

just happened to be loaded down with ribbons, most depicting missions he'd just as soon forget. "Why? I'd never hurt a woman. Well, unless she was trying to kill me," he amended.

"You reminded me of my father."

"You don't like your father?"

"I love him. But although you were decades younger, and just out of BUD/S training, while he was a vice admiral, I could see so much of him in you."

She sighed as she slipped into the low-heeled black shoes she'd carried in from the bedroom. "Which wouldn't have been so bad if it also hadn't made me feel too much like my mother."

"I met your mother at a cocktail party when I first came on staff," he volunteered, feeling a little twinge of regret as she covered up her breasts, which looked so soft and inviting beneath the gray silk blouse, with a somber black jacket that matched her slacks. "She seemed really nice."

"She is. She also spent most of the early years of her marriage trailing my father from post to post and having his babies. Partly, I think, to keep from being lonely all the time he was away at sea."

Quinn thought about that. "Makes sense to me. But maybe, if we'd given it a try, we might have been able to make things work out."

She splayed her hands on her hips. Lifted her chin. Although he might have discovered that this woman was the hottest he'd ever had in bed, all those orgasms she'd had last night obviously hadn't suddenly made her stupid.

"How?"

"I don't know," he admitted. "But it's a moot point, since we're talking bygones. I'm not in the navy anymore, and I don't recall asking you to have my babies."

She tilted her head. "Are you saying you don't want kids?"

Christ. Quinn felt the collar of his gray tunic getting

tighter by the minute. He was choking here, and he realized that whatever he answered, he had a fifty percent chance of being wrong.

"I like kids," he said. That much was true. "But since I didn't exactly have any role models as to how to be a dad, I've never figured I'd have any. However," he tacked on, holding up a hand to cut off any planned response, "since SEALs have to be flexible, I'm certainly willing to take any arguments under advisement."

"Well, that's certainly big of you," she said dryly. "Are you saying you want children?"

Could he be more confused? Quinn suddenly felt as if he were crossing a conversational minefield.

She blew out a long breath. "I don't know."

Quinn glanced down at his watch. "Well, since we both have jobs to do, maybe we'd better table this discussion for now."

She nodded. Scooped up her bag from the table. "Agreed."

"But you know," Quinn said, as they left the apartment, "just because neither of us is ready to start making babies, there's nothing to prevent us from keeping in practice. Just in case we might change our minds down the road."

She laughed. "Now that's definitely an idea I can sign on to."

The shooter stood across the street from Magnolia Flowers and Gifts, watching through the plate-glass window as the florist took six bloodred roses from the cooler and put them into a long white box, while the man on the other side of the counter, as instructed, wrote a message on a card, which the woman in the pink smock then put into the box.

She was chatting away, a smile on her face, as she tied the scarlet ribbon around the flower box, then rang up the sale.

The man came out of the shop.

"All done," he said.

"What were you talking about?" the shooter asked.

It was the sixty-four-thousand-dollar question. If the guy answered wrong, he was a dead man. If he answered right, he'd live another day. Unless, of course, he walked in front of a bus or something.

"The lady was talking about how Valentine Snow is her favorite newswoman," he said.

"And you agreed?"

"Well, sure. I mean, why the hell would I be sending her roses if I didn't like her?"

"Good point." Deciding the guy had followed instructions, the shooter took two twenties and a ten out of his wallet and handed them over. "You never saw me."

"Roger that," the vet said. Pocketing the money, he walked away.

Letting him go was a risk, the shooter knew. But if everything went according to plan, by the time the cops tracked the guy down, he'd have pulled off his grand finale.

Then, after getting rid of Special Agent Cait Cavanaugh, he would blow this town.

But not alone.

With thoughts of all the things he wanted to do to Valentine Snow, with her, the shooter was humming as he drove toward the academy.

60

There could not have been more security if the president had decided to pay a visit to the Admiral Somersett Military Academy. As it was, three U.S. senators who were ASMA alumni had been asked not to come, for fear of making the target even more appealing.

Although the politicians were understandably not happy about losing such super photo ops, particularly in an election year, each reluctantly agreed to stay in Washington. Where, natch, they were also all going to hold press conferences explaining why they wouldn't be on hand to honor two of America's finest.

"Like the maid and the crossing guard don't count?" Cait muttered when the SAC filled her in on the discussions with the various staffers.

Despite the weather, people had lined up two and three, even four people deep on the sidewalk along the route the cortege would be taking from the funeral home, to which the bodies had been moved after Drew Sloan had finished the autopsies, to the academy. Although caissons had been suggested, because of the rain the decision had been made that the flag-draped coffins would be transported in two black hearses.

Adding to the pomp and circumstance, a pair of bagpipers would follow the hearses, and behind them would be two riderless horses, a symbol of a fallen leader that, the academy's protocol officer informed

Cait, went back to President Abraham Lincoln's funeral procession.

A perimeter had been established, enclosing a two-block area of the academy's grounds.

Rope lines were being manned by uniformed police. Inside, in concentric circles, were more cops, ATF, FBI, and Secret Service agents.

Heavily armed and armored SWAT teams from all three branches were on rooftops overlooking the street.

One good thing, Cait thought, as she looked up at the gloomy gray sky, which continued to drizzle over the city, was that the viewing and the memorial service had been moved from the parade ground into the academy's rotunda. Which allowed better control over the situation.

The rain kept the Secret Service agents from wearing their trademark sunglasses, but they all had the requisite microphones on their wrists and their radio receivers in their ears. Their eyes were never still, scanning the crowd, looking for that one person who appeared out of place.

As good as she'd always thought she was, as good as the FBI was, Cait had to admit these Secret Service guys might just have the edge.

Which was a good thing. Because she'd sure as hell be willing to be topped in the security detail if it meant preventing an incident.

Anyone trying to breach the security would have to get past not only these guards but also the armed guards at the tall stone gate leading into the academy grounds. Because the shooter had been able to kill his second victim by aiming straight through the gate, down the row of trees to the parade ground, a black canvas awning, completely opaque, had been erected between the curb and the doorway of the rotunda building.

The plan was for each hearse to back up to the

front of the awning, which would allow the two caskets to be unloaded out of view of any would-be sniper.

In addition, anyone entering the building would have to show ID and pass through a metal detector.

Meanwhile, nearly every patrol car in the SPD was cruising the streets in a five-block area and law enforcement helicopters circled overhead. Although the media had squealed like stuck pigs, the Secret Service—the one agency no one was allowed to argue with—had grounded their television copters.

Cait knew there was no such thing as perfect security, but they had done everything possible to prevent an incident at the academy.

Provided that was what their killer was targeting.

61

The Reverend James "Jimmy" Thornton had spent the past six weeks in small towns throughout the Low-country preaching the word of the Lord. While he might not have the fire of Billy Graham, or the popularity of Rick Warren, and definitely could never live up to the golden tongue of Elmer Gantry—though he'd been fictional and a fraud to boot—he was pleased with how the revival had gone.

The tent had been filled, and hundreds had responded to the altar call. And although saving souls was his true mission, his wife would be pleased to learn that not only had he finished the tour in the green, but there'd be enough for that belated honeymoon on Swann Island he'd been promising since their marriage six years ago.

He would've even managed to eke out a bit more profit if the price of gas hadn't skyrocketed. It seemed to be costing more every time he filled up the Econoline, and as he stood by the pump watching the numbers click by, this time the sticker shock was even worse than it had been last week, in Tallahassee.

He'd just taken the charge slip when the bullet crashed through the front of his skull, exiting the back of his head and shattering the window of the Circle K behind him.

The Reverend James "Jimmy" Thornton was dead before his body hit the asphalt parking lot.

Coincidentally, the patrolman assigned to break the news to Mrs. Thornton had attended last night's revival. Still riding the emotional high of being saved, he would assure her that the reverend was now in a far better place.

Which proved scant comfort to the pregnant widow and mother of three children, all under the age of five.

Dr. Drew Sloan would not be attending the memorial service at the academy. Nor would he be watching the coverage, which was scheduled to be broadcast on national television.

Realizing that time was of the essence, and wanting to do his part to apprehend this madman before he killed again, Drew had rushed the autopsy of the partially charred corpse, sending the samples of DNA testing both to the FBI and to the Armed Forces Repository of Specimen Samples for the Identification of Remains in Washington, D.C., which, it had been reported, had a new high-speed tracking test. High speed if you happened to get pushed to the top of the waiting list, and Drew was hoping to use the high profile he'd achieved over the years, along with the ongoing threat, to fast-track the test.

Although the military hadn't recognized the value of DNA testing as an adjunct to traditional identification efforts until 1991, the repository now had more than 4.6 million specimens for all the service branches, as well as DOD civilian employees and contractors. It was, admittedly, a shot in the dark. But sometimes, Drew thought, you got lucky.

And if there'd ever been a case where he needed luck on his side, this was definitely it.

The white van with Magnolia Flowers and Gifts painted on its side in pretty green calligraphy pulled up in front of the WBUC television station, at precisely ten forty-five in the morning. The kid delivering the flowers, wearing jeans and a white polo shirt with the shop's logo on it, was stopped by the receptionist from entering the back offices behind the locked double glass doors.

Because she was pretty and blond, and made it very clear she was available, he lingered, flirting a bit and assuring her that although the box of flowers he was carrying might be for Valentine Snow, she was a lot sexier than the station's high-profile newscaster.

By the time he left the station it was ten minutes after eleven and the blonde with the D-cup breasts had agreed to meet him at the Black Swan tonight after she got off work.

Patti Ann Cosby watched him climb into the van, thinking he had the cutest damn butt she'd seen on a guy in a long time. Because Valentine Snow had already left for the academy, the receptionist put the white box aside on top of a filing cabinet, then picked up the phone and made a reservation at Clips, Tips, and Toes for a mani-pedi during her lunch hour. If she had time, maybe she'd run by Chantilly Lace and pick up a teddy. Or perhaps even a satin demi bra and matching thong.

Sometimes a girl got lucky, and it was always good to be prepared.

Unfortunately, Patti Ann would be sitting in a vibrating chair, leafing through a copy of *People* magazine—catching up on Brad and Angelina, and Britney and Lindsay—while a young Vietnamese girl painted her toenails Hearts and Tarts Pink when Valentine returned to the station.

Which explained why it would be another four all-important hours before the white box with the red satin ribbon would finally be opened and anyone would read the shooter's fatal message.

62

Although, as a homicide cop, Cait had witnessed a lot of death, she detested funerals, memorial services, any of the programmed responses that so-called civilized societies had thought up to supposedly ease the passage of a member into the afterlife.

She understood, on a rational level, that the ceremonies were more for the living than the dead. And as much as she would never want to deny survivors any comfort or healing, that didn't stop her from hating the flowers that clogged her sinuses, the tears that tore at her last nerve, the dirges, all the words, many of which she knew to be as fake as the makeup that funeral directors seemed to insist on plastering onto corpses.

At least in this case she didn't have to check to see how well the bullet wounds had been covered up, since both General Jacob's and Captain Davis's caskets were closed, draped in American flags, and surrounded by a thick gold rope and a uniformed armed guard from the academy to keep anyone but the immediate families from getting too close.

After the public viewing and the—please God, hopefully brief—eulogies, the general's body would be flown by a military aircraft from nearby Beaufort Air Station to Washington, D.C., for a funeral and interment in Arlington National Cemetery. Captain Davis's remains would be staying in town; his funeral was scheduled for tomorrow at St. Brendan's, after which he would be buried at the Queen of Angels Cemetery.

It seemed that along with Quinn, all the rest of the staff—and their spouses—had shown up to pay their respect. Ryan Hawthorne was still looking a bit shell-shocked by the event, and his wife was far more subdued than when she'd been sobbing on the porch of her pretty little bungalow after it had been turned into a murder scene.

There was a physical distance between Ryan Hawthorne and his wife. Not only did Cait not see any touching, but they appeared not to exactly be on speaking terms either. Which wasn't surprising. What was a bit of a surprise was that Mrs. Hawthorne had the guts to show up in the first place, given the gossip that had to be swirling around the academy.

Cait detected alcohol on the breath of Mrs. Stockton, an attractive brunette who had employed the murdered housekeeper and was the wife of the general who, if rumors were to be believed, would be appointed commander of the academy. Watching everyone closely, Cait thought she detected just the slightest smugness in General Stockton's wife's eyes as she greeted both widows with a hug.

The elder of the two widows, Mrs. Jacob, was a tall, stately woman with a long face and silver hair pulled back into a tight twist at the nape of her neck. She stood military straight in a severe black suit, black alligator pumps with three-inch heels, and black pearl earrings. She did not weep. Rather, as she accepted the condolences of the hundreds of people who passed through the receiving line, she remained the epitome of grace under pressure, reminding Cait a bit of an older Jacqueline Kennedy. The only thing missing was the delicate black lace mantilla that would forever remain etched on the memories of Americans who hadn't even been alive when President Kennedy had been assassinated.

Although Cait wouldn't have thought it possible,

Kristin Davis, standing beside the widow Jacob, appeared to have lost at least ten pounds since Cait and Quinn had shown up at her home to break the news to her that her husband was dead. Her hair, which she'd been wearing in that stylishly loose French twist the other day, flowed like a waterfall over her shoulders. Her suit was also black, but a bit more chic than her counterpart's, with its nipped-in waist, silk lapels, and pleated skirt that fell just above her knees.

She was pale as a wraith and trembling so visibly that if it hadn't been for the two cadets, each seeming to literally hold her up, Cait wasn't sure she'd have been able to stand unassisted.

She was wearing dark glasses, the better to hide eyes, which, given her outward appearance, were undoubtedly red-rimmed from weeping. When Quinn went up to her and took her in his arms, she clung to him, her sobs shaking her slender shoulders.

Watching him comfort the young widow, his broad hand stroking her sleek fall of hair, his head lowered so he could murmur words meant solely for her into her ear, Cait felt not jealousy but awe that somehow fate could have given her yet another chance with this man.

It appeared that where Quinn McKade was concerned, the third time really was the charm.

Things were going well enough until the Hawthornes reached the widow Jacob.

Which was when General John Jacob's wife, in a very un-Jackie-like manner, hauled off and slapped Ryan Hawthorne's wife so hard that her head spun nearly as far around as the kid's in *The Exorcist.*

The sharp sound rang out, bouncing off the stone walls of the statue-lined rotunda like a rifle shot, not a good thing considering the circumstances. Cait saw several military men in full dress uniform—including, unfortunately, the two cadets supporting Kristin Davis—actually duck.

Sensing the inevitable, both Quinn, coming from

one direction, and Cait, from the other, raced toward the line.

With his longer legs, Quinn beat Cait to the wisp-thin young widow.

Unfortunately too late to catch her as she fainted, yet again.

The shooter decided that perhaps he'd miscalculated. Granted, Jensen had been a head case, but at least he'd managed to drive the damn car, allowing him to concentrate on his shooting.

Now, trying to do both on his own was slowing him down. At least all the cops in town seemed to be at the academy, which was giving him more free rein. But if he wanted to live up to the quote he'd promised Valentine Snow, he was going to have to figure out a way to up the ante.

63

"Well, that was fun," Cait muttered once they'd managed to separate Mrs. Jacob and Mrs. Hawthorne.

Kristin Davis was currently lying down in the infirmary. The two shamefaced cadets had been banished to the barracks, and Cait left the widow being tended to by ASMA's staff physician, who'd inserted an IV for what he'd described as dehydration. Also on hand to comfort her, not in his former role as a priest but merely as a friend, was Mike Gannon.

"It certainly added some excitement to the day," Quinn agreed.

"As if we haven't had enough lately. God." Cait shook her head and sighed. "I'm beginning to understand why Joe used to fantasize just driving off to Maine and becoming a lobster fisherman."

"Yet he didn't."

"No."

And neither would she. Cait knew she would go nuts from boredom in a week. But surely there was some middle ground.

"Maybe once you nab this guy, we could go away," Quinn suggested.

"Like a vacation?"

"I hear they're enjoyable."

Cait was tempted. But . . .

"What would we do?"

He shrugged. "Zach's got a boat. We could borrow

it and take off to Key West. Make love. Drink some piña coladas and mai tais with little umbrellas in them. Make love. Walk on the beach, looking for shells. Make love. I even hear they've got this deal where everyone gets together at the end of the day and celebrates the sun setting into the water. And after that, we could go back to our little beach cottage—"

"And make love."

"See?" Despite the seriousness of their situation, he ruffled her hair. "Now you're getting with the program."

"I'll take it under advisement," Cait said.

It really did sound fabulous. And she couldn't remember the last time she'd been away, having jumped straight from SPD to the FBI, where her life revolved around what color the daily terrorist threat code might be.

"Darling," she heard a woman's voice behind her say.

She turned to see her parents headed her way. She felt an urge to smooth out the wrinkles that she could practically feel crinkling her FBI black suit.

"Hello, Mom." She touched cheeks with her mother and did the air-kissing thing, careful not to mess up the smooth, sleek bob her mother kept blond with monthly visits to Mr. Joseph, at the Cut Above salon.

Her mother's fashion maven eyes swept over her. "You look lovely, dear. Very law enforcement official, but feminine at the same time. And black has always been a good color choice for you."

"Thanks." While her mother had always been supportive of her choices, it was not often Cait received a positive statement about her wardrobe. Which caused a twinge of suspicion that she put aside as she turned to her father.

"Dad." She'd learned not to hug her father while he was in uniform.

"Cait." He glanced over at the two caskets. "It's a tragic day for the academy."

"Yes," she agreed, "it certainly is. And even more so for all the families who've lost loved ones."

"True. But at least the FBI's put their best agent on the job."

She was a grown woman. Praise from this larger-than-life former vice admiral should not give her such a rush of pleasure. But it did.

He turned to Quinn. "McKade. Good to see you again."

"Thank you, sir."

As she watched those broad shoulders square and his chin come up, for the first time Cait saw Quinn in full military mode. Although he looked fabulous in the dress uniform, it was obvious that clothes didn't make this man. Like her father, he might not be active military anymore, but he was obviously a warrior to the bone. The odd thing was that the idea no longer bothered her.

What a difference a few days could make.

"Quinn." Her mother gave him her best smile and held out a perfectly manicured hand that had Cait thinking that she probably would've been happier with Valentine Snow as her eldest daughter. "It's good to see you again, though as my husband says, I wish it were under any other circumstances."

Her speculative maternal gaze moved from Quinn to Cait, then back again. "Thinking about it, we're having a little family get-together at the house tomorrow. Cait's sister Megan's daughter, Cassidy, is going to be baptized."

"So Mike Gannon told me."

"Did he? He's such a darling man. I was hoping he'd be able to perform the ceremony, but of course now that he's no longer a priest, that's not possible. But"—she brightened visibly—"I do have two other single daughters, besides Cait, of course. So, I suppose it's always good to have another prospect out there."

Cait managed, just barely, not to roll her eyes. Nor did she dare look at Quinn.

"Did I mention the affair's going to be casual?" Her mother pressed her invitation. She'd obviously clicked into full matchmaker mode. "Of course, you're welcome to join us at the cathedral as well, if you'd like."

"I'm sorry." Either Quinn was an excellent liar or he really meant it. "But I'm afraid I have to go out of town tomorrow."

What? Wondering when he'd planned to share that little piece of information with her, Cait had just turned toward him when the cell phone that she was wearing on her belt vibrated.

The news was not good.

She closed the phone and looked up at Quinn. "So much for Key West. The bastard's struck again."

Belle and Candice Sandman had had a rocky relationship over the years. Belle, who was a member of the United Daughters of the Confederacy and bled Republican red, hadn't been at all pleased when her fourteen-year-old daughter had handed out flyers for Bill Clinton at the Sweet Potato Festival in 1992 and, worse yet, had shown up at a fund-raiser luncheon Belle had given for that nice George Bush, Sr., wearing a blue PUTTING PEOPLE FIRST Clinton button on her sundress.

Then, if all that hadn't been humiliating enough, after a short-lived flirtation with Goth (blessedly abbreviated when her daughter had discovered it hurts like hell to get your tongue pierced), Candice had refused to come out at the cotillion, which had been the most important social event in Somersett since before the War Between the States. Belle had been planning her baby girl's ball gown since she'd been in the womb, so having her only child refuse to join the family's debutante ranks had been like a knife to the heart.

Still, time, as they say, heals all wounds.

Although she'd never gotten to see her daughter dance with her daddy, and do the cotillion dip-curtsy in that white, off-the-shoulder Southern belle hoop-skirted gown created from cascades of shimmering organza tiers and studded with seed pearls that she'd dreamed about for years, at least Candice had pledged Kappa Kappa Gamma at Clemson—which all the women in Belle's family had belonged to for generations and which was, in her esteemed opinion, not only the best at the university but in the entire country—and she'd also been homecoming queen.

And although she was still unmarried and, sigh, a Democrat, for heaven's sake, at least their weekly mother-daughter spa days were free of the strife that had once caused Belle to occasionally wish she'd grown up Roman Catholic so she could have joined a convent and embraced celibacy rather than giving birth to such a stunning but thankless child.

They'd been buffed, polished, and spray-tanned and had shared a spa lunch of fresh ginger elixir, lemongrass shrimp salad, sweet tea, and as a decadent treat, Swann Tea's to-die-for chocolate mint brownies.

"Be sure you call your daddy," Belle was telling Candice as they left Southern Serenity Spa. "You know how worried he gets if he doesn't hear from his princess at least once a week."

"Yes, Mama," Candice responded with an indulgent smile.

And well she should, Belle considered, given that Sandy had gifted her with a shiny new red Nissan Z roadster for a thirtieth birthday gift last month.

Belle's last thought, an instant before the bullet pierced her skull, was that if she could live her life over again, despite all their earlier troubles, this beautiful young Democrat was precisely who she would've chosen for a daughter.

Two down.

Only three more to go.

And there were still plenty of hours left in the day. He should have thought of multiple shootings earlier.

It was, he thought, as he'd watched the women fall, one after the other, like a really great spare down at Buccaneer Bowl, a more efficient method.

The shooter wondered if Valentine had received his flowers yet. She had, after all, been at the academy all morning. He'd been listening to her broadcast on simulcast as he'd driven around town, searching out his targets, and it hadn't sounded as if she'd read his message.

As if conjured up by his thoughts, her beautifully modulated voice suddenly broke into a commercial for Sandman's Nissan.

"This just in." Although the average listener would hear her trademark calm, knowing her as well as he did, the shooter could sense the excitement in her tone.

"A shooting has occurred at the Circle K on Palmetto Drive. A man who had stopped for gas has been reported down. It is not known if this is the work of the same shooter who has killed others in Somersett. Police are on the way to the scene now. Stay tuned to WBUC for more updates."

"No way I'd fucking miss them," the shooter said as he drove away.

The ferry should be coming in from Swann Island soon. If he hurried, he should be able to greet the disembarking passengers with a surprise they'd never forget.

64

"Ms. Valentine?"

The new receptionist, the third this month—what the hell was her name? Pammi? Patsy?—stopped Valentine as she arrived back at the station.

She'd done her stand-up as near to the pumps as allowed at the gas station. And another across the street from the spa. While she would have liked to get closer, the cops had taped the crime scene off, searching for clues.

Good luck, she'd thought. So far the entire task force had been doing a bang-up job.

Now she needed to run through some voice-overs for the six p.m. newscast.

"What is it . . . Patty?" That was it!

"You received a package today."

After buzzing her and Joe Gannon—who'd been like a silent shadow all damn day—through the double doors, the receptionist, *Patty,* handed Valentine a white florist's box. Dodging her bodyguard's attempt to grab it from her, she carried it into the newsroom.

Which was, as always, chaotic. Cardboard coffee cups littered desktops, phones were jangling off the hook, and writers were hunkered over their computer keyboards, madly typing away as the evening deadline approached.

When Valentine had first arrived at the station, after walking away from her lucrative job and swanky digs in Manhattan, Talmadge Townsend IV had offered her not only her own hairdresser and makeup person but her own private office as well.

All of which she'd turned down. If she'd wanted the celebrity perks, she would've stayed in New York. What she'd wanted was to remember what it had felt like to be a working reporter. And, even more important, after Iraq she'd wanted to do that reporting somewhere she didn't have to worry about people she'd come to care about being blown up by IEDs.

She put the florist box down on the metal desk that was one of many shoved into the crowded newsroom, only to have it scooped up by Gannon.

"Let me," he said.

"It's only flowers."

"You sure of that?"

When memories of a Hummer being blown apart reverberated in her mind, Valentine put her hands up and backed away.

"Be my guest," she said, knowing that as annoying as she'd found the former homicide detective today, if he died trying to protect her, she'd never forgive herself.

She watched as he untied the red satin ribbon. Held her breath as he lifted the top off the box, revealing half a dozen perfect crimson American Beauty roses nestled on a bed of white tissue paper.

She was reaching for the small white envelope tucked into the dark greenery when he caught her hand.

"Let me." He paused. "I don't suppose you happen to have any tweezers?"

"Not on me." Talk about overkill. They were only flowers. And the envelope was standard florist's fare, too small to hold a tarot card. "But Sunny, the makeup woman, probably does."

She did.

With a deftness that Valentine suspected came from

his years of collecting evidence at homicide scenes, Joe Gannon opened the envelope and pulled out the card.

" 'Dear Valentine,' " he read aloud. " 'While these roses can't begin to equal your beauty, I hope you'll enjoy them. There are six. One for each of the people who'll die today. I suspect that little coincidence will prove appealing to the network brass, who'll undoubtedly give you your own sniper special . . . Love, your most loyal fan.' "

Because she felt on the verge of fainting, just as Kristin Davis had done earlier in the day, Valentine sank into the chair behind her desk as Joe took out his cell phone and called the task force.

It was worse than Cait could have imagined in her worst nightmares. Moments after she received Joe's call about the flowers, the report about the shooting at the ferry terminal crackled across the police airwaves.

Three tourists had been mowed down after a day of sightseeing on Swann Island.

Making a total of six murders in a single day.

"At least, if the note in the flowers can be believed, he's done. For now," Quinn, who'd stayed by her side all day, said.

" 'For now' is the definitive statement," she said. "God."

She scrubbed both her hands down her face. A few hours ago she was scorching the sheets with this man. Now she was looking at six bodies. Seven, counting the guy in the trunk of the burned-out Altima.

"I'm sorry about having to leave you tomorrow," he said.

"Don't worry about it. My mother is a lovely woman, but she's an unrepentant matchmaker and can run over you like a velvet bulldozer if you let her."

Her embarrassment regarding her mother's behavior at the academy had almost flown her mind, replaced by far more vital issues. Such as how the hell were they going to catch this psycho? Before he killed again?

"She wants her daughter to be happy," he said mildly. "Can't blame her for that. And I'd be happy to go to your niece's baptism party. But I got a call while you were setting up the defensive perimeter with your partner. Seems something's come up."

There was a stress in his voice she'd never heard before. A little surprised, she looked up at him.

"An emergency?"

"Of sorts," he said. "But nothing I can't deal with. And I'll definitely be back by tomorrow night."

She hated to admit the rush of relief that statement gave her. Because the truth was, she had the sinking feeling that things with this shooter were going to get a lot worse before they got better. And Quinn had definitely been right when he'd said sex was a great stress reliever.

Though it was more than that.

The absolute truth was that she felt better when she was with him.

Ignoring the fact that her behavior was totally unprofessional, she linked her fingers with his.

"I'm glad," she said, "that you'll be back."

As if oblivious to the crime scene experts buzzing around them, Quinn bent his head and touched his mouth to hers.

"I'm glad," he said, "that you're glad."

The kiss was quick. Light. But it still managed to make Cait feel as if he'd lit a candle in the icy darkness the shooter had created inside her.

65

"I can't believe this," Valentine murmured, much, much later that night.

Although she'd wanted to run home and hide beneath the covers, she'd managed to get through the six o'clock and the eleven o'clock newscasts with both Joe and Brendan—who'd shut the pub early again—watching over her.

Now she was home, sipping her second glass of wine while wrapped in the Irishman's protective embrace.

"Murder isn't usual for Somersett," he agreed.

"It's because of me."

She took another sip and stared out the floor-to-ceiling windows. Usually she found pleasure in the night view of the brightly lit bridge and dinner cruise ships, but in her mind's eye she was seeing all of today's bodies and, even worse, a Humvee in flames, viewed from the air as the military plane had flown her safely out of Baghdad International Airport.

"It's not the first time people have died because of me."

"Now isn't that talking foolishness?" He brushed a kiss against her hair. "Even if the man has fixated on you, these killings are in no way your fault."

"Have you ever wondered why I left New York?"

"I assumed you wanted a change of scenery. Something, given that I moved here from Ireland myself, I could certainly understand."

He drew her a little closer. Nuzzled her neck. "I assumed that if there was more to your reasoning, you'd be telling me when you were ready."

"You don't push."

It was one of the things, along with his friendship and absolute steadfastness, she'd come to love about him. That and, although it might be shallow, the fact that he was one of the best-looking men she'd ever seen.

"We Irish are not only a tenacious race, we can be patient. When it serves our purpose."

"I was in Iraq on assignment. Although things had grown increasingly worse since I'd first been embedded during Shock and Awe, for some reason I never felt at risk. It was as if all that death and carnage couldn't touch me."

"And can't I identify with that?" he murmured as he took a sip of the whiskey he'd poured for himself.

She looked up at him, surprised, and was about to ask him what he meant, when he merely touched his fingertips to her cheek.

"Go on," he said.

It was not the first time she'd gotten the impression there was more to Brendan O'Neill than the easygoing, sexy pub owner persona he showed to the world. But since she'd already begun to share her dark and painful secret, Valentine was determined to get it out.

"We were warned to stay in the Green Zone. But since access to real Iraqis was too limited, all the reports coming out of there, at least to me, were sounding the same. I'm ashamed, looking back on it, that I wanted more. I wanted to stand out. I had a reputation of being one of the most fearless war reporters—man or woman—to protect."

"There's no harm in ambition."

"No. Not unless it puts others at risk." Because it still hurt, she tossed back the rest of the wine.

"Would you like a refill?"

"What, and get falling-down drunk and have you witnessing a crying jag?"

The odd thing was, she hadn't been able to cry. The pain had cut so deep and so harsh, she feared that if she let it out, she would never be able to stop the flow.

"I wouldn't be minding."

"You know," she said, seeing the truth in his eyes, "I actually believe that."

"I'm not saying I haven't lied in my past," he said. He brushed his thumb lightly along the smudges beneath her eyes that revealed a lack of sleep. "But we're talking about you," he coaxed.

"There was a group of soldiers at Camp Victory. That's this base that sort of sprawls around the airport."

"I've heard of it."

"Most of them were so young. They could have been my baby brothers, but they took me under their wing and drove me places around the city that no sane person probably should've gone."

"I watched those reports. With my heart in my throat for you, thinking you were the bravest woman I'd ever seen."

"Or the most careless."

"It's a thin line at times. Between courage and carelessness." Again, she had the oddest feeling that he knew what he was talking about.

"I was on my way back, with letters they'd written to their families. And videotapes I'd made. One young corporal's wife had just given birth to a baby. The other men had made this big congratulations sign for him. Everyone in his unit had signed it. I was taking it home to his wife and new daughter."

A lump rose painfully, familiarly, in her throat. As she tried to swallow it back down again, he merely rested his chin on the top of her head and remained silent. Giving her the time she needed to collect herself. To share the most painful memory of her life.

"They have to take this special maneuver going in and out of the airport because of all the rocket attacks."

"A corkscrew," he said. "I've seen it described."

Yes. He would have. Because she'd been one of the hotshot foreign correspondents reporting on it.

"Although I was advised against it because of the possibility of attacks, I was watching out the window. I could see the Humvee leaving the tarmac, headed back to camp. I knew they couldn't see me, but I was waving good-bye anyway as they turned onto the roadway."

She drew in a deep, shuddering breath. "One minute the Humvee full of young men I'd come to think of as my friends was there." She began to tremble. "Then there was a huge blast that shook the plane." How was it that she could still feel the heat from that blast, even now, but still felt so cold? "And then they were gone."

She closed her eyes. Which didn't prevent her from seeing the scene.

"If they hadn't been there. On that road. At that time. Because of me . . ."

A sob pushed its way past the lump in her throat as he took her into his arms, holding her close. She buried her face in his shirt and allowed the tears she'd held back for so long to begin to flow.

And all the while he was murmuring words in his native tongue, words she couldn't understand but that she knew were meant to comfort. Which they did.

Finally, all cried out, she pulled away. Just a bit.

"Your shirt is soaked."

"It'll dry." He cupped her wet face in his palm, brushing at the tears on her cheeks with his thumb. "Would you be feeling better now?"

"I am."

She sniffled, then thanked him when he pulled a clean handkerchief out of his pocket. She'd had no idea men still carried those things around. Then again, there were many things she didn't know about Brendan O'Neill. Things she wanted to know. Needed to know.

Because, although she'd always thought of herself as a rolling stone, unwilling to settle down long enough to gather moss, she realized that Brendan wasn't the only one who'd been falling in love over these past months.

"We need to talk," he said, as if reading her mind. "There are things about me you don't know."

"There are so many things about you I want to know." She managed a wobbly smile through her tears as she felt her once shattered heart beginning to mend. "But they can wait. Because right now, what I really want, and what I need, is for you to make love to me."

He smiled at her. With his wonderful mouth and his warm, liquid blue eyes. "And here I was beginning to worry you'd never ask."

66

As Quinn drove over ridge after ridge of steep mountains, the country music twanging from the rental car radio accompanied by the threatening rumble of thunder coming out of the fast-moving clouds racing through the mountains, he felt as if he'd landed on another planet. At the very least, the scattered settlements of weather-beaten cabins and split-rail fences, with cattle and sheep roaming at will along the narrow, winding roadside, gave the impression that he'd stepped back in time.

Camp Cupcake, as the federal prison for women located two hundred and seventy miles southwest of Washington, D.C., was nicknamed, didn't exactly look like his idea of a prison. The facility, his research had informed him, had housed blues diva Billie Holiday, along with Lynette "Squeaky" Fromme and Sara Jane Moore—both of whom had tried to assassinate President Gerald Ford—and most recently Martha Stewart, had no guard towers, no tall stone walls with razor wire topping them.

In fact, the landscaping was nearly as lush as that of many of the homes he'd seen in Somersett. And how many private homes had he ever visited that had their own tennis courts?

Yet, a prison it was. One from which, his mother's

lawyer had told him in the call yesterday morning, Julia Van Pelt was about to be paroled.

He did not go inside. Instead, he waited out by the road, where the attorney had told his client he'd be waiting to pick her up. The attorney, who'd kept Quinn informed all these years, had taken it upon himself not to inform his client that he'd made other arrangements.

Quinn stayed in the BMW, watching as the woman, accompanied by what was obviously a prison guard, walked out of the brick building.

They exchanged words. And smiles. The guard held out her hand and the former inmate took it in both of hers.

Then squared her shoulders and began walking toward the car.

Quinn had remembered his mother being reed slim. She still was. Her hair, which had once been a dark chestnut, was now gray and curled lightly around a face that, while more lined than the last time he'd seen her, was still lovely.

Her step was slower. And when she stopped once, and glanced back at the prison, he had the oddest feeling she was fighting the urge to go running back.

But she shook it off and continued toward the car.

She was about twenty feet away when he climbed out of the driver's seat. Came around the front of the car and stood there.

Waiting.

Hoping.

Ridiculously, all the things he'd thought of to say, the practiced words of greeting he'd memorized on the long and winding drive up into the mountains, fled his mind.

So, like the eight-year-old boy he'd once been, he said the only thing he could think of: "Hi, Mom."

Her first expression was shock. He waited for the anger born of betrayal, but instead she burst into tears.

And began running. Not back to the only life she'd known for more than two decades. But toward her son.

She launched herself into his arms, feeling as light as a feather as he spun her around.

She was laughing and crying at the same time.

And damn, she wasn't the only one.

"You shouldn't have come," she scolded as they drove away from the prison.

"You couldn't have stopped me," he said. "Not this time. Not anymore."

She looked at him, drinking him in as if she'd been crawling across the Sahara and had suddenly stumbled across a sparkling, palm-tree-lined oasis.

"My baby boy's definitely grown up," she said. "We have so much to catch up on." She shook her head. "And I know it's all my fault, but—"

"I know." He reached across the space between them and took her hand in his and lifted it to his lips. It was the first time he'd kissed his mother in twenty-five years. "But I understand. And we've all the time in the world to catch up."

He flashed her his best grin, pleased when she managed a wobbly smile back.

"I've found you a house," he said.

After moving to California with her new husband, Joe Gannon's sister, Tess, had kept her bungalow as a rental, which fortunately had been available when Quinn had called her yesterday.

"I think you'll like it. It's in Somersett, a real pretty town in South Carolina's Lowcountry. Then, after you get settled in, there's someone important I want you to meet."

This time her smile was brighter. "A woman?"

"*The* woman," he corrected.

67

"I've come to a decision," Valentine announced.

Amazingly, after the sweetest lovemaking she'd ever experienced, she'd spent her first night in a very long while completely free of nightmares. But the images of the shooter's victims had returned as she was getting dressed. Although Brendan had tried to talk her into taking the day off, she knew she couldn't really rest until the man who had already taken so many lives was captured.

"And what would that be?" Brendan asked as he put a steaming mug of coffee down on the breakfast bar for her.

"It's obvious that as good as Special Agent Cait Cavanaugh is, even with all those varied members of the task force working on the case, they're continuing to play defense. The son of a bitch has been setting the agenda from the start."

"I'd not be arguing that."

"So the thing to do is to set a trap for him."

He caught her chin between his fingers, lifted her face, and brushed a kiss against her lips. "And now you'd be a detective?"

"No. Now I'd be the bait."

She watched as comprehension dawned. His eyes hardened, and storm clouds moved across his handsome Irish face. "Impossible."

"Why?" She pulled back and eyed him over the rim

of the mug. The more she'd thought about it while he was in the kitchen, intent on fixing her breakfast, the more the idea had made sense. "It's me he wants. He's obviously doing all this to get my attention. So the logical thing is to let him believe he's going to get what he wants."

"There's nothing logical about it. Nor will I allow it."

"Excuse me?"

"You heard me. Even if the authorities would permit a civilian to take such a risk, which I'm daring to bet they would not, there is no way on God's green earth that I'd be allowing the woman I love to put herself in harm's way. Especially not after—"

He shut his mouth so fast and so hard Valentine could have sworn she'd heard his strong white teeth slam together.

"After what?"

He tilted his head back. Stared up at the ceiling as if seeking help from some divine source. Then said, "It's what I was going to tell you last night. About another who died because she became involved with me. I will not risk it happening again."

"I see."

She didn't. Not at all. But she'd been a reporter long enough to know how to conduct an interview. Even one with a subject as unwilling as Brendan O'Neill looked to be.

He sat down on the stool at the counter next to her. Swiveled the seat so their knees touched. "I told you I was a barrister. Back in Ireland."

"That's right. In family law." She smiled a bit at the memory. "Because you didn't want to wear those frightful wigs."

He didn't smile back, as she'd normally expect him to. "Aye. That was one reason. But there was also some satisfaction in helping young mothers, who were, as a rule, the majority of my clients.

"There was one who came to me needing a job.

She'd come down from the north after her husband was killed."

"Killed as in murdered?"

"Aye." His lips were set in a thin, tight line. "She was Protestant, you see. Her husband was Catholic. They met while they'd both been volunteering on a peace project during the Troubles."

"Which side killed him?"

"No one initially knew. Well, obviously there were those who did, but they weren't telling. There were rumors it was the IRA, who wasn't that fond of the idea of their men having children with the enemy. Others claimed it had been the Provos, because they could be just as vicious with those of their own who made the mistake of crossing to the other side.

"She was a widow, four months pregnant, when I gave her a job doing secretarial work. She was eight months pregnant when shot down like a dog while walking to the bus stop after work by an IRA operative who'd slipped across the border into Dublin."

"Oh, my God. I'm sorry. But it couldn't have been your fault."

"Perhaps not in reality. Just as it wasn't actually your doing that those soldiers were killed by that IED. Given that they undoubtedly went back and forth between their base and the airport, along that same road, several times each week.

"But along with our tenacity and patience, one of the things we Irish do best is guilt. And we're also ones for tending our grudges."

Despite the seriousness of the subject, she smiled at that. "I'll keep that in mind."

"You'll never have any reason to be concerned. There is nothing you could ever do that would make me find you less than perfect."

"Hah. Wait until you find my drying underwear hanging over your shower rod every morning."

"And isn't there a simple way to get rid of that problem?"

"I should give up wearing underwear?" she guessed.

It was his turn to manage a faint smile. "Ah, and didn't I know you were an intelligent woman."

Then he sighed and looked out over the harbor, which this morning was draped in a silvery morning fog.

"So, that's when you gave up your practice and went back to the west to run your father's pub?"

"No. That's when I used all the sources I'd acquired during my years in law, including a member of the Guarda, to track down Siobhán's murderer. So I could make the man pay. Slowly. Painfully."

Valentine stared at him, unable to believe the man who'd treated her so tenderly could have ever been a cold-blooded killer.

"I don't believe that."

"The assassin certainly did when I showed up at his door. I suspect he became more of a believer after I'd beaten him to a bloody pulp."

"But you didn't kill him."

"Only because a neighbor called the Guarda. They broke down the door and finally pulled me off of him. But not before I'd broken one of their noses."

He absently rubbed the fingers of his right hand over the knuckles of his left, looking down at them in a way that made Valentine wonder if he was still seeing the killer's blood on them.

"I can understand you *wanting* to kill such an evil man. But that's an emotion, Brendan. If you'd truly *intended* to kill him, there wouldn't have been enough police in all of Ireland who could've stopped you. And he would've died that day."

She'd never spoken words she believed more.

"Well, we'll never know, will we?" He dragged a hand through his hair. "After the bastard got out of hospital, he was imprisoned. By then I'd lost my taste for all things legal, so, since my father fell ill about the same time, I returned to the west and took over his pub, where I was living quite happily. Until the assassin was released in a prisoner exchange."

"But he was a murderer."

"Although he'd admitted to killing Siobhán, boasted about it, in fact, to me, the evidence against him was circumstantial. Also, those were dangerous times during the Troubles, and he had some powerful support on his side of the political wars. Since I've family still in Castlelough whom I didn't want to put at risk, I thought it was time I emigrate. I traveled around a bit, decided I liked the Lowcountry, had an opportunity to buy this building, and, well, that's my story."

"And no one here knows?"

"Only you."

Valentine was overwhelmed that he'd trusted her enough to share it with her. It also told her how truly he did love her, to be willing to open himself up and share his tragic tale to try to talk her out of putting herself at risk.

"I can understand why you don't want me to do this," she allowed. "But it's also obvious that you know a lot more about killers than the usual pub owner does. And you've got to realize that this one is going to keep killing until the cops get lucky and catch him on a traffic stop, or jaywalking, or some such thing. Or if he's trapped."

He shook his head. "You are the most hardheaded woman I've ever met. Are you sure you're not Irish?"

"Actually, although I almost hate to bring this up after that story, my ancestry is English and French, with some Dutch and Swedish thrown in."

"My favorite blend of nationalities," he said. "What if I suggest a compromise?"

"What type of compromise?"

"We'll call Cait. Perhaps she'll have an idea of how we can use the killer's obsession with you and still keep you safe." He drew her into his arms and kissed her until her head spun. "Because, Valentine Snow, I have several long-range plans for you."

"Promises, promises."

Wrapping her arms around his neck, Valentine kissed him back. And marveled at the twisted paths each of them had taken that had brought them here, to this place, at this time.

68

"You know," Cait said thoughtfully, "it's not such a bad idea."

"What are you talking about?" Brendan nearly exploded. "It's a fecking dangerous plan!"

"Well, using Valentine to draw him out is stupidly risky," she allowed. Then slanted a glance toward the newswoman. "No offense intended."

Val folded her arms. "I'll hold off judgment on that," she decided, "until I hear you come up with a better idea."

"I'll take your place."

"No way," said Quinn, who'd returned from his mysterious trip.

"Just because we're sleeping together doesn't make you the boss of me," she said, flashing him a falsely sweet smile.

"You two are a couple?" Valentine asked.

"About time," Brendan said.

"Which is why I'm not going to let you put yourself out there as a target," Quinn said, in that no-nonsense, I'm-a-big-bad-killer-SEAL-and-you-will-not-argue-with-me way Cait was getting used to.

She'd certainly heard it enough times growing up with her father, the vice admiral. Which also meant there was no way Quinn was going to intimidate her.

"I've got an idea," she said. "If you two males will

just dial down the testosterone for a few moments and hear me out."

The shooter had been pleased with the media coverage. He wished there'd been more footage of the ferry murders, but all in all, given the time constraints of local news, he thought Valentine Snow had done a remarkable job. In his opinion—and he was, after all, an expert on her—she'd even topped her Desert Storm war coverage.

The only bad thing about all that success was that when he'd called St. Brendan's to verify the time of Cait Cavanaugh's sister's baby's baptism, he learned it had been postponed. Which he had to assume was due to overkill on his part.

He smiled at the double entendre, even though he experienced a twinge of regret that he hadn't been able to blow the FBI agent away on the cathedral steps, as he'd hoped.

Oh, well . . . there was always next time.

He was sitting at the table in the studio apartment he'd rented in Cotton House—a former warehouse in the harbor district that during slave days had served as a shipping point for Sea Isle cotton leaving for England—cleaning his rifle and waiting for the noon newscast, when a bulletin suddenly flashed onto the screen.

"This just in," said the male anchor with a toupee that looked like raccoon roadkill sitting atop his head. "The Somersett sniper appears to have struck again."

"What?" The shooter stared at the screen. "That's fucking impossible, you moron."

"The victim is our WBUC's own Valentine Snow, who was shot in the head this morning on her way into the station. She was rushed to St. Camillus Hospital, where, according to doctors on staff, she has undergone surgery to extract the bullet. We're now returning to regular programming. Stay tuned to WBUC for updates on this breaking-news situation."

As the scene on the screen switched to a bunch of broads sitting around a table, chewing the fat about God knows what, the shooter pointed the remote at the TV and darkened the screen.

His actions had obviously triggered a copycat.

Whom he'd have to deal with.

But first he had plans to make.

"Are you sure you've got everything set up?" Quinn asked SAC Brooke Davidson for the umpteenth time.

"Yes, Mr. McKade," she said with what even he had to admit was extreme patience. "We've guards in plainclothes posted in the parking lot, at all the entrances, and in the hallways up and down the surgical recovery floor. No one without the proper credentials will be allowed to get anywhere near Special Agent Cavanaugh."

From what she'd seen of Cait's boss, the woman was intelligent and hadn't earned her position at the top of the South Carolina FBI chain by any affirmative action, but by being one of the best at her job. He'd checked her credentials, which were gold.

But that didn't mean he was just going to sit back with his thumb up his ass while other people who still didn't have his qualifications protected his woman.

Who was currently lying in bed, wearing a bandage wrapped around her head and one of those backless hospital gowns she'd complained mightily about, at which he'd reminded her this had been her idea.

If the special agent in charge was right, the shooter wouldn't even make it this far. But they were going to have to let him try, in order to catch him.

And when he did, Quinn would be ready.

Dr. Drew Sloan had bodies piling up like planes over Atlanta's Hartsfield-Jackson Airport during a thunderstorm. Which was why he didn't immediately concern himself with the fax he heard coming into his office outside the autopsy suite.

A minute later, his administrative assistant came in carrying two sheets of paper. "This just came in with a top-priority notice," she said. "It's from someplace called the Armed Forces Repository of Specimen Samples for the Identification of Remains."

His interest spiked, Drew pulled off his gloves and went over to check out the report. The good news was the military had gone ahead and put a rush on the test and had identified the body found in the trunk of the Altima.

The bad news was that the name and the photo meant nothing to him.

"Call Michael Gannon at the free clinic across from St. Brendan's," he suggested. "Maybe, with luck, he'll recognize this guy."

The shooter wasn't worried about getting into the hospital. That would be a piece of cake. The problem, as he saw it, was how the hell he was going to get up to the surgical recovery floor to see Valentine Snow.

The latest report was that she was in a coma. Which was impossible. Because if she died on him, it would mean all he'd done over these past days, all the people he'd killed, would have been for nothing.

One lucky thing. Cotton House happened to be just four blocks from St. Camillus. The proximity to the hospital, along with its relatively inexpensive monthly rents, made it a popular choice among interns and residents of the teaching hospital. During his three months in the building, he'd learned the shift rotations, which was why he was waiting in the shadows as the elevator came down to the parking garage.

The first elevator held three people, which was two more than he needed.

The second held two, both of which were females, which didn't do him a damn bit of good.

He hit the jackpot on the third when the metal door opened and a single male he recognized as an ER resident stepped out of the elevator and headed toward the black and chrome bad-boy Honda VTX 1800 motorcycle he kept chained to a concrete pillar.

He'd unlocked the bike and was putting his helmet on when the shooter strolled up behind him. He glanced back and began to smile in recognition when he noticed the silenced Sig.

His eyes widened. He might be a whiz in the ER, but he wasn't fast enough today. Having the advantage of surprise, the shooter pulled the trigger before the resident's brain could send the message to his legs to run like hell.

69

Michael Gannon had just finished diagnosing a seven-year-old with chicken pox and was on his way to examining room A for a routine check on a young woman who'd come in for her monthly prenatal checkup, when his nurse came running up to him and handed him a fax. She was breathless, and the hand holding the paper was shaking.

"This just came in from the medical examiner. It's the man whose body was found in the trunk of that burned-out car in the marsh?" Her voice went up, turning the statement into a question. "The ME thinks he might have been working with the shooter."

Mike recognized the face immediately. Which wasn't really a surprise, given that the former vet, who'd already suffered one tragedy, could have been unduly influenced by another, stronger personality.

And he knew exactly which one that would be.

A second thought came storming into his mind. Something the chicken pox patient's mother had just told him. That Valentine Snow was currently in the hospital after undergoing surgery for a gunshot wound.

Knowing that the shooter harbored an obsession for the newscaster, Mike feared he was at this very minute on his way to her hospital room.

And damn it all to hell, he was the one who'd given the killer the key to St. Camillus.

* * *

The shooter wasn't surprised by all the guards at the doors of the hospital. Some were in uniform and armed. Others, in hospital scrubs, were obviously plain-clothes officers, since he would have recognized them if they'd actually been on staff.

He thought it was a clever touch to have actual hospital security checking IDs at the same time. Having always prided itself on being a state-of-the-art hospital, in the years since 9/11, St. Camillus had installed a thumbprint identification system.

He greeted the guard at the kitchen employees' entrance, as he had five days a week for the past month. Ran his thumb over the glass scanner. The former priest had arranged for the job, which was scut work that paid only minimum wage, but at least it had given him a respectable enough cover while he planned his killing spree.

Fortunately, his salary wasn't the only money he had coming in. Otherwise there'd have been no way he could have afforded to buy his arsenal. And better yet, live at Cotton House, which had proven to be a stroke of luck today.

Once inside the hospital, he bypassed the kitchen entirely, going instead to a janitorial supply closet down the hall, where he changed from the white kitchen staff uniform into a pair of blue scrubs. Then pinned a badge reading DR. JAMES FITZPATRICK onto the cotton shirt.

Having just promoted himself from dishwasher to surgical resident, the shooter left the closet and headed for the bank of elevators.

"What the hell's taking the guy so long?" Quinn grumbled from the bathroom adjoining the surgery recovery room where Cait had been lying in that damn bed for the past two hours.

"Maybe he got stopped by all the guards," she said

dryly. "I tried telling everyone the uniforms were overdoing it, but would anyone listen to me? No." She answered her own rhetorical question.

"Well, excuse us for not wanting you to be the wacko's next victim."

"I'm an FBI special agent, McKade," she reminded him. "I'm trained to be even more armed and dangerous than our guy. In fact, I'll bet, on a good day, I might even be able to outshoot you. At least with a handgun," she tacked on.

"That'll be the day."

"I outshot Joe once. Actually twice. And since he beat *you* on the range—"

"He told you about that?"

"Sure. We used to share everything—well, most everything—when we were on the force. That's what partners do."

"Speaking of sharing, there's stuff we need to talk about."

"Like your parents being antiwar terrorists who were involved in the robbery of a Brinks truck that ended up with a guard being killed?"

The question, asked in such a calm, casual tone, nearly took his breath away.

"How long have you known?"

"After you mentioned your dad's suicide and hedged about your mother. You're usually the most forthright person I know. So, since it seemed we had a thing going, although I'll admit to an invasion of privacy, I ran a background check."

Deciding that the killer wasn't going to come bursting into the room anytime soon, and that the system was set up to radio him once the guy did get into the hospital, he came to stand in the doorway between the two rooms.

"I was going to tell you."

"I figured that." He heard the truth in her voice. "And I'll apologize. But when you left on your emergency yesterday, I was worried about you." Her eyes, softening with concern, backed that up. "So, how is she?"

"As well as can be expected. It'll probably take some time to adjust. She's had her life regulated for so long, she looked a little lost when I left her at the house."

"Tess Gannon's house."

He lifted a brow. "You have been busy."

She shrugged. "What can I say? I'm good."

"She didn't have anything to do with that shooting," he said. "She wasn't even there. But she was a member of the VWPA." The Vietnam War Protestors Army, which had spun off from the infamous Weathermen.

"Only because she was kidnapped because her parents were rich."

"And refused to pay the ransom."

He'd always wondered what would have happened if they had, but according to the court records he'd read, the FBI had been adamant against dealing with homegrown terrorists.

"Yeah. Then later disowned her when she seemed to join them. I don't think it was like all the papers reported," he said. "That she got Stockholm syndrome. Granted, I was just a kid, and you never know about anyone's marriage, least of all your own parents', especially since our lives were anything but normal. But I believe she really loved him."

"Well, whatever." Since he'd never been able to resist this woman, he gave up his cover to cross the room and take the hand she stretched out to him. "I'm glad she stayed with him. Because if she hadn't, you wouldn't have been born. And you wouldn't be here with me. Right here. And right now."

As serious—and potentially dangerous—as their situation was, Quinn chuckled at that. "Yeah, like this beats the hell out of Key West."

She grinned, her eyes sparkling beneath that fake bandage. "You know what they say. It's not the place. It's the company that's important."

He bent his head and was about to kiss her when a voice came in over the earphone he was wearing.

"We've got a dead resident over at Cotton House," the crisp, controlled voice of SAC Brooke Davidson said. "Name of Dr. James Fitzgerald. And guess what, boys and girls, I also just received a call from Dr. Michael Gannon that our shooter has been working in the hospital kitchen for the last month. And proving that bad news comes in threes, he just checked past security five minutes ago."

Frank Angetti was pissed. Bad enough that because of that damn interview, he'd been stuck answering phone calls about barking dogs and trash collection. Now here he was, dressed in green janitorial scrubs, mopping a damn hospital floor over and over again, waiting for some stone-cold killer to come around the corner and whack him.

At least that SEAL had pulled rank and insisted on taking the inside position. The guy wasn't even in law enforcement, but having spent years killing people for a living, along with being the size of the Incredible Hulk, he had kept that new SAC from arguing.

Angetti had been spreading the damn wet suds over the same twenty feet of tile for the past hour. Since they couldn't shut down the hospital just on the off chance that newswoman's cockamamie idea might actually pay off, he kept having to put up with the constant traffic of people pushing gurneys, which was why he paid no attention to the scrub-clad doctor pushing the cart toward the room where his partner was waiting for his signal.

70

So far, so good.

The surgical floor was nearly deserted, indicating they'd probably pulled all but the most vital hospital staff off the floor, waiting for him to show up.

Like that guy mopping the floor. Were they so stupid they didn't realize he'd recognize him from when he'd shown up at the crime scene at the academy?

Usually the shooter liked to get away as soon as possible after a hit. But since the captain on the parade ground had been his primary target all along, he'd stuck around, joining the crowd of lookie-loos, to make sure the guy was good and truly dead.

The fake janitor was no Efrem Zimbalist, Jr. That was for damn sure. Whatever he was thinking about, from the scowl on his face, he was so pissed off about something that the shooter could have strolled by carrying his entire damn arsenal and the guy wouldn't have noticed.

Unlike in so many movies, a gun's silencer is never actually silent. Which was why the shooter decided against risking detection and pulled out the KA-BAR he'd used on Captain Jack.

As he passed the agent, he shoved it deftly and deeply into his chest, almost tempted to shout out "Timber" as the fat guy slid down to the soapy floor.

There was an open door to the left. The shooter debated dragging the agent into the empty room, then decided he would just end up leaving a trail of blood anyway, so what the hell, he was so close to his target, he might as well just leave him where he lay.

Satisfied with that decision, and still carrying the chart that had listed Valentine Snow's room number, the shooter strolled on, confident that there was now no one and nothing between him and his objective.

Cait had just about decided that the entire plan was going to prove a wash when she heard a cart being wheeled up to her closed door. At first she thought it must be Angetti with his wheeled bucket, complaining, as he always did, that his prostate wasn't what it used to be, and by the way, even FBI special agents deserved a piss break more than every three hours.

But when the door slowly opened, the first thing she noticed was that she didn't smell the cigarette smoke that always surrounded her partner like a noxious cloud.

Holding her breath, confident that Quinn was in the adjoining bathroom, watching through the slit in the barely open door, she felt the man enter the room.

She could hear the squeak of the rubber-soled shoes on the vinyl tile floor.

Then a surprised and very pissed-off voice, saying. "Fuck! You're not Valentine Snow!"

71

His last mission may have ended up a disaster, but there was no way in hell Quinn was going to allow anything to happen to Cait. He'd been against this idea in the first place, but when he'd realized there was no way to talk her out of setting herself up as a target, he'd reluctantly gone along with the program. So long as he could be the one closest to the action.

Proving yet again that the best battle plan never survived contact with the enemy, he burst out of the bathroom, gun drawn.

And came face-to-face with the familiar former military MP who'd given the speech at Mike's vet group. The tenth of the twelve steps, about taking personal inventory and admitting you were wrong.

The guy who was dragging Cait out of the bed and holding an ugly black Sig Sauer to her head.

"You come one step closer, McKade," he said, "and your girlfriend's toast."

"I'm standing right here," Quinn said, his heart, which he'd learned to control so perfectly during his sniper days, pounding so hard and fast in his chest he wouldn't have been surprised if it had broken right through his rib cage and out of his skin.

"Smart guy." The guy's eyes were as dead as a shark's. "Now, drop the gun."

Normally, he knew, he could pull the trigger before this guy got a shot off. But normally the bad guy didn't have the barrel of a gun pressed against the temple of the woman he loved. Not wanting to risk her life, Quinn did as instructed. The Glock hit the green and white tile floor with a thud, putting it out of reach for the moment.

"Lucky for you, I'm not into killing fellow vets."

"Try telling that to Jacob and Davis," Cait said, making Quinn want to wring her neck. He loved her to distraction. He also wished she'd keep her damn mouth shut. "And Jensen," she tacked on.

"Jacob and Jensen were collateral damage," he revealed.

Like Davis wasn't? Quinn suddenly had an ugly thought. And from the way Cait's eyes had widened, he realized she was, once again, thinking the exact same thing.

"We can get you out of this, Sergeant," she said remarkable calm.

Then again, Quinn figured the FBI probably taught hostage negotiation tactics at the academy. Something that hadn't been necessary in his former line of work.

"Yeah. With me lying on a gurney on some death row with needles stuck in my veins," he said.

"It's bad," she agreed. "I'm not going to lie and say you'll walk out of here a free man if you let McKade and me go. But you've still got a card to play. You can tell us about Captain Davis's wife using you to get rid of her husband."

Quinn watched him stiffen. Prepared to jump the guy if he made another move toward Cait.

"I used to talk to her about Valentine Snow," Sergeant Matthew Johnson, former USMC, said. "How watching her was the only thing that kept me from feeling mad all the time. I told her how I didn't think it was fair the network got rid of her just because they wanted to put that young blonde in her place."

Quinn had had no idea why the newscaster had left the network. But she'd insisted at the time it was her decision and he'd never seen any reason to doubt her.

"So, she suggested a way you could help Valentine get back to the top," Cait said. Her voice remained calm, but her always expressive eyes revealed the pain Quinn knew she was feeling from the loss of all those innocent lives. "Having her be the top reporter on a serial sniper story."

Collateral damage, the shooter had called them.

Yet another example of government-speak, designed to pretty up something ugly.

"It can still work," the shooter suddenly decided.

His shark eyes were no longer flat as the idea struck home.

Reading those eyes, Quinn dived for the Glock.

At the same time, the shooter shoved the blue metal crash cart at Quinn, then dragged Cait out of bed and out of the room.

72

He was dragging her down the hallway toward the stairs. Even as adrenaline was screaming through her veins like the civil defense sirens all the bases she'd lived on as a child were always testing, Cait's mind stayed surprisingly calm.

She'd been trained for this. Well, not exactly this, she thought as she felt the gun jammed into her side so hard she figured she could end up with a broken rib. Which, considering the circumstances, sure as hell wouldn't be the worst thing that could happen.

She had a brown belt in karate. And had been taught all sorts of other esoteric defense methods, and although she might not be able to break bricks with her bare hands, surely she could handle one whacked-out guy who had a shitload of problems of his own and undoubtedly couldn't be thinking all that straight right about now.

And then, of course, she had a fail-safe backup.

Big bad SEAL Quinn McKade, whom she could hear charging right behind them. Having no doubt that he could shoot this bad guy dead without touching a hair on her head—which was currently covered up in a bandage, but still, that didn't change the concept—Cait nevertheless decided it was time to bring her skills to their partnership.

The shooter was yanking open the metal door to the stairway, which didn't give him a free hand.

Taking advantage of the opportunity, Cait twisted away, landing a kick at the back of his knee, causing it to crumple and sending him tumbling headfirst down the stairs.

"Are you okay?" Quinn paused as, now only a second behind, he reached her.

"I'm fine," she panted, assured that she'd be able to breathe again sometime in the next century. "Just go nail the guy before he kills anyone else."

"Roger that," Quinn said.

He'd wanted to stop. To drag her into his arms and kiss her senseless. He'd never been so fucking scared in his life as when he'd seen the shooter holding the gun to her head. And worse yet, dragging her down the hallway, with so much adrenaline pumping through Quinn's system he hadn't dared risk getting off a shot because it would only have been the most important shot of his life and he couldn't have guaranteed his hand would've been steady enough to pull it off without hitting Cait.

At which time there wouldn't have been enough PTSD therapy in the world to fix him because his life would simply have not been worth living.

The fall hadn't proven fatal. From the clatter on the concrete stairs below, it was obviously the shooter had made it to his feet.

Quinn's second clue was—*pop*—the nearly silent shot that came whizzing past his head, hitting the wall behind him, sending plaster flying.

He picked up the pace, clattering down the stairs, ducking as another shot nearly grazed his shoulder.

The shooter was good.

Quinn was better.

Having scoped out the stairway ahead of time, as any good sniper would, he knew that one more twist around the bend and he'd have a view of a straight stretch of stairway leading to the metal door opening to the next floor.

Which just happened to be the pediatrics floor.

Like, yeah, he was going to let the psycho loose on that one.

He stopped at the railing. Lifted the Glock.

Drew in a breath. Exhaled.

And waited.

Inhale. Exhale.

Count it out.

One.

Two.

Three.

Just as the shooter lunged for the door, he glanced back over his shoulder. His gaze locked on Quinn's.

There was a brief flicker of resignation in the man's eyes as Quinn eased back on the trigger, then gently pulled the trigger.

One shot.

One kill.

73

After leaving Angetti in the ER with a tube in his lung and bitching about the rib the damn shooter had broken with the knife, Cait and Quinn showed up at the Davis mansion on Palmetto Drive.

This time Kristin Davis did not faint.

Instead, displaying the same inner steel that had allowed her to use her profession to manipulate a depressed veteran into killing all those innocent people to make her husband look like just another random victim, as soon as Cait had read her the Miranda warning, she'd lawyered up.

"Joe always said murder's about who benefits," Cait murmured later, as she and Quinn lay in bed, wrapped in each other's arms, passion temporarily spent.

"And she planned the other shootings as a smoke screen, to take the focus off her husband," Quinn said.

Christ, he'd had dinner with them. Played basketball with Will Davis. Comforted the widow. If he wasn't feeling so damn good, he might just have felt like a chump.

"I've been thinking about that offer Joe made me," she murmured, as she trailed her fingers down his chest. "About going to work for Phoenix Team."

"You'd be one helluva an asset."

"That's what Joe keeps telling me. Meanwhile, I turned in my shield today. Whatever I decide, I think I'd like to take you up on that vacation."

"Zach's already got the boat gassed up. We can leave for Key West, or wherever else you'd like, first thing in the morning."

"Key West sounds great. Beachcombing, tropical drinks." She nuzzled closer. "Celebrating the sunset."

He skimmed a palm down her back from her shoulder to her butt. "Don't forget the most important thing."

"How could I forget that?" she said on a rich, throaty laugh Quinn knew would still have the power to make him hard when he was ninety. "Since I'm already wanting you again."

She rolled over on top of his aroused body. Bracketed his chest with her arms on either side and smiled down at him.

"And after we get back from Key West, there's something else I'd like to do."

"You name it."

"I understand this is a difficult time of transition for her, and since your house isn't going to be finished for a while, you're going to have to stay here, and I'm not exactly the best cook in the world—I mean, to be perfectly honest, nuking frozen Lean Cuisine is usually about the best I can do—but Sabrina and Titania would probably be willing to help out, especially if I agree to go along with the bridesmaid deal at their wedding, so . . ."

She took a deep breath. It was not often Quinn had seen his Cait nervous. This was one of those few times.

"Since it seems we've got this couples thing going, which makes her family, do you think your mother would, just maybe, possibly, be willing to come to dinner?"

Even as the feel of her, soft and warm, and the piña colada scent of her hair were beginning to cloud his mind, Quinn laughed. Because sometimes life was just so damn perfect.

"I'd like to see you try and stop her."